P9-BZU-493

Eggshell Days

Eggshell
Days

Rebecca Gregson

Thomas Dunne Books

St. Martin's Press ❦ New York

THOMAS DUNNE BOOKS.
An imprint of St. Martin's Press.

www.stmartins.com

Library of Congress Cataloging-in-Publication Data

Gregson, Rebecca.
    Eggshell days / Rebecca Gregson.—1st U.S. ed.
      p. cm.
    ISBN 0-312-31041-2
    1. Dwellings—Maintenance and repair—Fiction. 2. Cornwall (England : County)—Fiction. 3. Inheritance and succession—Fiction. 4. Female friendship—Fiction. 5. Communal living—Fiction. 6. Simplicity—Fiction. I. Title.

PR6107.R445E34 2003
823'.92—dc21

                                                            2003040615

First published in Great Britain by Pocket Books, an imprint of Simon & Schuster UK Ltd.

First U.S. Edition: August 2003

10 9 8 7 6 5 4 3 2 1

To my girl

Acknowledgments

I am indebted to Hugh Lander and Alyson Rugg for sharing their extensive knowledge of historic Cornish buildings so readily and to Ben and Hussey for letting me use such a great example of one. Also, a big thanks to Tina Jackson, who once lived in a bus, and to Tim Smit for putting me right on a journey to Exeter.

Prologue

FOR ONCE, THE GOD OF SEATING PLANS AT WEDDINGS HAD SMILED UPON
them. Actually, putting them all at the same table wasn't a divine plan at
all, it was the bride's. She told her mother there was absolutely no point
in splitting them up, since they always migrated toward each other
within minutes of the speeches anyway, so they might as well finish
where they started. Besides, their peculiar intimate banter could be a
bit alienating for anyone who didn't know them.

"But single people are precious fodder at weddings, darling. And if
they're not together, there won't be the banter, will there?"

"Oh, but there will. It will just go on over other people's heads
instead. Honestly. Believe me. I know what they're like. And only two
of them are single anyway."

Luckily for the four of them, the bride's mother lost.

"Fantastic," Emmy said, peering at the name cards from under the
brim of her Portobello Market hat. "At bloody last. I was sure I was
going to be stuck with that idiot in the embroidered waistcoat. Is this
the perfect wedding or what?"

It was hard to argue. The service in the abbey had lifted them all with heavenly music and beautiful words. Then, from the Gothic arches, the congregation had spilt onto the school's sweeping Somerset lawns elegant heels sinking slightly into the early spring grass, which popped with crocuses and champagne corks and rose-petal confetti.

Black clouds rolled above them but they felt like the chosen few, kissing and laughing and getting mildly pissed under the only patch of sun in the country. When the tent sides rolled up to reveal twinkling trees of contorted hazel and underlit tablecloths of crisp damask glowing like campfires in the dusk, everyone clapped at the sheer theater of it all. Apart from Emmy and Sita, who made a beeline for their table to assert their domination.

"Wait, don't get too excited," said Sita, circling. "We've still got a Nick and Jane Sansford, a Moo Danby and a Kathleen Rice to worry about."

"Worry?" Emmy said. "You're not allowed to worry about anyone today. Today is going to be entirely worry-free." She took another slug of champagne and squinted at the names on the cards. "Niall can have the Kathleen. He's always good with shy people."

"How do you know she's shy? Do you know her?" But Sita knew who Emmy did and didn't know.

"I can tell by the name."

"Oh, right, so you're being thoughtful," Sita said, raising her dark eyes as if to say: like hell you are.

"Of course."

"He'll meet someone one day, you know."

"I know he will. He's just not going to meet her today."

"Clearly."

Sita switched the cards around quickly and Emmy smiled her famously contagious smile, the one that made her look as if she would spontaneously combust with gratitude, the one that made you fleetingly think she and Maya did share something of a resemblance after all.

Sita, of course, smiled back. "Moo can go between the married ones," she said.

"They might not be married. They could be brother and sister."

"Who cares? I can't be bothered to find out, can you? So how far have we got? We'll have each other. And, um, I want Niall on the other side." Emmy took off her hat and tossed it onto her chair, shaking her hair free and rubbing her scalp. She had had enough of being groomed.

"Like I don't know," Sita said.

Emmy blew a few strands of her suddenly static-filled brown hair out of her eyes. "It's no good. I'm going to have to tie it up. I should have had it cut." She took a tie from her wrist, where she had hidden it among a collection of silver bangles, and pulled her hair into a simple ponytail. "That's better."

But Sita was still concerned with the seating arrangements. If a job was worth doing, it was worth doing well. She put the place names back and double-checked. "Good. That works. And the other advantage is that this way you can supply me with discreet fags."

"Since when have you ever had an indiscreet one?"

"I used to smoke openly at college."

"No you didn't. You used to hang out of the window if you knew he was coming round."

On cue, Jonathan walked up with Lila on his hip and a rattle between his teeth.

"Oh no!" Sita said, putting a finger in the chubby out-stretched hand and taking the toy from her husband. "What are you doing here, baby?"

"She screamed every time I put her in the cot and it's not fair on the others. They've got a private cinema going on up there."

"What are they watching?"

"Don't ask. You don't want to know."

"I'll feed her before we eat," said Sita, instinctively putting her palms on her Chinese silk blouse to check her breasts, "then she's going to bed regardless."

"You put her down, then."

"Jonathan! She's not an old dog!"

Niall's wit radar was working well. He arrived at the table just in time to catch the line.

"Which is more than I can say for . . ." He gestured at a blond woman in a tight glittery sheath who was laughing loudly at everything. "What's she called again?"

"That's Sooty."

"Jaysus! Does anyone have a proper name around here?" He was already loosening his silver tie and working up to taking off his morning coat.

"Don't be so rude. She's really sweet," said Emmy.

"Sweet? Why are you always so nice? She's a feckin' maneater."

"You can talk."

"I've never eaten a man in my life."

"No, but you look like an old dog. Did you sleep in that morning suit?"

"I did. You told me not to be late."

"Liar." But with Niall, it was quite possible he was telling the truth.

The four of them settled down. Lila, wine, cigarettes and breadsticks passed between them as they huddled together, blissfully unaware of how intimidating they looked to the Moos and the Nick and Jane Sansfords of the world. They talked quickly of who they'd seen so far, how much they'd aged since the last wedding, where the weight had gone on and which couples were still together, but really nobody interested them more than themselves.

Astonished to find herself at a wedding she was actually enjoying, Emmy raised her glass. "To Sara and Sean and their fantastically unimaginative seating plan," she said.

"Hold on, hold on, we haven't toasted you and Maya yet," Jonathan pointed out. "I think we should do that first. Marriages are two a penny."

"That's true," said Niall. "You rich bitch!"

"Hardly," Emmy said, embarrassed. "You should see it. The place is falling to pieces."

"I have seen it."

"Yeah, ten years ago. Time takes its toll, you know. You'll see what I mean."

"Great, is that an invitation?"

"You don't need a bloody invitation. None of you do."

"What about next weekend, then?"

"Okay. Then you drop the heiress bit."

"A Cornish manor is a Cornish manor, darling," Sita said, signaling for a puff on Emmy's cigarette.

"It's not a manor, it's a farmhouse," she corrected, but exuberance bubbled up through her words, making her finish with a small laugh.

"Bollocks! It's a bloody mansion and you're just too grand to admit it," Niall said.

"Well, whatever it is, the photos make it look amazing," said Sita, seeing Emmy's neck getting blotchier with embarrassment by the minute. "I think the decision to live there is extremely brave and we're all seething with envy. Maya's already told me three times that she can't wait."

"That's only because I've promised her a surfboard when she's eleven."

"Nothing wrong with a bit of bribery."

"You could all come and live there with us," Emmy suggested, meaning it.

"We'll remember that when I finally get the sack," Jonathan said.

"Next month, then."

They all cheered, even though his situation at work was far from funny.

"To Emmy and Maya and their inheritance," he said. "May they live happily ever after in their rural idyll."

"To pneumonia and bankruptcy," Emmy added, blinking furiously to hide her pleasure at the realization that she was, at last, the subject of at least some sort of toast.

She could feel Niall's left shoulder lightly brushing her right. Every time he leaned over toward the others, the brush turned into a press. There was nothing secret about it, but she couldn't help thinking that only they knew it was happening.

LATER, SHE WISHED SHE HAD CHERISHED THOSE FEW MINUTES A LITTLE more, because suddenly there was a waft of unfamiliar perfume and his shoulder had gone.

A woman had arrived at the table wearing the sort of clothes that looked even cooler than they were for giving the impression that she had left it till the last minute to decide what to wear. A bias-cut murky green dress, a tiny fern print chiffon jacket and no hat. Her short, spiky blond hair was waxy and her lipstick was a startling pink.

"Hi," she said lazily. There was a transatlantic something to her voice. "I'm Kat." She pulled out the chair next to Niall's.

"Niall O'Connor," Niall said.

Emmy felt the space where his shoulder had been become an icy wasteland.

"So, Irishman," Kat drawled for all to hear, "have you got a wife here or what?"

"I'VE LOST HIM," EMMY SAID TO SITA OVER PUDDING. SHE WAS ON THE other side of her friend now. If anything, witnessing Niall and Kat's rapid sexual progress from a distance was even worse. She could see every detail face on.

"Stop that," Sita said. "You know what he's like. He's just a serial flirt."

"No, but look."

The newcomer put a confident hand out to take a cigarette from between Niall's lips and immediately brought it to her own. Two thin wedges of tarte au citron sat untouched on big white plates in front of them, the dusting of icing sugar undisturbed, like midday snow outside a honeymoon chalet.

"What does that tell you?" Emmy seethed.

"That she's not the kind of Kathleen you thought she'd be?"

"I've lost him," Emmy said again as Niall took another cigarette from the packet and lit it off the one Kat had in her mouth. She could see their hair touching. "I'm going for a walk. I'll check on the children."

"No you won't. They're fine. Jonathan has just been and the crèche staff sent him straight back down again. They said they'd come and get us if there was a problem."

"There *is* a problem."

"Only in your head. Now, listen, you're going to sit here, and talk to me, and smile and look as if you're having the best time in the world. Laugh, Emmy. Look at me and laugh."

Emmy picked up her glass and held it to her friend's.

"He'll be back," Sita said. "You know he will."

"Will he?"

"Yes."

"God Almighty, what would I do without you?"

They clinked conspiratorially and drank to their friendship, but through the glass Emmy saw a pair of pink lips and the burning tips of two Camel cigarettes which for once had absolutely nothing to do with her.

MIST ROLLED OFF THE WATER. TWO SWANS MOVED BY, CAUGHT IN THE lakeside spotlight. There was a distant babble from the tent, where the music had slowed down to a smooch. Kat sat on the edge of a picnic table, her legs round Niall's hips, her dress hitched up like a miniskirt, his jacket round her shoulders. His shirt hung out over his trousers. He had one hand on her waist, and with the other he was smoking over her head.

"Do you think anyone saw us?" she asked, playing with the triangle of chest hair that was an inch away from her face.

"No, not unless they were looking."

"So how are we going to go back in as if nothing has happened?"

"We're not. We're just going to disappear into thin air."

"Are we? What about your friends?"

"Oh, don't worry about them. They're the last people you need worry about."

"All of them? Even the one who was watching you like a goddamn hawk?"

"Yeah, even her. Especially her."

"That's good. I don't do friends you have to worry about." She took his cigarette again and forgot to give it back. "Where's this thin air, then? Where are you staying?"

"I think we're in one of the boarding houses."

"What, in a fucking bunk bed? That's a little too thin for me. I've got a king-size all to myself."

"Not anymore, you haven't," he said, taking the cigarette from her mouth and flicking it into the darkness. "I'll catch up with them tomorrow. We're all supposed to be traveling back on the same train."

"WHERE THE BLOODY HELL IS HE?" EMMY SNAPPED OVER HER CROISSANT in the school canteen. It might have been devoid of boys in uniform and free from the smell of gravy, it might even have had flowers on the tables, but it was still a school canteen.

She had asked the dinner lady, who had been thinly disguised as a waitress for the entire wedding weekend, to bring Niall a full English breakfast, even though nobody had seen him since ten o'clock the evening before. It was now congealing on the plate. "Well, he'll just have to make his own way to the station."

"Ignore her," Maya told Jay and Asha. "She's got a hangover."

"So have I," said Jay.

"No you haven't," his younger sister said. "Thirteen-year-olds can't get hangovers. You're just showing off."

"Piss off, weirdo," he hissed.

"Jay!" Jonathan shouted. "If I hear you use language like that again, I'll . . ."

"You'll what?" Jay smirked.

"Right. Get up."

"Leave it, Jon," Sita said wearily. "Just go and get the bags, would you? We'll see you in the hall."

By the time the two taxis arrived, fifteen minutes later than they should have done, Emmy was boiling with anger. "What are we supposed to do? Go without him?"

"He's a big boy," Jonathan told her, herding his children by the backs of their heads toward the two huge doors. "He can look after himself."

Sita walked out of the bursar's office, where she had settled the bill. She had put everyone's, including Emmy's, on her MasterCard. Because she could second-guess its reception, she tried to say lightly what she had to say: "The secretary has just told me Niall called ten minutes ago and left us a message. He says he'll see us at the station, if not on the train."

"Oh, right!" Emmy exploded, her voice ricocheting off the wooden panels and polished floor. "Well, how kind of him to let us know. God, how bloody selfish can you get?"

"MUM, THIS ISN'T GOING TO BE ONE OF YOUR EGGSHELL DAYS IS IT?" Maya asked in the cab. Jay was in the back with her and she was taking advantage of his presence, using him as an unwitting shield.

"Sorry," Emmy winced from the front. "Am I being that bad?"

"No, you're okay," Jay said. "It's better than pretending. Mum and Dad put these stupid fixed smiles on their faces when they're in bad moods in front of people. Haven't you ever noticed?"

"I don't think Mum counts," said Maya.

The taxis were in a twenty-mile-an-hour convoy behind a milk tanker. Behind them was a metallic blue Golf. In the cab in front of theirs, Sita turned round and tapped her watch through the back window.

"We're going to miss the train," Emmy told the driver.

"It's this blessed tanker. He must be able to see us. He should pull over." He sounded his horn.

"I hope we do miss it," Jay told Maya when he could see Emmy was in conversation.

"Why?"

"Then we won't have to go to school."

"We'll just have to get the next one. There'll be one every hour. Some people commute from here, you know."

Jay sighed. "They must be mad. All grown-ups are mad."

"Is Monday a bad day, then?"

"Every day's a bad day."

"Is it?"

"Yeah, it is. I hate school."

"Do you?"

"Yeah, really. Sometimes I don't bother going."

"What do you do instead?"

"Go home."

"What do you tell your mum and dad?"

"Nothing. They're not there, are they? I just pretend I've been at school. If they can pretend everything's fine when it's not, I can too."

"What's not fine?" Maya asked. It had never occurred to her that things in Jay's family might not be fine.

"Do you want a list?"

"Anyway, I thought your mum was at home all the time now Lila has been born."

"Well, yeah."

"So how do you skip school?" She didn't believe he did, in the same way that Asha didn't believe he had a hangover.

"Well, that's one of the things that aren't fine, isn't it?"

"All right, you two?" Emmy asked, looking round.

"Fine," said Jay, putting on what he thought was a stupid fixed smile.

"Hey, Niall's behind us!" Maya shouted, waving frantically. "What's he doing in that posh car? Who's that girl?"

"Maya, will you just turn round and sit properly," her mother barked.

Maya recognized only too well the edge in Emmy's voice, and when that edge was present the only sensible option was to do exactly what she was told.

I

THEY WERE HAVING THE TRAIN-CRASH CONVERSATION AGAIN.

"Right, okay, I think we should stop this," Emmy said. "Now that we're here." She gripped the solid edge of the table, just to be sure they really were. Toby's table. His kitchen. Her kitchen. *Their* kitchen.

"That's rich, coming from you," Niall said. "You're the one who usually starts it."

"That was back then." She smiled. It was the contagious smile, the one that gave that glimpse of Maya. "Before my fairy godfather waved his magic wand." It must have been magic, because it didn't even matter to her anymore that Kat was on Niall's lap. Being at Bodinnick made up for all sorts of things. "We missed the train," she carried on. "It crashed. We could all be dead. We live here now. End of story."

"Don't you mean beginning?" Sita corrected. "This should be where it starts to get interesting."

"We hope," said Jonathan.

A blown fuse meant it was dark in the huge room, but it was a clear evening and there was a full moon, so they could at least see each other.

"Well, there are two ways of looking at what we're doing," Niall said, peering through the candlelight at the boxes of belongings all over the floor. "Essentials for simple living" was what they had all agreed to bring. It didn't look like it. "One is that we're all as mad as bollocks, and the other is that everyone else is."

"At least we don't have any secrets," Sita said quickly to reassure herself, forgetting Emmy's huge one, which was forgivable since Emmy had almost forgotten it herself. "At least we know, more or less, what we're in for."

One of them had already hung a clip frame on the flaking kitchen wall to prove it. Twenty years' worth of changing photographic technology showing them freckled, plaited, big haired, tanned, pale, bearded, bare, tear-stained, pregnant, fit, anorexic and not. It was a reminder that their bold and hasty decision was not such a risk, a reminder that everyone had seen everyone else cry at least once. Except Kat, and for most of them she didn't count.

"Downsizing," the weekend property pages annoyingly insisted on calling the move from city to country, but that hardly seemed the word for it. All three of their London addresses would have fit easily into the rambling manor with room to spare. Admittedly, the four-story Fulham terrace that Jonathan and Sita had packed up and let at top speed took up considerably more space than Emmy or Niall's rented broom cupboards, but no one was inclined to toy with architectural puzzles. The premise was that everyone here was equal. *Animal Farm* it was not.

Cold Comfort Farm was more like it. Two days ago, Emmy had phoned to ask the farmer's wife to light the Aga and put the heating on in readiness for their arrival, and Eileen Partridge had replied, "What heating would that be, my bird?"

Anyway, freezing or not, spring was definitely back on course after its wintery blip, and Emmy was sure Bodinnick was relieved to be full again. In fact, earlier, it was as if the house had winked at her. She was standing by the sundial just as it was getting dark, looking up at the grand façade and realizing she had waited all her life for this moment, and someone had opened and closed an internal shutter on an upstairs bedroom window. Brilliant, she'd thought, almost winking back. The house has got us and we've got each other. How can we possibly fail?

Even the near-Gothic moment of flicking on the hideous kitchen strip light and fusing the entire ground floor seemed part of the big romantic conspiracy. Candlelight made it feel as if the adventure had finally begun.

It was as if the place was welcoming her back, delighted that she had brought properly passionate people with her this time, not just a few spiritless siblings—although even with five adults, three children and a baby, it wasn't what you could call bursting at the seams. Once everyone got used to the space, though, it would shrink. Familiarity shrinks everything, she'd promised Sita and Jonathan's middle daughter, Asha, who hated bigness, hated the high ceilings, the deep windowsills, the huge, heavy doors, hated the whole idea.

It was now dusk and the excited clamor of arrival had died down to a collective sigh of relief. At last they were dining in at home instead of dining out. Dining in together, for the first probationary night in their shared kitchen in the middle of nowhere, with a leg of Cornish lamb bought from the kitty and the children pottering around the vast upstairs, metaphorically peeing on imaginary boundaries to mark their new territory.

If they were feeling lucky, it was fair enough. Britain's worst rail crash for sixty years, with a death toll of a hundred, and they should have been in it. "Carriage C," Emmy could remember Jonathan shouting when they'd first heard the news, still stranded at the station the morning after Sara's wedding. "Carriage C, Carriage C." She could even remember the way his hand burrowed frantically in his inside jacket pocket for the tickets to prove his point. "All right, all right," Sita had snapped. "We believe you." But nobody believed it really, still didn't.

"My God, we should be dead," they kept saying to each other in the days that followed. "Why aren't we dead?"

And the only answer they could come up with back in London, as they'd watched repeated television footage of the mangled lump of metal dangling from the crane's teeth, was that it hadn't been their time.

"If it had been our time, would we have died happy?"

It was that terrifying question which had started the whole ball rolling, from hermetically sealed sitting room to drafty manor kitchen in less than seventy days.

Admittedly, it helped that they had all had such a stress-laden two months, during which time the ball had careered relentlessly through their lives, apparently hell-bent on collecting every possible reason for them all to seek pastures new.

First, Niall's flat had been burgled as he lay under his duvet playing with Kat. His CD player, his tape deck, his computer and his TV all yanked from their sockets, his credit cards, mobile phone and the keys to his motorbike gone for the third time in as many years. He'd been initially furious, and then, when he found a spattering of what looked like blood across his bathroom sink, frightened.

Not as frightened as Sita had been when she witnessed a mugging at the end of their street, though. Three men, two of them standing over a third, kicking him. She, a doctor, had run for her life. For nights and nights afterward, she could not forget the clicking of her heels on the pavement, racing blindly for home in the dark, round the corner and up the steps to safety, knowing that she should have offered her help. Later, she read in the paper that the victim had died in the ambulance, of a punctured lung.

Jonathan had lain awake next to her all those nights, too, taking deep, measured breaths and feigning sleep, too depressed to ask his wife why she was troubled, too obsessed with his boss's newly cold shoulder and his secretary's suspicious sick leave to take on anyone else's pain.

All he needed to ask was "Are you okay?" but they were three little words he couldn't muster.

Things could hardly have been worse between them but then Jay's persistent truancy came to light, when they were in the grip of the worst bout of flu either of them had ever experienced, and they hardly had the energy to get down to the school to discuss it. In fact, for the first appointment, they didn't.

In the end, there was no contest. There was no point in hanging on to their sanity for dear life. Life was simply too dear. If Emmy was brave enough to give it a go, so were they.

"Is it socially interesting that the women take an entirely different view from the men on this?" Niall asked now, taking an unlit cigarette from his mouth for the second time and dipping the tip in and out of the candle flame.

Emmy didn't know whether she couldn't believe they were living under the same roof again—a leaky moss-lined slate roof with missing tiles, from which you could see the sea one way and green fields the other—or whether she had always known it would be so. It was just a shame Kat was such a wrench in the works.

"We don't."

Niall raised his eyebrows. Both knew damn well he'd only asked the question to get an argument going.

"Would ye come out of denial? Jonathan and I are totally fatalistic about it, whereas you and Sita keep going off on some great romantic journey about the what ifs."

"Sita has never gone on a romantic journey in her life," Jonathan said affectionately, "have you, darling?"

"Don't have time," she answered. "Not with four children to look after."

"Three," Kat corrected.

"She means me," he whispered. "It's an old joke."

She might as well wear a neon sign over her head saying "I don't fit in," Emmy thought.

"So what 'what ifs' do the women do that you don't?" Sita asked Niall.

"What if we had got the train? What if you hadn't witnessed that mugging? What if Jay hadn't been picked up by the police in the middle of a school day?"

"What if your flat hadn't been burgled? What if your computer hadn't been nicked? What if you hadn't met Kat?"

Kat purred. "Do I make you feel reckless, darling?"

"Wrecked, more like it," Niall said. "Anyway, those aren't what ifs, they're why nots. That bloody larcenist took so much of my stuff I had nothing to lose, did I? No, I'm right. The men do the why nots, and the women do the what ifs."

"So why not do a what if for a change and see what happens?" Sita said quickly.

As Niall tried to work out what she had just asked him to do, Sita licked her finger and air-painted one point to her. It was a relief to remind herself that she was still the clever one, even though she was so often drunk with tiredness nowadays. Lila, living proof that even a doctor can make a contraceptive mistake, finally dropped off her breast, and she quietly adjusted her bra. There was no need for discretion; it was just the way she was. Whenever Emmy had fed Maya ten years previously, it had been an orgy of leaking nipples and tangled straps.

"Is she asleep?" Jonathan asked.

Sita nodded, tucking some of her dark, thick bob behind her ear and revealing one of the curls of gold he had given her the day Lila was born. Jewelry on the birth of a child, flowers on wedding anniversaries, a savings account for godchildren. Jonathan did everything by a book that Niall didn't even know how to open. And here they all were, banking on the fact that their differences were their strengths.

"Jaysus, Sita, that baby could suck for Britain. Ye must be knackered."

"What's with all this sudden Irishness then, Niall?" Kat asked, inspecting her toenails. Jonathan wasn't sure it was exactly what he wanted to watch at suppertime, but there were clearly going to have to be compromises. "Are you hoping for Celtic solidarity or something? E-mail me when he starts chewing straw, will you?"

When she said things like that, even Niall was relieved she hadn't chosen to go the whole Cornish hog. She had kept them all guessing, though. Yes, she would come, no she wouldn't, yes she would. In the end, she had agreed to keep her lucrative modeling work going, and live with him at weekends and holidays only. It seemed a perfect compromise.

"What's that?" Emmy asked, watching her fiddle with a piece of blue foam.

"A toe separator. Do you want me to get you one?"

"I don't paint my toenails."

"So I noticed. Maybe you should start."

Niall waved his cigarette in the air. "No, no, no, stop. A toe separator is not an essential for simple living."

"It is in my book."

"Well, your book is too feckin' high-maintenance by half."

"Speak English, sweetie. Pass me a candle. I need more light."

"Okay, Sita. Here's me doing a what if. Which single thing that went wrong that morning conspired to save us?" he persisted. He was going to have the train-crash conversation again if it killed him.

"The milk tanker!" all four others shouted, as they'd done a hundred times, but even as they did, the image of the colossal steel beast, nose in hedge and tank skewed across the narrow country lane, still shook them.

"It should never have tried to pull over to let us pass."

"It was my fault. I made our cabbie flash his lights. I remember asking him."

"Ah, you're all obsessed with the milk tanker. That's just because it was a big fecker. What about all the other little twists and turns?"

"Five minutes, tops. The milk tanker delayed us by fifteen," Jonathan said.

Emmy went to fill his glass but his hand planed automatically over the rim.

"Go on, you're not going anywhere, not for three months, anyway," she coaxed.

He relented by showing her an inch with his fingers as the discussion rolled on, and only Sita saw him rub his chest with the flat of his hand. It didn't make any difference how many times she told him the tightness was just stress. The one shelf that ran round the crumbling walls of their antiquated bathroom upstairs was already piled with his mail-order vitamins and health supplements.

"Except they weren't the crucial minutes," Niall argued, dragging on his cigarette as if his life depended on it. Sita realized Jonathan had been rubbing his chest in anticipation of smoke. "How many times has your plane left late and made up the delay during the flight? It wasn't the milk tanker. It's too obvious."

"Why did it jack-knife, then?"

"Because the roads were wet, for feck's sake."

"Niall, that's three fucks in the last two minutes," Kat pointed out. "That shows you think you're losing the argument."

"Or that I'm frighteningly sexually prolific."

"Hello? This is your live-in partner speaking."

Emmy wanted to laugh. They'd only known each other for nine weeks.

"Not anymore, you're not."

"I will be when it suits me. That's the beauty of a recreational relationship."

"A *what*?"

"A recreational relationship. Didn't you know? That's what our sort of arrangement is called."

"By who? *Cosmo*feckin*politan?*"

"I wouldn't bother finding work, Sita. Just go out and buy a swear box."

"Actually," Niall said, "I think one of the rules for the next three months should be that we use the word 'feck' a bit *more*."

"You couldn't use it a bit more. You'd never finish a sentence."

"It's very therapeutic, the linguistic combination of an 'f' followed by a hard stop. And you know, we could all do worse than give way to the occasional feck."

Niall winked at Kat. Jonathan raised his eyebrows at Sita. Emmy looked at the floor.

"That's so eighties," Kat said. "Hasn't anyone told you no one cares about the word anymore? It's lost its power to shock. It doesn't sound cool these days, it just sounds goddamn rude. And you must try harder not to do it in front of the children. Don't let him do it in front of the children, Emmy."

"I don't," Niall said.

"You did today."

"Come back and sit on my lap, you bossy tart."

"My nails aren't dry yet."

"So, had we already missed the train by the time the cabbies made their detour?"

"Why did Sara get married on a Sunday not a Saturday like normal people? When else would we be busting a gut to get back to London on a Monday morning, for God's sake?"

"Why didn't we drive?"

"And if we weren't meant to be dead, how come we booked those train seats in the first place?"

"That's what I mean," Niall said, flinging his arms into the air and letting his Camel cigarette drop its ash behind him. "Which link mattered? Which one was it that saved us?"

"The milk tanker!" they all shouted again, as he leaned back in his chair and inhaled again, grinning through the smoke like the devil's favorite advocate.

"Right," Emmy said, banging her hands on the table, "that's it. That really was the last time, okay? The last."

She supposed they had to go through it all again, to mark the remarkable just one more time. Eight weeks ago, the prospect of an evening like this hadn't existed in so much as a flicker of a candle flame. Eight weeks ago, it was going to be just her and Maya. But then, of course, her fairy godfather had made them miss the train.

Prodding a puddle of freshly spilt wax, she reminded herself that the candles were hers. So were the candlesticks, the drawers and cabinets she'd found them in, the tables and sideboards—and even the bricks and mortar, for that matter. Or they would be for the next three months. That was the deal. If things worked out the way they should, Bodinnick would eventually belong to them all. The finer details of who would own what stake rested with the sale of Sita and Jonathan's home in Fulham, but the general idea was that they would probably end up owning half, Emmy would own the other half, and Niall would buy into her share with whatever he thought he could afford, which might be anything between ten and two hundred thousand, depending on the state of his wine-importing business. It was a loose arrangement, to say the least, and that was the way she liked it. The small print didn't interest her. What was hers was theirs.

She picked up some stapled sheets and fanned them in the air. Everyone knew what they were. On the long and boring journey down, Maya had given them a title sheet. *Rules*, she had written in neon gel pen.

"Right, to shut you up about the bloody train crash, I'm going to read these out."

"Could you add a ban on toe separators?" Niall asked.

"And put in swear boxes," Kat said.

"Of course. We can have monthly subscriptions to *Cosmo*feckin*politan* if we want. This is a work in progress, remember?"

"No, thanks. It takes me all month to get through *What* feckin *Car*," Niall said.

Everyone had to admit it, he was good at making them laugh.

"Are you sitting comfortably?"

"Not yet." Niall lifted a buttock from his chair.

Well, he made them laugh sometimes.

"Are you sure you want to come down at weekends, Kat?"

"I'm sure."

" 'Course she does," he said, winking across her.

Emmy cleared her throat as Kat pushed her chair back, moved across and settled her tiny frame back on Niall's.

"Toes dry, are they, darling?"

She nodded and pulled his arms round her waist again. He put his hand up her shirt and left it there.

"So," Emmy said quickly, "are we all up to speed with the legalities?" She was overconcentrating on the first sheet. She didn't want to see Niall's hand up Kat's shirt.

"What legalities?" Kat pounced.

"Well, just the private mortgage, really."

"What private mortgage?"

"Oh. Didn't you tell her, Niall?"

"No, he didn't," Kat answered.

"Well, to be fair, we only finalized it yesterday. I thought Sita was going to tell everybody, or maybe, well, I think I assumed Niall would."

"No. No one told me anything."

"Oh."

They all sat there in their first awkward silence, everyone waiting for someone else to break it.

"Emmy?" Sita said at last.

"Oh, well, I mean, is there any need for Kat to take it on board anyway? She's not implicated in any way."

"No, but I think it's important we all know everything," Niall said, "so that there's no sense of, you know, someone feeling they have a bigger right to be here and all that."

"Okay, that's fine." Emmy shrugged. "Well, Jonathan and Sita are putting in forty thousand from their savings."

"Not *from* our savings, that *is* our savings. We're cleaned out."

"Jeez," said Kat. "What for?"

"To carry out urgent repairs to the roof, the plumbing and, er, the wiring," Sita said, waving at the darkness around them.

"In return, they have that sum secured by a private mortgage on the property, to be repaid to them if and when it is sold," Emmy added. Her voice was soft with appreciation, and yet it hadn't occurred to her that, in fact, she was the generous one. Giving came naturally, which was a good thing, since taking also could.

"Which it won't be," said Niall.

Emmy winked at him. "Niall's ten thousand—Sorry, you do know about that, do you, Kat?"

"Yes."

"Excellent," said Emmy, meaning the opposite. "So Niall's ten thousand will also go into the repairs, but on a private loan arrangement with me, to be paid back after any sale, once Jonathan and Sita have retrieved their money. Are you sure you don't want anything in writing, Niall?"

"It is in writing."

"Well, in something other than felt-tip."

"No. I trust you."

"Fool," she joked, knowing that he was right to, "and on the day-to-day front, we've already arranged equal access to a joint bank account opened in Sita's and my names, with Jonathan and Niall as signatories. Our contributions to it will be reviewed after a fortnight to see if we got the sums right. A petty cash float of a hundred and fifty is already here"—she patted a locked tin—"and we'll keep it on the top shelf of the Welsh dresser. It'll be topped up weekly and used for agreed communal spending."

"Like what?"

"Well, we said routine household expenses, didn't we? Petrol, groceries, that sort of thing."

"We won't manage to feed nine of us on a hundred and fifty quid a week."

"We might. Well, we'll try, anyway, and if we can't, we'll up it. But we've got the bank account too, remember. If we get stuck, we'll just dip into that."

"No," said Jonathan firmly. "That's there for electricity and heating, phone and Aga fuel." He held a photocopied version which had appeared from seemingly nowhere but had in fact been pinned—by him—to an old cork board earlier that day.

"It's soundin' a bit feckin' fierce to me," said Niall.

"That's only because you have a problem with taking anything seriously. Do you want more? There's reams of it."

"Yeah, go on, hit us with the lot."

"Okay. Sita's going to use my car for work, Sita and Jonathan's is going to become the communal car. Niall's motorbike is totally bloody useless, of course, and we're going to use buses whenever possible."

"Oh, we are, are we?"

"I know what this reminds me of!" Niall exclaimed. "Your birth plan, Em. Maya was going to be born underwater to the sound of whale music and you weren't going to have any pain relief, remember?"

"So how was the epidural?" Sita laughed.

"Bloody marvelous."

"What's that got to do with buses?" Kat asked, confused.

"You'd know if you'd seen the back end of her in labor like I did," Niall said.

"I beg your pardon," Emmy shouted.

"Buses," said Jonathan. He could see things getting out of hand. "Where do we get buses?"

Everyone thought of the only one they had seen so far: the one they'd got stuck behind for the final mile of their journey, an ancient hand-painted jalopy with curtains at the window and a motorbike hanging off the back.

"Mrs. Partridge told me today that the nearest stop is at the bottom end of Cott," said Sita.

"We should grow our own vegetables," Emmy said. "Fresh peas and new potatoes. From garden to table in an hour. Unbeatable."

"And in the meantime, we have to rely on local seasonal produce."

"That's swede and daffodil pie for the next three months, then," said Niall.

"Who said anything about pastry?" Sita asked him.

"What about Cornish pasties?"

"I think they count as local seasonal produce."

"As in year-round seasonal?" Niall asked with one raised eyebrow.

"Exactly. Oh, this is a good one, I don't remember this," said Emmy, looking at the biro scrawl on her sheet. "Discounted wine courtesy of PopCork Online."

Kat spluttered. PopCork Online was Niall's dot com business, one of the early ones that had miraculously survived. Miraculous not so much because of the famously precarious nature of such companies, but because of Niall's somewhat unorthodox approach to stock control.

"Did you really say that, Niall?"

"Yeah, why not?"

"Is that okay?" Jonathan asked, looking at the four empty bottles on the table. It seemed a bit generous.

"Sure. I've always got bin-ends hanging around, so unless you're all going to start drinking as heavily as me . . ."

"That's not likely."

"Not possible."

"Then it's fine."

"You'll never be rich," said Kat, looking cross.

"Don't want to be," said Niall.

"That's good," said Emmy, thinking his girlfriend really did know nothing about him. "Do you want to hear more or have you had enough?"

"We want to hear it all."

"Okay." But she read the next bit quickly to herself. "Washing machine operational during off-peak times only. Nonessential phoning done during cheap-rate hours. E-mailing and letter writing for longer communications preferred. Hair and beauty treatments kept in house. Haircuts from personal budgets, appointments to be scheduled in conjunction with other necessary trips to town. Newspapers to be read on screen during free internet access time. Books to be borrowed from library. Gifts handmade or 'promises,' wine from Niall. All exercise, apart from swimming, must be free. All new clothes an individual expense." She could remember them writing it in all seriousness in the sitting room at Sita and Jonathan's one earnest Sunday afternoon. "Basically, we're not supposed to be spending any money," she said grimly.

"God, London is sounding better and better," Kat smirked.

"Anything else?"

"Yes. To avoid chaos in the kitchen, children breakfast first, overseen by Jonathan, Sita or Emmy. Cooking on rota. Weekday suppers to include children, weekend suppers later, to exclude children who will be fed a proper meal at lunch-time. Niall and Kat to have their own timetable if required. Shopping to be done twice a week, with strict list, on rota basis. Laundry overnight, individual's responsibility. Jonathan and Sita four nights, Emmy and Maya two, Niall one. General household cleaning to be run in conjunction with cooking rota. Family bathrooms and loos individual responsibility."

"Jawohl."

"What about *my* laundry?" Kat asked. "I don't get much chance to do it in my flat. I'm never in."

"Your clothes are so bloody small, you can rinse them under a tap in a British Rail bog on your way down."

"So I can just do it whenever, can I?" she said, ignoring Niall.

"Yes, Kat. No problem," said Sita.

"I don't want to have to join a queue or anything. Not if I'm just here for one night."

"That's fine. I'm sure we can work round you."

"Thank you, Sita."

"Go on, Emmy."

"Niall, you get exclusive use of the library for your office, and I get the en suite dressing room to your bedroom as my sewing room."

"Isn't there another room you could use?" Kat asked suspiciously. "It doesn't seem an entirely logical choice."

"You don't need it for anything, do you?"

"No, I was just thinking of privacy."

"Well, the only planned nakedness in there should belong to the dressmaker's dummy."

"I was thinking of *our* privacy, actually."

"Ah, don't worry about that," Niall said. "She's seen it all before, haven't you, Em? And you're not really going to be needing a sewing room anyway, are you?" He winked at her. "We all know about you and your great plans."

"You're on dodgy ground, mate," Emmy said.

"Yeah, but so's your business. How long has it been in the planning stage?"

"We did put something in about privacy, didn't we?" Sita asked speedily.

"Yes, we said that if you want to be left alone, you shut your door."

"But an open one doesn't necessarily mean 'Come in,'" Kat underlined unnecessarily.

Emmy didn't know if it was just prejudice, but Kat did come across as a sour old cow sometimes. Young cow. Younger cow, anyway.

"We'll all have to get into the habit of knocking," Sita said.

"And that's it," said Emmy, folding the sheets. She'd had enough of rules now. She wanted the lovely familial warmth back.

"Oh, what about the final reminder at the end?" Jonathan asked.

"No, there's no need to go into that," she said hurriedly.

"Why not?"

"Well, it's not quite in the spirit of things, is it? You and Sita didn't have a prenuptial agreement, did you?"

"We did, actually."

"Oh."

There was a gunfire of laughter from all of them.

"To be fair," Jonathan said, "it's probably the only rule we need."

"Okay," said Emmy reluctantly. "You read it, then." She pushed it across to him.

"Sure. Well, it just says that if at any stage any one of us wishes to move out, we can call a house meeting and the decision to put Bodinnick on the market will be discussed and put to the vote. If the vote is overwhelmingly to stay, that person or persons shall be bought out. And Emmy's decision is final."

"How do you call a house meeting?" Kat asked.

"Like this." Niall cupped his hands round his mouth and shouted.

Lila jumped in her sleep and Jonathan frowned.

"You just have to ask. Make it clear you want us all to sit down and listen to you," Sita said, feeling Emmy's foot press against hers under the table. She pressed back.

"As I was saying, it's all a bit feckin' serious," Niall said, grabbing a second set of stapled sheets from the heap of stuff in the middle of the table. This time, Maya had used glitter glue to spell out *The Bodinnick Manifesto*.

Jonathan had started this one by e-mail. That was when everyone knew they were on to something. If Jonathan, in the cold light of London, could carry the vision of a new life to work with him, so could the rest of them.

Niall handed it to him. "Go on," he said.

"What, read it?"

"No, eat the bloody thing."

"Do you want me to? Okay." He cleared his throat. "*The Bodinnick Manifesto*."

Niall coughed on his Camel. "It's not a feckin' by-election."

"*The vision. Jonathan Taylor——*"

"Conservative," said Niall in a stage whisper. Kat giggled.

"*To cut down the stress, to get out of the rat race, to find the confidence to be different, to find out if I can, to kiss goodbye to the Heathrow Express*—Oh, come on, I didn't put that."

"Ah, y'see? Typical bloody Tory, ye've changed your mind already."

"*Sita Dhanda——*"

"Labor, three times, incredibly painful."

"Yes Niall, it was, thank you."

"*To adopt a simpler lifestyle with more free time to concentrate on the things that matter. To show our children a nonmaterial world.*"

"I'm still going with that."

"Hear hear."

"*Emmy Hart——*"

"Monster Raving Loony."

"Okay, Niall. Joke's over."

"*To say thank you for everything you all are to me. To provide Maya with a sense of family. To shout from the rooftops that I am living the life I want.*"

"Rooftops?" Niall said. "What are you? Mary feckin' Poppins?"

Kat giggled again.

"Niall O'Connor—"

"Wanker," whispered Emmy, to loud cheers.

"To never eat sushi again."

"That's pathetic."

"Even you have got to come up with a higher dream than that."

"There is no higher dream."

"Kat Rice: To get away from aggression and pollution. To give my mind and body the attention I deserve. To spend more quality time with Niall."

"Quality time? With Niall?"

"You've got the wrong bloke."

The shouting and laughter around the table became rowdy enough to draw the children down from upstairs.

"What's so funny?"

"Why are you banging on the table, Dad?"

"Hold on, hold on," Jonathan said. "I haven't finished. I haven't done you lot yet. *"Maya Hart: To climb trees. To have a purple bedroom and a dog. To have an adventure."*

"Purple, Mum, got that?"

"Jay Taylor: To leave school."

"Prosaic as ever," said Sita, managing to put her hand on her son's head before he ducked and moved away.

"Asha Taylor: To climb bushes. To have a pink bedroom and a rabbit, a guinea pig and a chicken. To have a safe adventure."

"You copied Maya," Jay said.

"No, I didn't."

"Yes, you did."

"Hey, we didn't invite you two in here to argue."

"You didn't invite us at all."

"And you were arguing anyway."

"He started it."

"No, I didn't."

"Yes, you did."

"And finally," shouted Jonathan over the noise. "Let's not forget Lila. This sounds remarkably like her mother to me but it is apparently Lila's intention *to stop waking everyone up too early, to learn to sit up unsupported, to feed myself, walk, dress myself, cook, drive, clean.*"

"Did you write that, Mum?"

"No, Lila did, you pillock," Jay told his sister.

"To the *Manifesto*," said Jonathan, raising his glass.

Everyone raised their glasses too.

"Is anyone missing sushi yet?" Emmy asked.

"Oh, it's okay," Kat said. "I brought some with me."

2

IT WENT WITHOUT SAYING THAT ASKING FOR SUSHI WAS A LONG-TERM no-no at the Londis shop in the small south-coast village of Cott, but you wouldn't necessarily be able to pick up directions to Bodinnick there, either.

This was more to do with the store's permanently changing part-time staff than with xenophobia, although flashes of the latter were hardly unknown. On the other hand, if you were lucky enough to stumble across a nonxenophobe who had a grandparent buried in Cott churchyard, they would ask you if you wanted the dower house, the farm or the big house itself.

These separate dwellings had enjoyed their own approaches since the First World War, when all four seventh-generation Trevivian sons had been killed in the space of a year, and their diminutive widowed mother had barricaded herself in the dower house, letting the farm go to her gamekeeper for a song. Bodinnick itself was shuttered, locked and left to grow mold on its windowsills until the old woman died in 1955 and a distant cousin with an eye on an Oxfordshire vicarage, rather than a Cornish manor, felt it was high time such an engaging family home was properly enjoyed.

Emmy's uncle and godfather, Toby Hart, might not have been the kind of family man the broker had in mind, but he nurtured a particular set of reasons for buying Bodinnick. His childhood home in Kent was a house so eerily similar that, as an old man in Cornwall, he often found himself looking for the missing back dairy or wondering how a third window could have been added to the drawing room without him noticing.

But Ledbury belonged to his elder brother, Emmy's father, Lieutenant-Colonel Anthony Hart, whose sole purpose on earth seemed to be to provide perfect heirs, which he did with military precision every two years until he had sired his own beautiful regiment. Emmy had been the last and the only female recruit.

Toby's seed was never going to be able to compete, for it was clearly made of different stuff, and when Bodinnick came on the market there was no question that it was meant to be his. Cornwall was six safe counties away and the solution suited everyone well. So well, in fact, that by 2000, no one could remember anyone called Trevivian living at Bodinnick. Bodinnick was where Mr. Hart lived.

All this meant that Emmy and Maya Hart's route to acceptance in the village was already mapped out, but the others would have to prove themselves in other ways. They quickly realized that not asking for sushi at the post office would be a start and that even soy sauce might be pushing it—a risk recognized in the early appearance of a running household joke.

"Excuse me, do you sell shiitake mushrooms?"

"No."

"Fresh udon noodles?"

"No."

"Liquid dashi?"

"*No!*"

"Chicken Tonight?"

"What flavor, my bird?"

The crack was aimed mainly at Kat, who, a week later, was still having difficulty accepting that Japanese vegetarian cookery had yet to penetrate Cornwall, let alone Cott.

"But Bodinnick was once important enough to warrant its own stone signpost," she argued.

"What's that got to do with the price of bread?" Niall asked.

"That would be the white sliced variety, would it?"

Kat could afford to be sniffy about food. Her cooking skills, learned during her days as an Aspen chalet girl, were undeniable. Much to Emmy's deep annoyance, on the second day, when they had all been too tired to go to the supermarket, she had made a passable meal from a few rusting tins left in Toby's store cupboard. Spanish squid à la Campbell's cream of mushroom soup. Nobody had died. In fact, Jonathan hadn't even needed a Rennie, although if there was such a thing as jealousy pills Emmy should have popped a few.

"This isn't London," everyone kept telling Kat when she railed against the lack of choice.

"London? This isn't even bloody Slough."

"Never mind," Niall said. "You've served a week already. Your initial sentence is nearly over."

"A *week*?" said Emmy, looking up from the newspaper behind which she'd been counting the number of hours if not the minutes before Kat went back. "Is that all? I've lost track of time."

"I knew this would happen," Sita said, coming in with Lila tied in a sling on her hip. Her collarless shirt, which was covered with splashes of previous London-based decorating efforts, had been ironed. She had a paint scraper in one hand and a dirty nappy in the other.

"What *have* you been doing to that poor baby?" Niall asked.

"What?"

"Paint scraper? Nappy? Oh, never mind."

Sita didn't laugh. She was in a bad mood. "When are we going to take out these units?" she asked, slapping the much-maligned wood-effect melamine worktops. "The sooner the better, quite frankly. And we should take up all the lino, too. I bet there's slate underneath. The stuff in the hall is already coming up at the bottom of the stairs and one of us is going to break a leg on it in a minute."

"Shouldn't we wait for the electrician to finish?"

"Finish? It would be nice to see him start."

"Antsy, are we?" Emmy said, tugging the hem of her friend's shirt as she went by.

"Well, it's not supposed to be a holiday, is it? We're supposed to be getting this place in some kind of order, remember?"

"What do you think those blokes are doing up on the roof, then? Staging a prison protest?"

"They're being paid." With our money, Sita didn't say. "But we can't pay for everything. We're going to have to do some things ourselves. Look around you. The place is falling to pieces."

"Hey, that's my line."

"Well, I'm using it now, because you seemed to have stopped."

"Oooooo," Emmy teased. "You and your bloody work ethic."

"Asian parents." Sita shrugged with her back to everyone. She untied the sling, pulled a few old cushions off the armchair in the corner and plonked Lila in an old dog basket on the floor. "What d'you expect?"

Sita often claimed she couldn't remember school holidays, but that was because, in effect, she'd never really had them. Her father made her and her sister stay in their bedroom studying, while he ran the shop downstairs. "Education can transform your social position," he used to tell them. "You can go up in your status," he'd say. They would imitate him wobbling his head during their lunch breaks and take it in turns to look out for each other so they could listen to music on their Walkmans, or read their secretly bought magazines about boys and makeup. Somehow, she hadn't yet got round to telling him that his son-in-law had become a house husband.

Jonathan came through the door. His hair was covered in flakes of old white gloss paint from scraping the skirting board in their moldy bathroom, and he had on a pair of trainers that he only wore for DIY.

"How come I'm the only one up a ladder around here?"

"At least my dad taught me how to get things done," Sita said defensively, "which is why we can now afford for you to lead a life of leisure."

"Leisure? Married to you? Living here? You've got to be joking."

"*And* which also goes a long way to explain why Sita, as the daughter of a shopkeeper, is now a GP, and Emmy, the daughter of a colonel, is a waitress," Kat said. Her protestations that she really didn't have a problem with Niall and Emmy's past sometimes appeared a little flimsy.

"Ouch," said Niall. No one else could quite believe she had said it.

"Former waitress," Emmy reminded her. She broke open an orange and piled the scraps of peel on top of each other. That was the thing with Emmy, she never bore a grudge. She was aware enough to know that her own behavior was so often left wanting that her best bet was to forgive almost everyone almost everything. "And future owner of the most successful children's fancy-dress mail-order company the world has ever seen."

"We're waiting," Kat said.

"Don't hold your breath," said Emmy, thinking that if she didn't say it someone else would.

Niall sucked in air noisily.

"You can talk," Sita said to him. "Is your computer even plugged in yet?"

"It can be. I sorted your hard drive this morning," Jonathan said.

"I thought that was my job," Kat said.

"What's that about my hard drive?" Niall asked, looking up from his cigarette paper. He was wearing the same baggy drawstring trousers and tweedy roll-neck sweater he'd had on all week.

"It's not floppy," Emmy said looking up, "apparently."

"This is very true."

Sita listened to the increasingly irritating banter as she washed her paintbrush, comforting herself by thinking of the patterns of behavior that *had* been established. The children—who were upstairs playing a game they had played almost obsessively all week, involving a wardrobe and some old coats—were getting the hang of which loos they could and could not use and where to find their parents at dead of night. She and Jonathan had a system of laundry up and running, Emmy had a permanent home for her tampons, and Niall knew which way to turn at the end of the drive to get to the nearest pub. It was progress of sorts.

As Niall had so delicately put it, "The house was almost feckin' tailor-made." The layout of the second floor could not have been designed more appropriately to accommodate their three essential clusters of living if it had tried, so the feared task of divvying up had, in the end, been stress-free. There hadn't been one moment at which needs clashed, apart from the small hiccup over Emmy's sewing room, which was still very definitely the dressing room next to Niall's.

Sita and Jonathan and the children had taken over a suite of rooms at the top of the stairs. Jay and Asha shared a huge, light bedroom to the right, which took in the west front corner of the house and had three sash windows with deep sills which they had been warned in no uncertain terms never to attempt opening themselves. "If you fall out, you'll kill yourselves," Emmy told them. She was only repeating something Toby had once told her, except she didn't embellish it with the rocking-horse ghost story as he did. She knew all about Asha's threshold for fear after spending an hour eating popcorn with her in a cinema foyer while her own daughter sat all on her own in Screen Two, happily watching Harry Potter meet Voldemort for the first time.

The plan was one day to divide the room with a large curtain, because both Sita and Jonathan secretly hoped that Jay would soon start showing signs of puberty. Once upon a time, they had thought he was hormonally precocious, but then they realized he was just a moody little sod. His upper lip was still very bare, barer than nine-year-old Asha's, even. He was a bit of a shrimp.

Next to Jay and Asha's room, but enjoying the front aspect only, was a baby-sized dressing room with no access from the landing, leading to another big bedroom which had an old but serviceable en suite bathroom on the other side. This had been Toby's room, so it was furnished with a tapestry half-tester over the king-size bed and an antique leather sofa running between the two windows, not that you could see the finer details of either against the dark red walls.

With a lick of cream paint, Sita, Jonathan and Lila were the ideal successors, particularly as their three rooms were at a slightly lower level than the landing, fed by one door and a couple of steps, reinforcing the feeling of trespass for anyone who needed it.

Maya, now ten, knew instinctively where it was and was not all right to go. She always knocked before entering even an empty bathroom—a trick she'd learned a few years ago when she'd found her mother having her back scrubbed with a Body Shop loofah by a man she'd never seen before. It wasn't the man she'd found alarming, it was the way Emmy had lurched from being wild with indignation to begging for forgiveness in the space of about five minutes.

To the left, the wide, long landing, with its two threadbare but valuable Persian runners, ran for long enough to accommodate Jonathan and Sita's bedroom and bathroom, and then dropped down again into the rooms allotted to Emmy and Maya.

Theirs was an L-shaped collection of smaller chambers, with their bedrooms along the front of the house and a separate lavatory and bathroom a few steps across the corridor, looking east. It was the end of the house where Emmy had slept as a child, and most of the old furniture was still there—the kidney-shaped, marble-topped dressing table with the gathered chintz cloth and ornate white mirror, the not-quite-matching marble-topped bedside tables, the serpentine lamp bases with their slightly wonky raw-silk shades. For a man so unconventional outside the home, Toby had certainly succumbed to traditional tastes within.

Emmy was thankful that the original architect had been sensitive enough to put the larger bathroom window on the eastern wall, not the western, otherwise it would have looked across a narrow outside passageway right into Niall's bedroom, and, like it or not, Niall's bedroom was also Kat's.

She also liked the fact that, since she and Maya were at the end of the house, there was no reason to venture down the last flight of landing steps except to come and see her. This was less for privacy than for reassurance. She'd always liked to know her visitors came from desire, not by default.

Another happy coincidence was that Niall and Kat's largest window faced north, which might cut out the sun for them but at least also cut out the chance of being accidentally caught in the act, and, as Niall had insensitively pointed out, they were the most likely candidates for impromptu sex, so it was perfect.

"I object to that assumption," Jonathan had said over dinner and then wished in the ensuing amused silence that he hadn't.

As compensation for Niall and Kat's rooms being the darkest, they had the biggest bathroom, which Emmy was already doing her best not to look in every time she walked down the landing. If she averted her eyes slightly, she saw her sewing room. She had just ordered three more rolls of fabric and a new machine, so it would look the part, if nothing else.

Downstairs, though, the layout was less easy. The sitting room was north-facing, a fact which wasn't helped by the old blue carpet and its distance from the kitchen. The dining room table was so long and wide that they would have to dismantle it to get it out, so there was little they could do in there but eat, and the kitchen was better for that. Then there was a music room, a library, and a very small one-windowed room which Toby had used as a study and which the children had already claimed as a den.

"Why don't you use that one as your sewing room?" Kat had suggested.

"It's a bit too small," was Emmy's excuse, but that depended on what it was too small for. Sitting and staring into space was an activity you could do in a shoebox.

The big, sunny kitchen was already established as the heart of the house. Big and sunny was good, but it was universally agreed that the melamine units, the lino and the strip lights were very, very bad. They decided early on to make it their first project.

"If only because, if everything goes belly-up, a new kitchen will make it easier to sell," Jonathan had said.

"Go wash your mouth out," Emmy had told him, trying to stop her head filling with beech worksurfaces and aluminium storm lamps. Bodinnick's kitchen was not born to be beautiful. It was born to feed hordes of hungry, busy people. It was also where, according to Sita's timetable, the assembled throng should have been gathering for their first house meeting.

"We should have at least one, before Kat goes tomorrow," Sita insisted, putting her brush to dry on a piece of newspaper on the Aga lid.

She looked around. Niall was rolling a second cigarette, his latest money-saving wheeze, even though he hadn't yet smoked the first. Kat was painting her toenails again. Emmy was drawing on the inside of her orange peel with a pen. The exposed patch of bedroom floorboards where a chunk of ceiling plaster had collapsed and brought supper to an untimely close on their first night still sat over the table, waiting to be fixed.

"Right. I'll be upstairs if anyone wants me," she said a little brusquely. Unfortunately, her point was lost in the sudden clamor of fighting siblings.

"I want to go home," Asha wept, rushing in. "I want to go home. Please Mummy, can we go home?"

"This *is* home," Jay shouted, snapping at her heels. "You'd better get used to it."

"No it isn't. It's not *my* home, *my* home is in London."

"Hey hey hey, you two!"

Everyone saw Asha's painful little think bubble. It showed her old bedroom, with the unicorn stencils and white cupboards and night light. It showed her pink walls and her glittery curtains, her fitted carpet and her miniature desk and chair.

She had spent her whole life in a house where you could find anyone within a couple of minutes, where the paintwork didn't peel, the floors didn't creak, the fire didn't smoke. Even if you were on your own, you were never more than twenty feet from someone else. At Bodinnick, she sometimes thought she was lost forever. Outside her bedroom window, there was nothing. Nothing to worry about like overhead cables which might sway and break in the wind and electrocute someone in their bed like there were at some of her friends' houses in London, nothing like really tall trees right outside that burglars might climb up and break in like there were at Niall's old flat. All there was at Bodinnick was a lovely big garden. And she was terrified.

"My home's back in London," she kept crying.

"Not anymore, it's not," Jay taunted.

"Emmy, this isn't Narnia, is it? Is it? Maya says it is. She says there's an evil queen in that wardrobe and Jay told me to go through the coats, and . . ."

"But you've read *The Lion, the Witch and the Wardrobe*, haven't you?" Emmy said, not as gently as she meant to. She wasn't in the mood to have Maya blamed for Asha's neuroses, but at the same time she couldn't bear to think that the move might be making any of them unhappy.

"I don't like it. Daddy stopped it. It scared me."

"They're just playing it out."

"I don't want them to."

"Why not?" Emmy's parenting skills didn't stretch to reassurance. There had never been the need.

"I just don't."

"You could be Lucy."

"I don't want to be Lucy. I want to be me. I want to go home."

"Well, you know what?" Emmy said. "This is better than Narnia—this is Bodinnick."

Which wasn't entirely the right thing to say. Asha needed fitted carpets and double glazed windows, not magic and mystery. In Emmy's defense, she knew very little about children like that. The prosecution might say she had no desire to, either.

Suddenly, from the floor there was a dull thud, a split second's silence and then a blood-curdling scream. Lila had fallen from her nest of cushions and was hanging backward out of the brown plastic dog basket, her head resting on the hard, cold lino.

"For God's sake, who put her down there?" Sita shouted.

"You did," Emmy said.

"Well, it's about bloody time she learned how to sit up!"

"Wellies on, kids," Emmy said quickly, realizing the household could take no more. "You ain't seen nothin' yet."

It was true. The house, just as Emmy had promised, was shrinking, but the grounds and outbuildings were still an unknown universe, with secrets lurking behind every hut and hydrangea.

3

EMMY FROGMARCHED THE CHILDREN TO THE CHAPEL FIRST, BECAUSE SHE thought the walk would do them good.

In truth, the perfect little medieval building nestling in the corner of a field on the other side of the lane that led from the manor to the farmhouse had always left her slightly cold, but she blamed Toby for that. The past hadn't been kind to men like him, and the Church certainly hadn't, so even as a child Emmy had picked up on the fact that the place represented something stifling and repressed.

She was right about the therapeutic aspect of the walk there, though. By the time they got to its arched door, all three children were laughing again. She and Asha had collected fallen camellia and azalea blooms on the way, big blousy pink ones, wistful cream ones and yellow trumpets, floppy with frost.

They floated them in the rain butt and put the ones with stalks in a jam jar on the altar, and then, after a few minutes, they shut the small wooden door again and Emmy knew the flowers would be dead the next time anybody saw them.

Somewhere in the back of her mind, she accepted that the chapel deserved more, but she and Toby weren't the only perpetrators of injustice. Bodinnick's sale details in the top drawer of the walnut bureau in the library didn't make much of it, either. The fading document described a formal early-Regency house of robust nature, built in 1820, with the addition of a servants' wing in 1870.

The chapel was almost an afterthought, included in the garden paragraph and referred to as a "former private chapel currently being usefully employed as a tool and potting shed." Beyond it, there was, in the description's carefully vague wording, a "much older" building, insulated from the servants' wing by a wall, with access from the outside only. This "older building" was where they all went next.

It was the early equivalent of the modern-day shed, and when Toby took ownership of Bodinnick in 1960 it was full of the detritus of farm and family life—hen coops and lunchboxes, broken chairs and tractor tires, sacks of seed and tins of furniture wax—and was known as the "store." He'd done nothing to alter its role but had added to it with his own rather more quirky mark—faux marble columns for a New Year's Eve Roman orgy, speakers the size of junior-school children, a twelve-foot pennant of Prince Philip in nothing but the crown jewels for the Silver Jubilee, and a sit-up-and-beg bright pink bicycle complete with tinsel-twined basket, a veteran of his gay marches in London.

As she watched the starburst effect on the children, Emmy's memory threw up a very vague recall of Toby's one-time intention to turn the store into an art gallery. He'd been forever coming up with ideas for the place. Maybe this very minute he was sitting on a fluffy white cloud, stroking his goatee beard and thinking, "Go, girl!"

She hoped she could do him justice. He deserved success, even if his death—or rather his bequest—had been the shock of her life. It was ironic, really. Part of the reason for the move from London was rejection of the material world they all felt they'd been sucked into, and yet if Toby hadn't made her the recipient of such gain, none of them would be here at all.

The need to possess had never been her thing. Even having Maya ten years ago and finding herself wholly responsible for another person hadn't changed that, so when she'd first heard that she was the sole beneficiary of the will, she'd felt like the pretender to a very grand throne.

She had been dreading the funeral, but in any event, it had turned out to be so much like a party that she'd had to keep reminding herself afterward that Toby hadn't been there in person. And not one finger had been pointed about the will. It really did seem that she was the only one who hadn't seen it coming.

"No one knew Toby better than I," his poor old boyfriend Julian had said after the burial, holding her gloved hands in his cold, scaly grasp. "And he believed that no one knew you better than he."

"I think that may be true."

"Then you have one duty to him, and one duty alone."

"Which is?"

"To make the most of your joie de vivre. He used to say you inherited it from him."

"That may be true, too."

"So you must let Bodinnick make you as happy as it made him. Make your life exactly what you want it to be."

"It would help if I knew."

"He always thought you did know."

"Ah," Emmy had said feebly. "But what about you? Are you sure you don't want to stay on?"

"Thank you, my dear, but I couldn't bear to be there without him. My cottage in Totnes will serve me more than well until I go and join him."

Once she knew that, she had been brave enough to ask the rest. She'd tried not to focus on the drip hanging from the end of his long, thin nose.

"Do you think I could share the house? With friends? A sort of cooperative, so that all of us and none of us own it? They're good friends, *best* friends, they're more important to me than my family. I'd trust them with my life."

Julian had said, with a nod so definite that the nose drip fell and settled on his mustard cashmere scarf, that he thought that would make Toby very happy indeed. He said Toby knew all about friends being more important than family, present company excepted.

Amazing, since the wedding and the train crash were, at that stage, still a whole week away. Spooky, even.

Perhaps the manor had been nurturing her all her life for this. Her responses to the place had always been different from the rest of the family's. She was the only one who never got scared here as a child, the only one who came and stayed with Toby on her own, the only one who wanted to play in the attic, poke around the rooms, make dens in the garden. Her brothers used to pester for a day on the beach or a tent in the field, but Emmy always preferred to be within striking distance of its thick granite walls. Being inside its grounds was like having her own fortified town. She never wanted to be queen, just inhabitant. Besides, it had already had its queen.

"Be careful!" she shouted to the children as one of the fake marble columns wobbled. It was verging on the disrespectful, the way they were suddenly lost in the desire to possess. Half an hour ago, they had been tearful, taunting and homesick. Now they were behaving like a crack team of consummate carjackers. Well, they hadn't been near a shop other than the village one for ten days, which must be a record.

"Uh, I need a man!" Maya shouted, trying to drag the pink bicycle free from its prison of ropes and old chairs.

Don't we all, darling? Emmy felt like replying.

"Jaysus! It's Liberace's dressing room."

Oh my God, she thought, leaping out of her skin as Niall appeared from nowhere. I can do thought-transference. Wish him, and he appears.

He had his arm round Prince Philip. "I'm beginning to see what your family were up against," he said, moving the figure to one side.

"Careful. Toby's ghost lives on, you know. He'll come to haunt you with his feather boa and Judy Garland record collection."

"I hope so. It'd be nice to see him again."

"Wouldn't it."

"It would. This is great," he said, looking around. "God almighty, that's an amplifier and a half."

"That was for his electric guitar."

"Where's the guitar, then? Is that still around?"

"Don't even think about it."

"Too late. The seed has been sown. It's years since I played."

"And you were terrible even then."

"Get on. I was great."

They both thought of the first time he had sung to her.

"That train was a stroke of luck," he said.

"And which train would that be?" she asked coyly.

"That would be both of them."

"Is the right answer."

That now beatified journey of her youth on the Paris-to-Rome sleeper had been Hitchcockian in its potential for menace. Nineteen years old, alone in Europe and picking her way in the dark over twisted heaps of travel-weary bodies and scuffed rucksacks, she had almost been able to hear the soundtrack. It had been no surprise at all when the Moroccan guy leaning against a carriage partition had swung his pitted oily face in her own and blocked her path with his reeking body.

"Excuse me?"

"Beer? Spirit? Drink with me?" he'd slurred, waving a bottle at her. "Pretty girl." He had rubbed against her breast.

She could still remember the lack of effect her then seven-and-a-half-stone frame had against his hot, sweating bulk, but at least the struggle had caused enough commotion to wake the sleeper at her feet.

And when that sleeper had stood up, the relief of seeing someone a good foot taller than her aggressor was immense. It might even have been love at first sight.

"You havin' a problem there?" His hair was sticking up in clumps for want of a good wash, but his brand of personal hygiene, or the lack of it, was immediately familiar. Student-based. Non-threatening. Welcome.

"Beer, lady? You want beer? Drink with me?"

"No, I don't think she does, mate," the sleeper had said, "and she's with me, okay?"

So her first date with Niall had been a trip to a railway loo at midnight, and he'd held the door for her while she tried her best not to make a sound or pee all over the floor. Then they'd returned to her carriage, sat together with their legs on their bags, smoking and talking and strumming until Turin, where they'd kissed on the platform and arranged to meet in Milan.

And that was it. It wasn't the pregnancy that broke the beautiful spell of the next two years, it was the abortion. She was twenty-one in the summer after her finals and Niall was twenty-four.

"I'm going mad," she'd told him two months after it was done. "I think our love was encapsulated in the baby and now we've chosen to get rid of that we've also got rid of ourselves."

"We're still here."

"No, we're not. We're in the medical wastebin with our baby. You're not, and I'm not, but *we* are."

There wasn't anywhere else they could go with that, so they'd walked away from their shared bedroom in a shared house and left everything, absolutely everything, behind.

Weird that it had taken another train to bring them home again, to another shared house, with other shared bedrooms. Except that he shared his bedroom with someone else now. Only at weekends, though. And they never referred to *it*. Ever. But it was okay. It really was okay.

She smiled at him again.

"What's on the other side of this?" he asked, tapping the solid stone. He knew those smiles and they usually meant trouble.

"The kitchen."

"Perfect. We'll knock through. I'll get my brother to draw up the plans for free, and Murphy can come and build it."

"Build what?"

"How about a sitting room people actually want to sit in."

"Don't you like the one we've got?" Emmy felt icy panic claw at her chest.

"I don't know. It's too cold to stay in there long enough to assess."

"Is it a disappointment here? Did you think it would be better than this? I wish it was the middle of summer—it's so beautiful here when it's hot and sunny. Give it a few weeks and—"

"God, Emmy, relax. It's just feckin' cold in the sitting room, that's all."

"Do you think I should get some heating put in? I know it's already nearly May but even if we don't stay until the winter, it might, you know, well, at least then we could—"

"Stop. Right now. Everything is fine, everyone's happy, we're all pinching ourselves at being lucky enough to . . . you know." He put his hand to her hair and pulled a strand away from her face. "It's just colder inside than out, that's all."

Emmy changed the subject. "Did you say Murphy? You've got to be joking."

"Paddy Murphy's the man, builder par excellence."

"Except we'll have to use local tradesmen, or you won't get served at the pub."

"Good thinking."

"What are you doing in here, anyway? I thought Kat wanted you to hump furniture."

"I'll hump later. How're the kids?"

"See for yourself." Emmy gestured.

"Don't do smug."

"I'm not. But look, Asha's fine. She's completely forgotten about it. They make too much of it. She'd be fine if they just ignored it."

"That's great. Just don't forget that everyone has a different way, that's all."

There were a few words implicit in his comment. What he meant was "everyone has a different way from *us*." Emmy bristled with pleasure.

"It's all about diversion, isn't it? It's such an easy trick."

"Divert me, then."

Emmy didn't bother to take him up on it—she'd heard it all before. Sexual innuendo from Niall had very little to do with whether he was attracted to you.

The girls had freed the bicycle and were rubbing the cobwebs away, feeling its tires, emptying rubbish from its basket.

"Look at that. They say that one man's junk is—"

"Another man's treasure?"

Maya heard his voice and looked up. Niall blew her a kiss.

"You haven't been too hard on her, have you?" he asked accusingly.

Only he could suggest such a thing. Emmy knew that he knew she was sometimes too hard on Maya, that she leaned too hard, punished too hard, loved too hard.

"No."

"Go easy. It's new for us all."

"I know, but tell me it's not just me who thinks it's odd that Asha's got all the trappings of security she could wish for, and she can't say boo to a goose, and then there's Maya, who's been dragged up without a father, with a mother who lurches from one emotional crisis to the next . . ."

Niall put his hand in his old cord coat pocket to find his cigarettes, and shook his head. "That's not right, though, Em, is it?"

"It is."

"No, it's not."

"Why?"

"Well, for a start, we both know you think Maya's better off without a father."

"I do. I'm not ashamed of that."

"Nor should you be, but don't do all that 'dragged up without one' thing. Not to me, anyway." He was sailing close to the wind. "Because I know you think you have the more rounded child as a result—that given the choice you would actively advocate single parenthood."

"I do. I think it does you good to have the corners knocked off you at an early age."

"You don't have to be the child of a single parent for that to happen."

"I know, but you get less attention, and that has its benefits."

"Do you?"

"Maya does."

Niall didn't think so, but he didn't say so. "You'd hate to share her, wouldn't you?"

"You try it. It's bloody hard work."

"That's not in dispute, but c'mon, Maya is hardly deprived of stability, and what are your emotional crises? A couple of useless boyfriends? She's one of the lucky ones, and you know it."

He watched the girl climb over an old tractor seat and jump down the other side. He might be the only one who could get away with talking to Emmy like that but he also knew when to change tack. "But you're obviously doing something right."

Emmy nodded, accepting the compliment. She thought *she* was one of the lucky ones too. Single parenthood was what she would choose. It meant the accolade belonged entirely to her. Maya was her achievement. Her only achievement, maybe, but still all hers.

Niall shrugged. "I can't help it."

"Can't help what?"

"Being so proud of her."

You have no idea what hearing something like that does to me, Emmy thought. "Don't help it, then. You know how much you mean to her."

"I do now. She's already given me my pass to enter her room whenever I like." He produced a credit-card-sized piece of board with his name and a password on it. "No one else is going to have one, apparently. Not even you."

One of Maya's early paintings flashed up in Emmy's mind. *My Family*, it was called. Niall was in it, along with the goldfish and the hamster, and it had been on the fridge door for years. Emmy liked him playing Dad, but only because he knew things. For a start, he knew he was playing, and secondly he also knew the point at which she would do the Lioness thing and swipe him with her paw.

"Not that I'm going to be allowed to use it much," he said, putting the pass back in his pocket. "Not at weekends, anyway."

"What? Kat? She's not *still* got a thing about her, has she?"

"Don't be too hard on her, Em. She's just trying to find her feet. She's really keen to make this work, not just between her and me, but here."

"Or is she just putting up with us lot as a means of getting you?"

"What do you mean, getting me?"

"Keeping you, then."

"I'm not going anywhere."

"Good. Don't."

"I won't. I don't help, though. I told her the reason I wasn't up for a kid just now was because I felt I already had one."

"She wants a baby?" Emmy's heart thumped a little.

"Not really. Only when she's pissed."

"That's ridiculous."

"Is it?"

"Well, you tell me."

"You're a bad girl sometimes, Emmy," Niall said, shaking his head at her. "Most of the time you're irresistibly lovely, but every now and again you're rotten to the core."

"Sorry. Anyway, you told her you already had one?"

"I told her I felt I did. It's true, you know it is. Maya feels like mine, even if she isn't."

"She certainly behaves as if she's yours sometimes."

"Swears like a trooper, smokes herself half to death."

"All that."

There was a long pause, which Emmy wanted to go on for even longer. It happened sometimes, their past coming to illuminate their present, and when it did her world was a better place. She had tried to be clear about it to Sita once, but she'd ended up being about as clear as pastis and water. What everyone except Kat did seem able to understand was that, even though Niall wasn't Maya's father, she engendered in him something so like paternal love that he might as well have been. Even Jay and Asha had got as far as that.

"So Kat knows everything about us, does she? I mean, like everything?"

"She knows I was there at Maya's birth. That'll do."

It was the closest they had ever got to referring to the termination. Everything else before and after was permissible, but the abortion and the maelstrom of emotion that swirled around it were not. They went near it at their peril.

"Did you ever put Toby right?" Niall asked suddenly.

"Nope."

"Good."

"Good you said good."

Toby Hart had only met Niall O'Connor once, when his postnatal niece had brought him to Cornwall on a trip to introduce her baby daughter. Their baby daughter, Toby supposed. The evidence for his paternity was all there. What man would offer to change the dirty nappy of another man's child?

He'd promised himself to take the secret to his grave, but not before dancing on another one. The Victorian family values that had so damaged his own life were being swept away by a demographic tidal wave before his very eyes. He'd caught wind of the blast of heartfelt disapproval over Emmy's untimely pregnancy and was furious. If Emmy chose to be a single parent and Niall respected that, then good for them. Why should she name the father if she didn't want to? Why should they live like man and wife? It was after that short weekend visit that he made up his mind. Bodinnick was Emmy's if she wanted it, and if she didn't, well, the money would help her stick two fingers up to the lot of them.

Toby took his unswerving belief about Maya's parenthood with him, never suspecting that he could possibly have read it wrong. The truth was that she couldn't have been Niall's child, much as they all might have wished it. By the time her little seed had been sown, so much water had rushed under the young couple's bridge that the timing wasn't just out, it was long gone. Emmy knew it, Niall knew it, and, by osmosis, Maya knew it too. Not that minor details like that mattered.

Maya was the size if not the shape of a watermelon when Niall first laid hands on her, through the skin of Emmy's tightening stomach. Feeling the familiar landscape of his ex-girlfriend's torso with the touch of a friend and not a lover had been the only gesture in the whole reunion that hadn't come naturally. The effort not to slide his fingers round her widening waist and squeeze the flesh of her newly ample bottom again was superhuman, but he owed her at least that. Three years had been a hellishly long time without contact.

Her letter when it came had been short. *I'm pregnant again*, she'd written, *and I need to explain to you why I am going to keep this one*. But she never really had explained.

As soon as he realized the father wasn't going to feature, he was willing to listen. His first call, her first visit, their first laugh all came easily, without regret. But the hands-on-bump thing was different. It affected him in a way he couldn't describe.

"Are you the father?" the student midwife asked him as he helped Emmy count her way through a contraction. "Not this time," he said. The midwife thought he meant that he would be the next, not realizing that he had been the last. "If you play your cards right," she joked.

Anyway, he'd seen Maya take her first breath, and no one, not even her real father, could take that away. Holding the baby while Emmy was stitched up, studying Maya's freshly peeled rawness, he'd fought a dark desire to merge her with the unborn one, the one that still existed between them. He never spoke about it, but for a split second in the delivery suite the two lives had become one. Maya's wet black hair had become even wetter as he put his head as close to hers as he dared, but Emmy was not only drugged, she was so completely out of sorrow by then that she didn't notice. It was a lifetime ago, literally.

"Ow!"

The echo of a dusty collapse somewhere behind an old screen made the thick store walls shake.

"We're okay," Maya shouted.

Now that she was so far removed from the image of that helpless prawn, Niall would look at her and recognize not the unborn but himself—his own tilt of the head, or his way of standing with hands in pockets, one hip lower than the other. The secret longing to hear her call him Dad was too corny even to contemplate, but the fear of another man standing a better chance still occasionally loomed. His usual comfort lay with Maya herself, who appeared entirely unconcerned about the identity of her father. He could almost see her think bubble: I've got Niall, so what's the big deal?

His own think bubble, when Kat pushed him into considering their own child, sometimes read more or less the same. Maybe not the best thought to share with her, but possibly a better one than the other that often possessed him.

He had known Emmy for nearly fourteen years. To break it down, that would be two years of young love and endless sex, two months of blinding panic, one year of grief, another two of emptiness, ten quick minutes of reunion and a remaining eight years of pretty perfect platonic friendship. They were doing quite well, considering. Just as he was wondering what the next three months might bring, a blond wig came flying through the air.

"Hey, that's enough, you lot."

The children screamed with laughter and clattered on.

"You're not related to Barbara Cartland by any chance, are you, Em?" Niall caught the missile and spun it round his fist but the tight curls stayed perfectly in place.

"It's quite possible," Emmy said. "Is she or isn't she?"

He held the synthetic hair up to the light. "Oh, definitely, without a doubt."

"Is she or isn't she what?" came an accusing voice from the large oak door. It was Kat, and when Kat heard the word "she," she always assumed it referred to her.

"Wearing hairspray," Emmy said, turning round and feeling guilty for no reason.

"What? Who?" Humorless was one adjective you could use to describe her. Beautiful, rude, talented and demanding were four others.

"No, you've come in too late. The joke's gone." Niall dismissed her inquiry with a wave of his hand. "How are your legs? Ripped raw?"

"Smooth as a baby's butt, thanks."

"Why didn't you wait until you got back to London?" Emmy asked, a little too accusingly. Asha's crying wasn't the only reason she'd taken the children outside. Sita and Kat had started making girly attempts at bonding.

"Sita's very good at waxing, actually. You should let her do you. Apparently, it makes even more difference if you're dark."

"Or you could just say Em's got legs like a caveman."

"Ug."

"I didn't mean that. It's just that I'm so fair that you can't really tell when I need a wax, can you, Niall? So I don't know why I waste my money."

"Sita charged you? Jaysus!"

Both women laughed, although Emmy's was the more generous sound, full in the knowledge that the dig was at Kat, not her.

"Can you give us a hand with this bike?" Maya shouted.

"Not me. These suede trousers cost a fortune to clean," Kat said, taking a step back.

"All dry cleaning an individual expense, rule number twenty-three," Niall replied. He didn't bother to suggest she go back and change them. He knew why she was wearing them: they made her bottom look like a peach. Why was it, then, that he felt more like sinking his teeth into the plumper pear that was Emmy's? She had on a pair of checked surfy things that looked as if they might once have been a curtain, and he could see her flesh gently rippling underneath. The last time he had made love to her, she'd been like a rake. He wouldn't mind seeing what she was like a couple of stone heavier.

"Niall, I want you to come back to the house with me," Kat carried on. "I need you for something."

"Can't it wait?"

"Have you forgotten that I'm going back to London tomorrow?"

"No."

"Or that you're going to Ireland next weekend?"

"So? I'm coming back, y'know. It's only another passin'-from-purgatory moment."

"You're going to Ireland?" Emmy asked. She didn't want him to go anywhere.

"Funeral."

"Whose?"

"Kieran Kennedy, my brother's mate from way back. Heart attack, forty years old."

"You'll see Cathal?" There was a catch in Emmy's voice but his name had to be pronounced with a bit of throat clearing—Ca'hul—so she got away with it.

"He better be there. I'm only going to keep him sober."

"No chance."

"Kieran was a fat bastard. Drank himself to his grave on Saint Patrick's Day."

"But that was in March."

"I know. It took him a long time to let go."

"God. There's a lesson in that for you both. When did Cathal call?"

"A few days ago. Maya answered the phone and brought it to me when I was in the bath, remember?"

"No, she didn't tell me that."

"Does she tell you everything?" Kat asked irritably. "Niall, did you actually notice me come in and start speaking to you? Only . . ." She whispered in his ear.

"Mary, mother of J, we've only just got up. What was wrong with suggesting that an hour ago when we were still in bed? I can't do it to order, anyway. Where's your spontaneity, woman?"

"You're not trying to put off all that humping you promised you'd do, are you, Niall?" Emmy asked.

"Would I?" he said, smacking Kat's tiny bottom.

Kat had no choice but to try out her most generous laugh, too.

4

Niall's "recreational relationship" went back to London on the same day the children started at their new schools, so it was hard to tell what the catalyst for the sudden burst of activity was. Maybe it was the hint of summer breeze that blew through the house after Jonathan opened all the sash windows, heaving and pushing until their ancient gloss seals cracked and the swollen wood retreated. Maybe it was the way the house martins swooped in and out of the eaves as if they were solar-powered. Or maybe it was just the basic truth that, in Emmy, Niall, Sita and Jonathan's case, four was company and five was a crowd.

"Come on," Emmy said, leaping up from the kitchen table on the first Kat-free morning. "Let's get this show on the road. This lino can go for starters."

She kicked at a cluster of tiny lumps under the green marble-effect flooring and managed to take the tops off them. A spray of ancient grit stuck in her toenails and in the rubber sole of her flip-flop. "Ugh, that is revolting."

Sita knew opportunity when she saw it, but the breakfast things were still on the table and she hadn't yet found time to get out of her pajamas. "We should clear up first."

"What's the point? We can do it later." Emmy was teasing her a little, overplaying their differences, but Sita was ahead, as always, and said, "Sure. Actually, could you paint my toenails first?"

"Yeah, right. I thought you'd want to strike while the iron is hot."

"Oh, the iron's on, is it? I'll just—"

"Bugger off," Emmy laughed, beaten at her own game. She was already on the floor, picking at an upcurled corner by the Welsh dresser.

Sita tried not to feel too much like a performing baby elephant as she lowered her bulk to the floor to join her and rested gingerly on her knees.

"No one's going to approach me from behind, are they?"

"You should be so lucky."

The flooring was tacky with years of neglect, a black line of grease running along the dresser's plinth where the mops of a decade of domestic helps had failed to reach.

"Uuch! It really is disgusting!"

"Yes, but it's rotten as well. We can just pull it off. Look."

It came off easily in a pleasingly wide strip big enough to reveal a triangle of the original floor underneath. That was all it took for their idle peeling to become frenzied stripping. Suddenly, with that enticing glimpse of smooth gray flag, they saw a whole new world. Craftsmen-built units in sycamore, polished granite tops, a light-filled living space, part workshop, part heart and soul. Easy meals, music, newspaper mornings, homework and flapjacks.

"We could knock through to the store."

"Run a massive sofa along one wall."

"No stainless steel. I hate stainless steel."

They developed their own techniques. Sita used a paint scraper to make sure she got under the loose pieces, Emmy just picked and pulled, taking her chances. Piles of discarded lino mounted up between them, and every now and again they found themselves pulling at the same bit. When that happened, they took more care, enjoying the challenge of seeing how big a strip they could draw before it broke. Sometimes, where the glue was bone-dry, the vinyl shattered and sent splinters shooting across the floor. Other times, where moisture had got into it from a spilt drink or rising damp from the suffocated slate, it was like wet wallpaper, coming off in dank layers.

It was a filthy but all-consuming task, so only when Sita's bottom bumped the table leg did they stop to assess the situation.

"We need to move the furniture," said Emmy urgently, her cheek smeared with the lino's black glue. "Why don't we carry it all out onto the lawn?"

Jonathan, back from the first, surprisingly easy, school run and expecting to find them where he'd left them, drinking coffee and bitching about Kat in the kitchen, ran into them in the hall. He was just in time to see them take a chunk of plaster off the wall with the table corner as they passed.

"Watch out! What are you doing?"

"Waxing each other's bits," Emmy said. "What does it look like?"

"It looks like you're wrecking the joint."

"You do it, then," Sita said, putting her end of the table down. "I need to get out of these pajamas."

"Me too," said Emmy. "Jon, go and get Niall out of bed and tell him we've got more humping for him to do."

TWO HOURS LATER, THE CIRCLE OF FRESHLY MOWN GRASS IN THE MIDDLE of the drive outside the front door looked like the dregs of a house-clearance sale. The kitchen table, the chairs, the settle, the top of the Welsh dresser, the leather armchair, the bottom of the Welsh dresser, and the old electric cooker that no longer worked were stacked in a precarious pile in the center. Around it were boxes containing crockery, saucepans, Tupperware boxes without lids, rusting cake and biscuit tins, tartan Thermos flasks, ancient food mixers, enamel teapots, wooden and steel canapé dishes, corn on the cob skewers and far too many smoked glass trifle dishes. They had taken every single thing out of the kitchen which was now not much more than an echo, but less was already more. Even the boys could see that.

"Did Toby ever buy anything after 1970?" Niall asked, prostrate on the lawn. It was still only eleven o'clock in the morning but his second beer was going down very well.

Emmy put her foot on his chest, and held open a black bin bag.

"No. He wasn't materialistic, remember?"

"Right, that's the tea break over," Sita said. "Let's get on."

"I don't think we should let half this stuff back inside," Emmy said, flicking the black sack. "Everything we think we can live without goes in here."

"You're not going to chuck it away, are you?"

"No, I'm going to car-boot it next weekend at the playing field in Cott. I saw the advert on the gates yesterday. It's a fiver a car. It'll be a good way to meet people."

"Yeah, right."

"You'll be suggesting a feckin' barn dance next," Niall said, lifting his head and squinting into the sun.

"Now there's an idea."

"You're on your own, then."

"Okay, I'll start. Do we want this?" Sita asked, holding up a chipped orange jug.

"No." It went in the bag. "This?" It was a beige coffee percolator.

"No."

"This?" Jonathan asked, picking up a flat broomhead. "It hasn't got a handle."

"Get rid of it."

"This?"

"Out."

"This?"

"No."

"This?"

Niall rolled over and held Lila's fat little hand. She was propped in a nest of cushions, watching them. "How much would we get for the Buddha?"

When he stood up, he took his shirt off, even though it was still far from summer, and Emmy pulled hers out of her jeans and tied it in a knot at the waist. They caught each other's eyes and smiled, and when they could they put their hands on each other's backs and pretended it meant nothing.

THE BONFIRE IN THE TOP FIELD WAS STILL SMOLDERING WHEN NIALL threw on the old blue carpet from the sitting room. As he flumped it on the dying pyre, it created a mushroom of air and then fell down in a heavy flop, smothering the last few orange embers and billowing the ash into the air and faces of everyone standing around it.

"Niall!"

"It's okay. I'll get it going again."

Everyone was so busy kicking the dead, cold carpet and wiping white and gray flakes from their cheeks that they didn't notice him disappear on his new toy—a four-wheeled quad bike he had bought off the farmer at the weekend—and come back with a can of petrol that Jonathan had bought for the lawnmower.

It wasn't so much the final destruction of the motheaten blue carpet that he wanted to achieve, as the resurrection of the fire. He unscrewed the lid and splashed the fuel around like an experienced arsonist.

"Stand back," he shouted, but before anyone could react he'd tossed on a match and a furious ball of blue flame rocketed toward them like a costly special effect from a Spielberg space adventure.

Jonathan and Sita ran, the wall of heat chasing them as they stumbled over the humps and bumps of the grass.

Emmy was floored by it. She ducked, and in her shock lay flat on the ground, screaming, "You bloody pyromaniac! Did you mean to do that?"

"Well, how else are we going to get rid of it?" he shouted back over the furious crackling, laughing nervously. Thick black smoke belched over them and, for a second, he disappeared behind it.

"Just tell me you wouldn't have done that if any of the children had been here," Sita said crossly when he reappeared.

"Course I wouldn't. What do you think I am?"

"A bloody liability," she told him. "I'm going back to check on Lila. Don't do anything else stupid, for God's sake."

"Come on! I'm not as dangerous as I look, I promise you."

The fire blazed, spluttered and spat behind them as it consumed the ancient synthetic wool and rubber of Toby's dreadful carpet. As the heat subsided and the flames sank to a safer height and color, Emmy decided that, actually, she quite liked it. At least, she quite liked the energy it was throwing out.

Niall was pacing round it, excited. He had his sweater off and had tied it round his waist, and most of his shirt buttons, including the cuffs, were undone. "Well, now it's going, we should get the rest of the stuff. Do you think we could burn the useless old sofa from the music room?"

"And all that old wood from the kitchen?"

"God, the heat."

"Bring it on."

Jonathan looked at them from a distance. He had spent an hour stacking the wood in question in a neat pile by the back door. He was going to chop it into manageable lengths and store it for winter firewood, but it was pointless to make a bid for it now. When Niall and Emmy teamed up, opposition was more or less useless. He was beginning to understand that fact better than he ever had in London.

Niall climbed back onto his quad and revved the engine. Emmy was there like a shot, climbing up behind him, legs akimbo on the back of the ripped black seat. Her knees clamped themselves to his thighs almost instinctively as he pushed his foot down on the accelerator and bounced off over the field grass.

"Keep an eye on it, Jon," he shouted as they sailed off into the sunset. "Give it a poke if it needs it."

Jonathan watched them go. He wasn't sure if his face was burning from the fire or from some horrible recoil that had started to combust from inside.

The conversation with Sita at first light had made them both touchy. He'd woken feeling aroused, and this time had decided not to dismiss it as just another run-of-the-mill morning erection, so he had asked her to come and join him on the sofa. "No," she'd said, "I'm too cold."

"I know how to warm you up," he'd said from his antique exile on the sofa under the window. The women in his life had set up a feminist camp in the marital bed and showed little sign of allowing him back in. Asha was refusing point blank to sleep in the room she had been given, even when Jay was there. It was too big, she said, and if Lila was allowed in with Mummy, why wasn't she?

"No, thanks," Sita had said. So he told her she made him feel unwanted, unnecessary, surplus to requirements. He wanted to know how she'd feel if he disappeared off the surface of the earth.

"At six o'clock in the morning? Look Jon," she said, "I've had five hours' sleep, broken by a night feed. I'd be deeply pissed off if you disappeared off the surface of the earth, not least because I wouldn't wish single parenthood on anyone. What do you want me to say?"

She had barely said goodbye when he left on the school run, and then when he came back, it had been all lino and carpets and beer, and he hadn't got a look in edgeways. Not communicating wasn't like them. Or perhaps it was. Perhaps he just had more time to realize it now he wasn't constantly rushing to catch a train.

Or maybe the rejection wouldn't have lingered so long if Emmy and Niall hadn't been behaving the way they were. Breakfast without Kat had been almost too much. Why had they eaten scones, anyway? What was wrong with cereal and toast?

"Cream with your split, sir?" Emmy had said. She'd been wearing a long shirt with nothing underneath. Okay, it was a nightshirt, but Jonathan got the message even if Niall didn't.

"With my what?"

"Your split."

"It's a scone," Sita said.

"No it's not. It's a split. There's a difference."

"Not to the naked eye, there's not."

"Say it again."

"What, naked?"

"No, split."

"And again."

"Sp-lit."

"You two, please," Sita interrupted again.

"I can't help it. I've always fancied servile women."

"Is that why you liked me as a waitress?"

They could have gone on for hours if Jay hadn't come in and started nagging for someone to take him to the bus stop.

"Walk," Niall told him. "It's only down the lane."

"Can I?" he'd asked his parents keenly.

"I don't see why not," Sita replied, without even so much as a look at Jonathan.

"No you can't," Jonathan had said. "It's your first day. That's ridiculous."

"For God's sake, Jon, he needs to know we can trust him," Sita said huffily, as if Jay's previous truancy had been Jonathan's fault.

Children were experts at interrupting, his in particular. He accepted that his sex life had always been a bit off and on, but it had never been quite this off for quite this long. Jay, stop start, Asha, stop start. And now of course there was Lila. They were talking nearly thirteen years of scrappy sex here. At forty, that set a pattern. Welcome to middle age, Sita said whenever he tried to talk to her about it.

Suddenly, he didn't want to be anywhere near the bonfire by the time Emmy and Niall got back and began stoking and fanning and all that crap, so he started to walk.

In the garden, the ground in the shaded areas where the rhododendrons arched to form a canopy was still mushy—a thick soup from last autumn's leaves and winter twigs. Already a path was beginning to form from all the recent exploration. He could see imprints of children's trainers and his own much larger boots. The track from Jay's BMX bike skidded off to the right just before the gate and the sight of it made him feel better. It used to be practically impossible to lever his son into any open-air activity, and now he wanted a wetsuit. At least Cornwall was benefiting one of them.

Jonathan didn't get other people very much, not even—if he was being absolutely honest—his wife or his closest friends. He loved them, but he knew they were sometimes different to him. Sometimes it seemed as if everyone was always different to him.

The pond was a classic example, he thought as he walked past it. Emmy had taken them to the optimistically named "water garden" just after the chapel, and they'd all torn their skin and clothes to pieces fighting through the bamboo and razor-sharp grasses to get to it.

A pond was just about visible to the naked eye but it was dank and dark, covered in a mass of succulent weed, like flat cacti, and the Gunnera grew like giant rhubarb round the edge. The musty, forgotten water stank. Tar-black midges hovered across its hidden surface. Someone had spotted an elderly Koi carp lurking beneath the gloop and they all whooped and screamed and clapped their hands as if they were falling upon hidden treasure. But for a medieval chapel, nothing. Not even a raised eyebrow. When Emmy had first taken them to Bodinnick's chapel, his jaw had practically fallen on the floor. He couldn't believe she hadn't mentioned it before. It was one of the most perfect examples of a simple rural medieval building he had ever seen.

Her lack of interest made him wonder if his life might have been easier if his passion had been for motorbikes, or new music, or exotic travel. He was always telling his children to look above the shop fronts, to see what hid behind the hideous façades. "But they prefer the hideous façades, darling," Sita would say.

He walked quickly past the pond, keen to get where he now knew he was going. After the rhododendrons, the planting fizzled out into random hollies and hydrangeas. One large pink camellia stood apart, neither random nor sited, as if it had fallen off a wheelbarrow years ago and no one had bothered to pick it up.

He lifted and twisted the rusted metal latch on the arched gateway in the brick wall and pushed the door open as far as it would go. A ridge of soft mud collected behind the rotting wood, and he had to turn sideways to slip quickly, almost furtively, through the gap.

As he came out of the shade and across the tarmac track that ran from the road behind the house and into the farmyard, he blew through his hands and coughed. He coughed again for the purposes of self-diagnosis, not sure if he was wheezing or not. The ball of fire from the burning carpet might have scorched his lungs, and he was sure he had inhaled some of the acrid smoke.

The five-bar gate was tied with a loose chain so he climbed it to save the trouble of resecuring it. There was no hint of chest pain as he did so, and he jumped off, quickening his pace, feeling stronger.

Walking up the slight incline through the meadow grass and over to the smaller kissing gate, he felt cross with himself for not telling anyone he had been to the reference library yesterday. One of the pages he had photocopied about historic buildings in Cornwall even included a short paragraph on Bodinnick. Why hadn't he told them? Was it a desire not to be called Captain Sensible again? Or was it selfishness?

The revving of Niall's quad broke the stillness, so he almost ran toward the boxy little building beyond the tangle of grass, weeds and self-seeded trees, employing the same rhythm of breathing he used to use on the treadmills at the company gym.

The small field was covered in sheep's droppings, but mysteriously there were no sheep and the stepping-stone path to the door was all but covered by the invading grass. It felt like a forgotten place, which suited his mood.

The first thing he did was run his smooth office hands down the small wooden entrance. A Tudor arched doorway with strap hinges, according to *Cornish Houses from 1400 to 1700*, which he'd found in Bodinnick's own library yesterday. At breakfast he'd read a chapter about the "robust and unruly" people who lived in these places, people who lived piratical and dangerous lives, surrounded by treacherous coastlines which increased their feeling of separation and "encouraged an attachment to God and their homes."

He had no idea what it would be like to be robust and unruly, or to have an attachment to God and his home, but he wished he had.

The lichen on the granite side buttresses was both slimy and rough, but he had an idea it only grew in pure air, so he took a deep breath and tested his lung capacity again. This time he counted to five, not four.

He took his hand off the latch and walked around the outside, savoring its scale. It was small but confident and surprisingly lofty.

There was a tiny square chamfered window, then a narrow rectangular one, then two large centered windows on both the east and the west sides with carved decorations to their surrounds. The slate roof had been renewed within the last thirty years, he guessed, and the other clue to recent interest was what he suspected was a late-twentieth-century granite cross on the gable. He wondered if it was a replica of the original or whether Toby had simply got it wrong. He entertained himself with the thought that he might be in a strong position to take it down, to make decisions about this building. No one else was going to, that was for sure.

The door resisted a little, then, with a slight push, creaked and flung open, revealing a light gray arc scratched on the slate floor where the door had been opened and closed over the years. Not that many years: the slate was modern, too neatly cut for antiquity.

The door shut behind him, coming to rest on the ridge of slate that had caused it to resist on opening. He pulled it back, but as soon as he let go it shut again. Emmy was right about one thing: the smell. It was damp. In pursuit of a through draft, he found a stool to prop it open with, and when he'd done that he took a detailed look around.

The exposed wagon roof looked sound enough. The timber curved seamlessly, the distances between the beams were mathematically accurate, the edges of the wood were smooth.

He tried to bring to mind the medieval carpenter who'd made it and a mason perhaps, or an apprentice, but he couldn't summon anything more than a vague sense of rustic competence. His mind was well and truly locked in the twenty-first century. Visionary he was not. He needed the written word to form a mental image of anything, and to reassure himself he patted the back pocket of his jeans, from which poked a few stapled pages.

The step up to the sanctuary, or altar, looked original. He stood on it, then stepped off again and back a few paces to take in the larger picture. A small wooden table sat below a large three-paned cinque-foiled leaded window, flanked by granite pillars set into the stone. There was a jam jar in the middle of the table, its insides stained with brown rings and dying floral debris. The decay offended him so he took it off and put it in the corner on the floor.

When he looked up, he saw the "upper chamber, accommodation for a resident chaplain with projections on either side, on the south for a staircase, and on the north, for a recess and a fireplace," he'd read about, and for a moment he tried to conjure up the chaplain, too, but as with the carpenter he failed.

Buildings he could see. He had enough knowledge to bring up in his mind the appropriate architecture for most periods, so if someone talked of a Georgian house or a Gothic window, he knew what they meant, but people remained as text. His imagination couldn't go that extra distance.

He needed the security of someone else's knowledge, and he pulled the pages from his back pocket and started to read.

"Virtually all medieval buildings were constructed with lime. Lime was slower to build with, and required skill and patience, but produced durable, attractive and healthy results. Damp was allowed to evaporate away harmlessly, and the soft but tough lime worked in harmony with seasonal changes in humidity and temperature."

He thought about the quick-fix culture they had lived in in London and felt a new rush of achievement in their efforts to leave it behind. He brushed his hands over the wall and bits fell out, down his sleeve and onto the floor.

"Cement sets very hard and is impervious to damp. Any moisture finding itself drawn in will be trapped and will cause problems. If it is used in a building whose underlying structure is of the more flexible lime, problems will undoubtedly occur."

He looked carefully at the internal pointing of the stones round the altar and along the sides. His angst with Sita and his jealousy of the others faded away. He thought of Emmy and Niall by the bonfire, leaping around with the same intensity as the flames, and he no longer cared. He was more interested in a large, clumsy patch of ugly gray cement.

"Repairing lime-based buildings with lime-based materials is the answer. There is little mystery involved: a grasp of the basic principles combined with common sense and perseverance is all that is required. After using lime, most people realize just what a marvelous and invaluable material it is, become 'converts' to the cause and start to encourage others to try it for themselves."

A convert. He liked the sound of the word. His hand went automatically back to the crumbling mortar and his fingers rubbed the crevices. Grit fell easily out, and the more it fell, the more he dug.

He didn't know how long he dug and scraped and picked, but by the time he walked back past the bonfire Emmy and Niall had retreated to the house and the flames were just a gentle flicker.

5

SOMEWHERE, IT HAD BEEN RASHLY WRITTEN DOWN THAT EVERYONE HAD their say at Bodinnick, and when it got to the stage of choosing paint colors the children took it upon themselves to put such political indulgence to the test.

Jay wanted the universe on his ceiling, glowing dark stars against a midnight blue, but Asha wanted fluffy white clouds and a rainbow. Maya, as she had stated in the manifesto, wanted purple.

"No, not that sort of purple," she said every time Emmy showed her a paint chart. "That's too Barbie. Too royal. Too light. Too dark."

"God help their future partners," Sita said as she stepped over the pots in the hall in the first pair of shoes with heels she had worn since they arrived. A threadbare Turkish rug was rolled to one side and the black and white tiled floor was covered in damp flattened cardboard— old boxes from the store that Toby used to ship his art sales in. "Lawyers, the lot of them. Particularly Asha. I call a nine-year-old persuading her parents she needs a cot a serious result."

She couldn't conceal her disapproval at Jonathan's capitulation over the outlandish request, and he couldn't conceal his disappointment that indulgence was definitely not on his wife's list of personal tendencies anymore.

"You look nice," Emmy told her. She could see the effort Sita had made with her gray boxy linen jacket and skirt. The jacket wouldn't do up and the skirt was tight over her post-natal tummy, but then the suit had been bought fifteen months ago when she was at her slimmest ever, just before she discovered she hadn't done with childbirth after all. At least it was getting its wear now. Three weeks' cover for a local GP had landed in her lap sooner than any of them would have chosen.

"Do I? Is it a bit smart? I don't know."

"You look lovely," Emmy repeated. Jonathan could have stopped pretending he was too busy stirring emulsion and joined in, she thought.

"I don't know. I don't want to look too London."

"You don't."

"You don't even look too Cornwall," Jonathan said to Emmy. She was wearing a very old chambray boiler suit that had never seen a hardware store in its life and she had one of Toby's ties round her waist.

"Good."

"Why *are* we building her this ridiculous cot, for God's sake?" Sita snapped when she stumbled over a plank of wood.

"If that's what it takes to make her feel safe, what's a bit of MDF?" Jonathan replied equally tersely. "We all have our props."

He was defensive about Asha's lack of confidence. He knew it came from him. But Sita wasn't feeling confident either, and she went over to Jonathan with the intention of apologizing by way of a hug. The old shirt he had on smelled of the City, something to do with the over-ironing and stress that had resigned it to the dump bin in the first place, and because he only returned her insecure squeeze with a dutiful pat, she said, "Ugh, that shirt smells."

"Well, we all lean on something from time to time, don't we?" Emmy said, levering off a lid with a screwdriver.

"What do you lean on?" Jonathan asked. He was pouring a watered-down creamy glue from a two-liter plastic container into his tin of emulsion, and even that made his wife cross. Why couldn't he just slap up some straightforward matte like the rest of them? Why did he have to pay so much attention to detail all the time?

"Can I lie?" Emmy asked.

"No. Rule 465. No lying."

"Well, okay, Maya. I lean on Maya."

Jonathan looked embarrassed. He hadn't expected an honest answer, and he hadn't wanted one, either. He added water from a kitchen jug with more concentration than necessary.

"Serves you right for asking," Sita said, putting the lid on her lipstick and throwing it in her bag. "I'll take the girls. Oh, and Emmy, don't lean on Jonathan in my absence, will you? You'll end up on the floor." The door slammed.

Emmy said, "Are you two all right?"

"Of course," Jonathan said, as if she were mad to even ask. "What do you want, a brush or a roller?"

"THAT WAS MY MUM AND MY SISTER," JAY TOLD SCOTT AT THE BUS STOP, as Sita gave him a hoot from Emmy's rusty old car. "It's her first day at work."

"Up the abattoir?" his new friend asked, as if it went without saying.

"The what?"

"The abattoir. There's loads of jobs going up there at the moment. My dad's thinking about going for one but my mum don't want him to."

"Why not?"

"Her boyfriend works there."

"Oh, right," said Jay, sliding off the curb. "No, not there."

"Where, then?"

Jay kicked the toes of his new school shoes against the granite shelter. "In the village, I think. She's a doctor."

"Nurse, you mean, you div!" Scott told him.

"She's not a nurse, she's a doctor." Jay looked at the ground, hoping Scott wouldn't mind. He liked him, and not just because it meant he wasn't the smallest in his class anymore.

"Oh. I never knew you could have lady doctors. I thought they had to be nurses."

"So who's the div now?"

"I am." Scott laughed, stamping on his friend's feet with his filthy trainers.

"Cor-rect. You are the weakest link. Good-bye."

"Good-bye."

They barged each other with their backpacks and Jay felt his flask leaking through the nylon.

"Is your dad a doctor, too?" Scott asked.

"No."

"What's his job, then?"

"He hasn't got one," Jay said proudly.

"You should tell him to go up the abattoir."

"I will."

"Do you want to come fishing later?"

"I haven't got a rod."

"Nor have I."

"What do you fish with, then?"

"A stick."

"A stick? Do you ever catch anything?"

"No."

They fell against each other, laughing so loudly that the bus driver had to sound his horn to tell them he was waiting.

SITA SAT IN HER BLUE SWIVEL CHAIR LOOKING AT THE FRAMED STUDIO shots of some other doctor's chubby blond children on the mock-leather surface of her new pine desk. Above the desk was a blown-up photograph of a sailing boat called *Kontiki*, with the same two children in matching life jackets waving from her deck. Under it was a pair of smart black leather court shoes two sizes smaller than Sita's, and hanging on the back of the door was an equally small stone-colored mac which she recognized as from the Gap because she had nearly bought one herself. She felt replicated but different. The same model in a different finish.

"I bet you'll be the first Asian doctor Cott has seen," Niall had said at breakfast, at which she had been the sole topic of conversation. "Make sure you give them the full works."

She wished he hadn't said that. She felt like a fish out of water as it was. The practice manager had popped in with a truly terrible cup of filter coffee which tasted as if it had been sitting on its hotplate for days, and just as she was tipping it down the small steel sink the woman had appeared from nowhere again, saying, "Just leave it if you don't want it." It wasn't a good start.

In the drawers she had found three packets of eucalyptus chewing gum, a tube of honey-and-lemon hand cream and a nautical-clothing mail-order catalog. There was a box of toddler-friendly toys on the floor, full of the kind of discarded bits and pieces that could be picked up at school fêtes all over the country. It was every doctor's surgery everywhere, and yet it was all utterly foreign. She felt like phoning Asha and telling her it was okay to be homesick.

Her first patient was a woman with short dark hair and glasses. She was wearing floral jeans, a denim jacket and flip-flops and she made Sita feel ridiculously overdressed.

"Oh!" the woman said, failing to disguise a double take.

Sita's hackles were up before she could stop them. Yes, an Asian doctor, she felt like saying. What are you going to do now?

"I, er . . ." the woman said. She neither moved forward nor backward.

Sita stayed sitting and smiling. Inside she began to burn.

"I . . . I thought . . ."

The woman clearly didn't know where to look. How about in my face? Sita thought.

"Is there something wrong?" Sita asked eventually. "Apart from whatever it is you have come to see me about?"

"Er . . . I'm sorry, I didn't realize you were . . ."

Sita looked down at the woman's notes but couldn't focus on a single thing. She was already back in the kitchen at Bodinnick, telling Emmy.

"This is . . . I think, um," the woman began, "I . . ."

"Sorry, were you expecting someone else? I'm Dr. Dhanda, covering for Dr. Bryant for three weeks."

"Yes, yes, I know. They told me that. Perhaps I should . . ."

The woman was clearly flustered. Her face was pink and behind the lenses of her spectacles, her eyes darted everywhere but in Sita's direction.

"Do you want to sit down?" Sita asked. She'd been expecting a certain rural suspicion, but not this. The fish out of the water was in its last dying spasms. London seemed more attractive than ever.

"I . . . well . . ."

"Would you prefer to see someone else? Dr. Hall is back from his holidays today, I think."

"No. I asked to see a female doctor. It's just that you . . ."

"Are Asian?" Sita heard herself say.

"No!" the woman cried. "Oh, no, not that, not at all." She was even redder in the face now, but Sita stayed sitting, her head tilted slightly to one side. She tried not to look as nervous as she felt. In fact, she thought she might have cricked her neck.

"Oh good, because there's not much I can do about that."

They both gave small uneasy laughs.

"It's just that, well, your daughter has just started at Cott school, hasn't she? She's in my son's class. I've seen you in the car park."

"That's right, she has."

"Miss Davey's lovely with the kids."

"It seems like a nice school."

"Not that she stands much nonsense, mind."

"Good."

They stopped. The woman looked as if she wanted the floor to swallow her up. "My problem is a bit delicate," she murmured.

"Don't worry," Sita said, feeling her neck ease. "Doctors are used to delicate problems."

"What about seeing you in the playground? Won't we feel . . . ?"

"Not in the slightest. What is said in these four walls—"

"No, it's not that, I just . . . well, I came here because I promised my husband I'd talk to someone about . . . my . . . my, er . . ."

Sita waited. Her neck felt normal again. Slowly, she tried to right it. "Take your time." She had never said that in London.

"My, er, my lack of interest," the woman said. She stared at the floor. "I don't really know why I'm here, except I promised him I'd try. I don't know what you can do to help. I don't know what anyone can do. I've just gone off it, that's all. It's not him, it's me."

There was a brief mutual sigh.

"I understand," Sita said.

"Do you? Do you really?"

"Yes," said Sita again, "yes, I really do."

JONATHAN DIDN'T UNDERSTAND MUCH OF WHAT WAS GOING ON, EVEN though he could hear every word from his bedroom.

"It's not purple, it's Real Indigo. Jaysus, it even says so on the side of the can."

"Oh, and I suppose you're painting your shelves Memory, and not just gray, are you?"

"That was yesterday. Would ye keep up!"

"Anyway, who said you could look at my paint charts?"

"Kat did."

"Well, she's not here, so she doesn't count."

"It *is* purple."

"It's Real Indigo. Anyway, where's the dog?"

Niall was at the foot of a ladder in Maya's bedroom, looking up at Emmy's dripping brush. He waved a paint-slopped copy of the *Manifesto*.

"What?" Emmy barked down at him.

"It says here, '*To have a purple bedroom and a dog.*' And this is a Real Indigo bedroom with no dog. On the other hand, not a morsel of sushi have I let pass my lips in the last month, therefore I win and I claim my prize."

His hand ran quickly up the inside of her leg and she flicked the brush just as quickly toward his hair. Real Indigo mingled with the Natural Aubergine he had been painting his own walls with before Kat changed her mind. She kept e-mailing him with instructions and links to paint-company Web sites.

"You clash," Emmy told him. "Now bugger off. You've got work to do before you go to Ireland."

"You don't really mean that."

She climbed two steps down the ladder and put herself in a dangerous position. Hips level with lips. Niall gave a small groan.

"Yes I do, and you need to sort out the lid on your box," she said, bending her head to his ear. "It keeps flying open."

"That's because you keep prying it open."

They meant the box they had always kept their relationship in, shut away and labeled, where it couldn't cause any trouble.

"I don't."

"Ye do."

"I don't."

"Niall?" Jonathan shouted from the corridor, having skinned his knuckles for the second time trying to take off the gloss on the skirting board with a rusty paint scraper. "Have you got the blowtorch?"

The explosion of laughter was almost the last straw. "I'm sorry? Why is that so funny?" he asked, putting his head round the door. "And what are you doing in here anyway, Niall? Kat will kill you if she comes back and you haven't finished."

"I'm not in here. I took an earlier plane to Dublin, remember?"

THAT EVENING, SITA AND EMMY SAT AGAINST THE WALL OF THE HOUSE, drinking beer, catching the last of the sun and watching Maya and Asha try to get Lila to sit up without falling over. Each time, she rolled over, first sideways, then backward, then to the other side. The older girls shrieked with amusement, using the baby like a heavy-bottomed toy.

"She should really be sitting by now," Sita said. "The other two were."

"She's fine," Emmy told her. "All babies develop at their own rate. You should know that, of all people."

"But—"

"No buts. You want her to run before she can walk, you do."

"No, I just want her to sit up, that's all."

The girls stuffed Lila back into her car seat and started to practice cartwheels on the lawn. Jay was fishing in the pond with his strange little friend, Jonathan was inside on the computer, looking up limewashing on the Internet and Niall was on his quad in the field, pretending to tidy up the remnants of the bonfire but really seeing how fast he could corner without tipping.

"This is how it should be," Emmy said hazily, but in the silence that followed she felt obliged to add, "Isn't it?"

"Kind of," Sita said.

"Hard day?"

"Pretty much. They all are when you've got kids, aren't they?"

"Why don't you go and have a bath? Go and have a lie down with Jonathan."

"I can't."

"Yes you can."

"No," said Sita emphatically. "No, I mean it. I really can't."

6

CATHAL O'CONNOR WAS ALWAYS SLIGHTLY ALARMED WHEN HE SAW HIS younger brother again after a break. Greeting Niall at Dublin airport that afternoon was like advancing on one of those fairground mirrors in which characteristics you didn't know you had are distorted for comic effect. You aren't supposed to take the deformation seriously, but you can't help but think there is some truth in it, that the lines under your eyes really are that dark or your hair really is that wild.

Niall always looked unwashed and hung over, but at least he usually managed to dress without putting his sweater on inside out. Cathal, on the other hand, spent his nowadays in a suit which lulled him into a false belief that he had left the *Men Behaving Badly* look behind. But as soon as he saw the shambolic figure of his brother walking out of the arrivals gate, he knew without being told that his own shirt was hanging out at the back, his tie's innards were unraveling and his jacket pockets gaped from all the junk he carried around in them. As an architect, he was immaculate. It was his own personal spacial design that needed attention.

"You look like a bag o' shite," he told his brother as they made their way down Temple Bar. The gentrification of their old haunts annoyed them both intensely, but they still went there, if only to moan and scowl at the English stag-nighters.

"That's because I am one," he replied.

"Look at yer." Cathal flicked the label sticking out below Niall's unshaven neck.

"So I got dressed in a hurry."

"Her husband came back, did he?"

The line of mutual attack was normal. It always went on for the initial hour of their reunions, a nod to their teenage years when a public display of disrespect was the thing that shaped them. Playing the same game on the cusp of their forties helped them feel buoyant, although occasionally it also made them feel hopelessly depressed. Only when they looked at it through the bottom of their fifteenth pint glass, mind you.

Their one hundred relatives still held extensive post mortems about the O'Connor brothers' discourtesy. Such a shame when you came from such an innately courteous family, they'd say, but there it was. Never mind that the brothers were now only mildly irreverent, the mud had stuck. Their three sisters more than made up for it, though, securing sensible husbands and fifteen children between them before their younger brothers had even left university. Thank God for girls, the one hundred relatives agreed.

You could hardly put Cathal and Niall's uselessness down to the male genes. Joseph O'Connor, their father, had always been the very model of civility and safety. He didn't drink, he didn't swear, he kissed his children and adored his wife. When he'd died in their early twenties and they had sat next to his peaceful body in his satin-lined coffin, not knowing how to cry, both of them had realized with a weird pride that they were somehow less than him, even though they'd set out to be more. Outclassed by quiet averageness. The problem by then was that their personalities were set in stone—or pickled in alcohol, as their mother said—and they found that, no matter how hard they tried, they couldn't be another Joe. So what did they do? Panicked, some would say. Cathal married a woman he'd known for only five minutes, and Niall went traveling.

Niall's trip to France hadn't been exactly planned. One minute he was maneuvering his bike through Richmond on his way to work as a restaurant manager at a mediocre hotel, and the next he turned right instead of left and ended up in Bordeaux, with the clothes he stood up in, his wallet and his Marlboro cigarettes. When he came back to England a year later, he knew so much about wine that he would have been a fool not to use the advantage. The other life change was that he now smoked Camels.

It was the age-old mistake of spending more time in the pub than he did at home that scotched Cathal's marriage, which was why his children now only got silent kisses down the phone. He missed his two boys even more than he missed his father, but they didn't seem to miss him. Not enough to take him up on his frequent invitations to stay, anyway.

"Oh, you come here, Dad," eleven-year-old Christopher said in response. "That'll be only the one flight, and anyway it's easier for you."

But it wasn't that easy to cross the Atlantic, and it made life difficult for them when he arrived. Their mother's American boyfriend was a little jumpy. A little jumpy and a bit big, but that was what steroids did for you, Cathal tried to joke, but it was hard to find the funny side when his youngest, Billy, was already picking up a Boston accent.

So not for the O'Connor brothers the semidetached family home in a suburb on Dublin's more affluent south side. Not for them the extension over the garage for the fifth bedroom to accommodate the results of Catholic contraception. And not for them the lifestyle the brothers had been weaned on, the kids coming home for lunch on their bikes, their father on foot from the factory, the whole family round the table for grace before chicken salad. Their adult worlds could not have turned out more differently if they had tried. In other words, in O'Connor family terms, they were long gone.

Without consultation, the two brothers turned on their heels at exactly the same time, and walked into the bar they always went to first, an establishment which brewed its own porter on the premises. It used to be one of those pubs you would go into only if you were looking for a fight.

An open iron staircase linked the three floors, beyond which you could now see the brewing chamber with its huge copper vats, pipes and wheels. Niall sniffed the mildly hop-flavored air appreciatively and tried to ignore the glittering brass bar counter. It was far too clean for his taste.

"Two pints of Guinness Extra-cold and two Powers chasers, please," he said to the black-haired, black-clad, black-eyed bar girl. When she turned her back, he asked Cathal, "Is she someone we went to school with?"

"Maybe the daughter of someone we went to school with, ye bloody eejit!"

It was Niall's eternal problem. He still thought he was twenty-one. Cathal, on the other hand, sometimes felt like an old old man. It was something to do with which side of forty they each lay. The whiskies went down in one synchronized move, even before the Guinness had settled in the drip tray.

"Didn't even touch the sides," said Cathal. "Another two, please, sweetheart. So come on, then, who made you put yer sweater on in such a hurry?"

Niall didn't answer. Instead, he raised his eyebrows and downed the second chaser in one as well. "W'd ye feck off."

Their lads' laugh trailed away as they watched the last milky swirl of the agitated Guinness settle to its velvety black. In a minute, they would relax enough to talk properly. The banter was wearing as thin as their hair, but they would always want to go through the motions. It was what they did.

"C'mon, tell me." Cathal tried again. "How's it going in Cornwall? Is it everything you hoped it would be?"

"Yeah, it's great," Niall said, lighting up and concentrating on the first draw. "Ah, that's good."

"Well, go on, gobshite."

"That's it. It's great."

"Is that all you've got to tell me? It's great?"

"Well, it's early days but y'know." If Cathal had asked him yesterday, it would have been easier.

"No, I don't know. You look bloody terrible."

"Thanks for that." Niall flicked ash into an ashtray and reached for his glass.

"The move isn't irreversible, is it? I mean, y'know, if it's clearly a mistake and all that."

"Who said anything about a mistake? No, it's good, really, it's great."

"Is it like the back of beyond there or what?"

"You should come over, see for yerself."

"Yeah, I could do with a break, but I was thinking Goa, really."

"Ah. Goa it is not."

"It's been pissin' it down here for weeks, too."

"Can't help you there. We've hardly seen the rain. Cornwall's practically tropical."

"Fantastic. So go on, how's PopCork Online? Still raking it in without the team?"

"Ticking over. I'll go back to it properly after another fortnight, but I want to concentrate on the move for a bit. The household needs to bed itself down." Niall tried to let his bad choice of words wash over him, but the silence got the better of him. "I don't really look terrible, do I?"

"Yes, you do."

"I was only coming to see you. I didn't think I needed a tie or anything."

"A wash would have been enough."

"I am washed."

"Well, you look bloody awful," Cathal repeated with concern.

"Sorry."

There was a silence which was neither sullen nor awkward. Niall understood his brother's need to get rid of some excess paternal sentiment.

"Heard from the boys?"

"Not much. I got a nice card from Billy the other day, but I've not seen them for six months, y'know."

"I thought they were coming over at Easter."

"Well, they were, until Christine's mother changed her mind and went over there instead, one of those last-minute things her family is so bloody good at. I tried to get a flight, but there wasn't a seat to be had by then."

"Where did you go, then? Mum was at Maeve's."

"I stayed on my own in the flat."

"What did ye do that for?"

"I wanted to."

"You're jokin'. Does Mum know?"

"No, and you're not going to tell her, either."

"You should go and see the boys yerself."

"I haven't been asked."

"You don't need a feckin' invitation. Ask yerself."

Cathal knew he probably should, but his need, his desire, stopped just a little short. He didn't know why. It wasn't lack of love, it was more a self-fulfilling disappointment with himself. I have disappointed, I am disappointing, I will disappoint. There was a brilliant father inside him wrestling to get out, he just needed to put on a bit more muscle.

"No. I'll wait for them to ask me. It's better coming from them."

"Ye might have a long wait. Think what you were like at ten."

"It's too long ago for me to even try."

"Thirty years."

"Thirty-one, actually."

"Oh, well then."

"Did ye know it was Dad's birthday yesterday?" Cathal had spent all day thinking about it.

Niall had remembered on the plane, when he saw the date on the *Irish Times*. "I realized this afternoon. Did you see Mum?"

"Yes. She was all right. A bit quiet maybe, but all right."

"Good. I must get to her tomorrow."

"She's doing us lunch before the funeral."

"What, to line our stomachs?"

"I'm sure. Now, c'mon," Cathal said, repositioning the spotlight. "You're feelin' either really bad or really good about something, I can tell. You're being too attentive."

"You're full of shite. I'm fine."

"I'm not and you're not. C'mon."

"No, it's nothing, honest." Niall had decided on the plane to shelve what had happened, box it up, padlock it, shove it away in the aisle of his mind that didn't deal with things. If Emmy could do the same, they'd be okay.

"So how about you tell me the bits that don't involve women."

"You're a bastard." Niall laughed with a great gush of relief. "It's got nothing to do with women."

"I'm a bastard and you're a liar," Cathal said. It was the second time that day that Niall had been called such a name.

EMMY HAD NO IDEA WHAT WAS AND WHAT WASN'T THE TRUTH ANY-more. In fact, she had lost the ability to judge anything. Whether she was behaving normally, whether any other member of the household had any idea what had gone on in their absence that morning or not, whether what had happened was a good or a bad development, an inevitability or a mistake.

"Oh dear," she muttered out loud, not that it mattered what she chose to mutter since there was no one around to hear her. The curtainless kitchen with its skeletal shelving and doorless units was like the *Marie Celeste*.

Sita, Jonathan and the children were in various permutations of their beds, Kat was back in London (well, of course she was), and Niall was in Ireland, damn him. Which left her staring at the same mess she'd been staring at this morning. Before "it" had happened.

Supper bowls lay puddled with olive oil and tomato, the radio was still burbling on, a heap of Maya's clothes in a washing basket sat at the end of the table. In the bedrooms, the smell of sleep hovered and duvets lay warm and crumpled. Twelve hours had made all and no difference.

"Leave it, I'll do it, you go," Emmy had urged Sita after breakfast that morning, perhaps a little too keenly, in retrospect. "I've got to hang around and wait for the plumber, anyway. Go on, disappear, flee, shoo. Take Maya."

But she hadn't done it. She'd left the milk and the cereal flakes hardening round the rims of the bowls, she'd left the toast crumbs on the Aga plate and the half-drunk cups of coffee and she—they—had done something else instead, almost as soon as backs were turned.

Leaning against the dresser with the taste of his lips still on hers, it was difficult to make sense of it all. Panic and relief wrestled for position inside her like ferrets in a sack. How *could* we cross the one boundary that defined our world? Thank God we did. Which way do we go to get back? Maybe we don't need to get back.

The truth was that it had been on the cards from the word go, and today they had both played their joker. A kiss. A near miss. They had stopped just in time.

Niall would be drinking with his brother by now, any residual wistfulness blown right away with his first chaser. Emmy had seen the signs of recovery before he'd even finished his cigarette.

"We're not to lose the plot over this," he'd said as they sat shaking at the kitchen table, twisting each other's fingers in their own. "We'll box it up, okay? Keep it safely locked somewhere special. We'll be fine. Nothing's changed."

"Sure, yes, of course, that's right," Emmy had lied through her teeth, taking a Camel for herself. The box, the box, the bloody box. Nothing's changed. How impossible a concept was that? Every single thing was now another color. And yet, at the same time, it was all still exactly the same.

She poured herself a glass of water and looked up at the exposed patch of ceiling where the plaster had fallen off. "The world isn't going to fall on our heads," he'd said—but that was because it already had.

Well, if she did have to put it away in a box like Niall said, it might as well be neatly folded. In a few days' time, she knew, he would walk back in as if nothing had happened and she needed to be ready for him to do that.

She walked back to the chair by the Aga, her hand clamped over her mouth. Was she stifling a smile or a scream? My God. Do I regret it? When had the hints of sexual tension started? From the first weekend? From the train crash, even? Was this the end of their perfect post-termination affair?

Which link mattered? she wondered, and then she imagined for a split second that she heard the others shouting, "The milk tanker!" from another room. She laughed. The whole thing was a disaster. She was right. She was mad. But she was happy.

In retrospect, the writing on the wall had turned to frantic, uncontrollable scribbles at breakfast. It was the "Oh, we're going to be alone" moment that confirmed it, followed by a flicker of eye contact, one unnecessary hand on a shoulder in passing, a superfluous flattering remark. And that had been it. Smack bang snog. His tongue was in her mouth the moment the sound of Jonathan's wheels on the gravel had faded to silence.

"Hi," he said, putting his hands on her upper arms.

She'd been wearing an old red cotton vest with no bra, a soft gray sweater with unraveling cuffs, an ancient denim skirt and sheepskin boots. She might as well have completed the look with a tea cozy on her head but then he'd not exactly been dressed to seduce, either, in that stinky tweedy roll-neck thing.

"Hi." Well, what else was there to say?

"You look nice."

"Thank you. I've been up since six, perfecting the look."

"Emmy?" His hands were still on her arms.

"Yes?"

"I've got a confession to make."

"What's that?"

"You're not allowed to be cross."

"I won't be."

"Well, it's like this. I've been wanting to kiss you."

Her heart must have stopped, just for a second. "I wouldn't. I'll taste of Marmite."

"Is that a promise?" He took her face in his hands. "Can I, Emmy?"

"Yes," she said, although it came out as a hoarse whisper.

He brought her to his mouth as if he was going to drink her. "God, I'd forgotten how good Marmite tastes." His hands were in her unbrushed hair, his lips all over her unwashed face.

"Liar."

They kissed necks, cheeks, hair, lips and tongues, then she pushed her hips forward, just a little. He stopped first, though.

"Emmy, what are we doing?" he asked into her neck.

"Being stupid."

"How stupid?"

"Don't care."

He hitched her skirt up in response. "Oh God, Emmy."

"I know." So the two of them hadn't died then.

Up against the dresser, she'd wrapped one booted leg round him. She could feel him against the thin cotton of her pants. Then suddenly he looked right at her, cupped her face again and said something completely at odds with the urgency that had overtaken them both.

"This is our last chance to stop."

"No."

"Yes, we should, but it's too late," he said. "It's too late."

When he said that, did he mean too late for him or too late for them? She'd not responded to it, anyway, because it was too late for her by then. She'd allowed him to touch her in a way he hadn't touched her since before the abortion. She'd let him back in again in a way she had never meant to.

But they had stopped, just short of going the whole way, and somehow, after one of them had moved away and the other had made a joke and the sexual energy had dispersed into the air like kettle steam, they had calmed down and talked. They'd spluttered with laughter and disbelief at their moment of madness and Emmy felt like telling him that love had just swallowed her whole. They'd wrapped hands and fingers, kissed cheeks and locked eyes. But then he'd done the plot-losing locked-box speech, and the moment had passed, like a burst of summer sunshine in a long wet winter.

"Nothing will change," he kept saying, as if the more he said it, the more it might actually be the truth.

"No, it's always been like this," she'd said as casually as she could. "Thirteen years, if you count it from—"

"God help me, I was counting it from Maya."

Emmy didn't want Maya to come into it. "It's no good appealing to God now, you bad Catholic boy."

"Well, if I only sin once every thirteen years, I should be okay."

So he saw it as a one-off, clearly. Something to be moved on from.

Did she? Emmy walked away from the window and realized she was going to be glued to the spot for a long time yet. Would he tell his brother? Should she send him a text message and ask him not to? Would Cathal's knowledge matter, anyway?

WHAT CATHAL DID AND DIDN'T KNOW WOULD TURN OUT TO BE CRUCIAL, but for now, he was happy to know only what his brother was prepared to tell him.

The girl who had served them their first drinks suddenly appeared the other side of the bar. She had apparently been cloned three times, and all four of her stepped up onto a raised platform which a minute ago had been covered in drinkers.

"Oh shite, it's the feckin' Corrs," someone shouted, not noticing four male musicians following her, carrying a drum, a flute, a fiddle and a squeezebox. All eight members of the band were in head-to-toe black.

"It's worse than that, it's Riverdance," Cathal shouted to Niall over the noise. "I saw them last week—they're not even dire. C'mon, let's go."

Outside, they crossed the street and headed for the bar that they always, for no good reason, went to second. It was much more self-consciously cool, trying as hard as it could to be Continental, but at least there wasn't going to be any clog dancing, and they could talk in normal voices. The music was piped jazz, and the space round the kidney-shaped chrome bar was empty. A black, domed ceiling was pierced with hundreds of tiny star lights which, if you had had enough to drink and were on your back, looked exactly like a night sky. They ordered two bottles of Coors Lite at Cathal's suggestion.

"I can't drink Guinness in the quantity I used to. It fills me up."

"That would be just the ten, then?"

"About that," Cathal said. They weren't entirely joking. In their youth, they regularly drank up to fifteen, and then went on to shorts. "You know the drink we should be drinking now?"

"Horlicks?" said Niall.

"And you can feck off. No, vodka and Red Bull. That's what they all drink these days. We'll give it a go later, for that fat bastard Kieran Kennedy."

"What, you want to die as well, do you?"

"No, but I want to be still pissed when I say goodbye to the old gobshite tomorrow. It wouldn't be right to do such a thing sober. Now, come on, talk to me. Tell me what you've done."

"Ye'd make a terrible priest, Cathal."

"That's the nicest thing ye've ever said to me."

"But I'll tell ye anyway."

"No no, only if ye want to. If it'll make ye feel better."

"I'm not feeling bad in the first place."

"Y'are."

"I'm not."

"Y'are."

"Okay. I am."

"I know y'are. But why?"

Niall bit his lip and then spoke. "Emmy and I crossed a line this morning." He stopped and stared into his pint.

Cathal looked at him expectantly. "And?"

"Oh, y'know."

"No, I don't."

"Ah, I don't know, either. It was the first time we'd found ourselves alone together since moving down and you know what it's like. Sometimes it feels right, y'know, I mean, not just right, but more than that, almost kind of predestined. But then we also know we can't go back there again, and yet sometimes it just feels, sort of, you know, *stupid* not to. That's all."

"What's all? It doesn't sound like a 'that's all' situation to me."

"It just felt . . . well . . . things got . . . We had . . . It went . . . Oh, well, ye know."

"You and Emmy had sex?"

"No."

"What then?"

"We kissed."

"Where?"

"In the kitchen. What do you want to know that for?"

There was a barely perceptible silence before Cathal composed a reaction. Was he supposed to be shocked? He presumed, like everyone else, that his brother and Emmy had the kind of relationship where a kiss in the kitchen might or might not happen, depending on the opportunities available to them, and that Maya was a possible product of one of those opportunities reaching its natural end.

"That's disgustin'. The kitchen is a place for food preparation, you evil dog. How many times do I have to tell you, you must only ever kiss a member of the opposite sex in the bathroom, where hot water and carbolic soap are immediately to hand."

Niall didn't laugh. "It's just that I wish it was clearer in my head about what we are to each other, that's all."

"It's always seemed clear enough to everybody else."

"Well, it's not. You've got it wrong."

"Or maybe *you* have."

"No. We shouldn't have done what we did this morning. Emmy and I don't do that."

"Don't you?"

"Not for a very long time, anyway."

"So you do now. It's not rocket science, Niall."

"Have you forgotten about Kat?"

Cathal's face froze for a second, and even colored slightly. "Oh shite. D'ye know, I had, I honestly had. I'm sorry, I really had. But I've never met the girl, have I? To be fair. And ye've not mentioned her since you arrived. I'd forgotten her name to be honest wid ye."

There was another small silence.

"The thing is, Kat isn't really the problem. I mean, she is in one way, but in a much bigger way she's not. I don't . . . it's not like . . . Oh, I think I might just be the most useless bollocks in . . ."

"So what *is* the problem?"

"I don't know."

"Is it good old Catholic guilt? Because I can't help you there."

"No, it's more complicated than that."

"Jaysus, more complicated than Catholic guilt?"

"It's got something to do with Maya, Emmy's daughter."

"Niall, I know who Maya is, for God's sake."

"Well, you didn't know who Kat is."

"Oh, and she's been at the center of your life for years, has she? Of course I know who Maya is. Not only have I actually met her on several occasions, but are you aware you talk about her as if she were your own kid, my niece?"

"Well, she's not, I can assure you of that. But she's important to me, really really important. She trusts me. And being involved with her mother is, y'know, probably not helpful."

"Helpful to what?"

"I don't know."

"Did she see?"

"No, of course she didn't."

"So? Does it matter?"

"What if we can't redraw that line?"

"Draw it in another place." Cathal shrugged. "Look, you and Emmy, maybe—"

"No. It's too complicated. We've done all that. We work fine as friends."

"You expect me to buy that?"

"Yeah, you should."

"So just tell me again. Maya isn't my niece?" Cathal was teasing his brother, trying to catch him out in a lie. At least, that's what he thought he was doing. Later, he'd wonder if he was digging for something else.

"Maya's not your niece," Niall said slowly.

"Thank you."

"It's a pleasure."

"Okay, so let's talk about Emmy. Does she want to redraw the line?"

"We didn't talk about it. I had to get the plane."

"God, Niall, you're a dog."

"No, we did sort of talk about it. It'll be fine. I've just got to stop jumping the gun."

"It sounds to me as if you've already discharged the feckin' thing. Why don't you think these things through before you do the deed, not after?"

"I know. It just happened."

"D'ye love her?"

"It's not that easy, y'know. She and Maya come as a package. It's not just about whether I——"

"You love her."

"I don't know. Yeah, of course I do, but . . ."

"You love her, and you're attracted to her. What's the problem?"

Niall shrugged this time. "History. She's hard work sometimes. I'm not always the best person to deal with her."

"Do you want it to happen again, to go farther?"

"I don't know."

"Okay, how would you feel if she met someone else? Brought him back to the house? If you had to watch them go up to bed together?"

"I don't know. I think I'd be okay. I mean, that's what I do, isn't it?"

"Jaysus Christ, Niall, will you tell me something you do know?"

"Okay. Kat wants a kid."

"Wait wait wait wait wait." Cathal poured the rest of his second Coors Lite into his glass and downed it as if he hadn't had a drink for a fortnight. "What are you? Bus Atha Cliath? Nothing for ages and then the whole fleet comes at once. A *baby*?"

"Well, I don't mean a goat, do I?"

"Is it that serious? You've only just met her."

"At our age everything's serious, isn't it?"

Cathal ignored him. It hurt too much to think of how unserious his liaisons were lately.

"Do *you* want one?"

"No, probably not."

"Would that be because ye've already got one?"

"What d'you mean?"

Cathal looked at his brother suspiciously out of the corner of his eye.

"She's not mine," Niall told him forcefully. He took a photograph out of his wallet and handed it over. "I wouldn't mind if she was, but she's not."

Cathal held it with both hands and studied it carefully. Maya had a Gallic hint about her for sure. Her long auburn hair reminded him of his sisters; she was sitting on a dark wooden staircase in a T-shirt and wellies. She was all leg.

"Is this Bodinnick?"

"Last week."

"Looks woodwormy."

"I'll get it treated. What d'you think?"

"Well, she's grown a lot since I last saw her. Still looks like you, though, don't you think? She's got your . . . your . . . your something."

"But that's the whole point. She hasn't. She hasn't got my anything."

"Is that right?"

A dire but distant possibility floated obliviously from Niall's mouth and as Cathal breathed in, he took it with him, down his own throat and into his stomach where it sloshed and sploshed around with the American beer, making him feel unusually sick. In danger of becoming instantly sober, he called for the familiar velvety comfort of his favorite drink.

"Another two pints of Guinness, please," he said sharply to the barman. "Ordinary, this time." Then he turned to face Niall instead of looking at him in profile. "So are you saying you really aren't Maya's father?"

"Yeah, that's what I really am saying. What's wrong with that?"

"Nothing," said Cathal, swallowing and sniffing. "Nothing. I've just spent ten years being absolutely sure you were, that's all."

They took the Guinness to their lips and sucked it in, then Cathal raised his eyes to the starry ceiling.

"Here's to life, the universe, Kieran bloody Kennedy and everything," he said, thankful for the mask of drunkenness.

7

"LOOK UP," JONATHAN SAID TO HIS SON IN THE PITCH BLACK AS HE CLOSED the chapel door. He was wise to the latch now, and he knew to wait for the creak, which came just before you had to lift the whole thing up and yank it. Each time, on opening or closing, it scraped deeper into the light-gray arc on the slate floor. The more scrapes he made, the better he liked the floor.

"Wow!"

A small explosion happened somewhere in Jonathan's heart. Jay, the boy who had stopped using superlatives years ago, had just said, "Wow!"

"I never knew it was this big." Jay's neck was at right angles to his body as he let the night sky fall into his face.

"That's because you've never really seen it before."

"Yes I have, I've seen it loads of times."

"Ah, but in London, you didn't see it *properly*. There's too much light pollution. All those street lamps and buildings get in the way. You just get a tiny section of it."

Jonathan didn't want to make too much of the chapel's magical properties but there was a lot to be said for the visual impact of a few days' manual labor. In London, he had spent his life dealing with intangible money used to insure against indistinguishable events, and in the end he felt he had become invisible himself.

These days, as he picked out clumsy gray lumps of cement with a pointing trowel or cleaned out the grit with a stiff bristled brush, he felt he was shading himself in again, becoming more noticeable for taking the opportunity to make even the smallest visible contribution. I did that, he could say now. I stopped that bit of wall from falling down. I made Jay say, "Wow!"

His trousers were white with the dusty crystals that had been seeping out of the chapel's granite walls since he had started work on it. The dustier they got, the better he liked them. He also liked imagining the building's relief at being able to let it out, and it reminded him of all those meetings, all those stifled coughs, all those breathing exercises against closed lavatory doors. It was as if something was at last able to seep out of him, too.

When Emmy first showed him the chapel, he'd really believed for a moment that he'd smelled God, or at least a presence bigger than himself. Ever since, he'd half been expecting the wagon roof to open up and a great shaft of light to beam down, and God's voice to say "Yes, you, Jonathan Taylor. It's *you* I want," but the only disembodied voice he'd heard in there so far belonged to the mid-morning presenter on Radio Two.

Not that God was what he wanted anymore, not now that he had the enticing Tamsin Edwards to look forward to. He thought about the morning's events again, meeting her, the way she spoke, the things she said, the frequency of her laugh. It was a surprise even to him that Historic Buildings Advisers could be so young and so interesting.

Jay put his thumbs together and made a frame with his hands, like a photographer sizing up his shot.

"How many stars can you see now?" Jonathan asked.

"Nowhere near as many." Jay put his hands back in his coat pockets.

"See? They've got nothing to compete with here, have they? You get the whole thing all at once."

Jay suddenly realized he had nothing to compete with anymore, either. The boys at his new school were like him. Their skateboards were just as knackered, their Game Boys just as old, their parents just as cautious.

"I like it in Cornwall, Dad."

"Good. I like it, too."

"Do you think we'll stay?"

"It's not just about us, unfortunately. Everyone has to want it."

"But if you had to put money on it?"

"If I had to put money on it, I'd say . . . I don't gamble."

Jay went back to the stars and Jonathan felt that familiar twinge of regret that he was who he was, that he always, for one reason or another, stopped short. One day, he wanted to go the whole distance.

"It's just like that planetarium I had," Jay said. "That was so wicked. I should have brought it with me."

"You don't need it anymore. You've got this."

Jonathan suddenly had an urge to talk to his son about insignificance. If his own father had told him about insignificance at thirteen, too, he might just have seen it coming and been able to jump out of its way. But his own father hadn't spoken to him about much at all. He could barely remember one single interesting thing the man had said. But perhaps insignificance came anyway, whether you resisted it or not.

He was so tired he could have fallen asleep there and then, against the damp granite wall with Jay leaning against him like a human hot-water bottle, but at least it was a different tiredness from the one he had felt in London.

In London, tiredness had come from a permanent proximity to people, a knowledge that you should never take your eye off the ball, a ceaseless traffic noise in your head. In Cornwall, the tiredness came from realizing that, at last, it had all stopped. Well, that and the fact that he was still sleeping on a leather sofa which needed urgent reupholstery.

His back hurt, his neck was stiff and he couldn't remember the last time he had woken up and felt physically refreshed. Sita kept telling him his aches and pains were to do with spending so long on his knees in a damp environment, but then she had a different agenda. She wanted him inside, with the paintbrush and the sander where he could be put to good use.

He knew she looked on the chapel as a selfish frivolity, and to a certain extent she was right, but why shouldn't he be selfish for once? Could she not hear the distant hope flickering or see the little flame that had started to burn again, the tiniest bubble of excitement in his voice?

No, of course she couldn't, no more than he could see her gritted determination to get things done at last, so that she could fan her own flame, too. Which was? He realized he didn't know anymore.

Whatever. Such worries had just for now ceased to matter. Jay— the boy who used to shy from fresh air even at the height of a summer noon—had actually been the one to suggest walking back out to light the candles so they could see the shape of the windows against the night sky. Such times were not to be sniffed at.

He tucked his son's neck into the crook of his right arm, resting his right hand on the boy's slight shoulder and holding Jay's arm with his other hand. A month ago, their physical connection had been the occasional friendly punch.

"Can you see the Milky Way?" he asked, drawing his finger across the cloudy banner that streaked the sky. "It starts there. Keep watching it. The longer you look, the more you see."

They stood, watching without talking, until the galaxy turned itself inside out and became a million holes in a huge black cloth, backlit by the fiery white heart of another universe.

"What's beyond them, do you think?"

"The future, I suppose."

"Not ours, though," Jay said pragmatically. "We'll be dead before anyone gets that far."

Jonathan didn't know how to answer that one. When anyone had died in the leafy suburban street he'd been brought up in, his parents drew the curtains of every front-facing room, out of respect. Death was never mentioned, but you could tell when it had happened because of the hushed tones, his mother furtively sniveling into handkerchiefs in the kitchen, the head-shaking and clicking of tongues. He was going to add silent mealtimes, but it hadn't taken a death to make a silent meal-time with his parents. That was one of the great joys of Bodinnick, the noise level round the table. Noisier, he sometimes wanted to shout, noisier.

"I wonder what it's like being dead," Jay carried on.

"You'll find out one day."

"Yeah, but you'll find out before me."

Hope so, Jonathan thought.

"Dad?"

"Yes?"

"It makes me feel really small."

"We are really small."

In one way, Jonathan wanted to say, that's what this chapel thing is all about. It's about having had enough of feeling small and pointless, and wanting to explore the possibility that it needn't be like that, about giving yourself enough scope and space to see if there is something else out there that you have missed, about seeing what you can achieve with-out anyone else's help, about not always doing what other people want you to. Do you see, Jay? Do you get it? But he knew how hard it would be to put that across to a thirteen-year-old boy, especially in terms of chiseling out cement, so he stayed silent. It was best not to draw up sides, while Sita was reacting.

When he'd gone to the chapel that morning, he'd been feeling lethargic, aware as he budged the door open that he had given up his early expectation of finding anything redeeming within its walls. And then at that very low moment, Tamsin Edwards had floated into his view.

"Hello," she said, her vague Cornish burr bouncing off the salty walls. "I was just admiring your work."

As he watched her running her bitten pink fingernail along his neatly executed grooves, he'd realized it wasn't just the walls that were being given the opportunity to breathe again. Feck, as Niall would say. He should leave well alone. Young bright women never went down well when Sita was postnatal. Her father had brought her up to believe that if you stand still someone will overtake you, which was one of those truths that were so horribly true, it wasn't even worth thinking about.

"Tamsin's the adviser I've been talking to," he'd said a bit sheepishly when Sita found them talking rapidly over coffee in the chapel, and Sita had looked back at him as if he'd just told the most blatantly transparent lie in the history of their marriage. Maybe he had.

"Hello, Mrs. Taylor," Tamsin replied cheerily. "Fabulous chapel you've got here." Well, how was she to know Sita preferred Ms. or Dr. Dhanda?

Sita's distrust was Jonathan's fault. If he'd been more confident about displaying his interest in the chapel, if he'd been open about his trips to the library and phone calls to the council and subscriptions to specialist magazines, his familiarity with Tamsin wouldn't have seemed so odd. But it was odd, particularly to him. He could remember every single thing she had told him.

"Lime mortar has to breathe," she'd said. "This stuff suffocates it, keeps all the damp in. Can't you smell it?"

Her creamy complexion had flushed with the mildest red again. Pink maybe. The lightest pink flush. "I can't work out why it isn't listed. The house is, but the chapel isn't—though the remains of fifteenth-, sixteenth- and seventeenth-century buildings in Cornwall are so numerous that they sometimes get overlooked on purpose."

"But this isn't a remain, it's a complete structure."

"True, but you sound as if you want it listed."

"Don't you think it should be? Early-sixteenth-century domestic chapels with slate roofs, coped verges and granite ashlars can't be all that common."

"You know your stuff, don't you?" Tamsin had smiled, and Sita had caught him doing that excruciating gesture of false modesty, a quick downward brush of the hand.

He'd taken some of her lines to the supper table with him. "It has to breathe," he told everyone. Every time he said it, he breathed too. "Modern cement is impervious to damp but if there's a tiny crack and moisture gets drawn in it gets trapped, it's got nowhere to go, it can't evaporate. That's what the smell is."

"That's possibly enough about working with traditional building materials, thanks," Sita had said, thinking she could smell something else as well.

"But lime works in harmony with the seasonal changes. It's softer, more flexible."

"Just like Tamsin," Niall had commented, and three of the four of them had laughed like drains.

It was getting cold now and he and Jay would have to go in soon. His hands and knees were aching, and if he wanted a bath before midnight he would have to start running it now. The water pressure needed sorting, which was another job Sita wanted him to do. He was exhausted by the mere thought of it. The muscles in his calves ached from squatting for so long, chipping away at the rock-hard mortar, grueling work for a man who had spent the last twenty years sitting on a padded swivel chair talking into a telephone.

He wondered what, if anything, would happen should he stay out here all night. It was the kind of behavior that people like Niall got away with all the time. People like Niall could sleep in their clothes, go missing for days, drink wine for breakfast, and not a word would be said. So why couldn't he? Stuff went on without him the whole time. Nothing ever stopped because of his absence. And yet at the same time he was required to be ever-present. What impact would his death have on the world? Other than meaning a little extra work for Sita, obviously?

Was it his fault for accepting, even if he didn't entirely understand, the boundaries of his restrained personality? If Niall was a human version of Bodinnick, wild, sprawling, spacious, others saw Jonathan as the equivalent of a modest home in suburbia.

Tamsin would never list *him*. In architectural terms, he was the kind of man who recognized the social importance of correct cornicing but would never have the guts to rip it out if the mood took him.

But that's where his acceptance of who he was stopped. If he didn't want to be that kind of man, why was he? What had shaped him? What had led him down the path to commonplace? If the answer was himself, why did he sometimes fantasize about being someone else?

What could he pass on to Jay about all that? Don't follow paths just because they're available. Hack through the undergrowth and discover something new. Be brave, take chances. He knew that, to the outside world, it looked as if he himself was doing just that. You don't give up your job, let your house and move your family to the southwest tip of Britain to lead a more simple life if you aren't at least a little adventurous. But of course, you do, because he just had, and he was the most boring man in the universe. Captain Sensible and Mr. Anorak.

THE PATH THROUGH THE SCRUB FROM THE CHAPEL WAS EVEN MORE defined now, and he realized he'd been making the same journey four times a day for a fortnight. Back and forth he went, once again the commuter—just like the one in the poem who spends his life riding to and from his wife, shaving and taking trains. In fact, just like the one he used to be in London. Was routine his addiction?

Sita's anger over his interest in the chapel managed to swap focus at random. How could he justify spending so much time on it when there was clearly more than enough to do in the house? What did he mean, he was taking Lila there with him? Lime is dangerous: it can blind.

"I've taken advice and I know what I'm doing," he'd said, "but if you really don't like it, why don't you take her to work with you?" Which was when she'd called him a bastard and left the house without saying goodbye. She'd never ever called him a bastard before.

The whole point of uprooting their lives from city to country was to increase their feeling of togetherness, not to wreck what little they had. At this rate, they'd be lucky to see the three months out still married. That would be the ultimate irony. To renovate a house at the expense of their own personal bricks and mortar. To see a house rise out of the ashes and a family sink without trace.

But he didn't say any of those things to Jay. Instead he said, "We should go in. Mum will be wondering where we are."

Sita was wondering about him, actually. She was wondering what on earth had happened to the man she had married, and whether he was wondering the same thing about her. She was also wondering if Emmy had told her the whole truth about her and Niall, why she was feeling such deep-green shades of jealousy, and what the hell they were all doing here. But the worst of her sleepless wonders was why she no longer bothered to share any of them with Jonathan.

They used to be such a team, confronting challenges together, trusting each other's judgment, knowing without being told that each had the other's happiness higher up the list than their own. That was their sex, really. They had never been wildly active, not in the way she knew some of her friends were. They'd never done it in a public place. They'd never used a sex toy or props. She had never even played out a fantasy in her head, let alone admitted one to him. They did it—or rather used to do it—in bed at night, usually with the lights off. It was good when it happened, but they got their kicks in other ways. And there was the "used to" phrase again.

She thought about the holidays they had taken before Jay was born—mountain climbing in the Italian Alps and river canoeing in southwest France. While most other young couples would have gone straight to bed with a bottle of massage oil, they went to a bar with a bottle of beer and spent hours exploring their individual weaknesses, their confidences, what scared them, what excited them. They took it in turns to lead. One minute, he needed her advice, and the next she sought his. Those conversations were their version of foreplay. Very often, after a joint achievement, they would be on a high for weeks. It used to be like taking their marriage vows all over again, remembering that they were a team, that they worked better as a unit than they did as individuals.

She could remember coming home from one such holiday and Emmy asking her why she had ever bothered to leave the Girl Guides. Jonathan had whispered, "She's just jealous," in her ear. It must have been at the peak of her and Emmy's estrangement, a strange few years in which they had focused on their differences. Sita married and pregnant, Emmy single and very much not. But Maya had changed all that.

What goes around comes around, she thought. Maybe Jonathan and I will come around again soon. How though? And when? The children had brought with them a nasty little element of competition. Who was the most tired? Who worked the hardest? Who was the most put-upon? Now, not only did they not have sex, but they didn't have holidays, either.

Her two daughters moved their flawless coffee-colored limbs either side of her, and she tried to condense her maternal bulk into the dip in the middle of the old horsehair mattress. She was facing Lila, her left breast still released from its feeding bra, and she pulled the stretch-marked flesh back to study the baby's dark eyelashes and pursed lips. The horror at finding herself pregnant again had finally disappeared. Lila was surely the perfect gift.

She and Jonathan should be riding the crest of a wave, lying in a bed of smugness congratulating themselves on the products of their union, but instead, they seemed lost in a thickening fog of resentment. Why were they so cross with each other all the time?

She'd naively hoped the Cornish sun might be strong enough to burn through the fog, that the Cornish air might be clean enough to cure Jonathan's obsession with his breathing, that the Cornish wind might blow away their recent selves and bring back their old ones on a summer breeze. But so far, metaphorically anyway, it had mainly rained.

Would it help if she admitted that her main motivation for coming here was him? And that, if she wasn't going to benefit from his new self, they might as well pack up and go back? The difficulty was, she wasn't entirely sure they could go back, despite all the insurance policies they'd taken out.

He had been so much a shadow of his former self in the last year or so that she'd feared for their future. It was as if he'd left himself somewhere, under an office desk or in a computer program, and what she and the children had been getting was his shell.

She knew that the way she handled it only made it worse. It was the old chestnut about the talent of application again, the work ethic, the "If a job is worth doing, it's worth doing well" thing. Jonathan had been worse than useless in the last year, so she had taken on his responsibilities, too. Terribly efficient, businesslike, practical, competent. But cold? Undemonstrative? Bossy, even?

Frustratingly, she could feel her thoughts only licking at the truth. She had rendered him surplus to requirements. She hadn't meant to, but she had written him out of his own job description. She had become the mother and the father, the homemaker and the breadwinner. She was earning the money to feed them now and all she was managing to taste was his emptiness.

She'd tasted it at lunchtime, when she could have come home from the surgery for an hour. The distance between the practice and Bodin-nick was negligible, and her desire to see Lila, to feed her the puréed swede and carrot she'd prepared this morning and put her down for her afternoon nap, had been tempting. But not tempting enough. She'd spoken to Jonathan on his mobile to see if everything was okay without her and there had been that flat echo to his voice. He was in the bloody chapel again.

So he had seen or felt something over there that she hadn't—well, that was just too bad. She hadn't got time to explore her inner self. She was too busy shoving her nipple into Lila's mouth, while sorting out nightmares and angina, to get in touch with her spiritual side.

It had been her choice to keep her career going, but for the first time she was wondering if that was what she really wanted. It wasn't the money she was doing it for—they had enough with Jonathan's redundancy to keep them going for at least a year—but the prospect of them both being permanently unemployed was not one she would allow the family to face. At the same time, was she prepared to face becoming resentful in her role as the sole earner? How did grudges start? Was a temporary replacement's wage worth the risk? And since she was still working, how far could she fulfil her *Manifesto* wish to adopt a simpler lifestyle with more free time to concentrate on the things that matter? What *did* matter? Though usually so resolute, she had no idea.

The one thing she did know was that she was relieved to be back in a working environment. It made her feel less guilty than she had thought it would. She recognized herself in the surgery. Being a doctor was what she did. But she was also a mother and a wife. Was that where the guilt lay?

She heard his voice outside the door. "Thanks for keeping me com-pany, Jay," he was saying. "I enjoyed that." He sounded thankful and lonely. Then she heard the wobble of a hot-water bottle being thrown, a quiet laugh, and his footsteps move off again. The realization that he wasn't going to come in and kiss her goodnight made her want to cry.

But she didn't do crying—there wasn't time—so she sighed just once and closed her eyes. She had to sleep. She had to work in the morning even if no one else did.

WHEN JONATHAN CLOSED HIS EYES, ON THE LEATHER SOFA AT MIDNIGHT, he could still see the blurred glow of the chapel windows projected on his lids. He thought about cement, and suffocation, and rot setting in, and through-drafts, and how good it would be to feel that he could make a difference. He found himself thinking fleetingly about Tamsin Edwards again, too. Then he fell asleep, trying but failing to keep pace with the collective breathing of the female branch of his family, eight feet and a million miles away from him in bed.

8

CATHAL SAT IN FRONT OF THE PICTURE WINDOW OF HIS RIVERSIDE FLAT
at the desk his father had left him, and tried to stop his thoughts tramp-
ling over everything that was good about his world. There wasn't
much to trample on. His job, once fulfilling, now bored him. His ex-
wife, Christine, who once used to phone him twice a day at work, could
now barely be bothered to speak to him. His boys, once footballers,
were now into baseball. (It was worse than that, even, but the fact that
they were rapidly becoming another man's sons was too painful to
cite.) And on top of all that, the second most unthinkable thing was at
stake, too. Niall.

He used to be able to see the estate agent's point about it being
therapeutic after a hard day's work to look out at all those perfectly
restored barges twinkling on the Liffey, but now he wanted to push
wide the window and shout at them all to bugger off and twinkle somewhere else.

The view was rewritten history at its worst. The area used to be
strictly out of bounds to him as a child; not that he took any notice. But
with the wave of a developer's wand, the slums were now a chi-chi

enclave for city dwellers on fat salaries, a status symbol to go with the Armani suit and the Ferrari.

"The docks are not a suitable place for a son of mine," his mother had said when he'd told her where he was buying. And in one way, she was right. They didn't suit him, not now.

He'd bought the flat out of spite, to make Christine angry. She'd put their name down on the show home's Interested list during the death throes of their marriage and tried to use it as an ultimatum: either we buy one or I go. "Who do you think I am?" he'd said in front of her sister. "Bono?"

But now that she couldn't care less how or where he lived, it had lost even that limited appeal. When he looked out on the river, he didn't see the twinkling barges, he saw the generations of families who had been hounded out by the property pioneers. Where were they now? Where did they go when they needed their childhood back? He was so deep into the sentimentality of parenthood that it didn't occur to him most of them were busy trying to forget they had had one.

He didn't usually notice Dublin's incessant seagull chatter but today the birds sounded as if they were laughing at him so he got up and shut the window. Then he sat back down and picked up the photograph of Maya on the stairs at Bodinnick. He didn't know what he expected to see that he hadn't seen any of the countless other times he'd looked at it, but he looked all the same, waiting. Waiting for her face to become Emmy's, or a stranger's. But it didn't. He could still only see his own face staring back. That, and Niall's, blotchy with tears and disbelief, begging him to tell him it wasn't true.

Maybe it wasn't. At times over the last few days, he'd thought he must be going mad, that finally the divorce and the cruel removal of his boys to America had got to him. He wondered if the effort of hanging on to fatherhood by the skin of his teeth had sent him crazy.

"Get a grip," he said out loud. But there was no point telling himself to get a grip because he couldn't find anything to hold on to.

Why all this now? Why, after ten years of arm's-length contact, did he think he had the right to hold Maya's hand? Because that's what he'd been imagining himself doing, walking with her through the streets of his city, buying her something she pointed out to him in a shop, correcting her driving skills. He'd imagined his mum brushing her hair, and his boys asking him what she looked like, and his mum saying yes, she'd babysit, as long as he was back by ten.

There was one scene that had returned with a vengeance. It might have been the first time he'd seen her, or maybe the second. Eight years ago, he had called Niall from a pub down the road from his firm's Kensington offices and suggested a pint, and he had sat on a stool looking forward to a blokey drink and waiting to see his brother come though the swing doors. Which he had duly done—with a baby in tow.

"Don't tell Emmy," Niall had said. "She'd kill me. We're supposed to be at playgroup, aren't we, Maya?"

"I don't like playgroup," Maya had said. "I like pubs."

She'd been between two and three, although there was something adult about her, too. She had been such compelling company that he had almost ignored Niall and played a game flipping beer mats across the table with her. Even then, there had been an element of competition between them for her affection. More than that. A genetic familiarity. A sense of already knowing her.

"I don't wear nappies when I go to sleep," she'd announced standing on the chair and pulling up her checked skirt. "I jus' wear this one cos is very dangerous for boys to go in girls' loos an is very dangerous for girls to go in boys' loos, too. You can fall in big loos, and I dun wan a fall in big loos, do you? I just pee in this today. Not amorrow, jus today. Don't tell Mummy."

"I won't," he promised.

Another memory had the same element of collusion. Emmy had gone away with a new boyfriend for a few days, somewhere reachable and romantic—Paris, perhaps, or Prague—and Niall had come to Dublin with Maya, having been left holding the baby yet again.

One would expect Niall to be awkward around a child for so long, nervous at the prospect of being left in sole charge of a seven-year-old girl, hopeful of offloading the burden on his mother. But no. Niall had been in his element, taking Maya everywhere he could, showing her off, pretending to his mates she was his, letting her in on the joke. She'd called him Daddy the entire weekend.

Daddy. Cathal could hear her saying it and this time it wasn't so much of a joke. But if nothing had occurred to him then, why should it occur now? The lack of reason made it all the more sinister. Perhaps it was occurring because it was time for it to occur. Perhaps it was life catching up with them all.

The truth careered round the loop of his mind like an electronic rabbit on a dogtrack, always a few seconds faster than his brain. Distractions were like stepping stones to help him reach the other side of the day, but the moment he walked back into his flat on the "luxury" development his firm of architects had so spectacularly lost the contract for, the rabbit was out of its trap, going just slowly enough at first to let him believe it was worth chasing one more time and then *whoosh!*

It was going so fast now, it had persuaded him for a split second to give up the chase and take the easy option. To ask Emmy.

One hand rested on the telephone, his address book open in front of him, the other held the battered snap between thumb and forefinger. He felt perilously close to upturning many lives. The photograph had developed dogears since he'd acquired it—okay, nicked it—from his brother's wallet, which was hardly surprising given its movements in the last fortnight. Inside jacket pocket, back jeans pocket, briefcase, in tray, out tray, sittingoom table, kitchen table, bedside table. It had been propped against computer screens, alarm clocks, coffee jars. It had been shoved in cutlery drawers, desk drawers and glove compartments.

Sometimes, the need to look at her had been physical and he kept expecting the knot of hope to undo itself, but so far it had tightened and tightened, like wet rope.

Anger, if he could summon it, was productive, at least in the way a cough can be called productive. The more unpleasant phlegm he could spit out in private, the better he might fare in public. If Maya—he could barely think it without scaring himself half to death—if Maya *was* his child, and that information had been kept from him, then . . . well, then what?

But he couldn't maintain the anger, not when he thought about the timing. When he and Emmy had slept together that forgettable, point-less, lazy night, Christine had been at home in Ireland practicing her breathing for the birth of their first child. If he was angry at all, it was with himself for being so lethargic about his marriage. He didn't realize in those days that being a good husband allowed you to be a good father. He must have thought it was possible to be one without the other. He never used to think about wives and mothers being different halves of the same equation.

All those perfect moments he'd been allowed with Christopher would have been in jeopardy. That feeling that was slipping so fast from his memory, the knowledge that at last he had done something to be proud of, would have been tainted by knowing that he had also done something to be ashamed of.

The acknowledgment made his anger subside into a rather pathetic gratitude. Gratitude to Emmy for not blowing it all up in his face, grat-itude to Niall for being some sort of a father, gratitude to Maya for (pre-sumably) being the kind of child who took what she was offered without question. It was still possible, of course, that Niall had helped to deliver and raise the daughter of a complete stranger—but those eyes. They swallowed him whole every time he looked into them. Now the compulsion, the fixation, the need to know—he didn't know what to call it—had reached danger level. He was at his desk for the purpose of finishing work on an already overdue project but when he looked down at the lackluster plans for another two-story extension over the garage on another semidetached family home, he knew he could do it with his eyes shut, in his sleep, when sleep came maybe.

In the meantime, he thought he would go and see his mother. Fathers are all very well but mothers are something else again, he realized, glimpsing for the first time how his own two boys had made the only decision available to them.

His mother had no compunction about doing what she was doing with the kitchen scissors. Mary O'Connor tried her best to forgive most things, but when it came to messing up innocent lives for the sake of something as selfish as your own desires, well, that was different. Disappointment was not something she dwelt upon, but the fiasco of her eldest son's marriage and the version of family life her grandsons were being offered really hurt. She felt Joseph's hurt, too, even when he'd been the best part of twenty years in his grave.

Trying to eat her lunch while watching a woman apparently enjoy confessing serial infidelity to her reeling husband on live TV had been the last straw. She hadn't been able to eat her chicken and broccoli pie for the distaste she felt for it all. But then her pies never tasted quite the same now they were a shadow of their former selves.

Before she had succumbed to the scissors, she had cleared out her cupboards, and a pile of family-sized pie dishes now sat on the hostess trolley, ready for the church auction. There was no one she could hand them on to. Her daughters had all they needed and more.

Whatever happened to the sanctity of marriage? she wondered as she cut the same slim figure out of each photograph. Whatever happened to trust?

The wedding ones had gone straight in the outside bin, glossy white album with tissue interleaves and all, but there were others which had to stay. She couldn't bear to think of Christopher's or Billy's face staring up out of the rubbish at her, but nor could she bear to think of Christine's doing the same from the bookshelf. She didn't feel bad about her actions. She wasn't a vindictive or bitter person, she was hurt. When Joseph was alive, they'd shared their uglier emotions, taken them to church together, and silently left them there, but now she had to deal with them on her own. It would be easier to cut Christine out altogether, rather than be reminded every time she opened a book. And who would know? It wasn't as if anyone would ever ask to see them again.

Cathal arrived almost too soon.

"Oh, it's not Sunday already, is it?" she teased, bustling gratefully into action with cake tins and loose tea. The photographs were only just back in their places, the snipped remnants in the kitchen bin. She banged the lid shut.

"Sure it is. Have you not been to mass?" he said, bending down to kiss her soft cheek. His face was cold, having frozen half to death standing for the last twenty minutes on the touchline of a football match between two unknown teams of ten-year-olds in the playing field at the back of the house. The field used to be his shortcut home from school, and in those days the back garden gate had always been left unbolted so that his father could come and watch him and Niall play every Saturday afternoon and his mother could come and call them in for their tea. But today, of course, the gate was locked and long overgrown with ivy and he'd had to go the long way round.

"Never mind," he said. "Senility comes to us all."

"If we're lucky," she replied, touching his paunch and giving him a disapproving nod. She knew that curl of his lips well, from his being sent home from school camp for streaking, getting drunk at a funeral, taking his father's car without asking.

He was tempted to spill it all out there and then, among the neat Formica worktops and mug trees but her white hair lacked its Sunday grips and she looked tired.

"Are you okay, Mother?" he asked.

"Not so bad for one so old," she said. "Was that Isabel catching you on your way in?"

"No, why?"

"Oh, just that Theresa has made her decision. She'll be having the baby after all."

"She will? You'll be pleased about that."

"If pleased is the right word," she said wearily. "Are you going to tell me something cheerful?"

"Well . . ." He wished he could. "I'm actually after a photograph."

"Are you now?" She waited for more, checking the floor for evidence and thinking of the lacerated remains of his marriage sitting damply underneath the teabags.

"Would you help me find one for Billy?"

"A photograph for Billy?"

"One of me. He, er, he needs one for, er, I don't know."

If anyone wanted to lay their hands quickly on an image from the O'Connor archives, there was only one place to go. The collection took up a whole shelf in the vast reproduction mahogany-veneered wall display unit, red album after blue, chronologically ordered, every insert dated and captioned. His mother was the undisputed chief librarian, able to put her hands on any event, any year, within a minute of inquiry.

They walked into the sitting room and she watched him run his finger along the spines of her famous albums and pull out a red one. She put the tray down on the coffee table in front of the fire and turned on the shelving lighting. Glass cabinets flashed into life, highlighting junior boxing trophies, graduation portraits, vases so familiar they had lost their ability to shock with their frightfulness.

If it was a wedding photograph he wanted, he'd have to ask Christine now, although Mary doubted she had any left, either. She saw him swallow.

"Er, he needs a picture of me at ten years old for a project. Don't ask me why. I'm just doing what I'm told."

"Do you not mean Christopher?"

"No, Billy."

"It's Christopher who is ten, Cathal, not Billy."

"I know that, Mother. Jaysus, I know the ages of my own kids, for God's sake. I don't know what he wants it for and I don't get many opportunities to ask, do I?"

"You apologize now," Mrs. O'Connor told him quietly, moving back to her teapot.

"Sorry."

"I should think so, too, but you know, we've both made a mistake. Christopher turned eleven last September."

"So he did." Cathal felt as if he knew every single detail of that year.

"Ah, it's lovely that the boy's in touch, Cathal. Lovely that he asks his daddy to help him. All's not lost when a boy turns to his father like that."

Cathal nodded. "I'm sorry. I don't want to be angry."

"I know you don't. Bring a few books over here and let's see what we can find. You'll be wanting 1970."

They sat together on the horsehair sofa that had seen three separate upholsterer shops since 1950, and let their lives wash over them. There was something recuperative for Cathal in seeing his birthday cakes displayed religiously each year, plate gently propped on the very same table that his mother had just put a tin of homemade shortbread on. Five children, a cake a year for eighteen years. That made ninety cakes his mother must have baked and iced, and he'd bet he could find photographs of half of them. Food featured heavily in the O'Connor albums, and with every flick of a page he saw himself take shape. Fat baby, chubby kid, paunchy man.

"You fed me too much," he said. "No wonder I've got this." He patted his tummy through his blue cotton work shirt.

"Since when did I feed you pints of porter? It'll be the drink that's giving you that, not your mother's baking. But you take after me rather than your father, and there's nothing wrong with being cuddly."

"Not that anyone is putting that to the test at the moment."

"No?"

"No."

"You miss your boys, don't you?"

"Don't worry. We'll all get together soon, I'm sure."

"The trouble is," she said a bit wistfully, "that we all think we have time."

She patted his leg and he picked up the album he'd taken out first. Then she placed her hand lightly on his cuff.

"Don't go too fast, Cathal."

"You turn the pages then."

"That's Bessie's wedding. Would you look at me! What ever made me think I looked all right wearing something so short?"

"That dress was all right. Very soft, as I recall."

"There's quite a bit of it in the quilt in Maeve's room. Billy used to stroke it as a baby, do ye remember?"

Cathal nodded. He wanted, for a split second, to cry.

"That's our Limerick holiday," Mary said quickly. "That wee girl wouldn't leave you alone, said she was going to marry you."

"Did you keep her address?"

But the joke disappeared into thin air. A loose cardboard frame fell onto his lap, face down. As he turned it over, his stomach went with it.

It was Maya. There she was. Not sitting on the stairs at Bodinnick, but upright on a plain chair with a blue cloth background. In a striped tie. With his own face. Wearing his own school sweater.

"Would you look at you," his mother said fondly, but Cathal had momentarily lost the power of speech. The snap of Maya in his wallet started to burn a hole through the cotton of his shirt and the wool of his sweater, the mix of his suit.

". . . hated them, you did."

"What? Did I?" He recovered himself.

Mary was smiling.

"Did I really have that many freckles?" he asked.

"No, I drew them on afterward. Of course you had that many freckles, you eejit."

"Definitely ten?"

"A darn sight more than ten. You were pickled. They were even on your earlobes!"

"No, not ten *freckles*, you mad old woman. Was I definitely ten years old there?"

"About that."

"No, not 'about that.' I need to be sure."

"Does it matter so much?"

"Well, it does if I'm to do the right thing by Billy."

"Let's see, is there a date?" She turned it over. "Yes, look, you were definitely ten."

"Sure?" He was studying its every detail. "I'll take it then."

"As long as Billy promises to keep it safe. I've not got another."

Cathal shook his head. His mother was barely visible under the pile of albums, but she meant it. It was the only print of that photograph she had. If you didn't count the four smaller versions.

"You know, Cathal, some children grow up not even knowing their daddy. And there's Billy, asking you for a photo. All's not lost, ye know."

It might not all be found yet, he thought, giving her hand a squeeze. It was hopeless. His visit had made him feel worse. He had allowed his confusion to spill into ordinary life. Actually, it was worse than that. He had experimented with the idea that it *was* ordinary life. Involving his mother gave the wild chance a legitimacy.

"Will ye stay for a bite to eat?"

"Another bite?"

"A proper bite."

"Oh, go on, then."

———

THE TWO PHOTOGRAPHS WERE HIDDEN UNDER A SHEET OF PAPER—THE 8" × 5" portrait of him in his school uniform, and the 6" × 4" of Maya in T-shirt and wellies. More than thirty years separated them, but to him they were identical.

The opening sentence of his letter to Emmy was eluding him. Their union had been so brief that he'd all but forgotten it. He was about to attempt an intimate dialogue with a virtual stranger.

Eleven and a half years ago, he had been commuting between London and Dublin, setting up the firm's Kensington office and reluctantly staying with Niall at his shared house with a bath in the kitchen and an oven in the garden. One day Niall hadn't bothered to turn up—he'd obviously come across a better bed for the night—so Cathal, locked out and hungry, had phoned the only other person in London he knew.

Emmy had seemed keen enough to see him—even gone out of her way to do so. They'd met at a strange pancake place in Holburn which was vegetarian or Mexican or probably just cheap. It'd had a lot of green paint everywhere. And plants. A straggly little spider thing in particular, yellowing, hanging from a windowsill.

She'd been with a load of mainly female workmates, celebrating someone's birthday or sending someone off round the world or something. There had been cards and flowers and stupid little presents like chocolate willies, and as a man he had felt surplus to requirements. Eventually, she had tossed him the keys to her flat and said he could go back if he wanted to. And he had wanted to.

Sex had been the last thing on his mind when he heard the front door open and shut two hours later.

"You don't have to sleep on that thing if you don't want to," she'd said, looking at his feet hanging over the arm of the sofa. "My bed is big enough."

Emmy had worn a cloak of such unhappiness back then that he had hesitated. It had been a struggle to desire her. Not impossible, clearly, but he'd spent most of the night trying to avoid touching the starved hollows between her shoulder and neck and the wafer thinness of the skin round her ribs. He wasn't sure how much contact she could take without snapping. And even at the time, he'd known she'd slept with him because it was the nearest she could get to Niall.

Her fridge the next morning had been completely empty apart from someone's contact-lens fluid and a bottle of white wine, he could remember that. That and the condom.

Being married, he wasn't in the custom of carrying them around, and he was sure he could recall her reaching over him in bed and opening a drawer. She'd tossed it on the bed—"You'd better use one of these"—and he'd struggled to hang on to his erection while he put it on, with her lying there motionless next to him. Not watching or touching or helping, but waiting. Resignedly. Like, hurry up, then, let's get this over with. And what had she been wearing? Some impossible leotard that only she knew the way into and out of.

The condom thing worried him. His sexual promiscuity had been in the days when men supplied, or more usually didn't supply, the condoms, and he'd been a little shocked, even put off, by her taking control there. As if she did it all the time. His memory wouldn't play that kind of trick, surely. Then again, they weren't fail-safe.

Now, though, when that bloody little electronic rabbit shot out of its stall again and ran rings round the dogtrack of his mind, it got him wondering whether the condom girl had in fact been Emmy, or perhaps one of his other indiscretions that year. God knows, there had been a few. And he didn't know whether or not he wanted to be right about being wrong.

The table was covered with discarded scribbling. Searching through his old work diaries, he had already identified his trips between Dublin and London but he had always remembered the Emmy thing as happening on his first trip back, which was why, when Niall had told him about

Maya's birth, he had secretly thought, Bloody hell, she doesn't hang around, does she? But it had never occurred to him that it might have happened on the second. Or even the third. Both dates fitted his research.

A heap of crumpled rejects buried the newspaper. Maybe a phone call, then, to Niall, to find out Maya's birthday. Cathal picked up his mobile. If he rang while his mother was here, he could use her as a smokescreen. He stared at the numbers for a moment, urging himself to press one.

"Bloody Mary, mother of J!"

The phone sprang into life in his hand.

"Hello? Oh, did I say today? No, not busy, just, er, no, no. Give me half an hour. I'll be there. Forgive me."

Saved. He put the phone back in his pocket, let his head fall into his hands for a brief moment, then pushed his chair back and stood up. There was a convincing argument to let sleeping dogs lie. Or at least take the day off.

MAYA TREASURED HER "I'M ME" MOMENTS. SOMETIMES SHE WENT through a phase of them happening every day, and then they would stop and she wouldn't get one for months. It was nothing to do with mood or place. It was all and everything to do with her own secret self, and that was the only way she could explain it.

The first time she'd tried to verbalize the experience was nearly five years ago, in a Peckham park on her sixth birthday. Puddles of spilt orange fizz had formed in the dips of the waterproof tablecloth, crisp crumbs and half-eaten sausage rolls stuck to the abandoned crumpled paper plates. Her friends had gone home, the late May sunshine had turned to a milky haze and her loathed Little Mermaid swimming costume had finally broken its Lycra promise.

"I'm me," she'd suddenly told Emmy as she decorated their grubby toes with tiny padded stickers.

"Yep, you are."

"No one else is me, are they? Just me. Only me."

" 'Fraid so," Emmy replied. As a child, she'd often frightened her-self with the recurrent and profound realization that no one else can share the world with you. It loomed, like a storm cloud approaching, or the swell of nausea. You knew it was going to get worse before it got better.

"Think of that," Maya carried on. "Just me. No one else knows what it's like to be me. Not even you."

"Just shake it away," Emmy said. "It'll go in a minute."

"Why?" Maya asked. "I like it."

Emmy hadn't been organized enough to remember to take anything as sensible as a camera, of course, but as a result of the "I'm me" moment, she could still see the day as clearly as any carefully captioned snapshot. It was the point at which she realized her daughter possessed the inherent security she herself lacked. It might also have been the first time she saw Maya as a crutch, a stronger, better version of herself, but that was now so ingrained a view that she couldn't recall ever seeing it otherwise.

Sometimes Sita and Niall warned her about her tendency to lean on Maya. "She's only a child," they'd say. "You don't need to be quite so truthful with her." But she knew Maya better than they did, and she knew, too, that her daughter didn't get the whole truth. She only got the half of it.

Maya was having an "I'm me" moment that very minute, kneeling in the music room at Bodinnick, laying out on newspaper the materials to construct a medieval dwelling as part of Jonathan's brilliant idea for their first rainy Saturday. So far, she had a bucket of mud, some clay, and a pile of carefully selected willow twigs for timber supports. She knew what she was going to build. A single-cell wattle-and-daub cot-tage, like the one in the book Jonathan had got from the library.

As she concentrated on the engrossing task of sorting twigs into uprights and roof beams, it happened. A feeling of suspended animation washed over her. Stuff receded. There was only her. This is me, Maya Hart, ten years old, watching myself getting ready to build a model house. She sang a few tuneless notes just to hear her own voice in her head. She looked at her hands still moving around on the newspaper. I am ten but I am ageless. I am me, but there is someone else in me, too, someone I know but don't know. I am a spirit in a body. My brain isn't big enough for my thoughts.

She tried, as she always did, to see around the corner of the moment, but so far she had never got there in time. One day she felt sure she would. She looked up and then pop! Back to normal.

"Jonathan?" she asked.

"Mm?"

"Do you ever get 'I'm me' moments?"

"I get 'I wish I wasn't me' moments," he said, trying for the third time to fit the printer cable into the back of the PC.

"You don't, do you?" Maya was shocked. It had never occurred to her that anyone might prefer to be someone else.

9

"MAKE THE MOST OF YOUR JOIE DE VIVRE," JULIAN HAD TOLD EMMY AT Toby's funeral. Well, if ever there was a time to celebrate new beginnings, this was it. As luck would have it, it was the first of May.

"I need a maypole," she announced to the other three at breakfast, once the children had left for school, "or something. We should go to Padstow."

"Why?" asked Sita.

"Because it's May Day and that's where *everyone* in Cornwall goes on May Day."

"How do you know?"

"Well, for a start, I listen to the local radio and not Classic bloody FM," Emmy teased lightly, "but Toby took us once and I've never forgotten it. There was a monster horse chasing nubile wenches up and down the streets and people dancing and singing all over the place. We had to step over a drunk in the street."

"Sounds delightful," said Jonathan grumpily.

The sun was bouncing off the kitchen's freshly painted saffron-yellow walls, there were primroses on the table, wisteria dripping off the front of the house and unexpected geraniums breaking out all over the flowerbeds. Spring had sprung with such convincing life at Bodinnick that Emmy felt she could even forget Kat was coming back tomorrow. Almost, anyway.

"Feeling pagan, are you?" Niall asked, noticing with a little shiver of lust that she had let the hair under her arms grow.

"Yes," she muttered so Sita and Jonathan couldn't hear, "I am, actually, and if I were you I'd make the most of it."

Sometimes, she congratulated herself from the back of Niall's bike as they rushed up the A30, she had the best ideas. She put her arms round his waist, pressed her face into his shoulder and silently kissed his leather jacket. He wouldn't feel it so it wouldn't do any harm.

They were streaking up the outside of a mile-long tailback, passing camper vans with foreign numberplates, shiny Land-Rovers advertising London garages, surfy VW Beetles and anonymous station wagons packed to the gunnels with children and luggage, all of them bound for Padstow. Somewhere in the middle of it all were Sita, Jonathan and Lila in their ubiquitous SUV, but that was their lookout, Emmy decided, almost gagging on the rush of air that filled her open mouth as Niall put his foot down and took the lot.

The north-coast fishing village they were heading for really was the only place to go if you were in Cornwall on May Day. Even though tourists all over the world could pull details of this wild ancient custom off the Internet, it didn't stop thousands of them from believing, once they got there, that they were being offered a rare private glimpse of a primitive tribe at play, being let into a secret which had lost its roots in the mists of time—a clever trick which had as much vociferous local opposition as global support.

Plans to meet Sita and Jonathan in the car park proved to be a joke. There were too many car parks, too many people and too long a queue, so Emmy sent them a text message and they headed off.

Down in the primevally decorated town, it was impossible not to feel a little bit primeval oneself. Emmy walked the crowded narrow streets next to Niall like a ripe bud ready to burst into life. Even the stem of bluebells pinned to her red sleeveless vest made her feel like a bucolic maiden ready for the plucking.

Their shoulders were brushing again, as they had at the wedding, before Kat, and she could feel the swing of her breasts against the cotton of her top, imagining he could somehow feel them too.

The whole place looked like an Arcadian dream. Doorways and windows had been transformed overnight to arcane portals. Sycamore trees in the surrounding woodlands had been stripped of their best branches and young green leaves now fluttered competitively in the sea breeze with the brilliant nylon flags that zigzagged overhead.

Everywhere Emmy looked in the jubilant throng milling around the harbor, she saw a representation of youth. Plump rosy virgins (highly unlikely, she knew, but she was in the mood to suspend reality) flirted with their muscled admirers, who stood libidinously against the low granite walls. She couldn't help looking at the ways the boys advanced on their prizes, putting one arm against a shop front, a foot on a curb, pulling a ring from a lager can and spraying the opposition, standing just that little bit closer to each other. At the same time, the girls were easy prey, with open arms and happy faces.

"Everyone looks so hot-blooded," she said, lifting her voice above the clamor and the sporadic bursts of song.

"You don't look so cold yourself," Niall told her, his hand pushing her bottom through the horde. Keep it there, keep it there, she thought.

They shuffled along, following the stream of people round and round the cobbled streets, not knowing or caring where they were going, but trusting it would be somewhere good. Soon, they found themselves outside a formidable building which had clearly never tolerated any nonsense. Before they could draw breath, the swing doors of the Institute opened with a single thump on the drum. The crowd stilled. You could almost have heard a pin drop. Three more deafening beats, then out the monster came.

The town's entire population let out a roar as the May beast lashed and swirled its way into the crowd, the band weaving around it, teasing it with its pagan rhythm. Emmy and Niall's fingers crept toward each other and locked tight.

They called it a hobby horse, or 'obby 'oss if you were in the know, but the animal was nothing like the nursery toy the tourists expected. It didn't matter how meek the man underneath the wood and canvas frame was, it was a wild black whirling dervish of a stallion with its fierce hungry face that emerged to the baying of the mob.

"It's Nat Harvey's first time this year," Emmy heard someone say behind her.

"Bloody 'ell. Tamar better watch out th'n," another voice replied.

As the thump of the band approached, Emmy felt the rhythm hit her deep inside, melting her, making her tingle and want to run and dance. Fear and desire fell upon her and she had a crystal-clear sense of the world offering itself to her. Something opened up in her shut-down soul.

"Kiss me," she sang, swinging round to face Niall. "I need you to kiss me."

In that instant, they became different people, or maybe the same people operating in a different reality. He grabbed her by her bare shoulders, stopping dead in the middle of the pavement, sending people scattering and hopping out of their way. He pushed his lips—they were cold with the beer he had just swigged—against hers, and their mouths opened and joined. The rest of the world closed down for a moment, and when it started up again, the creature's mask—a stallion's head with snapping teeth and red eyes—was so close it could have taken a bite out of them. The revelers around it whooped and sang and clapped and cheered.

> *"Unite and unite and let us all unite*
> *For summer is acome unto day*
> *And whither we are going we will all unite*
> *In the merry morning of May"*

The song rose high and clear, and as the music reached an almost deafening climax, a rounded woman in her fifties, dressed in the day's traditional white shirt and white jeans, grabbed Emmy's hand and pulled her toward the 'oss.

"Like this," the woman told her, and took her into the dance. Her movements were large, practiced and confident.

Niall watched. He wanted Emmy for himself but the older woman's magnetism drew him in, and soon it was her he couldn't take his eyes off.

The horse noticed her, too. It flung its tail into the air and then brought it down in a controlled display of strength, sweeping the floor and the tips of the woman's shoes. It ran into the crowd, sent the girls squealing and Emmy flying back to Niall, then retreated to pay more attention to its prize. It reared and came, circled and swooped and then backed off before doing the whole dance again. The woman's hips rose and fell at each approach, her arms outstretched to embrace the challenge.

Suddenly, the hoop was up and over her head and she was under the skirt. Emmy imagined herself under there, her world turning black, the drums and the accordions becoming a muffled pulse. She imagined being the only woman in the world who could smell the horse's hot torso, the mix of tar and sweat and horsehair, the damp cloth of a T-shirt.

When the 'oss finally released the woman with a vertical toss of the heavy hoop, his sooty finger daubed her reddened cheek and she waltzed out laughing, branded with what some referred to as "the mark of life."

"Blimey!" Emmy laughed.

She looked at Niall, and Niall looked at her. They kept looking for a long time, long enough for there to be no doubt left whatsoever, and then he put his finger to her cheek and traced a line down her jaw.

"Oh, there you are," Sita said, almost on top of them. "We've only just been able to park the car. Have we missed anything?"

THAT EVENING, WHEN THE HOUSE WAS VERY QUIET, JAY HID HIMSELF away in Emmy's sewing room, perfecting his blanket stitch. He felt proud of his banner idea. He was going to hang it across the Welsh dresser tomorrow, so that when they all sat down to eat, they would know what they were supposed to be celebrating. If Kat was coming home for a party, a party they'd better have.

He was a bit annoyed with his parents for behaving as if they needed reminding to be honest. "No one said it would be easy," his mum kept saying when little things went wrong. "Don't expect it to happen just like that." But it sounded very much to him as though she was talking to herself.

What about that "period of adjustment" they had kept telling him about in London? Don't expect it to be plain sailing, Jay, they had said. Don't expect this, don't expect that. There will be times when you miss your friends, and hate us for taking you away from them. But give it a chance. We're doing this for you as much as for us.

Well, he didn't miss his friends because he had new ones, better ones, ones who made him feel he counted. And he didn't hate his parents for taking him away from London. He might hate them for taking him back, though, and that was his fear. That was why this banner had to be so big, so that they'd get the message.

Licking the end of the cotton as he'd seen his mother do, he took three attempts to get it through the eye of the needle. The floorboards creaked once, then twice, on the landing outside the door and he held his breath, but the footsteps moved on. Then he settled down to find the rhythm of the stitch he'd been taught in Year Two when he had made a miniature Christmas stocking out of red felt and cotton wool, and all the boys had teased him for being a girl.

When he got to the end of the seam, he bit the cotton off the needle and flattened out the joined sheet to admire his work.

At his feet was a selection of recently developed photographs, taken since their arrival at Bodinnick. Shiny faces grinning from kitchen tables, step ladders, and garden ponds.

He'd noticed when he was sorting them out that people always did the same thing when confronted with a camera. Emmy made the error of poking her tongue out in every single one, as if she didn't know how to smile to order. Niall had a tendency to put his arm round Maya, or lift her up, or do something to her. Always Maya, never Asha or him, or even Lila; always, always Maya. His mum tilted her head toward the person next to her and opened her eyes wider than she usually did, giving her a fake startled look. The only one his dad was in was the self-timer they'd done on the first night. He was holding up a load of paper and Maya's fingers were poking up like rabbit ears behind his unsuspecting head. Jay didn't like the way she'd done that—he thought it made his dad look stupid—so he Sellotaped it to one of the top seams where no one would see it.

In his favorite photograph, he was center stage, standing on one foot, the other in the air, his arms outstretched, overbalancing, obscuring both his sister and Maya. He wouldn't have done that a month ago. A month ago, he would have lurked at the edges. He spent thirty seconds admiring himself, pleased with what he saw, and then fixed it in a prominent position in the center of the banner.

Next to him was a carrier bag full of discarded tester pots which had been sitting on the landing for weeks. When he tipped them out, ready to paint the words, he realized that the paper seal hadn't been broken on some of them. Perhaps Scott's mum was right. Perhaps his parents did have more money than sense.

On his knees, paintbrush in his hand, he began. In capital letters of varying heights, purples and thickness, he painted "ONE Whole MONTH" along the length of the sheet. The cloth puckered under the upward movement of the brush, and in places the emulsion seeped through onto the threadbare carpet.

As he waited for it to dry, he worked out that if each match pot had cost two pounds, the household had spent at least twenty pounds on choosing paint colors. And that was just for Maya's bedroom. That wasn't simple living, was it? Who were they trying to kid?

OUTSIDE HER SEWING ROOM, EMMY SLOWED. THERE WAS THE THRESH-old to Niall's space—the space that would soon be shared with Kat again.

His bathroom door was wide open, a green towel was in a damp heap on the floor and puddles led to the bedroom. Beyond that, a radio burbled. Niall would be listening to it, wet and unclothed, preparing himself for the great return.

The thump of the May Day music was still beating inside her, making her want to burst in, throw herself on his bed, fling out her arms and give in. She wanted to dance with the 'oss just once, for old and new times' sake, but she knew she had to carry on putting one foot in front of the other until she reached her own room. It was almost too much effort.

Suddenly, she wanted something even more than the 'oss. She wanted closure on the last few weeks. She wanted to know where she stood, what would happen when Kat went back the next time, if their increased intimacy had changed things. All the issues that had been carried away with the beast this morning were back. The May Day music was fading to a feeble squeak.

Seeing his towel and his footprints, knowing that tomorrow there would be another towel and other prints, she just had to know. Even if the closure really was closure, she wanted it.

It took her ten brisk paces to get to her own space, where she picked up her mobile from the old walnut bureau.

ARE YOU DRY YET? she typed with shaking fingers. Then she put it back at the same angle, pointing toward the window where she knew the signal would be strongest. Even texting felt like a loss. Their recent messages had been a seamless string of not very important questions. Are you asleep? Did you get the bread? Fancy a beer? Just enough to keep them in secret touch.

Waiting for the bleep of reply, she sat on the bed looking at her swatches. As she picked up a red satin square, it rang.

"Hi," she answered, her voice as silky as the material she was fingering. She stood precariously at the edge of the dressing table against the wall. If she moved, he could so easily disappear.

"Yes I am," he said. "And thank you for asking."

"Are you dressed as well?"

"No."

"So you're stark bollock naked?"

"I am."

"Well, don't get cold."

"I won't."

She realized she was going to have to spell it out. "I, er, I thought we ought to have a talk."

"Is talking on mobiles when you're in the same house allowed?"

"Probably not." Emmy didn't care about rules anymore.

"So if we were being sensible, we would put our phones down and come and find each other."

"Yes, we would, but we're not, are we, so we won't. Anyway,

you'd have to put some clothes on for that." Damn. She frowned at herself for taking the conversation in the opposite direction to the one she wanted it to go in.

"I'm too hot for clothes," he said.

She began to feel the pound of desire again, which was no good for closure at all. "Hot baths are bad for you. You had better lie down."

"Had I?"

"A rush of blood can be very dangerous."

"So I've heard. What are you doing up here?"

"How do you know I'm up here?"

"I heard you go past."

"Did you? I nearly came in to see you."

"I know. I was hoping you would." He sat down. "What are you doing?"

"Standing up."

"Have you still got your boots on?"

"I beg your pardon?"

"Have you still got your boots on?"

"Why do you want to know that?"

"I just do. I want to know everything about you. So, have you?"

"Well, yes, I have."

"They're so sexy, those boots. What about your skirt?"

"You noticed."

"You knew I'd notice."

"Uh huh."

"Take it off."

Emmy laughed but she knew she would do what he'd asked.

"Go on, take it off," he said again. His voice had changed gear. It was slower, deeper. "Take your skirt off but leave your boots on."

"Why should I want to do that?"

"Because the visual image interests you," he said.

"You or me?"

"Me."

"What right have you got to tell me to take my clothes off?" she asked, unbuttoning her skirt and letting it fall to the ground. Then she moved her free hand to run her fingers over her stomach and across the top of her pants just to see if she felt desirable. She did. Her long legs looked good in her flat suede boots and she found herself mesmerized by the strong erotic image. "There."

"Have you done it?" He sounded surprised.

"Yeah."

"God, Emmy, have you really?"

"Yeah."

"What else are you wearing?"

"A black vest and my jacket."

"The denim one?"

"Yes."

She thought she heard him groan.

"Take the vest off and put the jacket back on."

"Why?" she asked again.

"Because you want to."

"Make me," she said.

"Make me make you."

"Just say that again a little slower."

"I can make you. I just have to ask you. Take your clothes off for me, Emmy."

He heard her put the phone down on a surface. She took her jacket off, laid it on the bed, threw her vest on the floor and put the jacket back on. She stared at herself, liking it.

"Can you see yourself in the mirror?"

"Uh huh."

Niall lay back on the bed, and they stopped speaking for a while, listening to each other's changing breathing patterns.

"Do you want me?" she whispered.

"I do, I really do."

"Tell me."

"I want you."

"Tell me again."

"Emmy, come here," Niall said in an urgent, quiet voice. "Come to me. Please."

"No. You come here." And she moved away from the mirror, her hand hanging by her side, holding the phone, her legs slightly apart, waiting for his footsteps.

He walked in, dropped his towel and took the phone from her hand, switching it off. Then he took her face in his hands and their tongues flicked in each other's mouths. Emmy put her arms above her head and he moved to kiss her breasts.

"And I want you," she said.

"You've got me."

"No. You don't understand. I want you forever."

"You've got me for as long as you want." She could feel his heart-beating through her skin.

They both thought of the single thump of the drum, the crowd's roar, the swirling dance of the beast. She took his finger again and pulled it down the side of her face. Now wasn't the time to hold him to any life promises.

10

"A MONTH," JONATHAN TOLD TAMSIN THE NEXT DAY, SUDDENLY REALIZ-
ing he was staring at the almost invisible downy hair that ran in a line
from her earlobe down her jaw line. The May Day beast had had its
effect on them all.

He knew he was a very changed man from the one who had left
London, if only because he was becoming so easily distracted. In the
city, he had been programmed to focus on specific things, yet in Cornwall his viewfinder was all over the place. There was suddenly a lot to
see, although, to be fair, he wasn't the only one looking. And none of
them had their zoom lenses pointing at the same thing.

With Sita it was children, work, house. With him it was children,
chapel, Tamsin. Or was it Tamsin, chapel, children? He couldn't
remember the last time either of them had put each other in the frame.

What was he doing in Tamsin's lilac VW Beetle anyway? He didn't
know whether he felt like her driving instructor, her date or her father.
Somewhere not so deep down, he blamed Emmy and Niall, but only
because that made him feel less guilty than blaming Sita. He certainly
didn't blame himself. Everyone else did that for him.

The medieval building they were heading for this stunningly clear morning was only an excuse. Open to the public every fourth weekend, Point Manor had a chapel of the same proportions as Bodinnick's, with the addition of two wall paintings which were apparently in a remarkable condition. It would be interesting to see them, but he could easily have gone on his own.

"Would you like me to take you?" Tamsin had asked him over the phone on Friday.

"I'd love you to," he'd said.

"Great, bring your children," she'd replied. But they'd both known he wouldn't.

"So you've got another two to go?" she asked, still five miles away and crunching the gears at every change.

"Two what?" He'd forgotten what they'd been talking about.

"Months."

"Oh, yes, well, that's the plan."

"Is it unsettling, not knowing?"

"Not knowing what?"

"Come on, keep up. Whether this is it or not."

Not when you've spent the last forty years not knowing, he thought, slamming his right foot automatically onto the floor as they found themselves staring up the back of an old bus. It had *Surfers Against Sewage* sprayed in big black letters across its boot and a thick curtain across the back window. It was the same bus they had all followed up the lane to Bodinnick on the last leg of their first journey.

"Well, who knows what they really want?" he said.

"I do. I want a job that I love that pays me loads of money which I can then spend traveling."

"What, like these guys?"

She pulled out on a blind bend. "God no. I've got no desire to be a gypsy."

"No?" If he hadn't been so preoccupied with her driving skills, he would have felt disappointed at that admission. "Anyway, I thought you liked the job you've got."

"I do. It just doesn't pay enough."

The engine was straining. Change down, for God's sake, he wanted to shout.

"Cornwall's full of mad people like this," she said, gesticulating rudely at the bus. "Britain is like a Christmas stocking. All the nuts end up at the toe."

"Thank you."

"Oh, not you. You're——" Don't say sensible, he willed——"Sensible," she said.

"Oh, you as well. Everyone thinks that."

"Are they right?"

"Not necessarily."

"Is it for me to find out?"

Her challenge made him lose his nerve and he changed tack. "Well, your job must pay you quite well to buy a brand-new car like this," he said, his foot flat down on an imaginary accelerator.

"Someone bought it for me, actually."

"Oh. Lucky you."

"It was a guilt thing," she said dismissively.

He knew she expected him to ask who the someone was, and what they had done to feel guilty about, but her slight arrogance had deflated him.

"Money's not everything," he said instead.

She finally found third gear. "You're going to tell me it can't buy you love next, aren't you?"

It was the first time their conversation had turned away from the professional, but he couldn't help wishing it wasn't happening while they were abreast of a thirty-year-old coach on a hairpin bend. He glanced up at the driver and was surprised to see it was a girl with what looked like a big stripy sock on her head.

"I don't know. I've never had enough of it to put it to the test," he said.

Tamsin looked as though she didn't believe him, and why should she? After all, he was a liar. As far as Sita knew, he was going on his own to a quarry to pick up some lime putty.

"They shouldn't be allowed to drive round in that heap. It's not roadworthy," she said angrily, beginning to scrabble in her glove compartment for a tape.

"What do you want? Let me get it. You just get on with overtaking."

"You choose."

He didn't recognize any of the names of any of the bands she had written on the cassette boxes, so he picked one at random and put it in, pretending he hadn't looked.

"Well done, good choice. Thanks," she said.

And because both the bus and a ten-mile stretch of road were now behind them, he smiled. She had both needed and thanked him in the space of a minute and he was grateful for that—even if he was very clearly in the passenger seat again.

"LET'S HAVE SOME MUSIC," EMMY SAID TO SITA, ROLLING HER SLEEVES UP and taking a deep breath of the clove-scented steam rising from the ham. She needed to fill the time, having already spun out her trip to the butcher's to a full hour, not that the person she really wanted to notice had noticed. Niall had been too busy sleeping off the effects of making love to two women in twenty-four hours to notice anything.

Kat really had come back from London last night just as she had threatened, and for the first time in nearly three weeks Emmy hadn't seen Niall all day. She knew what he was doing up there. He was kicking over the last few traces of his infidelity, undoing the spell. The problem was that she was still well and truly under it. She could still smell him in her bed, a mix of shower gel and smoke and mystic beast.

"Turn it up as loud as you like," she said to Sita, who was more than happy to oblige. She'd heard the movements upstairs too. "We can't have him emerging from his love nest into complete silence, can we?"

Sita shuffled around inside a cardboard box of organic vegetables which had just been delivered. "You okay?"

"Fine. Why?"

"Just that I thought it might be hard for you, with Kat coming back."

Emmy put her finger on the recipe. "Hold on. Add the sugar, lower the heat and simmer briskly. Sorry, what did you say?"

"Can't remember."

There was another noise from upstairs, an indistinct banging. It couldn't be the children. They were outside. Emmy turned the music up even more.

"What have we got this week?" she asked, peering into the box and speaking in a voice that sounded to her a few octaves too high. "Please not more kale."

"Carrots, potatoes, a rutabaga, a huge bunch of parsley."

"Hmm. Do you think we could get away with rutabaga and carrot with the ham?"

"No, the children are sick of it. We should try and do something festive. The food has got to be in the party mood, even if you're not."

"Oh, but I am."

"Yeah, and I'm a banana."

"See if you can find anything in there that uses swede and spuds, then," Emmy said, spinning the book across the table. The sound of Kat laughing seeped through the floorboards.

"What time did she get back? Were you still up?" Sita asked.

"No idea," Emmy said, remembering that the digital display on the clock radio next to her bed had said 12:12. She had heard everything. The motorbike, the front door, the low voices, the stairs. She even thought she had heard the clothes falling to the floor. "Right, this has now got to simmer briskly for an hour and fifty minutes."

Emmy peeled off her long-sleeved T-shirt to work in her vest. Sita noticed that someone had written "*Goodnight*" in ballpoint on the top of her shoulder. It wasn't Maya's hand. "That's not a brisk simmer, that's a gentle boil."

"What's the difference?"

"The same as the difference between you being in a party mood and me being a banana."

Jay saved them from the pointless discussion by walking in and asking if he and Scott could have a beer.

"No," Sita said.

"Why not? We're supposed to be celebrating, aren't we?"

"Not all day. You can have one tonight."

He made a face at his small friend, who looked relieved. "But Scott won't be here tonight."

"He can be if he likes."

"Cool. Can he stay the night?"

"I should think so. There's no school tomorrow. And if it's okay with his parents."

"It will be," Scott said a little sadly.

"Can I have this?" Jay asked, picking up a cast-iron saucepan lid.

"No," said Emmy. "I need it."

"This, then?" He picked up a knife block.

"No! What for?"

Jay tapped the side of his nose.

"Where are the girls?" Sita asked.

"Practicing their play. What about these? If we promise not to drink them?" He lifted a four-pack of beer by the plastic rings.

"No, Jay," said Sita. "Do you think I'm stupid? What do you want them for, anyway?"

He smiled secretly, Scott shrugged, and they both slipped into the room-sized larder, where they found a giant tin of coffee, a crate of shrink-wrapped baked beans and an economy-size box of washing powder, provisions bought weeks ago by Sita with the idealistic notion that bulk buying would make them all better people. In fact, all they had done so far was block the path to the fridge, stub a few toes and lurk like muttered reminders of their spectacular incompetence at sticking to the rules.

"These'll do," Jay whispered to Scott. "Give me a hand to get them up later?"

"Are *we* allowed a beer?" Emmy asked Sita when the boys had gone again.

"No, we're allowed champagne. We might as well make the most of being manless."

"When have I been anything but?"

"Don't give me that," Sita replied. "Jay may think I'm stupid but you're certainly not allowed to."

"IT'S QUITE A SORRY TALE, ACTUALLY," TAMSIN WAS SAYING TO JONATHAN who was trying not to concentrate too hard on his breathing.

It was a shame his difficulties seemed to have chosen this moment to return with a vengeance. A couple of times since they had got out of the car, he had felt his heart lose its rhythm. So far Tamsin hadn't noticed his panic-ridden gulping because he'd managed to cover it up with coughs.

"The building of the house was aborted in 1521 when Charles Pencarrow's wife and infant son both died of a fever. He couldn't bear being here anymore, because it represented everything he had lost. Basically, he went a bit mad."

Jonathan didn't want to think about wives or sons. "It's a shame someone else didn't come along and finish it," he said, drawing air slowly though his nose.

"No one would go near it. Everyone believed it was cursed."

"Cursed?"

"Yes. Two unexplained deaths, a madness. It didn't take much."

"Blimey. I hope it isn't."

"Why? What are you worried about then? Death or madness?"

He felt like saying just plain old adultery actually. "Death isn't exactly in my life plan. But places do have their own vibes, don't they?"

"No, I don't think so. I think the vibes are just about the people who are living in it at the time."

"Is that what you think?"

"Yes, that's what I think."

We're flirting with each other, he realized. "Well, *I'd* live here," he said.

"In your dreams."

He didn't want to think too hard about his dreams, either, so he opened the cream folded sheet of paper that he had picked up from inside the porch. "It says here that after the deaths Charles Pencarrow diverted all his wealth to the rebuilding of Saint Peter's Church across the valley."

"Oh, you should go to Saint Peter's if you can. It has this fabulous sculptured granite façade."

"You've been?" She nodded. She didn't tell him it was on a school trip six years ago.

"We could go together?" he suggested tentatively.

"Sure."

"That would be great. It's so good, finally meeting someone who's interested in the same things as I am."

"Oh, it's nothing."

And the way she said it, he really should have realized that she meant it.

"WHAT ABOUT CLAPSHOT?" SITA SAID.

"No, I've never had that. Is it treatable?" Emmy asked, fishing carrots and the green parts of the leek out of the ham pot.

Sita laughed. "It's something you can make from rutabagas and potatoes. Look." She pointed at a recipe in a book called *Hearty Vegetable Dishes*.

"Good grief! Who the hell would eat anything called clapshot?"

"Somebody who had a surfeit of rutabagas and potatoes?"

"Oh yeah!"

They were both a little drunk and Emmy had been tutoring Sita in the newly discovered techniques of phone sex.

"I think you should do it today," said Emmy. "Strike while the iron's hot."

"Wouldn't that burn?"

Their loud cackles were more or less unconscious now, but if they still traveled upstairs that was a bonus. If he heard them, Niall might wish he were downstairs instead.

"God knows we could do with a touch of originality," said Sita.

"Oh, you don't touch, and it's not very original. This is the age of the mobile, remember."

"It would be original for us."

"From what you've just told me, *any* sex would be original for you."

"This is true. Shall I phone him now?"

"He might have lime putty on his hands. Very caustic, I've heard. It can cause blindness. And don't you think that would be biting off more than you can chew?"

"I've never been able to do that, either. What do you do with your teeth?"

"Take 'em out, leave 'em in a glass of water on the side."

"It'll come to that sooner than we think."

"I know. My gums have already started bleeding when I clean my teeth."

"Stop," Sita said, making a disgusted face. "That's too much information, even for a doctor. Anyway, that's not caused by old age, that's down to careless brushing. Let's go back to phone sex a minute. Give me an opening line."

"You don't need me to tell you what to say."

"Oh but I do."

"Well, it can be anything, can't it? Just make sure you choose your words carefully—some words don't work."

"Like what? I need an example."

"Okay. 'Probing.'"

"Uuugh!"

"Or the 'c' word."

"I wouldn't say that anyway."

"And men don't like 'prick.'"

"I don't suppose they do!"

"So why do they like 'dick?'"

"Do they?"

"Don't they? I thought they did."

"I don't know, do I?"

Emmy filled their glasses with the last of the champagne. "Can you remember what—"

"Don't! I know what you're going to say and just don't!"

"Fingerbob!"

"I said don't! I'd forgotten him!"

They were dribbling helplessly, with tears streaming down their faces, and neither of them noticed when Niall walked in, barefoot. He checked the empty champagne bottle and decided not to mention how much it cost. It was worth every penny, anyway.

"Get on with sorting the clapshot, you old tart," Emmy snorted to Sita, rolling the rutabaga at her.

It was too good a line for Niall to ignore. "I thought you weren't on duty today, Sita."

"Oh, God! How long have you been there?" shrieked Emmy, spinning round. Her face was flushed with alcohol.

"Ages. I heard the whole lot." It was a fair bet. He knew what they were like.

"You liar."

"I did. And you're both filthy. You should be ashamed of yourselves."

"We are. Deeply."

"Well," said Sita, scraping her chair across the slate floor and picking up her mobile from the dresser. "Will you excuse me? I've got a phone call to make."

"You aren't, are you?" Emmy asked her.

"I am."

"Is nothing sacred?" said Niall, not really minding that he had clearly been discussed, and pointing to Emmy's shoulder to try and tell her about the pen.

"YOU ALL NEED TO LEAVE ROOM FOR MY DELICIOUS PUDDING," KAT reminded everyone. But fingers kept creeping back to the platter to have one more go at picking up the last few chunky flakes of rich pink meat, or to the chipped floral serving dish for some of the burned onions left from the clapshot.

She had spent the late afternoon spoiling Emmy and Sita's fun with her presence, and creating a complicated chocolate orange soufflé with ingredients from a selection of cappuccino-colored paper bags tied with gold ribbons. The bags still sat by the organic vegetable cardboard box next to the kitchen sink, making a statement similar to the one being made under the table by her high snakeskin-effect mules and Emmy's flat clogs.

"I'm not sure I could eat another thing," Emmy said, the ballpoint message still on her shoulder blade but hidden by a lime-green velvet wrap with a fringe of purple beads she had made for the occasion.

"Oh, you must."

Maya dipped her spoon in and licked it. "It's actually really yum!"

"There's loads of alcohol in it."

"How much?" Jonathan asked nervously.

Kat shrugged helplessly. "Oh, loads. I didn't think about the children."

"I'll have some," Jay shouted from the far end. He and Scott had already seen off two cans of beer each and he liked the Dutch courage it gave him. What's more, his banner had worked. He and Scott had hung it from the Welsh dresser, weighted down at the top by the contents of the larder. Everyone had cheered when he finally allowed them into the kitchen. He'd even let his mother kiss him.

"Arm-wrestle me, Dad."

"No. You'll beat me."

"Arm-wrestle me, Niall."

"No. I'll break your finger bones."

"A game of snooker, then?"

"We haven't got enough balls."

"Speak for yourself," Jay shouted bravely, basking in Scott's adoring admiration. "C'mon Scottie, let's go."

Sita and Jonathan smiled at each other side by side on the settle.

"Did you get my message at lunchtime?" she asked him under her breath.

"Yes. I didn't get back because I was already on my way."

"Pity."

"Why? What did you need me for?"

"You wouldn't believe me if I told you."

"Why not?"

"You just wouldn't."

"Try me." He wasn't sure but he thought he caught something in her eye he hadn't seen for a very long time.

"Phone sex," she whispered.

He looked around to see who was in on the joke. No one seemed to be. "Yeah, right. Don't tell me, Lila had run out of nappies and you wanted me to stop off at the shop."

"No, really."

"Really?" he asked. He was also whispering now.

"Yes, really."

"Bloody good soufflé," Niall said, scraping the last of it up.

"Not bad for a first attempt," Kat purred, pulling his arm round her neck.

"I think I need to lie down," said Emmy.

"Not before you tell us about your business," Kat said. "I took a look in your sewing room today. You've got a load of material in there."

"Oh, that reminds me, was there any post today?" Emmy asked quickly. "I've been waiting a whole week for some patterns I ordered."

"The post here is verging on bloody carrier pigeon, isn't it?" said Niall. "I saw the plumber, Roy Mundy, at the pub earlier and he said he sent his bill to us days ago. I'm sure we haven't had it. I reckon that chirpy little postie nicks stuff and hides it in the bushes somewhere. He's not right, is he? If he asks me to put a feckin' letterbox in the back door one more time I'll—"

"Language!" Asha shouted from the end of the table.

And then Jonathan remembered.

"Oh God, it's my fault," he said, the blood draining from his face. "I bet it's all over at the chapel. I intercepted the post the other day when I had Lila with me. I shoved it in her bucket seat. I was so keen to get away from him that I just took it and . . . I'll go and get it."

"Don't worry about it now, Jon. It can wait another day," said Emmy. "Anyway, it's pouring down out there."

"No, no, I'll go and get it now, while I remember. It's no problem. It won't take me two minutes."

"Don't be daft, Jonathan," Sita said, but he was already doing up his boots. She put her hand to her ear to mime a phone but he missed it.

"You're mad," Emmy told him.

"Completely bloody barking," said Niall.

"Probably," he said, and on the walk over there, he realized there was no probably about it.

THE RAIN WAS COMING RIGHT AT HIM, BUT IF HE KEPT HIS HEAD DOWN he couldn't see where he was going, because the lights of the farmhouse were his only pointer. The driving wetness found its way inside the collar of his coat and through the stitching of his boots within seconds, and the warmth from the kitchen flew out the top of his thinning hair and left him chilled to the bone. He would probably be cold all night now.

Not that he cared. The chapel door gave him its familiar greeting as he pushed it open and flicked on the light. A single unshaded lightbulb hung from a central beam and he made two mental notes. One, to have a proper think about the ultimate necessity for electricity over here; two, to get a doorstop.

The mail was still on the floor by the radio. It was covered in a film of grit, and the top envelope had a coffee ring on it. Two dirty cups were next to it. A slender bone-china mug that was far too good to be out here had marks of lipstick round its rim. In slow motion, he brought it up to his mouth and pressed it against his lips. Then he rolled it against his cheek and held it there. It wasn't the chapel he wanted to see again tonight, it was Tamsin.

When he got back to the house, a game of Chinese whispers was under way. What had started out as "Peas in a pod are good for the bod" had ended up as "Piss in a pot is good for Herbert," and he walked into the kitchen to hear his nine-year-old daughter deliver the final sentence with all the finesse of a navvy. Sita had gone to bed.

"Tenpence for the swear box, Asha," Niall shouted.

"Pot calling, I think," Jonathan told him, letting two envelopes fall into Emmy's lap. He put the mugs on the table but the lipstick mark was gone, wiped off on the inside of his pocket.

"Are you making a patchwork quilt or something?" Niall asked as Emmy undid the parcel and pulled out five different-colored squares of satin. He tilted a bottle toward her empty glass but missed—a splash of red wine hit the newly revealed slate floor with a wet slap. His attention had been caught by something else. The second letter she picked up had a familiar green stamp with a harp on it—the equivalent of a flashing neon arrow to an Irishman.

"Who's writing to you from Ireland?"

"I've no idea," Emmy said looking at the printed address, but her brain had finished sifting through the possibilities before the words came out of her mouth.

"Can I have the stamp?" Maya asked.

But her mother didn't hear. She had already started to pull the contents out and it was too late to stop. There was nothing to do but read it.

Emmy, I would very much like to talk to you. My work, home and mobile numbers are below. Please call me if you can. Cathal.

Her world receded like the shrinking crisp packet Jay had just set alight with a candle in the ashtray.

I I

MAYA DID SOMETIMES ASK ABOUT HER FATHER, BUT ONLY IN PRIVATE ON good days. She had learned to choose the right time from the experience of once choosing the wrong time, when Emmy had unwittingly made her feel, with just one look, as if she were the most ungrateful, insensitive selfish child in the whole world.

She knew the warning signs. Cigarettes in the house again, long telephone conversations in her bedroom with the door shut, canceled babysitters. Cigarettes were probably the most reliable pointer. Most of the time, Emmy only smoked Niall's. If she bought a packet herself, Maya knew things were bad. Mum had bought a packet a day for weeks and weeks after Niall met Kat.

On the other hand, the more obvious clues like crying didn't mean much at all. Mum cried over silly things like bumping her head on the door frame, or the car not starting, or being hopelessly late for school. As far as Maya knew, she hadn't cried once since they'd moved to Cornwall, but Maya suspected that was just because the doors were higher, there was always another car available, and here no one minded if you were late for school. Also, obviously, Niall was always around.

When Maya did want a sense of her own genetic provenance, it was easier to ask about Iona, her dead grandmother, even though she had heard it all before. Everyone was always happy to talk about Iona—about her being caught sitting on Grandpa's bed at Ledbury when they weren't even engaged, about her dressing up as a man to get in to a club in London, about her letting Emmy light one of her cocktail cigarettes and not minding when Emmy burned a hole in the curtain with it.

Because Iona had been dead for centuries, she didn't have the family taboo that Maya's father had. No one ever ever spoke about her father. They all behaved as if she had popped out of nowhere, like the product of a virgin birth or something.

At times, Maya thought she would prefer never to meet her dad, just invent him. That way, he could be whoever she chose him to be. He could be Niall, or he could be someone even better than Niall. He could be someone who was prepared to live with her mum, for example. Live as in live, involving beds and baths and things. And then at other times, she thought she probably would like to meet him, to see what he looked like and if she liked him.

She couldn't help being eternally intrigued by the fact that she was made up of bits of people she didn't know. Asha's mouth was exactly the same as Jonathan's—the lips went up in the middle under the nose like a little skateboard ramp—but Jay's was thinner, more like Sita's. She had to stop herself staring sometimes, because little details like that could change your entire face. If you blocked off their mouths, Jay and Asha were actually quite alike.

Maya knew she didn't have Mum's mouth. Mum's lips were full and bouncy and she could suck in her cheeks and do a really good fish impression, but her own lips weren't big enough for that. When she sucked in her cheeks, she looked more like an old woman with no teeth. So whose mouth was it?

"Can you do a fish?" she would ask her mother's boyfriends. And they'd have a go, thinking it was some sort of bonding ritual.

Often, when she was having her shoulder-length hair dried by Emmy in front of the mirror, she would try and surreptitiously work out which bits of them matched. On a really good day, she could persuade Emmy to put her face right next to hers and they would stare at their reflections together.

"Okay, how about chin?" asked Emmy once.

"Mine looks like a little bottom."

"No, it doesn't."

"Yours doesn't."

"Eyes?"

"No. Mine go like that and yours go like this."

"They're the same color, though."

"Do you think we look like each other at all?"

"People are always telling me we do," Emmy lied. But she didn't think so at all. She knew who she thought Maya looked like.

"Just describe him," Maya said.

"Oh, well, he had three heads, and eyes on stalks."

"Yeah yeah, and he was covered in purple fur."

"Pink, darling, get it right."

Emmy didn't understand that Maya needed it to be purple, even if it was a joke, so she could imagine she had inherited at least something.

"Pink, then. But . . ."

"Hey, look, our chins *are* the same shape."

"Why didn't you marry him?"

"Would *you* marry someone with three heads?"

"No, Mum, seriously."

"He didn't ask me."

"Would you have married him if he had?"

"Oh, Maya, you know I'm not up for all this."

Emmy's resistance didn't matter to Maya as much as the textbooks Emmy tried to avoid but couldn't help reading said it should.

Anyway, Maya had a distant plan which she told no one. She was going to find out about her father when she was older, when Emmy was less dependent on her, when she could meet him without anyone knowing, perhaps without even her father knowing. Out of curiosity, that was all. Just to check he didn't have three heads.

"What do I call him?"

"Why don't we just call him 'your dad?' " her mum had suggested once.

"No," Maya had replied, repulsed at the idea. "I don't want to."

So they called him nothing. He had been nothing for ten years and now it was three o'clock in the morning and Emmy was lying in her bed during the longest night of her life, trying to accept that life as they all knew it was about to change.

Would he still be Cathal? Or would he, God forbid, become Dad? She was seething with an ill-defined anger, not just against Cathal but against Niall, too. How could he be so bloody thick? Why had he never worked out the identity of Maya's father? Why had he always been so patient, so stupidly content to accept her refusal to discuss it? He should have pushed her, as he pushed her on other stuff.

"Who's it from?" Niall had asked when he spotted the green stamp. "Come on, what business have you got with my homeland? I demand to know."

"It's a fabric wholesaler," she'd said pathetically. "They've written to tell me they can't help me."

"Is that right?" he'd said. There was no suspicion in his voice. He genuinely hadn't got the foggiest.

The letter was in the drawer next to her bed, emanating a sort of evil. She knew its every detail already. The date of the postmark, the color of Cathal's ink, the number of lines. It was too frightening even to imagine it in there, and yet she kept checking, hoping to find it gone, or somehow rewritten as something harmless.

Her head ached with the effort of trying to believe that Jonathan had in fact not brought it back to the house but lost it forever somewhere en route from the chapel, that it had been taken by the wind, impaled on a high twig, made sodden and illegible by the rain. The fantasy kept madness at bay for a few precious intermittent minutes, until she imagined Niall climbing the tree and plucking it off. "Look," he'd say to Maya. "This is what your mother has refused to tell you all these years. This is what she has kept from me."

Emmy contemplated taking the letter downstairs and setting fire to it, sending it in black flakes up the chimney, but she knew that to destroy it would be to make the same mistake Toby had. Tidying his papers in the walnut bureau only a few days ago, she had found out that a Plymouth hospital had started calling him for X rays for a whole year before he kept the appointment. Tumor or truth, denial just made things bigger.

The option of sleep was no longer available. She stared at the ceiling, waiting for the answers to fall in her face, for something to guide her through the moral maze. Did Cathal have a right to do this? Did he really have a right? What would a reasonable, intelligent stranger think? Who was in the wrong here? Should she ring him now and get it over with?

She sat up and ran her hands through her hair, grabbing a bunch in her fist and pulling it gently as she thought. She was dehydrated, nauseous, dizzy. She must have drunk at least another bottle of red once they had moved into the sitting room. Her mouth felt sticky and her head was beginning to grow the mother of all headaches.

Now's not the time to make any plans, she told herself. I'm in shock. I must let it sink in. I must do and say nothing. I'm in shock. I'm in shock. I'm in shock. But Niall's voice came to taunt her, pulling her up as he so often did, forcing her to be more truthful.

"That's not right, though, Em, is it?"

"It is."

"No, it's not."

"Why?"

"Well, for a start, we both know you must have been expecting this to happen for years. Don't tell me you haven't. Be rational. Be honest."

But she had never been rational in her life. Even when a train she hadn't set foot on had crashed. She and Maya had escaped death. Not broken bones, not whiplash, not posttraumatic stress disorder, but death. Life was a drama. It was the way she was.

She crossed to her bathroom and stuck her mouth under the tap, taking great gulps of water. No one else would drink straight from the tap. They all messed around with filters and kettles, so terrified were they by the novelty of a private supply. But Emmy had been weaned on it, and the way she felt now she would have been pleased to catch some vile bug and nearly die. No one would dare to challenge a dying woman. Except she couldn't die, could she? She had responsibilities.

The house was quiet and dark, full of sleeping people. Untroubled people with uncomplicated lives. Why was that never her natural state? She walked barefoot past the door to Niall and Kat's room, imagining their naked bodies wrapped round each other. How dare he carry on as if nothing was wrong? He had used her. Played with her like a cat with a half-dead mouse, tossed her around with his paw just because he knew he could.

No, that wasn't true, she mustn't do that to herself. Or him. Cathal can't take everything away.

The cold water splashed against the lining of her stomach. A stab of intense loneliness stung the back of her eyes and she had to close them, for a moment.

Across the corridor, she could hear Lila beginning to cry, and the soft movements of one of her parents shifting in the bed to comfort her. I wish I was a baby, she thought. I wish someone always came to me when I started crying.

It occurred to her that if she was still in London, she wouldn't think twice about phoning one of them now. Even at three in the morning. The equivalent of barging into their rooms with a handbell shouting,

"Talk to me!" What else did she think was reasonable from one angle but, from another, clearly wasn't?

With each stair, she saw herself in a different light. A trooper. A cow. Misunderstood. Frightened. Sorry for herself. Protective. Hopeless. Selfish. A liar. How did other people see her? How would the courts see her? What would Maya think? She so wanted to do the right thing, and yet how could she, when she had already done the wrong?

Cathal, Cathal, Cathal. Her mind was rusty when it came to thinking about their sexual history. From the moment of the pregnancy test, possibly even before that, she had blocked him out. It wasn't that the memory was bad particularly; it was simply irrelevant.

By the time Maya had been born, the conception was verging on the immaculate. So it was easy, on the occasions she had bumped into him since, to treat him as just Niall's brother, or like the friend of a friend. It was impossible to pencil the other details back in, because they had been rubbed out so long ago that there wasn't even the slightest pressure mark on the page. There was simply no trace.

Even Sita didn't know the circumstances. That's how big and distant a secret Maya's father was. She and Sita had been remote during that awful time. It was a mix of things—different universities, Jonathan, a parting of interests, a silly standoff which friendships sometimes go through. Sita seemed to have found it all so quickly, so easily. And it all coincided with the time that Niall had been lost to her, too.

Emmy had been all at sea on her solitary raft and she had slept with Cathal out of a basic need for companionship. In his compliance, he had unwittingly thrown her a lifeline, given her a seed. "Given" was the correct word. You don't lend these things, do you? And he wouldn't have cared about it so much if his sperm had perished in the condom as he intended it to. Maya was hers. Cathal clearly had no claim on her.

True, he was the only possible father, with a year's margin of error either side. But he didn't know that, did he? No one did. He'd have to go all the way to prove it.

In the quiet night-time coldness of the hall, she tried to hold on to the bigger picture, to imagine them all there with her, embracing the inevitable. Maya darling, I've got something to tell you. Niall, don't hate me, please. Cathal, bring her back at six. Then she tried to find a way of how she could continue to deny it, but neither scenario had any basis in reality. The only reality was what used to be.

"You're so good at feeling sorry for yourself," Niall sometimes told her, and she knew he was right. She was pitiful, pathetic, worse than bloody useless. But was it her fault?

Her family had always tried to make her believe that there was shame in admitting that Maya had not been conceived within the framework of a relationship, and so, as a compromise, she had chosen to remain silent about it. People believed what they wanted. They had done that for ten easy years. What they wanted to believe, of course, was that the child was Niall's. Nearly right. So nearly right that it hadn't mattered. Until now.

"Please don't, Cathal," she whispered. "Please."

She walked into the kitchen and saw a dent in the chair cushion where Maya had fallen asleep. She blinked away the image of Niall carrying her up to bed, her heart as ice-cold as the stone she was standing on.

A pile of clean T-shirts were ironing themselves on the Aga lid, insulating the handle and making it too hot to lift.

"Shit!" Emmy dropped the lid back onto the plate with a clang. "Shit, shit, shit!" She waited for someone to come racing down the stairs to find out what the noise was all about, but no one did. And why should they? If they were sleeping next to the person they cared most about, what was a crash downstairs to do with them?

She dragged a chair out and collapsed in it, her head on her arms, at the top of the table. She hated her capacity for self-indulgence. It almost made her sicker than the letter itself.

Roy Mundy's plumbing bill sat on a clean plate, her patterns and swatches underneath. Asha's place names were scattered around the empty glasses like clues in a ghostly treasure trail. *"Daddy,"* she had written on Jonathan's, surrounded by love hearts.

What was this father—daughter thing? It was hype peddled by armchair child psychologists, who would have a field day with her own case. She didn't feel anything much for her father, even though he had been her sole parent for most of her life.

She forced herself to think of the possibility of Anthony Hart's death, which as he was eighty-nine was inevitably hovering, but all she could see was the stoic, capable and grieving face of her eldest brother. Her father existed only in relation to her brothers. She couldn't remember even calling him Dad.

Then she thought of her mother, Iona, with her cigarette holder and the long zips down the back of her sleeveless dresses; and the tap at the back of her tired eyes finally turned itself on. She didn't know how long she cried, nor what exactly she was crying about, but it was one of those cries which, she could tell even without a mirror, would leave its telltale evidence across her face the next morning.

She splashed her swollen face with cold water from the kitchen tap, dried it on a new striped tea towel and tried to drink her camomile tea. The drink had soothed her through many a troubled night, but this cup tasted slimy and sickly. The bag felt as if she had dragged it up from the bottom of a forgotten pond.

As she tipped it down the sink, she felt as if the last ten years were going down the plughole with it. Life was no longer at all the same. Cathal's letter had killed all things familiar.

Without the mug to concentrate on, she began to feel dizzy and feverish, as if she might suddenly throw up or faint. She held onto the back of each chair until she reached the old oak settle, where she began to dig around in the gritty contents of her sheepskin backpack for the little brown bottle. Her comforter, her fix, her prop. The longer it took to find it, the more fevered she felt.

Then her fingers grasped the cold glass with its soft rubber pipette and some of her anxiety subsided. Not bothering with the usual dosage, she unscrewed the whole lid and tipped a slug of Bach's Rescue Remedy straight into her mouth. The herbal curative washed around her gums and she held it there for a few seconds, its alcohol base numbing her thoughts. People always assumed she carried it for Maya. *To Comfort And Reassure*, it said on the label. But Maya knew how to do those things for herself. Emmy had never known. Maybe it was time to learn.

She drew measured air through her nose, exhaling through her mouth. Once, twice, three times. She would be okay. She would try and sleep.

"Maya, darling?" she whispered a minute later, bending over her daughter's bed. "Come with me, come and snuggle."

Maya half opened her eyes and moved obediently into a sleeping standing position. She knew the score. Emmy put her arm round the child's narrow, warm shoulders and let her lean against her until they reached the double bed.

"There you are," she said. "In you get. You're okay now," and, already feeling marginally more able to cope, she walked round the other side to crawl in beside her.

MAYA RECOGNIZED THE SIGNS AS SOON AS SHE OPENED HER EYES AND saw her mother lying next to her in the fetal position. Emmy's hair was tangled, which meant she hadn't gone through her usual routine before bed. On good nights, Mum went to bed with her hair tied in a little bun, and when she undid it in the morning it fell, like a glossy curtain, into a long straight bob. On those days, her skin had a glow to it, too, as if she'd just been for a walk. That was the night cream, apparently. Not today, though. Maya could see a triangle of cheek through the hair which looked pale and blotchy, black flakes of yesterday's mascara settled in the bluey creases under her eyes and she smelled of smoke. If

Maya needed farther confirmation, there was a packet of Nytol pills next to the bed.

It was an eggshell day, no doubt about it. Emmy called them that, although never at the time, only when it was over, when she had entered the apologizing stage. At the time, you didn't call them anything, but afterward, when it was all safely in the past, she would say, "That was a bit of an eggshell day, wasn't it? I'm sorry, my beautiful girl, I'm such a pain. I must be awful to live with." And Maya always said, "No you're not, you're lovely." And that was true. Her mum *was* lovely. She got a lot of stuff wrong, but she got loads and loads of things right, too, things that other people never noticed, like smiles across a table at just the right time, and private chats about confusing things that never became embarrassing. She was really good at those.

There was a technique, a recognized procedure, which Maya went through on eggshell days. It was best to give her mother at least an extra hour in bed, although it wasn't a good idea to creep away without saying anything. That made Emmy wake in a panic, which made things worse. She would feel remiss and she wasn't good with guilt. What Maya had learned to do was to whisper her intention to get up, and then come back an hour later with a cup of tea. She was a good tea maker, her mum said.

The same rules didn't apply when they slept in their own beds. Those days were easy peasy, and, since easy-peasy days happened almost all the time, eggshell days weren't such a big deal. This was the first one Emmy had had at Bodinnick and Maya was still trying to hold on to the idea that it could be a straight hangover.

"I'm getting up now," Maya whispered. "You stay there." But instead of her mother doing that familiar grateful half-smile and rolling back into sleep, she opened her eyes and spoke. She even put her arm out and tried to pull Maya back down.

"Don't go. Stay here for a little bit longer."

"But I'm not tired anymore."

"I'll get up too, then."

"No, I don't need you to. I'll bring you a cup of tea in a minute."

"We'll do something together today, just the two of us. I promise."

Which one was the mother here? The one with the eyelids that looked as if they'd been stung by twin bees, or the one who made sure the daylight wasn't glinting through the curtains?

Maya pulled on her jeans, which still had yesterday's pants inside, and a fleece and T-shirt, also still in one piece. Her trainers went on without socks. It wasn't a straight hangover, she knew that now. Straight hangovers could be identified by the grumpy groaning that passed for conversation.

"I don't want you going outside before I come down," Emmy said sharply. Her voice was wide awake even if her face wasn't.

"I won't," Maya replied, not bothering to ask why. On eggshell days, rules just popped up out of nowhere.

She ran down the stairs as if her life depended on it. A warm teapot was already on the table and she poured some into a nearby mug as fast as she could. There was only full-cream milk, and Emmy didn't like that but she'd have to put up with it today. She'd find her mum one of those cloth eye masks, and the Body Shop elderflower eye gel with the sunglasses for later. Maya was confident such "essentials" would have come with them. Walking shoes and waterproof coats might not have, but eye masks—they were a definite.

1 2

JONATHAN WAS WONDERING IF HIS EYES COULD POSSIBLY LOOK WORSE than Emmy's, and whether he stood any chance of looking better by the time Sita came home. At least the burning had stopped, although, when he checked in the mold-specked mirror on the chapel wall, they were still bloodshot and puffy. Was it too early in the year to hide behind the excuse of hay fever?

For a split second with the first splash of lime, the pain had been so intense that he thought about seeking urgent medical help, but thanks to the water straight from the outside tap it was now just a sting, as if he had been swimming in strong chlorine.

"It's your fault," he told Lila, who was giggling in her bucket seat. "Now, are you going to let me have them back?"

He felt happy, despite his eyes. Or happier, anyway. Asha and Jay were just outside the chapel door, which was propped open with a skateboard, practicing their trigger action with two large garden sprays, preparing to help him damp down the walls. They were still in their school uniforms and he knew he'd get shot for that, too, but he didn't care. It was refreshing to be in charge of all three of his children, and only his three children, for once, especially over at the chapel. He had offered to take Maya, too, but Emmy had said no, she wanted her in the house where she could keep an eye on her.

"What have I done wrong?" Maya asked. Interesting that Maya should see time with her mother as a form of punishment, Jonathan thought unfairly.

He was using Emmy's peculiar behavior since the party to dilute his own badness, although he was hardly having to exaggerate it. She had gone, for a reason she was not prepared to discuss, into complete retreat. Admittedly, withdrawal wasn't an unknown reaction for Emmy, but this time there seemed to have been no trigger, unless she was taking Kat's return harder than any sane woman should. But was Emmy sane? It had always been a moot point.

Every friendly effort to help—and they had all tried more than once yesterday—had been rebuffed with a "Just leave me alone, okay?" Already, the men of the household had reached the stage where they were taking her at her word. Maybe Sita would be able to have another crack at it once she got back.

Anyway, it did lessen the strength of his own deviance. He wanted to believe his interest in Tamsin was just curiosity brought on by lack of sex, that it wasn't affecting anybody or hurting anybody, not in the way that Emmy was. He wanted to believe he was finally just doing what most men did. Joining the club, sort of thing.

He put three more dollops of lime putty from the bag into the bucket and added the water.

"You told Mummy you would wear goggles," Asha said, coming in.

"If you can get them off Lila, I will." He added more water.

"You might get splashed again."

"I'll try not to."

"Are they still hurting?"

"No, I'm fine, darling. Stop worrying."

"I'm not. Is it true it can blind you?"

"Not this stuff. Now, would you say that was a thin cream? Bit too thick? What do you think?"

"A bit thick, I think."

"Best not to tell Mummy about the little accident."

"Why? Will she tell you off?"

Lila squealed and threw one of her paintbrushes on the floor. Jay came in, too.

"Leave the skateboard there, Jay. We need the air to circulate."

"I thought you didn't want it to dry out too quickly."

"Oh, good thinking."

Jay smiled proudly and Jonathan held his hand out like a surgeon in theater.

"Sieve."

Jay handed him a sieve.

"Bucket."

Jay handed him a bucket.

He began to work the lime and the water through.

"What can I do?" Asha asked.

"Grab me the goggles while Lila's not looking."

Asha handed him the goggles.

"This is good teamwork, kids," he said. "Thank you."

He'd purloined the flimsy white plastic goggles with foam-backed edges from Jay's chemistry set. They were too small for him and made him look like a cartoon ant.

When he put them on, Asha burst out laughing, but as soon as his five-month-old daughter saw him her bottom lip curled down, her face began to crumple, her eyes filled with tears.

"Oh no, come on," Jonathan said, lifting the goggles. "We've been through all this before. It's me, look."

Lila's crying stopped like clockwork.

"That's better," and he moved back to the bucket. "Now, we've got to work fairly quickly here. Dilute the mixture until it is the consistency of milk," he read from the photocopied instructions. "Does that look like milk?"

He put the goggles back on. Lila started crying again. "Oh, God. Lila, look! On, off, on, off." He put the whisk down, picked her up and made the fatal mistake of giving her what she wanted. Lila held the goggles by the elastic, bouncing them up and down and waving them in the air. Her bottom lip uncurled itself, her face uncrumpled and her tears evaporated.

"Goggles," Asha told her. "Say goggles."

Lila whacked her father in the face with them and Asha laughed again.

"Now give them back to Daddy."

Lila held tight, flailing them around his head as his old schoolteacher used to do with the blackboard rubber to unruly pupils. Not him, obviously. He was always the quiet one at the front.

"Goggles to Daddy," Jonathan said, trying to pry open her tight little fist.

The lip curled back down. The tears welled up.

"Okay, goggles to Lila," he said, admitting defeat. Women of all ages had him wrapped right round their little fingers. "You sit there and look after them," he told her, clipping her back into her seat, "and Daddy will be very very careful when he stirs."

He was planning, when Sita had a go at him, to get Asha to tell her the Lila story but he still knew he was in trouble. Jay had read a leaflet out loud at breakfast about the heat generated by a dustbin full of slaking lime being sufficient to set scaffold boards on fire, and Sita had made Jonathan promise he would be careful. "It's nothing to do with slaking lime," he told her. "This is lime putty. It's perfectly safe." Thank God he'd only burned his own eyes.

"Okay, kids, I'm ready when you are. You need to work fast. The thing is, if the wall is dry it'll suck out all the water from the limewash, and that's no good. It's your job to keep the surface damp, and it's my job to paint the wash on after you. Are you ready? Spray as fast as you can. Try not to miss any bits."

"We're ready."

"Go."

It was perfect synergy, and he wished Sita could see them.

So did Sita. Walking out of the house that morning had felt wrong and she hadn't been able to put her mind to work at all. Saturday night's party was supposed to have been a celebration, but it had ended feeling more like a wake. The usual spark in Emmy had died mid-evening, and her own embryonic rekindled interest in sex had died with it. Sunday had been a write-off. Monday, so far, was no better.

Patients had come and gone with their minor time-wasting ailments and carefully worded excuses for having a look at the new fill-in doctor, and she had played along, pretending not to know what they were up to, writing unnecessary prescriptions, making bland diagnoses, trying her best to win confidences and bury prejudice. But it had all left her unusually cold. She was tiring of a new surgery every other week. It was making her feel as if she didn't belong anywhere, not at Bodinnick, not at work, not even at Jonathan's side if she was honest.

Her mind kept going back to when Asha, as a toddler, went through a phase of refusing to join in anything. It didn't matter if it was a playgroup picnic, or pass the parcel, or face painting, or paddling in the sea, the child would stand on the edges, watching with wet eyes and a quivering lip, presumably wishing she hadn't kicked up such a fuss in the first place because that made it even harder to find a way back in.

Was that what she had been doing since she'd arrived in Cornwall? She'd made such a big thing of her desire for work, how could she now say otherwise?

Everyone was being sensitive enough to recognize the imbalance of her life and doing their best to accommodate it, but it wasn't easy piling on the makeup and blow-drying her hair after a night of so little sleep, while the rest of the house mooched around in baggy trousers.

Last night was a perfect example. She had heard Emmy bashing around in the early hours because she, too, had been awake, but she had been up since six and she knew damn well Emmy wouldn't surface until she felt like it. Then no doubt this evening, when she was so tired that she'd have to make her inevitable move for sleep at ten thirty, someone would call her a party-pooper. It happened so often it was almost a routine.

If anyone ought to be staying at home, it was her. Lila was still tiny. Anyway, work was supposed to be the part-time theme in this downshift, not family. But even though the others made the right noises, none of them knew what it felt like to come in after a hard day's slog and not know where to place yourself. By the time she got a look in, so much had happened at Bodinnick during the day that nobody knew where to start to fill her in.

Maybe today would be easier. She was on her way home again, even though it was only three thirty. The surgery had been very understanding, and it wasn't a total lie. She *was* feeling ill, it was just nothing to do with dodgy prawns.

As she drove up the drive eating a pasty out of a bag, she could see that Emmy's Golf was missing and she felt suddenly cross on behalf of Jonathan, who would be lumbered with all four children again. Her instincts told her she would find them over at the chapel and, without bothering to swap her good shoes for old, she took off across the wet grass. Shrieks of laughter reached her ears before she went through the arched gate, and the closer she got to the sound of fun the farther away she felt.

When she got to the gate and realized that Jonathan had only their own three, all to himself, she felt a sharp pang of jealousy. She looked at

Asha's unknowing face, Jay's slightly cumbersome lope and Lila's owl gaze and they seemed more consummately beautiful than ever—and yet, at the same time, the sight made her want to turn on her smart leather heels and run.

They hadn't noticed her. They weren't looking for her. As far as they were concerned, she was at work, and until she materialized in the evening she didn't exist for them. Never had she seen that truth more clearly.

Jonathan appeared from inside the chapel, pumping a garden sprayer and shouting something silly. He ran after a radiant Asha, and his hefty booted foot clipped the upright handle of Lila's car seat, missing the baby's head by an inch.

Sita's impulse to run out of the shadows was stopped in its tracks by Jay, getting his little sister out of the seat, picking her up, showing her the water hanging from the nozzle on the end of the sprayer, getting her little index finger and dabbing it on the drip. When Lila reached out for Jonathan, resentment blistered all over Sita's inner skin.

"What on earth is the matter?" she said, bursting onto the scene. She'd meant to say hello first, but somehow that hadn't happened.

"Nothing," Jonathan said. "Just having some fun."

"Daddy! Daddy, get me," Asha squealed, forgetting that her mother wasn't supposed to be here.

Jonathan lurched at her with a pretend growl. Lila squealed with delight.

"What are you doing back?" he asked with his back half turned to her. He was only half interested, too.

"Um, I've taken the rest of the day off." Then she meant to say that she missed them all, and could they give her five minutes to go and change and she could join in too, but those words didn't come, either. Instead, her rancor homed in on his red-rimmed eyes.

"What happened to you?"

"Just a little localized difficulty with the goggles, wasn't there, Asha?"

"Don't be cross with him, be cross with Lila. Get me, Daddy, get me!"

But the anger that came spitting out of Sita's mouth left no one in any doubt about who was cross with whom and suddenly, when she had said everything she thought she never would, she found herself playing her trump card.

"Right, that's it. I want that house meeting. This has all gone far enough."

"BLAME IT ON ME," NIALL SAID AS HE OPENED THE SWING DOOR TO THE communal changing rooms at the swimming pool and let Maya walk under his arm. He was pleased she still fitted. "You know what she's like sometimes."

Maya nodded, but she was getting a little sick of her mother's eggshell days. She knew they could sometimes spill into eggshell weekends, but this one seemed to be mustering enough strength to go on for weeks. Today, Emmy had even made Maya miss school. "Why?" Maya had asked. "Because you're looking pale. I think you're overtired," Emmy said. Keeping her out of school was a classic. It was so annoying.

In the back of her mind when they were packing their things to move, Maya had hoped that these days of Emmy's would belong to the past. She had thought for one silly moment that they were leaving all that miserable stuff behind, only taking the good bits with them. It wasn't very nice, finding out you were wrong.

"But if anyone else was in a bad mood for this long for no reason, Mum would be furious," she told Niall reasonably. "She's got double standards, hasn't she?"

"Thing is, Maya, what's sauce for the goose is not necessarily sauce for the gander with grown-ups."

He wanted to sweep her up and run away with her, and bring her back when it was all over, except that he felt it was all his fault. Removing himself from it now would make things worse.

"I'll see you in the pool," she said. "I'm going to teach you a surface dive."

"What's that?"

"It's what otters do. You just swim along, and then make a shape like this with your hands, and then you go underwater. It's really cool. People think you've disappeared. Mum really panicked the first time I did it because I stayed under there for such a long time. I can touch the bottom of the deep end when I do it."

"Otters don't have hands."

"No, but you have."

He put them either side of her peachy cheeks. "See you in there."

She scooted off across the wet tiled floor. What she wanted now was for someone to wave a wand and make it all all right again, whatever "it" was. When she said "someone" she meant Niall, because in her experience Niall was the only one who ever had the wand. That was why she'd asked him to take her swimming on her own. "I'd just like to have some time with the two of us," she'd told him. "God, you women, you're all the same," he'd joked, but he'd gone through hoops to make it happen, borrowing Emmy's car, making all sorts of promises to Kat about how he would make it up to her.

But now, Maya thought as she chose her cubicle, perhaps he doesn't have the wand anymore. Or perhaps he only waved it over Kat.

Niall was thinking something not entirely removed from that himself. He should have been more careful where he did and didn't wave his wand, or certainly where he did and didn't scatter his promises. He should have learned by now that when Emmy said everything was fine, what she meant was everything was fine at that precise moment. It didn't mean everything would be fine five minutes on. And he shouldn't have promised her she had him, because she hadn't.

The changing rooms were packed with noisy, wet school-children shouting and throwing socks at each other over the locked doors, but he walked obliviously through them. He'd been reckless. As Cathal would say, he'd let his dick rule his head and his sexual greed was now hurting the one person he hoped he would never, ever hurt. What he found even more painful was that Maya was only a short distance away from realizing it.

He could see that she didn't yet have enough understanding to put two and two together as he had. She hadn't yet done the Emmy plus Niall divided by Kat doesn't equal happiness sum, but he knew she would, soon. When she did, she'd realize it was his fault, and she would love him that little bit less. He didn't know if he could bear that.

What he also didn't know was that he hadn't added up correctly, either. He had the wrong equation. He wasn't even in it.

Emmy's mood since Kat's arrival had been atrocious. She could barely bring herself to talk to anyone except Maya, who she could hardly let out of her sight. It had been hard work even negotiating the trip to the pool. Why were they going on their own? she wanted to know. Were they meeting anyone? What time were they going to be back?

He kicked himself again for messing things up. It wasn't simply that he and Emmy shouldn't have made love, it was that they should have put themselves more securely back in their box afterward. But he had believed her when she'd said she was okay with it, that she would be fine if and when Kat came back, that it was just who they were, and she would deal with it in the same way she always dealt with it, by putting it in the box and keeping it safe until they next felt like taking it out.

But the box didn't exist anymore. They'd opened and shut it so frequently over the years that they hadn't noticed its hinges were shot, its lid was hanging off, and there was a bloody great hole in the bottom.

What he was thinking long and hard about now was that maybe Kat was the one who ought to be boxed up. But if he put Kat in a box there would be no need to open it again. The lid wouldn't keep flying open as it did with Emmy. He would shut it and more than likely lose the key. She wasn't the sort of love that wouldn't go away, she was more the sort that would sink without a trace.

He tried to loosen his swimming shorts but they were almost as old as Maya and the cord was already as loose as it got. His hairy tummy hung a little flabbily over the waistband as he padded into the pool area, and on his way he picked a bobble of Air Force blue fluff from his navel. He hated swimming. He was only doing it because Maya wanted to. He would go to the ends of the earth—or even into the deep end of the public baths—for her.

Maya's cubicle was caked with talcum powder and someone had written *Lauren loves James* in it on the bench. As she got undressed with a child's disregard for where she dropped her clothes, she wondered who Lauren was, and whether James loved Lauren too. She wanted to know what they looked like, how old they were, whether she would like Lauren best, or James.

She wanted to know if Lauren's enemy had written it, or Lauren's friend, or even Lauren herself. Or had it been James? Then she found herself thinking that James probably didn't love Lauren, and that the likelihood was he loved someone else who didn't love him. It seemed to be the way love worked, and not just at school. She hated that bit about Year Six. The I love him, no I don't, I've dumped her, she loves him now stuff. And yet she could see now how that got worse and worse the older you got. At least it was simple when you were in Year Six. At least no one cared.

She didn't want to put her clothes on the bench and rub the message out, just in case James or Lauren came back for a look, so she left them on the damp powdery floor. Her jeans, her fleece and her T-shirt were all filthy, anyway. Her mum wasn't doing any washing at the moment. In fact, she wasn't doing anything at the moment. She was locking herself away in her stupid sewing room, pretending to work, when everyone knew that all she was really doing in there was crying and smoking and getting herself into a state. Well, she was going to have to snap out of it soon.

She took her towel out of her bag and shook it to find her costume. Her goggles went flying and she had to retrieve them by kneeling on the floor and putting her hand into the next cubicle. She saw two feet jump, and then she heard a squeal.

"Is that you, Jade?"

"No," Maya said. "I just need my goggles."

"Who is it, then?"

"You don't know me."

"Yes I do. I know everyone."

"Well, you don't know me because I don't go to your school."

"Which school do you go to, then? St. Mary's?"

"I don't go to school," Maya lied. "I'm an orphan."

The girl didn't reply, but the goggles came skimming back.

As she walked past all the children again, lining up against the wall in their matching red school sweatshirts and hair soaking into their backs, she could tell what they were thinking. What was she doing there? Why wasn't she at school? Where did she get those body transfers from? She smiled at them all, hoping the rumor would spread that she really was an orphan.

The pool was empty. Too late now for a new batch of school lessons, too early for private ones. She'd beaten Niall and she'd thought about getting in but decided to sit on one of the hinged blue seats and wait.

The water was almost glass-still and she wanted to break its surface with a dive. Except you weren't allowed to dive. When she was a grown-up, she was going to take a leaf out of her mother's book and do exactly as she wanted. Emmy never did anything she didn't want to do. She didn't even get up if she didn't want to.

"Hi, darlin'," Niall said. He thought she looked a little lost sitting there. "Have you been waiting long?"

"Ages," she said, jumping to her feet and making a run for the pool. Niall ran too.

Dads, thought the lifeguard, blasting on his whistle from his high chair. Why don't they care what they look like?

When the phone rang that night and Emmy jumped to her feet, Maya did, too, pushing her chair back and sending it scraping across the slate floor.

"Leave it!" her mother shouted. She could have done with a lifeguard's whistle, too.

The sound of the phone surprised Emmy, even though she had been waiting for it to go all day. It was eleven days since Cathal had posted the letter.

"Hello?" Maya shouted happily into the Bakelite receiver. On noneggshell days, she and her mum would race to be the first to answer and she was claiming a victory on this one. "Hold on." She ran to the bottom of the stairs and Emmy waited.

"Niall? Niall, phone. Phone, Niall."

Emmy's next sip of blackcurrant tea tasted of morning sickness, metal and aspartame. She got up from the table like a robot and programmed herself to retrieve her daughter. Maya was walking back to the phone, her thick socks sliding on the shiny floor. Her hand went to pick up the handset again.

"Maya," Emmy shouted, freezing the frame in her head, "go back and finish your supper."

But her daughter had already started talking happily into the mouthpiece. "He's just coming. I think he's in the shower. We went swimming and his hair has gone all funny."

Emmy waited again. The voice on the other end was going to carry the conversation on. Of course he was. She could have written the script. And why shouldn't he? Cathal was an opportunist—he responded to combinations of circumstance. She of all people should know that. She swayed a little and felt warm blood whooshing round her brain.

"Yes," Maya said. Then a pause. "Nearly eleven."

Emmy's legs buckled. "Give it to me," she demanded, so loudly that Cathal would certainly hear.

"What?" Maya asked. "Why?"

"Because I said so." Emmy had her hand out. "Go and sit down."

Maya made a face and then remembered. Eggshell day. She pushed her feet across the floor in a skating movement once more and made another face at Asha. Asha made one back.

"Can I help?" Emmy said into the receiver, her voice shaking. Every last ounce of energy she possessed had fallen away.

"Is that Emmy?" It was the soft Dublin lilt of Mrs. O'Connor. "I was just having a word with your daughter. Where does the time go? How are you, my love? Is my son behaving himself?"

"Oh, Mary, I thought . . ."

"Are you all right, dear?"

"Yes, yes, I think—oh, he's just here. Thank you Mary, it's good to . . ."

"Have I called at a bad time?"

"No, no. Here he is."

She handed the phone to Niall, wet from another shower. Oh, someone help me, she pleaded silently. Sons, daughters, fathers, grandmothers, uncles, mothers-in-law. It was all too complicated.

His chat sounded normal, as if there was no family drama on the horizon, and that settled her. But the next thing she knew he was back in the kitchen, apparently talking to her in Swahili. "He says he wants to hear it from you, Emmy. God knows why. I've told him you're not the keeper of the key."

"Who does?" Everyone was looking at her. "What?" She hadn't heard a word anyone had said for at least the last five minutes. Mouths had been opening and closing around her and people had been coming in and out of the kitchen talking excitedly, but she hadn't engaged with any of it.

"Cathal."

"Sorry?"

"Cathal. Who did you think I meant?"

The blood drained from her face. She wondered if she was dreaming.

"He says he won't come unless you say he can."

"What?"

"Emmy?"

There was a barely visible shake of her head.

"But it's your mum on the phone, not your brother," she said. She could feel a stupid grin form on her lips. Was this all some kind of joke?

"Emmy? Are you okay?" Sita asked.

"Yes. I just don't understand what Niall means about Cathal. What does he want?"

"He wants to come and stay. He's doing a job on a house in Ireland of the same proportions and he wants to come and see Bodinnick."

"Like hell!"

"What?"

"I said, 'Like hell!' No."

"Emmy?"

"He's on the phone. Go and have a word," said Sita calmly. She was beginning to wonder if Emmy was clinically depressed again. There was an imbalance about her she hadn't seen for a long time.

"I mean . . . but it's his mum. I spoke to her myself." Emmy spoke more slowly now.

"Yes, but Cathal's there, too. Are you sure you're okay?"

"He's offered to help replace the sitting room windows," Niall said, "and have a look at the store. Go on, Emmy, it's our bill."

"No, it isn't." She found herself shouting again. "Mary rang here. Maya answered it. I'm not going mad. Stop making me feel as if I am."

Niall couldn't be bothered to tell her that Cathal had walked into his mother's house mid-call and that when his mother had handed him the phone it had gone mysteriously dead, or that when Niall had rung back Cathal had sounded more depressed than he had ever heard him sound before. It wasn't worth it. She was clearly in no mood to listen.

"I'll tell him yes, then, shall I?"

"Tell him what you like. As you said, I'm not the keeper of the bloody key." And she slammed out into the windy garden in her shirt-sleeves.

"My fault," Niall winked at Maya. "For sure." And yet he wasn't so sure.

13

CATHAL OPENED HIS SUIT JACKET AND TOOK A SHEET OF PAPER FROM THE inside pocket. His hands trembled a little and, what with that and his bloodshot eyes, an observer might think he was an alcoholic in serious need of a mid-morning drink. In fact it was dog tiredness. In the last few weeks, his body had forgotten how to relax and instead it was in a permanent state of vigilance. Emmy might get back to him at any time. Even with his limited knowledge of her, he knew she was just as likely to call at three in the morning as she was in the middle of the working day.

The paper was a copy of the letter he had sent her more than a week ago, the one that he had agonized over for so long, the one that had taken every ounce of steel to put into the postbox. It was also a letter that was having apparently no effect whatsoever.

"Peter, could I borrow you for a minute?"

One of his partners walked over to his desk. He was worried about the way Cathal had been looking lately. "Yes?"

"What do you think this means?"

Peter took the letter and read it in thirty seconds. "What are you asking me for? You wrote the thing, didn't you?"

"Yes, yes, but what would you think if you got it?"

"Well, that all depends on what's gone before."

"But if you had been sent it, would you get back to me as a matter of some urgency?"

"That all depends, too," his colleague told him carefully. "Hey, listen, are you okay?"

"Yes." Cathal folded the letter again. "I'm fine. Just trying to second-guess a woman. Thanks."

"Don't mention it. But you know what, don't you?"

"What?"

"It is a complete waste of time trying to second-guess any woman, but particularly one who affects you the way this one obviously does."

"No, no, she's not, er, of course, yeah, right."

As Peter turned away, Cathal read the letter one more time, just to be sure there really was no way anyone in their right mind could misread the gentle insistence. It was a question of whether or not Emmy was in her right mind, and from what he knew of her that was anyone's guess.

He had been sitting in his office all morning, his mobile phone right next to him. It hadn't rung, or bleeped, or lost its signal, but he kept picking it up and looking for the little envelope that would tell him he had a message. Then he would dial his home number, wait for his answer-machine message to kick in and press the hash key and his PIN number for access. Even before the computer-generated female voice began to speak, he knew what it was going to say: "You have no new messages." It was becoming the sort of obsessive repetitive behavior he saw more usually in the office juniors and he knew it was time to stop, to do something.

A new secretary was standing in profile at the photocopier. Cathal had taken her on last month, on the strength of her breasts, mainly. Today she was wearing a tight gray skirt and an even tighter pink sweater, but where he might once have found the stretch of wool across such ample flesh a major distraction, now it was barely a momentary observation. As a girlfriend had told him at the weekend, when he'd declined a previously popular offer of hers, the light in his boxer shorts had gone out.

He'd taken the girl at the photocopier out to lunch twice in her first week and she was waiting for him to ask again. So was everybody else. Peter, back at his desk and on the phone, was wondering why Cathal wasn't absentmindedly sizing up her legs as he usually did. She was showing enough of them.

Their firm of architects had lost office junior after office junior because of Cathal and his easy appreciation of women. Not because they didn't enjoy his attentions, but because for some inexplicable reason they took him up on them, and then when it was all over they got upset and resigned. It always surprised Cathal when they left. He always thought he'd done everything possible to make them feel at home.

He stared out of the window at the optician's across the street. *We can help you see the world more clearly*, the poster on the door claimed. There was only one person who could do that. And no, it wasn't God, he felt like shouting at the priest crossing the road.

The secretary finished at the photocopier and he got up to use it. As she brushed past him with a bristle of anger, he lifted the lid, placed the letter face down, and pressed the Copy button. A bright blue light lasered through his thoughts. Maybe he should just turn up in Cornwall, as Niall had suggested in all innocence. His brother had no bloody idea, did he? No bloody idea at all.

The machine churned on and he realized he had forgotten to alter the number of copies required. Five letters identical to the one he had shown Peter lay in the tray and a mad whim overtook him.

"Er, Bridget, could you make sure these get today's post?"

"Sure, but it's Belinda," she snapped back. "Look, if you've got something to say, I'd rather you just got on and said it."

"Sorry?"

Then she noticed that all five envelopes were addressed to the same woman and that her new boss was looking sick. Maybe it wasn't anything to do with her after all.

"Oh nothing," she said. "I'll just go for the post."

THE HOUSE MEETING, WHEN IT CAME, WAS A GRIMMER AFFAIR THAN SITA had intended. Its only saving grace was that it wasn't held in the kitchen, where there were all those candlelit memories and freshly painted hopes to think about. She chose the unknown territory of the dining room instead, and the rest of them sat there like strangers in a waiting room, fidgeting and picking their nails until she plucked up the courage to start.

"Okay, um . . ."

The north-facing room was a soulless place at the best of times, with its empty silver candlesticks lined up on the sideboards, its closed shutters and the almost pointlessly high lighting overhead. The paintings of hunting scenes and dead men didn't help, and nor did a glass corner cabinet which housed crockery untouched for a decade.

"Right, er . . ."

If she was honest, her initial anger or jealousy had quite quickly faded to mere dissatisfaction, but she had voiced her intention by then, and, as her father had drummed into her, you should always finish what you start.

She wasn't used to admitting defeat and, anyway, Jonathan had made it even more difficult by using that particular gene against her. It was as if he had been able to read her hesitation, and was punishing her by refusing to allow it breathing space.

Her demands had been met with predictable reactions, although none of the surprise or resentment had come from Emmy, who had retreated so far into her own little unreachable world that Sita thought you could have set Bodinnick on fire and Emmy would not flinch.

"Shall we . . . ?"

The five of them sat round the long table with the door shut. The girls were upstairs, asleep, but Jay loitered outside, alternately furious and curious.

"Well, we haven't come in here for a five-course gourmet meal with cabaret, have we?" Niall said, allowing a rare edge of savagery in his voice.

For once, there was no alcohol in their glasses, just filtered water as there would have been in any respectable boardroom. Everyone shuffled the papers in front of them, useless, meaningless words about private mortgages and visions for the future. Maya's gel-pen title pages looked up at them all like a Christmas card from someone who had just died.

Emmy hadn't brushed her hair all day. She sat, red-eyed and expressionless, between Jonathan and Niall, her nails bitten to the quick, her thin sweater hanging limply off her hunched shoulders. Kat was opposite, all clean tousles and clear skin, carefully self-styled to accentuate the difference. Sita sat next to her, another deliberate move. It looked to the others like a random choice of seating, but it was a careful ploy to dispel any idea of Them and Us, although the mere thought at that stage of any Us at all was laughable.

"Shall I start?" she asked.

The others nodded. Her neck tensed, as it had done in the surgery that day with the woman who had lost the desire for her husband.

"Okay. Well, I don't want to be in here anymore than any of you do, but it's got to be said. Basically, we've lost our way, haven't we?"

Her words were met with calculated silence.

"Oh, come off it. Surely it's not just me, is it?"

She stopped. Emmy was staring at the table top. Jonathan was looking straight at her, coldly. Niall leaned back in his chair, toying with a cigarette he had no desire, for once, to smoke.

Kat, on the other hand, looked rather pleased. If Sita had been able to see just how pleased, she might have said there and then, "Oh, this is stupid. Let's just try and make a bigger effort, shall we?" but she couldn't, so she carried on.

"Okay, I'll be even more frank. I get up tired and I come home tired, and the way it has increasingly seemed to me, I might as well be doing that in London, where I can at least earn decent money for it."

There was another silence. Someone scraped a chair.

"So, before it stops being a dream and becomes a nightmare, I think we should wake up. That's all."

There was the tiniest hint of insecurity in her voice which only Jonathan heard, and an instinctive loyalty kicked in. When he spoke, his voice was nervous and guarded.

"I promise you I'm saying this to Sita for the first time, okay? We haven't discussed any of this privately at all. But I think she is right. We do need to sort something. Quite what, I don't know, but now is our opportunity to discuss that. Maybe we should look at the point at which we started going wrong."

Niall raised his eyebrows and turned down the corners of his mouth.

"Or is it just that we're all having a few personal problems and, because we're now living in each other's pockets, those problems have become communal ones?" he asked.

Kat scowled at him. Emmy still refused to look up.

"But that is the nature of the beast," Sita said. "Unless we're a team, it doesn't work."

The word "team" stood out as much as "us." It made Jonathan speak again.

"Okay, let's work with that. Who feels as if this is a shared experience? Emmy?"

"I have no idea," she said. "I'm not the right person to ask."

"That is precisely the sort of unhelpful comment I mean," Sita snapped back. "If you of all people can come out with something like that, we might as well all pack up and go."

"Fine," Emmy said. "Why don't we? Don't mind me."

"Do you really mean that?" Jonathan asked.

Emmy shrugged. Niall lit his cigarette and sucked his teeth.

"What about you, Niall? Do you feel the shared experience?"

"Well, I don't think it's vanished without trace, has it? I mean, I know some of us have been—what shall I say—distracted lately, but if this sort of behavior was going on in London it would be dealt with in a few late-night phone calls between the girls, wouldn't it? We're in Cornwall, not feckin' Utopia, for God's sake."

"Some of you might have said it was one and the same thing a few weeks ago, sweetie," Kat said, pleased that she had waited for her debut.

She didn't realize it, but her comment did more to muster togetherness than anything that had gone before. Unfortunately, it wasn't enough.

"Okay, look, this is so painful I want to get it over with," Sita said. "I'm going to come out with it. I think the most sensible thing we can do—without any finality—is to get someone in to value the house, give us an idea of its marketability, and then we'll know what we're looking at."

"No," Emmy said. "That's even more pathetic than anything I have said so far."

"I don't think so," Sita replied.

"Yes it is. Either it's final or it's not." Emmy spun her papers across the table and leaned back in her chair defiantly, but her vigor died almost instantly and she followed up by flinging her head into her hands and keeping it there.

"Emmy, calm down," Niall told her. "Face it. It's not such a bad idea, if it lends some focus." But he could tell, even as he said it, that she couldn't see the wood for the trees.

"Vote," said Jonathan. "Come on. Let's get it out the way. I don't want to be in here much longer."

"No problem. Value it," Kat purred. Her voice added diddly squat. She paid her way at weekends but nothing more. She was really just Niall's guest.

"Me too," said Sita, which clinched it.

There was the merest nod of acceptance from the two men before the door was flung open, bashing the side of the cabinet and making the candlesticks wobble. Even Emmy took her hands away from her face. It was Jay, with an armful of stuff. His face was as brooding as the thunder clouds that had started to gather off the south coast.

"Here," he said, his unbroken voice offering the barest hint of maturity. "Have these."

He flung his booty onto the table. His prized Game Boy spun in a perfect trajectory toward his father, coming to a stop just before it fell off the edge. The new school backpack stayed where it was, a heavy lump of completed homework and friends' phone numbers. The banner from the party, which he had so carefully sewn with his best blanket stitch, unfolded and hung over the side. He had torn the photographs off in anger and they fell from their bundle onto the floor.

"Jay!" Sita said sharply. "What are you doing in here? I told you to stay out."

"Well, tough," he shouted. "I'm sick of being told what to do. Sick of you. I don't want to go, I want to stay. But you don't care about that, do you?" There were tears in his soft brown eyes.

Jonathan was on his feet.

"No!" Jay shouted. "I don't want your bloody stupid parents' pep talk shit. I don't want another walk round the garden telling me what I am and what I'm not allowed to do. I'm sick of you. You didn't ask us if we wanted to come here and now you're—"

"Yes, we did," his mother said.

"No, you didn't. And now, you're not asking us if we want to go, either. Well, it stinks. You're all selfish, and—" Tears were rolling down his face.

Sita was standing now, too. The others sat, motionless.

"Bed, Jay. It's late."

"Fuck late!" he screamed. "Fuck all of you. I hate you. I hate you!"

And he turned and ran out, slamming the heavy door as angrily as his puny arms would let him.

14

JONATHAN DIDN'T REALIZE HOW FAR THINGS HAD GONE UNTIL HE FOUND himself saying yes to another beer in Tamsin's flat at three o'clock in the afternoon. Even through the haze of lunchtime drinking, there could be no favorable explanation for them going back there after the wine bar. There hadn't even been a truly favorable explanation for the wine bar itself.

"To say thank you for last weekend," he'd said over the phone. "That's okay," she'd said, "you don't need to thank me. I enjoyed it." But they'd arranged to meet anyway. And Jonathan had lied to Sita for the second time. That for him was a habit.

Truth and lies swam around in his head like slightly pissed wasps. He swatted arbitrarily. Lie to Sita, swat. Toy with Tamsin, let it go.

He felt justified. He had tried hard to rekindle the brief foreplay he and Sita had enjoyed on the night of the party, but his wife had made it clear she was no longer interested, not since his ridiculous decision to go and get the post from the chapel in the pouring rain at eleven o'clock at night, not since the argument about the lime wash and his eyes, and certainly not since the traumatic house meeting, which had changed everything.

He didn't want to think about the almost freakish vacancy in Emmy's eyes throughout the whole gruesome deliberation. Actually, he didn't want to think about any of it. Even then, at that silent, awful table, the idea of Tamsin had popped into his head. He was almost getting used to it, the way she came to him at the most vulnerable times, like a silent shrug at their joint failure to make the most of the Bodinnick dream.

But if he had to pinpoint the exact moment he'd decided to take the Tamsin thing to the edge, he would say it was Sita telling him about Niall and Emmy's snatched moment of abandoned passion on May Day. She'd told him in their bathroom after the meeting, when he was standing in boxer shorts and socks rubbing cream into his chapped hands, and she was sorting the family wash into colors and whites. They had been pretending life was normal, that there was no significance in their decision to have the place valued, that it wasn't really all over but the shouting.

The way she'd said it made it sound as if it were entirely his fault that those days were so far behind them. And his first reaction hadn't been his usual acceptance of inadequacy, it had been anger: "Well, lucky old them."

"Quite."

"And what about Kat? Is it fair on her?"

But Sita had flicked one of Lila's sleep suits angrily into the air and said something along the lines of "You've got to take your chances when you can, haven't you?"

And so here he was now, taking his chance, already floundering. Not out of his depth, exactly, because being in Tamsin's flat was more like swimming to the shallow end of a pool and standing up to find that the water doesn't even cover your trunks. He was suffering from realizing he was overgrown, that he was too old for all this.

Nothing he could see in her twenty-something home had any reference to his life. In other friends' houses, there were familiar signposts, like a CD collection that echoed your own, or the same out-of-production Habitat mugs, or letters from school about hair lice or sports day.

Here, their fifteen-year age gap was visible even in the packets of food on her open shelving: flavored rice in sachets, tacos, a bottle of Malibu. A knee-length coat with a furry collar and cuffs lay over a perspex chair, and an ice-cream tub full of bottles of nail polish sat on the bare floorboards by a bright blue sofa with metal legs.

Because he didn't know where to look, he settled his eyes on a smooth oval boulder propping open a door leading into a room with cerise walls.

"I like your doorstop," he said pathetically. Oh God, please spare me from this humiliation.

"I got it from the beach."

"Is that legal?"

"Do I care?"

Until then he'd focused only on their similarities, of which, he was suddenly painfully aware, there was just one.

And yet for the past two hours Tamsin had laughed at his feeble jokes, flirted with him and flattered him. He couldn't remember the last time he had felt funny or sexy or worth listening to. And although it almost pained him to see her in this light, he at last understood the clear message she was giving out. To use the ugly shorthand employed by Niall, she was telling him in no uncertain terms that she was "up for it."

Her offer had been clear. "I don't want to make you late back," he'd said as they'd lingered over the last centimeters of wine in the bar. "Oh, I thought I'd take a long lunch," she'd replied. "Do you want to see my flat?" She'd been quite assured. Yes, her intelligent pale blue eyes had said. This is a sexual advance. Don't be shy. I'm not.

He had felt himself harden, but there was another dialogue going on in his head about quick fixes not being as satisfying as they used to be, about getting to the point in his life where he wanted to see beyond them, even if there was just an open vista or an empty space. But worse than all of that, the thought had occurred to him that it could all go terribly wrong. He was out of practice, big time.

He hadn't seen her offer coming, he honestly hadn't. Or at least not quite so fast. He knew many marriages were peppered with discreet infidelities but he had never understood, until now, how they happened. You just stopped caring too much about the consequences.

He still found women other than Sita attractive. He was even prepared to believe that some women felt the same way about him, but he could never work out how on earth anyone took such feelings a stage farther. Or why, actually. He'd never considered his own loyalty because he'd never thought he'd have to. And now he was being offered the perfect chance to test it.

Even his car full of family disorder hadn't seemed to distract her. What was going on in her head, allowing a man almost old enough to be her father, let alone anyone else's, to take her back to her flat in the middle of the day? He knew what was going on in his own head. It was an exercise in seeing what it might be like to be someone else, which was the only enduring fantasy of his life to date.

His heart had thumped all the way with guilt and fear. Desire reared its head every now and again but it was a third-party thing, and only because any sex, extramarital or otherwise, seemed such a long time ago.

In the wine bar, Tamsin had made him believe anything was possible, but that had been back in the safety of licensed premises. He'd believed in there, with the outdated red glass oil lamps and blackboard menus, that he could have a secret life, a soulmate, someone to talk to about love and lime when no one else cared.

What he felt now they were on their own in her big empty flat with the perspex and the Pop Tarts was that anything, particularly escape, was impossible. He also felt that both her image and his were irreversibly tarnished. There was something tacky about it all. He wanted to go. His career as an adulterer was over before it had started.

"This is it," she'd said breezily as she'd opened her front door, which gave straight from the street onto a flight of white painted stairs. Free newspapers, taxi flyers and three crushed cans of lager were piled on the floor. He'd imagined her sitting on the bottom step, waiting with her clubbing friends for a cab, drinking. Then he'd noticed his own brown brogues following her up the steps like a lost sheep. Or a lamb being led to slaughter, maybe. This is it, then. This is it. Immediately, he'd known it wasn't enough.

He'd taken the beer from her because he needed something to do with his hands, but she was already suggesting other options.

"Would you like to see the bedroom?"

"I'm fine here," he said.

"I know you are. I'm only offering to show you a few original beams."

"Oh, of course."

"I've got photos, if you prefer."

He sat down quickly on the sofa between the two bay windows. She came to sit next to him, making sure her thigh touched his.

"It's the same size as this. I wanted something old with good pro-portions."

"Is there a joke coming?" he asked.

"I don't know what you mean," she said coyly, passing him a blue envelope of mail-order processed snaps.

He tried to look as if he knew the routine, pulling out a cushion, thumping it and leaning back. "Just being facetious. Yes, it looks great. Did you reveal it yourself?"

"Yes. I'm very good at revealing things."

He wasn't sure if she was being serious or not. He put his hands behind his head, thinking it made him look less like someone who was about to start hyperventilating.

"Well, what shall we do now?" she asked, twisting her body toward him.

Clearly, women took control of such situations these days. Actu-ally, he acknowledged, as he clutched his stubby green bottle of Stella, they always had, as far as he was concerned. He had never made a sex-ual overture in his life. The number of women he had slept with equated exactly to the number of women who had made the first move.

He raised his eyebrows and put his hands palm up, but as he was trying to think of something suitably nebulous to say, she spoke again.

"I know. How about you kiss me?"

The effect on him was magical. He wanted to go home and make it all better with Sita, to cancel the appointment with the double-barreled chartered surveyor who was coming to value Bodinnick on the day ringed in red on the kitchen calendar, and to start all over again.

"I'd love to," he heard himself say.

"I know you would." She had even closed her eyes.

"But I won't, if that's okay."

Tamsin pulled back no more than a couple of inches. Her face managed a smile. "Yes, of course it's okay." Rejection hadn't ruffled her composure. Made her blush, maybe, just a touch.

"It's not that I don't . . ."

"Don't you? I really thought you did."

"No, I mean, I do, but . . ."

"Jonathan, it's okay. No one's died."

"No." He stared at the floorboards, wondering what he was mourning for.

"Hey, come on. I got it wrong, that's all. I thought you wanted me for something other than professional advice, and I didn't mind that. But I don't mind this, either. It's really no big deal. I do it lots."

"Do you?"

"Yes," she nodded. "I do."

"I should go," he said.

"Or we could talk about it while you finish your beer?"

"I'm no good at talking, Tamsin. Ask my wife."

"Better not," she said, getting up. "She might get the wrong idea."

———

BY SENDING ALL FIVE LETTERS, CATHAL HAD MADE SURE THERE WAS NO chance of Emmy getting the wrong idea.

"Someone's trying to tell you something, I think," the chirpy postman said as he handed her the identical envelopes with their Irish stamps. He had a smirk across his gnomic face as if he had just cracked the joke of the century. "Or is it one of those chain-mail things?"

He cocked his head and waited for the answer that he could take to Mrs. Partridge at the farm. Eileen Partridge liked to keep abreast of what was going on, and he liked the coffee and the sugar and currant Cornish "heavy cake" she gave him in return.

"Thank you," Emmy said quickly, shutting the back door in his startled face.

The first sight of the green harp was hardly a shock. In a peculiar way, it was almost a relief, since she'd been expecting it daily. But when she put it at the bottom of the pile to look at what else he had given her, she saw the second one and something hit her at the back of her throat. The third, fourth and fifth hit her somewhere much worse.

She leaned against the delicately fern-etched glass of the back door and stared into the dingy passageway known as the boot room, which still smelled of Toby's dogs, into wellies and weedkiller, into ancient tins of axle grease and oil dispensers with long thin spouts, and old seedling trays.

For a split second she thought she might collapse in a heap on the floor and lie there until someone carted her off, but the thought that the someone might be Maya was just enough to make her stay standing. She breathed in through her nose, a long controlled intake. Then she blew slowly out of her barely open mouth. She tried to swallow but couldn't. Her left hand went to her neck and she squeezed the glands below her ears, trying to collect her thoughts. Her right hand hung limply by her side, clutching the letters.

A door slammed upstairs and she heard raised voices. Somewhere in her head, she registered them as Niall and Kat's but the fact that they were having a row did not resonate. It was a detail that belonged to another life.

She opened the first letter while she was still leaning against the door. It was a photocopy of the one she had already received. She tore open the second, which was the same. And the third. Instead of being relieved that Cathal hadn't elaborated on his initial request, she felt chilled to the bone. Stalked, or hunted, or blackmailed. Had he gone mad?

She ripped straight through the fourth and fifth ones, once, twice, three times. She saw snatches of his photocopied words, and scared herself witless at the now familiar loops of his writing. The moment had something of the repetitive nightmare about it, as though she knew she was falling into it but couldn't help herself. A shadow passed across the glass behind her and she leaped away from it, as if any minute now the handle would go down, the door would be pushed open and he'd be inside.

The shouting upstairs still didn't sink in. Nor did the clattering of children in the kitchen just on the other side of the wall, the noise of cereal bowls and taps running, the sound of Sita calling good-bye twice.

Fury began to boil inside her head. Without thinking what she was doing or how she would explain it, she pulled from her trouser pocket a lighter which had lit her a cigarette every waking hour since the original letter had arrived, and set fire to the paper in her hand. As it caught and threatened to reach her fingers, she dragged out a coal bucket from between the boots and dropped the burning page in. One by one, the rest followed.

Standing over her pyre, she watched the long flames lick the Irish stamps, the typewritten address, Cathal's brutal demands. Her eyes burned with a warning. *You leave me and Maya alone. Just leave us alone.* She felt witchlike and powerful while the fire burned, but when it died her potency died too, and when the paper was just a pile of black ash she was left feeling like a wet rag.

————————

THE FLAMES WERE DEAD BY THE TIME NIALL AND KAT WALKED PAST TEN minutes later. A thin curtain of smoke hung in the air, but Niall's Camel cigarette rendered it invisible.

"I can't leave him here on his own," he argued. "He's coming to see me, not anyone else. The Irish house stuff is just a pretext. I've told you, he's got another agenda, I know him."

He was doing his best to keep up with Kat as she tore through the house, but she was in a fast and furious mood. She had her London clothes on again: a tight large-cuffed tailored white shirt and black cut-off trousers. Her black leather sandals had heels on them like the bottom of a bumper car and her lilac lipstick made her look like a mini version of Cruella Deville.

"But the deal was never me always coming here. You said you would come up to London sometimes, too."

"What are you talking about? What deal?"

Her car needed a new exhaust, the timer for the heating in her flat was refusing to work, and there was a party she didn't want to go to on her own. He *had* to come to London. "You know exactly what deal I mean, so don't be boring."

She kicked the bucket of paper ash to one side and opened the door, forcing herself and her hugely expensive bag through the space and out into the courtyard. Three bicycles were heaped in her way, the pink one from the store included.

"You were the one who wanted the recreational relationship," he reminded her.

"That was because you weren't offering anything else."

"I was. I offered this, full-time."

"Only because you knew I wouldn't damn well accept." She stepped round the bikes, brushing against the oil tank and getting the arm of her white shirt soaked with the warm rain that had just fallen.

"Not true. The offer is still open."

"I don't think so. Anyway, it doesn't sound as if any of you will be here much longer."

Niall had refused to talk about the house meeting. It was all too raw.

"I will come to London sometimes, but I can't come just at the moment. Why are you making so much of it?"

"Look, if you're not going to come with me, I need to know now. The train leaves in half an hour."

"Kat, watch my lips. I've told you. I am not coming."

"Is that your final answer?"

"Yes. It was my first answer as well. I don't see how I can be more clear about it."

"Well, you can live with the consequences then, you selfish bastard." She whacked Niall's legs with her suitcase.

"That was not necessary, Kathleen."

"Just take me to the bloody station. And I'm not going on your bloody bike."

"There's no need to swear," he said, knowing exactly how much he could wind her up. "It's very eighties, sweetheart. Hasn't anyone told you it has lost the power to shock?"

"Niall?"

"Uuh?"

"Fuck off."

SO HE THOUGHT, ONCE HE'D DROPPED HER OFF, THAT IT MIGHT BE TIME to take her at her word. It was a prospect that took less thinking about than he'd imagined, but he still felt it was a big enough decision to have to weigh up, and when he needed to weigh things up there was only one sort of place to go. It was no good going to the Cott Inn because people knew him there now—Roy Mundy the plumber, Jack Partridge the farmer, Jim Best the electrician—and they would want to talk to him, or, more likely, he would want to talk to them. The Aga was low, Partridge's sheep were still getting out and finding their way into the garden, and the wiring up the stairs was an iffy job which Jim really needed to take a second look at. Even if they were only getting it up to scratch to sell.

Instead, he followed a brown tourist sign off the main road which he had seen and failed to follow until now, and ended up at a low, thatched, elongated, whitewashed cottage on a creek. It didn't look much like his kind of pub from the outside, and he knew the menu would be more extensive than the beer cellar, but at least it would be totally and utterly anonymous.

The sky was a tie-dye affair of light and dark gray, confirming the forecast of rain. Boats bobbing on the churned and muddy water looked as if they'd had enough of the unsettled week. Across the creek, expensive bungalows with gardens running to the water's edge stared snootily down as if they had enough of looking at the boats, doubly offended to be forced to gaze upon a place that served al fresco chips in plastic baskets.

The wooden picnic tables along the jetty were slimy with the wet, as was the decking underfoot, but a rope prevented access anyway. An unhappy dog was tied to one of the bench legs, and jumped to its feet eagerly when Niall walked by. He patted it and it looked grateful.

The doorway to the Ferry Gate was a foot shorter than he was, and as he lifted the latch, he caught sight of the four-letter word—*Duck*— just in time. A wood and glass partition between the flagstone hall and the snug channeled him straight toward the bar.

The big car park had been practically empty so he was surprised to see how many people there were, until he realized they were the sailing fraternity and their expensive transport was moored outside.

The Gore-Tex gaggle looked up momentarily, but they could tell by his gray urban clothes that he had no interest in boats, so none of them bothered to acknowledge him as they might have done if he'd been wearing something stormproof in a primary color. Terracotta dishes and napkins littered their tables, and they all laughed loudly at each other's jokes.

The woman with bad highlights behind the bar looked relieved to see him, though.

"You a sailor, too?" she asked tentatively. She had on a low-cut long-sleeved white T-shirt and her breasts merged with the rolls of her tummy. Niall noticed a gold belt peeping out from among it all.

"No, why? Do you have to be to drink here?"

"Feels like that sometimes."

"Well, I hate boats. I felt a bit sick just walking in here from the car park, actually. I couldn't work out if it was the boats bobbin' up and down, or me, or the ground or what."

"You're all right, then. What can I get you?"

"Pint of Guinness, please."

She dropped her voice and glanced at the sailing crowd. "They're a noisy bunch, this lot."

"Don't worry about me."

"They're rude, too. I don't think one of them has said please or thank you yet."

"That's bad."

"I think they think the Cornish are thick."

"I bet you say that to all the Irishmen you get in here."

She smiled and gave him his Guinness, and because he sat at a stool against the counter she assumed he wanted to carry on talking. He looked like a man acquainted with the unspoken rules of country pubs. If you wanted to be left alone, you retreated to a table. If you wanted company, you sat at the bar.

"So what brings you here then? On holiday?"

"No, I live here. We moved down a month ago."

"And who is 'we'?" She picked up a beer towel and began to wipe between the pumps.

"Well, that is the golden question," Niall said mysteriously. "That is the golden question."

EMMY PICKED UP NIALL'S MOBILE PHONE, WHICH WAS CHARGING ON the Welsh dresser and pressed the Menu button. Information. Phone Book. Messages. She pressed OK. I'm going to do this. I really am. Call Voicemail. Received Messages. Select. Even as she typed in the text, she didn't believe she would send it. She thought she was going to remain immobilized forever by fear. "PLEASE DO NOT SEND ANYMORE LETTERS AND PLEASE DO NOT COME TO CORNWALL. EMMY."

Enter number. She tapped it in from the piece of paper she had pulled out of her pocket. She could still scrub it. Send message. Would she? She pressed OK. Message failed. Resend? OK. Message failed. Another breath. Resend? OK. Message sent.

Oh my God. Her decision to make contact was now irretrievable. She put the phone back on the dresser as if it was about to explode, and her legs turned to jelly. The little green light flashed back at her. She stared at it, waiting. Nothing happened. She stared some more. Still nothing happened.

Five minutes passed and the world had not fallen in. She boiled a kettle and shook some coffee into a mug because she was too lazy to find a clean teaspoon. She drank the coffee, even though it was too strong, and then forced herself to go and find Maya and apologize.

As she was on her way out of the kitchen, feeling for the first time in more than a week that she might have brought a small amount of control back into her life, the phone shrieked. Three sharp tones which pierced the silence.

She dived back to it. Message. Read Now? She didn't know about that. A door banged somewhere in the house and it shook her into realizing she had no choice. OK. His message flashed up. (1—New) "AM ON MY WAY. I COME IN PEACE. CATHAL." View Options? Delete Message? It was Niall's phone and it would be a cruel way for him to find out the truth of something he didn't even doubt. Select? OK.

Then she forgot about finding Maya and instead went straight to her bathroom, locked the door and threw up, holding onto the cold enamel rim of the lavatory as if her life depended on it.

"THOUGHT OF THE ANSWER YET?" THE BARMAID ASKED NIALL. "THREE pints of Guinness should be enough to lubricate even an Irish brain."

"Yes, but I've forgotten the question."

"It was the golden one."

"Oh, that one. I remember. It's either 3.4 or Val Doonican."

She laughed and was summonsed by an angry ring of the brass bell at the other end of the bar. "See what I mean?"

Niall nodded and went back to the thought he'd been having before she'd interrupted him.

The tape of Elvis Costello playing in the background had triggered it. He and Emmy had seen him at the Glastonbury Festival once, years ago, before she'd got pregnant, before the mud.

He could remember them parking the bike in a dusty summer field and, as the thump of airborne music from a faraway stage pumped through him and she had humped her sleeping bag over her shoulder and walked through a swirl of tiny glittering particles of hay, he'd thought he could never love anyone more. They had slept in a one-man tent and one night they had built a fire near the pyramid stage and curled up in their bags like padded silkworms, stoned and happy, and fallen asleep to the sound of some now-forgotten band. So far, he hadn't been proved wrong.

He put his empty glass down on a brass drip tray, waved to the barmaid and walked out. He did know who he wanted to live with. He'd always known. And this morning Kat had given him the perfect opportunity to make it all a lot clearer.

15

As she sat on the edge of her bed waiting for the very first glimpse of the hood of Cathal's car, Emmy realized at last the significance of her recurring dream. She'd had it for almost as long as her daughter had been able to talk, but in it Maya had always been as she was now, long-haired and long-limbed, freckled and complete.

It came as a dream within a dream. The empty room always appeared first, coming into sharper and sharper focus, and then, when the detail was really clear, Maya would walk in. She was always alone, calmly looking for something as if she knew she would find it eventually. She was never in a hurry and would wander through room after identical room in a peaceful trance.

At the very end of the last room there was an old tower with a winding staircase, and Maya would mount it without hesitating. At the top of the stairs, she would open a narrow door into a little room and, as she disappeared, she would look back and smile at someone in a way that Emmy didn't recognize. Then the door would shut behind her. It was Maya's smile that always woke Emmy up.

She hated that dream, but at least she knew now what it was all about. Cathal was her Rumpelstiltskin. He was the thirteenth fairy at the Sleeping Beauty's christening, hiding in the tower with the poisoned needle, ready to inject the spell of separation. He was a Brothers Grimm goblin of the twenty-first century. And she was like the mother in "Tom Thumb" who by some stroke of magic had found herself with the child she never thought she'd have, or the sad barren wife in "The Gingerbread Man" who is so desperate to have something to love that she bakes herself a baby.

Emmy actually shouted out loud when the first unknown car came into view. She had no desire to be this story's pathetic victim, the one who waits all her life for one good thing to happen to her and then lets it go because someone else has other plans for it.

"Leave us alone!"

Her hands, inadvertently in a praying position, were tucked between her thighs and she pressed them down even farther, digging through her clothes into her flesh. On the floor, an old carpet bag gaped open. In it were toothbrushes, nightclothes, underwear and credit cards, ready for her and Maya to flee at a moment's notice. And this was surely the moment at which the notice should be posted. Except there was no getaway car. Sita was at work and Jonathan had disappeared.

Her throat tightened again, a Pavlovian reaction to the thought of Cathal and her mind started to scramble around for alternative scenarios. It might not be him. The car was a white four-wheel-drive Japanese monster. It was definitely not the organic vegetable delivery or the plumber, but she couldn't see the driver's face.

Mind over matter, she willed herself. She stared at its double set of headlights, pushing them into reverse with her eyes. But the car loomed closer and closer. It parked and someone got out. She shut her eyes and waited for the sound of the door pull. Then she opened them again.

A bundle of For Sale signs pressed against the back windscreen of the car. Culworthy-King and Simpson. Chartered Surveyors. Auctioneers. Valuers.

"Mr. Culworthy-King?" she heard Niall say beneath her window. "We weren't sure what time you had arranged with Jonathan. He's, er, he's tied up elsewhere for the moment."

It was the bloody real estate agent. Emmy took her hands out from between her thighs and held them to her face, pushing the ball of her little fingers into the corner of her eyes. The man who was going to search for the perfect buyer for Bodinnick was almost welcome in comparison. She breathed again and steadied herself, buying a little more time.

She watched Niall and the agent walk across the circular patch of grass in front of the house and stand by the birdbath to admire the façade. Then she watched them walk back and disappear into Bodinnick's beautiful bowels. But the visit neither interested nor disappointed her, only prompted her to resume her position on the edge of the bed. Her hands clasped tight again and she waited for Cathal.

When the right car finally came, it was Italian, not Japanese, and front- not four-wheel drive. It was blue, with a throaty exhaust note she knew he would find appealing, and as soon as she saw the vague outline of the driver's head she knew it was him and that this was the instant she had been dreading all Maya's life.

She heard the thump of his music, recognizing the rhythm but not able to place it. Then suddenly both the engine and the music stopped.

She listened for the door. Open. *Slam. Crunch.* Any minute now, he would be in the house. In her house, looking for her daughter. My God! What was she doing, just sitting there?

"Maya!" she screamed down the stairwell, remembering nothing of the journey from the bed to the landing. "Maya? Maya!"

There was still time. She ran down the stairs two at once as Jay always did, her hand sweeping along the polished wood of the banister, her feet barely touching the ground. As she faced the challenge of the hall, she heard him try the antiquated bell. *Clang clang.* It was a death knell.

Passageway, kitchen, back door, another passageway, courtyard. Fresh air. She gulped it.

Jay was there, fixing a puncture on his upturned bike, seething with hatred for Culworthy-King.

"Have you seen Maya?" she puffed.

"No. Who's that man with Niall?"

"Will you help me find her?"

"Is he a real estate agent?"

"If you see her, tell her to go straight to her room."

"Is he going to sell Bodinnick?"

But Emmy had already gone. Garden, shrubbery, path, arched gate.

"Maya? Maya? Maya." The name drifted out of her mouth like a gentle song. She didn't know whether to scream or whisper.

"Mum?" Maya's face appeared from a hole in a rhododendron bush. Asha's appeared a second later.

"Oh God, Maya."

"What's happened?"

"Oh," Emmy panted. "Nothing. I've been looking for you, that's all."

"What for?"

"Er, I need . . . I need to measure you."

"Not now," Maya moaned. "Do you have to? We're playing a really good game."

"Yes, yes, I do. It's important."

"This is our spy headquarters and we're the secret agents and if that man Niall is talking to—"

"Please."

Emmy pulled her daughter out and dragged her along by the hand. Asha followed, grabbing Emmy's free hand, just in case. Arched gate, path, shrubbery, garden, courtyard.

"Stay with Jay, Asha," Emmy ordered, flinging the child at her brother.

"Who's that man, Emmy?" Jay shouted after her.

"Mum!" screamed Maya. "Mum, you're hurting me. What's the big rush?"

Passageway, kitchen, passageway. And then . . . hall.

"Oh!"

Cathal was standing in the middle of the tiled floor, his bag at his feet. He didn't look much like an evil fairy in his blue canvas trousers and gray polo shirt.

"Cathal!" Maya shouted as her face lit up. She went to him without a flicker of hesitation and he put his arms out before he realized what he was doing.

"Maya, how you doin?'

"Great."

"Emmy." Cathal nodded and tried a smile.

"Cathal," Emmy said glacially.

"Mum?"

And there they stood at three points of a triangle. Mother, father and daughter. Together in the same room for the first time in their lives.

"Niall?" Emmy suddenly hollered up the stairs, still rooted to the spot. *"Niall?"*

JONATHAN HAD LEFT THE HOUSE ON PURPOSE. HE DIDN'T WANT TO BE either a part of Sita's control freakery or a punching bag for Jay's anger.

"We're just asking you to be civil," he had said when Jay announced his intention to tell anyone who looked remotely like a real estate agent to get lost.

"Well, what about doing what *I'm* asking you to do?" his furious son had shouted. "You never ask me what *I* want! You just think about yourselves the whole time, don't you?"

"Well, what *do* you want?"

"You *know* what I want. I don't want to go back to fucking London."

"That is enough, Jay."

"Well I don't—"

"If I hear you using that word again, I'll—"

"You'll what?" Jay spat. "You're always saying you'll do something and you never bloody do. What word, anyway? Fucking? The word Niall uses all the time? The fuck word?"

Jonathan left him, screaming to himself in his bedroom. He couldn't get out of the house fast enough.

Because of the wind, Crannock beach car park was empty apart from an old red and black bus sitting in a far corner in what looked like a jumble of gas bottles, flexi-pipes and water tanks. The spot had been carefully chosen. It was sheltered and unobtrusive and he thought of Tamsin, even though he was trying not to. "God no, I've no desire to be a gypsy," she'd told him. Her words sounded distasteful now, like the memory of food poisoning from the one spoiled mussel in an otherwise delicious bowl of bouillabaisse.

He read the words on the back of the bus—*Surfers Against Sewage*—and realized it was the vehicle they had overtaken on the blind bend on the way to the manor, the one they had followed up the lane on their arrival at Bodinnick. He felt vindicated. Tamsin had made it sound as if the county was crawling with undesirables, and here was the only evidence of travelers he had so far seen, albeit three times. And it looked far from undesirable to him.

The girl bus driver with the sock on her head was nowhere to be seen, but in his desire not to intrude Jonathan swung his shiny gas-guzzling car as far away as possible, parking outside a wooden beach café.

He got out and headed for the dunes beyond, with the excuse of finding two or three large pebbles or small boulders for doorstops at the chapel and Bodinnick. At least he had something to thank Tamsin for.

There had been a lot of door slamming lately, and it wasn't just the through-draft.

As he got closer, he could see that the confusion of pipes and bottles around the bus was in fact not a confusion at all but an ordered system of domestic supplies. There were curtains at all the windows, there was a chimney in the roof and boots by the door. Envy hit him so hard it hurt.

So simple living was alive and well, but just not at Bodinnick. The certain disappointment in himself that he always carried around had become even heavier lately. What use was he?

The irrational preoccupation with Tamsin had subsided, but there was something worse than anticlimactic about what had been left in its wake. Worse, he supposed, for the lack of climax in the first place. She had coaxed the one little glimmer of recklessness out of him, and although he knew he was better off without it he now felt utterly empty.

When they had got up from the sofa in her flat and walked back down the stairs, he waved good-bye to the part of himself he was leaving behind on the cushions, a part which had only just been born, a helpless wriggling little scrap of fantasy which would have needed so much nurturing it had hardly ever been viable. He wondered what Tamsin had done with it, whether she had nurtured it and grown it into the man she wanted it to be, created an entirely different encounter that she could tell her friends about, or whether she had scraped it off the canvas and binned it with the empty beer bottles.

She certainly wouldn't want to have anything to do with the bits that were left—the dull dependable bits, the Sita bit, the children bit, the chapel bit. The bits he needed to nurture and help grow into the man he wanted to be.

The wind was strong enough to whip the dry top layer of sand off the dunes, making him bow his head as he walked across the car park and up the railway-sleeper steps to the beach. But the sun was shining, too, and the clouds were dispersing quickly enough to give frequent blasts of the most unnatural blue. Once out of view, he brought his face to the wind, getting stung by the gritty dust.

From the ridge, where the sand was soft and sifted, blown in from the grassy tussocks rather than washed up by the sea, he could see for miles. The beach had graded itself not only in bands of color—demerara, corn, sludge—but in strand lines of seaweed and litter.

He began to walk down, looking for doorstop-size stones, and as his legs found a rhythm he began to feel better. He breathed in, feeling his lungs fill with fresh air, and he suddenly realized his chest pains had vanished. How long ago? Were they gone for good? Was this the first sign of progress?

He bent down to inspect a smooth small rock but its underneath was smeared with oil. One could ignore the occasional abandoned jelly shoe or bucket handle at the top end, the end where holidaying families with young children set up camp either through lack of imagination or stamina. But farther on, where the real grime began just as your feet stopped sinking into powder and instead began to crunch on the gritty shingle, the ugly detritus was so prolific that the scene could have been an artistic experiment in waste.

Rubbish imitating life, a collage of crap. Orange nylon rope lay in tangles between rocks, like families of dead octopuses. Oily lumps of rubber disguised themselves at a distance as large black boulders. Plastic lids, hundreds of them sea-rinsed to faded blues, pinks and greens sat like prize shells among the gray builder's gritstone. For some reason, he thought of the straw-yellow sand that he used to buy in sacks for the children's sandpit, and wondered what the hell toy shops did to it to make it so clean.

The flat, wet expanse stretched for quarter of a mile in each direction, book-ended by huge twin rocks rising from the spuming sea which seemed to be saying, "We were here first, and we will be here last, before human disregard and after it, too. We don't change."

Jonathan kicked a concertinaed water bottle and watched it scud across the hard ripples sculpted by the outgoing tide. Half a mile of human trash, dragged in and out twice a day, added to hour by hour, at sea and on land. The world was awash with scum.

He was halfway to the water's edge when the sound of crashing waves quickened his pace and made him want to run. In his head, he was in the salty waves, feeling the fresh foam wash him, smack him, sting him, stir up his anger, baptize him with something else, wash his infidelity away.

Had he really thought he would find something in the chapel? Or with a girl half his age? What? Satisfaction? The pleasure of change? Where would he find his purpose?

The chapel had given him a brief sense of it, but that was all. It was almost over now. Painting the chapel walls would take him another two days at most. He wanted to have done with them, inextricably linked as they were to Tamsin, but he was frightened. What then? Another project to keep the wolf inside him from the door?

He had maneuvered himself into his own tight spot, limewashed himself into a corner. He supposed he could throw himself into the children for the last few weeks. But what did he want to do with them? Why couldn't he find himself? Why? Why? Why?

He shouted the words into the wind, which swallowed them up and took them away from him as if he'd never even uttered them. He held his arms outstretched to feel the force-six rush off the sea.

Such indulgence made him oblivious of the two figures who had appeared from the distant dunes hauling two black binbags behind them. They saw him, though, as they saw most comings and goings on the beach, and for a while they watched him. Something about his flailing arms and his closeness to the water concerned them.

"Do you think he's all right?" the girl with the stripy sock hat asked her boyfriend.

By the time Jonathan turned to walk back to the car and resigned himself to make the peace at home for his unexplained departure, the young couple had decided he wasn't about to walk into the ocean and end it all, so they had stopped watching.

At which point he noticed them. They would walk a few steps, bend over, pick something up and then move on. They were moving across the sand in a straight line, too far apart to be holding any reasonable conversation.

Somehow, with the entire beach between them, the three of them migrated toward each other—a mutual curiosity that would never have found its way out in the city. When they got close enough to view each other in detail, Jonathan saw that the lad with the fuller bag was picking up litter. He was about twenty, with matted dirty brown dreadlocks under his huge hooded fleece. His beard was darker than his hair, thin and soft and tufted. He had a ring in the rim of his nostril. The other was the girl bus driver and she seemed to be collecting seaweed. He was surprised to see she was about eight months pregnant.

"Hello," he said, nodding. He intended to walk on, but found himself stopping.

"Hi," the girl smiled. She was very pretty. Her blond hair was in thin plaits and her skin had a rosy antenatal glow.

"Sorry about that. I thought I had the beach to myself."

"Sorry about what?" Her young voice betrayed privilege.

"All that running and jumping."

"Looked pretty sane to me, mate," her boyfriend lied. They hadn't met at school, that was for sure. He wore bracelets made of bike chains, and there was a thread of red shiny wire woven expertly in and out of the links. "It's big enough, innit? Makes better sense than sitting in a bloody deckchair all day."

The girl laughed and twisted the neck of her binbag. "We're trying to clean up a bit."

"It could do with it. I noticed how bad it was on my way down. I saw a syringe back there."

"Oh, you didn't pick it up, did you?" the girl asked, making him wonder how good a private school education she had rejected.

"No, I didn't," he answered unsurely.

"Very sensible." She waved her hands at him. They were both wearing heavy-duty gloves. "Don't touch anything like that without a pair of these."

"No, good point."

There was a lull, then Jonathan spoke again. "What are you doing it for? Fun, or money, or social conscience?"

"Because no other fucker will," the boy said, putting his thumb and forefinger on his nose ring and tugging it, but there was something stage-managed in his anger.

"Is that your bus in the car park?"

"Yeah. It's knackered at the moment, though. We tried to move on the other day, but I think I clipped the sump pump on a boulder or sumfin' and then we got wheel spin 'cos the sand was so wet, and, well, she couldn't help me push it, could she? Not like that."

The boy raised his eyebrows with a proud smile and Jonathan noticed that they were pierced too. "So I gave it some welly, and I think I fucked it."

Jonathan knew it was the point in the conversation where one would normally commiserate, give a mild verbal pat on the back and move on. But he didn't want to.

"D'you want a hand to get it going again?"

"Nah, you're all right, mate. We're not in any hurry to go anywhere. Not unless it's to the hospital for the baby and we'll get a better bus to take us then, I think."

They were walking together now. Jonathan bent down to pick up an unidentifiable gnarl of plastic.

"I really wouldn't do it if you haven't got gloves."

Jonathan nodded. I'm married, a father, he wanted to tell them. I have actually got a life.

Back in the car park, he watched her tip out the contents of her bin liner. A repellant heap of tampon applicators, nappies, condoms, loo fresheners and plastic strips from sanitary towels fell out, trapped in seaweed.

"That's what happens when people use the sea as a bin," she said. "We'll dry it out and set fire to it."

"The toilet, Mog, not the sea," said her boyfriend affectionately. "People use the toilet as a bin. That's how all this crap gets here. They don't just chuck it straight in the sea, do they? They might think that was too bad. But they don't think it's bad when they chuck it down the bog, do they?"

"We shouldn't really be taking the seaweed as well," said Mog, removing a glove to tuck a strand of hair behind her ear. "The sandhoppers need it, and the squat lobsters and the birds and everything. But this lot was so revolting."

"Doesn't look fit for anything very much, does it?" Jonathan said. "Are you sure it's a good idea, dealing with all this toxic stuff when you're pregnant? You're careful, are you?"

"Dean makes sure I am, don't you?" she said, clipping back on an ear cuff that had fallen off.

"Yeah, course. Sure you don't want a cup of tea?"

Shyness stopped him accepting. "Maybe next time. I should go."

"See you again, then. Bring your gloves."

"I will."

As Jonathan got back in his car, he wondered how soon would be too soon, and what made some people get to the point quicker than others. And he still hadn't got his doorstops.

"Mum won't open her sewing room door," Maya whispered to Niall on the landing. "She keeps saying she'll be out in a minute, but I've been waiting here for ages."

"It's not your fault, sweetheart," he told her, suddenly so incensed with Emmy's behavior that he banged on the door without effect. It had always been about extremes with Emmy—she had the capacity to be both happier and sadder than anyone else he knew—but this was getting silly.

Maya looked at him with her nose screwed and her lips slightly curled. "Who says I thought it was?"

Niall laughed, relieved. "No one. I just thought—"

"Oh, God!" Maya groaned. "Grown-ups are always 'just thinking.' I don't care whether she comes out or not. I want to go outside, and I've promised I will ask first."

"Since when?"

"Since Cathal came. Don't ask me. Eggshell rule." She shrugged.

"Right. Cathal? What's he got to do with it?"

"Search me. What's wrong with Mum, anyway? I thought she'd be happy now you and Kat have split up."

"Oh, we have, have we? Who told you that?"

"I heard Kat tell you to, you know, the 'f' word you're so fond of."

"That doesn't necessarily meant we've . . ." he said feebly.

"But you have, haven't you? I looked in your room and you've put her stuff in a box."

"I think I ought to tell Kat before I tell you, don't you?"

"No, not really."

"Well, when I've told her, you'll be the first to know."

Maya smiled, happy with that. "Okay, deal. Now will you find out why Mum won't come out?"

"She's busy working, I expect."

"Oh yeah, right," Maya said sarcastically.

"Anyway, I thought you didn't care," Niall teased.

"No, you didn't."

"It'll be something to do with the real estate agent's visit, I should think. I don't suppose she fancied bumping into him."

"I've already told her he mentioned a million. Jay and I were spitting at him from Jay's bedroom. None of it hit him. The wind made it all come back in our faces."

"Serves you right."

"We heard him tell you it would be upward of a million. Does that mean we'll be rich?"

"Hey, come on. I think you should leave this to the adults. It's not kids' stuff."

"Why? Everyone is equal at Bodinnick, remember? That's what it says in the rules."

"Yeah, but some are more equal than others."

"Great." She groaned again. Her foot was still against the wall and her hands were still in her pocket, as if she was waiting outside the principal's study on detention. "Anyway, it's not that. I know it's not."

Niall was inclined to go with Maya when it came to Emmy. Her instinct was usually right.

"Is she ill?" he asked.

"No."

"Is she cross?"

"No."

"Then it'll be one of those women things that kids and blokes don't get."

Maya shook her head. "If you mean her period, it isn't that, either."

Niall furrowed his eyebrows. "I can't think of anything else, can you?"

She looked puzzled, only half sure of herself. "I think she doesn't want to come out because Cathal is here. She wasn't very pleased to see him when he arrived. I don't think she likes him."

"Oh." Niall was taken aback. "He's okay, isn't he? Do you like him?"

"Yeah, of course. He's your brother."

"Cor-rect. Maybe she's cross with me for inviting people without asking."

"You did ask. When he phoned, remember? And she ran off into the garden."

"She did, didn't she? You're right. Am I thick or thick?"

"You said it."

"Will I try and talk to her for you? Is that what you're wanting?"

"Yes, please," Maya said quickly. "Now can I go outside?"

"I should think so."

And she scooted off, scuffing the Persian runner as she went. That was what she had hoped he would say. Niall was the only one who could get her mum out of herself sometimes.

He knocked a second time on Emmy's door, less angrily. He had been waiting for an opportunity to talk to her, anyway.

"Emmy?" he said through the door.

"Go away, Niall."

"No. Open up. I've, er . . . Me and Kat have . . . Well, I'm going to . . . I need to talk to you."

"I heard. So did the rest of the house, I should think. If you have to argue, try and do it quietly, can you?"

"Let me in."

The door opened, but she didn't drag him in by the shirt collar as she might have done a few weeks ago. Instead, she stood there limply.

"Can it wait?" she asked. It was years since he had seen her wearing glasses instead of contacts.

"What's wrong with now?"

"I've got to get this done." She waved a bit of fabric at him. "And I'm not in the mood for postmortems."

"Oh, you're working!"

"Yes."

"That's great." He felt more relieved than he'd expected to. "Maya was a bit worried. She said you wouldn't come out because Cathal was here."

Emmy made a nervous sound that was meant to come out as a laugh. "Cathal? What on earth made her say something like that?"

"I don't know," he said.

But actually he did, now. Emmy's reaction was too tense, too false.

"Look, as you pointed out, I'm working. Tell Maya to stop jumping to ridiculous conclusions, will you? Why she has to get you to talk to me instead of coming in here herself, I've no idea."

"Oh, really? Stop being such a bitch, Emmy. She's worried and I am, too."

"Well don't. I don't need you to worry and I don't need to be called a bitch."

"Thank you for your time," Niall said with a sarcastic nod but he didn't feel sarcastic. He felt gutted.

Emmy pushed her door to again, almost in his face, and went back to stand by the machine. She clenched her fist and held it against her mouth, listening to him walk down the stairs. What he was thinking? Did he really have no idea? Was he not in any way suspicious of his brother just turning up like this? There was something terrible about his apparent ignorance.

The floor was covered in piles of red satin, and remnants of the same fabric in orange were strewn around. It looked like a furnace in there, and why not? She was surely in hell.

It was a double-edged sword, hiding away like this. She sat on the satin on the floor, pulled her legs up and held them tight to her body with her arms. A tissue-paper pattern for a devil's outfit was partly unfolded next to her. She could see the outline for a pronged fork. She knew a devil transformed into an angel, but how in God's name was she expected to be able to create anything like that when she no longer believed in heaven? A discarded tabard of mock chainmail hung over the back of the chair. She felt as if her guts had been skewered on a lance and the dragon's flames had burned every cell of her skin.

There was another knock on the door.

"Look, unless you are Maya, I'm not in," she shouted.

The last person she expected to walk in was Cathal.

———

HE WENT STRAIGHT TO THE WINDOW.

"Come in why don't you?" Emmy snapped, jumping to her feet, but when she forced herself to look at him—the way his shoulders were slumped and his head hung from all the thinking—she almost felt sorry for him. "I'm sorry. I don't mean to be hostile."

She had meant to be, a few seconds ago. A few seconds ago it was her only defense. Now he'd even taken that away.

He didn't speak, but blew out, fogging a little damp circle on the inside of the window.

Emmy reminded herself of her carefully chosen catalog of facts. The last time they had been alone together, Maya hadn't even technically been a fusion of egg and sperm. That miraculous little explosion had happened only once Cathal was on his way back to Ireland to join his heavily pregnant wife. Maya had happened all on her own.

"I'm sorry, too," he said. "I know you don't want me here, but I gave up hoping you would reply to my letters."

"I sent you a text message," she said defensively.

"I was already on my way by then."

They were both looking out of the narrow window, knowing there was no point in clarifying what was blindingly obvious. Out in the garden, through the spotless panes of glass in the narrow sash window, they were looking at their daughter. Emmy had cleaned the glass herself that morning for something to do, and now she wished she hadn't. By doing so, she had put Maya into perfect focus. It was impossible not to want to claim some of her for yourself.

Their daughter was pushing Asha around in a wheelbarrow, trying not to let it tip. She knew she was being watched. She just wasn't sure where from, or why.

"I told her not to go outside without asking me."

"I know. Niall told her he didn't think you would mind."

Emmy bit her lip. "A mind reader, is he?"

"No, you're just transparent. While I'm here with you, there's no chance of her being outside with me, is there?" he said. "You're making me feel like a pedophile."

"That's ridiculous."

There was a silence while they tried to rein in their anger, and then he said it. It came out in a rush as he turned to look straight into Emmy's eyes, his muscles twitching, his lips taut.

"She *is* mine, isn't she?"

He hadn't meant it to be one of the first questions, but there Maya was, the living, breathing version of the photograph he had been staring at for the past few weeks, and it was all too much.

Emmy felt as if she had been punched in the stomach. "No," she said, bracing herself for the next hit.

"Is that true?"

She looked away from the window, trying to control the fog that had closed in over her head. She tried to remember the things she had thought of to say. "Anyone who knows anything about Maya will tell you she doesn't belong to anyone," she hissed.

"I'm not interested in that kind of ownership. You know what I mean."

"If she is anyone's, she's mine. Any court in the land will tell you."

"God, Emmy, please slow down."

"I can't," she said quickly. "You shouldn't be here. Look, I don't want to disappoint you, but she really isn't interested."

"That's because she doesn't know," Cathal replied quietly. His voice was so like his brother's, it was confusing. He was like a wolf in sheep's clothing.

"How do you know she doesn't know?"

"I can tell by the way she is with me."

A silence fell between them. The tiniest, tiniest part of Emmy wanted to stand at the window with him and bask in shared parental pride. The words "She's beautiful, isn't she?" wanted to form on her lips. It was so minuscule a part that she knew she didn't have to acknowledge it.

"I wish you hadn't ignored my letters," he said. "I feel like a bastard for turning up like this, but I didn't know what else to do."

"I didn't ignore them. I didn't get the first one straight away—Jonathan left it over at the chapel—and, well, it hardly matters."

"No."

"No."

"Which is why I was forced to come here instead."

"What do you mean, 'forced'? Who forced you?" She felt as if she were on the end of a seesaw. One minute she felt safe, the next she had vertigo.

"You did."

"Don't make me hate you, Cathal."

"Oh, I think you already do that, don't you?"

He watched Maya tip Asha out of the barrow. She stopped laughing and helped her up. Good girl, he felt like shouting down.

"I don't hate you, I hate what you're doing."

"I can't help what I'm doing."

"You shouldn't be here," she repeated. "We can't talk here."

"Then meet me somewhere. We don't have to make an evening of it. A layby would do. Anywhere. You know we're going to have to do it some time."

"Someone would see us. You don't know what it's like round here."

"Please."

"No. For the first time in my life, I feel I'm where I should be, with the people I should be with. And you're threatening that. You're invading it."

"I'm not invading it. I'm trying to make the best decision I can without hurting everyone. I haven't just got on a boat and come over here to shoot my mouth off and give you a hard time because I feel like it. I'm here because this isn't the kind of stuff you can ignore. It needs sorting."

"If you take this to its logical conclusion, you'll wreck all of it."

"How will I?"

She wasn't sure. She said the first thing that came into her head. "Niall will leave."

Cathal made a noise of disbelief and started almost to shout. "This isn't about Niall, Emmy. This is the one thing in your life that isn't about Niall. I know everything else is. I even know that sleeping with me was about Niall, but it isn't about him anymore. It's about Maya."

"And you. It's about you. The one thing it isn't about is me."

"You've had ten years to prepare for this. You should have worked all this out."

"But I didn't prepare. That's the point." She blew into the silence, fighting back the tears. She didn't want him to see her cry.

"Please don't cry, Emmy."

"It's too late for that," she choked.

"Let's not do this now."

"Let's never do it."

"Never isn't an option, though, is it? Never isn't fair."

Fair? she wanted to scream. Since when has my life ever been fair?

"I don't want to ruin anything, anything at all, I just want—"

"What? What do you want?" she spat. Soon she was spraying her venom without caution all over the room, because once she had started she couldn't stop. "If it's Maya you want, you can forget it. You can't pick and choose the right times to be a father—either you are or you're not, and you are clearly not. Did you hear that? You are clearly *not* a father, Cathal, so don't try and be one. You're not even a father to your boys anymore. Where have you been all these years? I know where you've been, you've been at home with your wife and kids, bringing them up, and now they've gone. Well, bad luck, but there is nothing here you can replace them with. Life isn't like that. You say I've had ten years to prepare for this, well so have you—don't you dare try and tell me it has never occurred to you before, because—"

Cathal interrupted. "No. You're wrong. It hasn't ever occurred to me, I swear. Really. It was just as much a bolt from the blue for me as it was for you. I saw her picture and I saw me lookin' back. That was it."

"Is that all you have to go on?"

"No." He looked ashamed.

"Then what?"

"I've got dates. I've checked."

Emmy made a noise somewhere between contempt and assent.

"I can't ignore it. It wouldn't be right." He was facing her now.

"Right for who?" she shouted as loudly as she dared. It was too loud as it happened, because downstairs, doing nothing very much, Niall stopped in his tracks and looked at the ceiling. Was that Cathal's voice?

"I'm thinking about no one else, I assure you."

"Liar!"

"Okay, we'll leave it there before someone hears. But I'm not going back until we talk about this properly, like civil adults, until we have some kind of view of the future."

"We?"

"*I*, then."

"You keep saying you want this and you want that, but you never actually come out with it, do you? What *do* you want?" It was a terrible risk. He might say he wanted Maya.

"I want it all to be out in the open."

"Don't be so . . ." Emmy grabbed her cigarettes and pulled open the door.

Cathal was on her heels. "Come for a drive. We need to talk."

"No. *You* need to talk, so get a fucking therapist. I'm fine if we never speak again."

As they went down the stairs, Niall came up. He stood to one side, looking at them rush by, not knowing what he was seeing.

1 6

Mog looked at Jonathan's tidy jeans sticking out from under the bus and, as the baby in her womb shifted, she wondered if it was true what people said about parental adrenaline being so strong it could lift juggernauts off trapped children.

Jonathan slid out and stood up. He'd never been under anything bigger than a car, but he could tell a broken sump pump when he saw one.

Black grease had smeared itself all over his bottom and up the arms of his all-weather fleece. It was in the back of his hair, under his nails, down the side of his cheeks. Mog forgave herself for thinking he'd daubed himself on purpose under there, like he was in the mechanics division of the Territorial Army or something. She recognized his over-whelmingly middle-class neatness, but what she didn't know was just how neat he used to be.

"There's not just a crack, there's a hole in the aluminium big enough to fit your finger through," he said.

Dean tugged at a tuft of his beard and Jonathan smoothed his cleanly shaven jaw.

"Well, we need either a brand new bus or a scrapyard, then," Mog said. "What'll it be?"

"Do you know where one is?" Jonathan asked.

"Yeah, it's about half an hour from here."

"I don't mind taking you there."

"That's all right, mate. I could take the blat," Dean said.

"If it had petrol in it you could," Mog said. "We never got any, did we?"

"The what?" Jonathan asked.

Mog held her hands in a hammock under her pregnant belly. "That thing." She nodded at a motorbike fixed to the side of the bus. "I don't know why he calls it a blat. Why do you, Dean?"

"It's what everyone called them at the camp."

"Why?"

"Dunno. A blat is anyfin' you use to get around, like a pushbike or a car or a bike, like. Saves you usin' your big vehicle, although some tossers would take a bus like this downtown just to pick up some fags, wouldn't they, Mog?"

"You used to live in a camp?"

"Yeah, until about six weeks ago."

"Why did you leave?"

Jonathan had accepted the offer of tea this time. It was the first time Mog and Dean had invited him past the water tanks and the gas bottles and the pipes that led in and out of the holes crudely cut into the pressed steel.

"It was the brew crew," said Mog. "They started outnumbering us, and it got a bit pointless in the end, being with people that were so pissed all day they had nothing better to do than shoot at empty beer cans."

"Special Brew. Carlsberg." Dean nodded knowingly, his dreadlocks flicking with the movement. "A quick way to get shit-faced."

Jonathan had seen cans of it on the beach.

"I started feeling embarrassed when we went into town together," Mog said. "We all got painted with the same brush."

"Do you think I've done the engine in, then?" Dean asked, offering Jonathan a worn green plastic tobacco pouch.

"It depends how far you drove without oil. No, thanks." Being taken, even for a moment, for someone who might be able to roll their own made him think briefly again of something that often kept him awake at night, about first impressions and other people's perceptions of you. About how wrong you could be.

"I dunno. Ten miles?"

"Let's think about fitting a secondhand sump first, then we'll worry about the engine later."

Dean hopped up into the driver's cab and started to unclip a carpeted hump. Jonathan remembered how the girls on his school bus used to take turns to sit on it and how the bus driver used to put his hand on their bare legs and no one thought it was odd, and he was back with other people's perceptions again.

"How do you get to the rest of it?"

"By taking the grille off the front."

Dean climbed across a couple of old water drums and turned the engine over, but Jonathan was none the wiser. He shrugged helplessly as Dean put his hand down the neck of his filthy knitted striped sweater to put his tobacco back.

Mog put her face to the slight breeze that was coming in through the door, and the wispy bits of hair around her cheeks that were once a fringe revealed her tiny studded ears. Miniature pieces of blue glass glinted in the sun. For a split second, she looked far too young to be a girlfriend, let alone an expectant mother.

He could smell the food that they had either just eaten or were still in the process of cooking, bringing to his tastebuds a vision of an earthy casserole of curried root vegetables, or chickpea soup. In fact, it was Dean's second Pot Noodle of the day.

Mog saw his eyes wander away from the engine and try to see round the door that cut off the driver's cabin from the rest of the bus.

"Would you like to see inside?"

"No, no, I'm sorry," he apologized, reddening. "I'm just curious. It looks intriguing."

"Please, I'd like to show you." He could see that she meant it. It was her home, and she was proud of it.

"Well, if you're sure I wouldn't be intruding . . ."

"I'm sure. Come and have a look."

She took her boots off, leaving them this side of the door, and he did the same.

"Thanks," she said. "It's just that if mud or sand gets in there, it's impossible to get it out."

He followed her into the main body of the coach, and even though he'd known that the rows of seats and the metal aisle and the mesh luggage racks and the notices about not smoking or opening the windows would be long gone, it was a surprise to find himself in a small but perfectly formed sitting room.

"Can you flick the lights on, Dean?" Mog called.

He turned them on from the dashboard and a mini-runway of half-shell lamps illuminated a faded red carpeted ceiling, broken up by two huge skylights. The metal trim where the bell would once have been was still there, too.

From the wood-paneled wall to the long, narrow window, it was no more than seven feet wide. There was a rug on the floor, cushions, photos in frames, books on shelves—*The Continuum Concept, The Magus.* He saw a row of orange-spined Penguin Classics and imagined her embryonic schoolgirl signature inside.

"Mog, this is amazing."

She smiled shyly. "It's not really. There's plenty of horribleness here. It's just all covered up." She lifted the edge of an embroidered indigo throw and revealed the arm of a tacky gold velour sofa with its back to the cab. "We got that from the trash. They didn't charge us for it because they knew no one else would be stupid enough to take it, but it's fine. It's quite comfy, actually. That one's even worse," she said, pointing to a second sofa beneath the long window. "It's just beat-up old foam mainly. I made the cover from a pair of curtains we bought at a jumble sale."

Jonathan thought about the number of rooms they had at Bodinnick. He thought of the number of rolls of fabric Emmy kept buying and doing nothing with, and he thought of the number of books they had left behind in London which no one had got around to reading.

Mog slid back a narrow half-light that ran along the top and let in a couple of inches of sunshine, knocking her shin on a fire extinguisher which had been converted into a crude wood burner. Its top had been cut off, and a length of flexible steel pipe from it led up through the roof. It stood on a sheet of metal on two bricks, and a little door had been cut into the wider part of its base. Inside, a wedge of mesh provided the grate.

There was a portable television on a painted shelf, part of an elaborate wall unit which also sported a CD player. Jonathan felt as though he was in a living museum.

"A television? How on earth do you do that?" he asked.

"Batteries. We've got three, one for the engine, one for the music and telly, and one for spare. We try and charge them every morning for about an hour—you know, just leave the engine running—and we store them in the belly boxes, those panels on the side of the bus. Dean's wired up the telly straight into one."

"Do you have to be careful how much you use?"

"Not really," Mog said. "Telly and music use bugger-all batteries really. They can last about a fortnight." Swearing sounded a conscious thing for her. "Come and have a look at the kitchen."

A floor-to-roof ply screen cut the galley kitchen off from the sitting area. He recognized the Lilliputian appliances from his caravanning holidays as a child and a forgotten, soulless wet week in Dorset came back to him.

A small cooker was being used as a food cupboard. He could see half a loaf of sliced bread and what he guessed was a block of village shop cheese in a white paper bag. There was a box of tea bags, a bag of sugar, a jar of rice and a few others of dried beans and lentils. A spotless grill pan was hanging from a wall. Neatly placed in the work surface was a caravan sink, complete with blue plastic pump and one of those curved caravan taps.

"You just work it, like this." Mog showed him, putting a cup under the tap to catch the short gush.

"Is it fresh?"

"Of course. Is yours?"

"Good point."

"It's sophisticated stuff nowadays. Some buses have Agas on them, you know. I'd love an Aga." She sighed wistfully, disappearing behind another partition.

"Grief, this is like the Tardis."

"It's actually a Bedford Twin Steer, I think from about 1967."

"Older than you, then? Good God!" he said. "A shower?"

"Well, this is a bit of a cheat. It was like this when we got it. The people who owned it first about, I don't know, twenty years ago—"

"Before you were born."

"Yeah, yeah, before I was born," she said good-naturedly. "They did it up as a camper van for their family, and they used to take it to Europe and live in it for a few weeks, but because they weren't proper travelers they had to have all the trappings, like the cooker and that, and they put this in. It's cool, isn't it?"

He looked at the Heath Robinson workings. A bin of water sat on a substantial shelf at head level. "How does it fill?" he asked.

"Well, that's the downside. You have to fill it yourself, with warm water, so it takes a bit of planning, but it's bliss once you're under it.

When we bought it, all the other travelers on the camp used to queue up to use it. That was another reason we left."

"Couldn't you just say no?"

"That wouldn't be in the spirit of things."

"You've got to be quick, though, I expect."

"Very." Mog laughed. "But it's such a luxury!"

"How come you ended up with such a smart pad?"

"I had some money," she said, reddening. "And Dean traded in his ambulance."

"Ambulance?"

"Don't ask. It was a complete hovel."

He caught a glimpse of the bedroom, a lower chamber at the very back of the bus.

"That's where we sleep. It's really cozy."

"What more could you want?"

"A loo?"

"Well, I didn't like to mention it."

"You dig a pit," she said quickly. "Or you use public ones. I could write a book about where to find the best ones."

"You should."

Mog put up her hands as if to say not me.

"Where do you get your water from?" he asked.

She picked up the kettle. "It depends. Mostly, we figure out where the natural springs are. You can find out by looking at an Ordnance Survey map, and we take it from there. You can be almost sure it's going to be a hundred times cleaner than anything from a tap, but here"—she waved the kettle toward the car park—"we get it from the bogs and boil it."

Jonathan nodded. As they walked back through the bus he thought of her parents, wondered whether they woke every morning feeling sick with worry at the thought of her empty bed, or whether it was possible that they no longer noticed.

Outside, Dean was still thinking about sumps.

"How much, then?" he asked.

"That's academic," Mog said, emerging and taking her very pregnant body carefully down the steps. "It doesn't matter if it's fifty or five hundred, we still can't afford it." She put her arms round his wiry frame. "Shall we have another cup of tea?"

"Let me go and get it," Jonathan said, putting his hand out for the kettle. She looked closer to the full term than he had realized.

"No, I need the exercise. Anyway, you're not allowed in the ladies."

"Let him get it from the blokes, then."

"Dean, there's roughing it and then there's roughing it."

"It's all the bloody same. Still gone through at least seven different livers by the time you drink it. And you're too bloody posh, you are." He smiled at her and she put her face up for his kiss.

Over a second cup of tea, since Jonathan was in no hurry, they talked about the baby.

"We think it's due in a fortnight. I was a bit slow on the uptake," Mog said. "I didn't realize I was pregnant for quite a long time."

"Which is the understatement of the fuckin' year," Dean said, picking tobacco from the end of a new roll-up.

"We'll have to get some petrol for the motorbike. We've timed it. It takes eight minutes to get to the bus stop, one comes on the hour every hour and it takes forty minutes to get to the hospital, so if we leave the minute I get my first contraction, we should be okay."

"We don't want to leave too early," Dean said. "If we get there too early, they'll be swarming round us like flies, telling us what to do, how to do it, probably even what to call the poor little sod. We don't want all that crap."

"The way we see it, childbirth has been going on for all time, so, you know, we want our baby to come into the world without all those bright lights and people in green masks staring at her and pumping her full of drugs or whatever."

"Him," Dean corrected.

"Her," Mog replied.

It was an innocent argument, delivered in a way that made Jonathan realize they thought they were the first to have it.

"What are your plans if something goes wrong?" he asked, feeling obliged to put it up for discussion.

"Like what?"

"Like a bus not coming?"

"We'll go on the motorbike."

"Or the motorbike not starting." He looked at it and tried to imagine it carrying a woman in labor.

"It will," Dean said. "It always does."

"Or Mog going into labor in the middle of the night?"

"I've got the number of a twenty-four-hour taxi firm."

"Have you got a phone?"

"There's one in the village."

"There's not much to go wrong, is there?" Mog added. "We'll be fine."

They looked so full of confidence that Jonathan didn't want to frighten them with the list of possibilities.

NIALL WAS ALSO TRYING TO DRAW UP A LIST OF POSSIBILITIES—ANY POSsibilities, all possibilities—since the most likely possibility was too impossible to even contemplate. There was almost half a pint of Guinness still in his glass on the bar which he'd gingerly been taking sips from since he'd heard what Roy Mundy had to say.

It was the first round at the Cott he'd been included in that hadn't been in return for one he'd bought earlier—a milestone in local acceptance—but the stout wasn't going down like it should. Something else was going down instead.

"Don't miss a trick, I don't," the spherical Roy Mundy kept chuckling.

Niall wanted the plumber to shut up, but Roy was in full flight. The more he teased, the higher he tugged up his trouser leg. Perched on a high bar stool like a portly gnome, he was now exposing a good six inches of mottled shin. Under normal circumstances, Niall would have had a laugh about it.

"But you don't have to tell us, does 'e, Dave?"

"No," said the landlord, "'cos if 'e don't, someone else always will."

"That's right, my boy," Roy cackled. "So, save for the odd bleddy cloak-and-dagger meeting in a rest area, how's it going up the road?"

"It's what you could call work in progress," Niall said, trying to ignore the cracks about the rest area. Roy and Dave were adamant they had seen him and Emmy in a clandestine rendezvous somewhere called Boxtree. "We've not quite found our feet yet."

"They'll be on the end of your legs," Roy said. His V-neck navy sweater, which reminded Niall of his old school uniform, was at least a size too small for his magnificent beer belly. "That's where I generally find mine."

Niall wondered if he ever got to see them. Perhaps if he did, he wouldn't wear those dodgy black lace-up shoes and nylon gray socks. He had another go at steering the conversation back to something less unsettling. Aga parts would do.

"I drove halfway round the bloody world looking for this place, and it turned out to be a lock-up in some dying factory with vegetation growing out of the middle of the road, with a note on the door saying 'Gone Surfing.' Is that normal?"

"Depends how many feet you've got," Roy said.

"Feet of surf," Dave explained with a pained expression.

As Roy hooted at his own joke, Niall heard Cathal's voice in his head again, muffled words coming from inside the sewing room that he couldn't piece together. "This isn't about Niall, Emmy. This is the one thing in your life that isn't about Niall."

By the time he came to again, Roy Mundy had changed the subject. "Well, then, I knew old Mr. Hart quite well. He was a case, w'un 'e? He was an old bugger, 'e was. I 'spect you've heard that, 'ave you?"

"Funnily enough . . ."

"I don't care, I don't. People can do what they like, can't they?" Roy sipped his beer. "What is it, some sort of hippy commune you've got up there?"

"Nudist hippy commune," Niall said. "I'm only wearing clothes now because I'm here. Usually we all walk around naked. Especially the women." His banter sounded hopelessly flimsy. He could hear Emmy in her sewing room with Cathal. "Right for who?" she was shouting.

"Nudist, is it? 'Ell! What's it you say is wrong with your Aga? Maybe I could fit it in this afternoon, hey, Dave?" He took a long sip, draining the last three inches of ale. "That's what they all think in the village, mind."

"Better not spoil their fun by telling them the truth then."

"Old bleddy Mrs. Partridge up there thinks you'm all on the wacky baccy."

"Jaysus, what a joke."

"We all think it is. We're all having a great laugh."

"Good. It's nice to know you're giving something back to the community."

Roy cackled some more and the two of them realized they liked each other. Niall wished he was in the mood to show it.

"Emmy is Mr. Hart's niece," he said, the Guinness still sitting unhappily in his stomach on top of the rest area conversation. "He left her the house in his will, and—"

"We know that," Roy interrupted impatiently. "And we know you've had Culworthy's up to have a look, and the colored maid who's taken over from Dr. Rawe at the surgery went home apparently sick the other day and then recovered enough to buy a pasty from Cott Stores and start eating it before she even got in the bleddy car. I tell you, we don't miss a trick, we don't."

"So you keep telling me. Anyway, Sita needs to eat, she's still breastfeeding."

"Spare me the details, boy. No, as I said, I don't mind. I like everyone, me." He tapped the bar with his empty glass.

"I'll get that," Niall said, nodding at the landlord.

"You're a funny lot, though, in' you? You've got all this space up there, and you have to drive a couple of miles up the road in separate cars just so you can talk in a bit of privacy."

"It wasn't me."

"Yes, 'twas."

Roy put a five-pound note on a pump, and Niall took it off again, pointing to himself as Dave Kemp filled the empty glass with a pint of Wreckers.

"You're a worse gossip than Eileen Partridge, you are," the landlord said.

"Get on! I seen 'im and his flash bleddy car in the rest area with Mr. Hart's niece, I know I did. Wos' think I am? Stupid?"

"That would be one word." Dave laughed.

"I'll tell you one more time," Niall said, trying to sound as if he was enjoying the wind-up. "It wasn't me. Prove otherwise and I'll buy you a beer every day for the rest of your life."

"That'll be till a week on Tuesday, looking at 'im," Dave said.

"Your twin, was it?" Roy asked.

"My brother, I expect."

"Your brother? I love to see a grown man squirm, I do."

"Was the hood up?" Niall asked.

"T'wadn't the hood that was up, boy."

"What was the other car? A blue Golf?"

"Course it bleddy was. You were there. All right, Jim?"

Jim Best, the electrician, came over to the bar. Same crowd every lunchtime.

"All right, Roy?"

"I'm just telling Mr. O'Connor here, the Boxtree rest area idn't as private as 'e thinks 'tis."

"It's your car there, is it? Partridge'll 'ave your guts for garters, boy. 'Ee can't get his car through the gate."

"I'll go and shift it," Niall said.

"I thought you said t'wadn't yours?"

"It isn't, it's Emmy's." He was relieved to have an excuse to leave after admitting that. He forced the last of his stout down. "Haven't you two got work to do? Like fixing my Aga, for a start?"

"I'll be there d'rec'ly," Roy said.

"And I'll be there just after that," Jim said, his face as straight as a poker.

As he shut the low white door that led from the public bar onto the road, he could hear the three of them coughing and laughing through their Superkings like a coven of witches.

He started his bike with a more aggressive kick than it needed, and pulled away from the pub, wondering where the hell Boxtree rest area was and why every hole in the hedge needed to have a name around here.

He took the first right, heading in the vague direction of Bodinnick but not down a lane he knew. Then he took a left, and at a junction of no fewer than five roads known locally, but not to him, as Star Cross, he took another right. It was like a labyrinth out to trick him. Every road had the same landmarks. Five-bar gates leading to timber companies, driveways to farms, private lanes to big houses.

Just when he thought he had completely lost his bearings, he saw it. Emmy's car, abandoned in the middle of a long, narrow rest area in front of some privately owned woodland. Tracks in the leafy mulch suggested the recent arrival and departure of another car. Well, he could be more specific than that if he chose to be. He could say the arrival and departure of a blue Italian front-wheel-drive with a throaty roar, which belonged to his brother Cathal.

He pulled in and took off his helmet with fumbling fingers. His mind searched for a more palatable scenario. Perhaps she had broken down, and phoned home for help. Perhaps Cathal had been the one to answer. Perhaps he had been hearing things when they were in the sewing room. Perhaps Maya hadn't really thought Emmy was refusing to come out because of Cathal. Perhaps he hadn't really seen them on the stairs, seen their faces.

He tried the door of her car and looked inside. Her bag was on the passenger floor and one of Maya's sweaters was on the back seat, the very thinly striped hand-knitted one he'd bought her at Greenwich Market that had stretched so much it now reached her knees. The hood was still warm.

He leaned against the front of the car, trying to work out why he felt so sick. Why *not* Cathal? He could see why she would find him attractive. But if they were together, how? And when? There were some pieces of the jigsaw that seemed to fit and others that didn't. He tried this way and that way to find the whole picture, picking up the same few bits again and again, turning them to the left, the right, upside down, forcing them. But he just couldn't see it clearly. Stuff was missing.

My God, he thought. What the fuck am I doing here? What am I doing acting like some crazed Peeping Tom? What will I say if they find me?

He heard traffic and panicked. As he turned his bike back toward the road, Cathal's car came over the brow of the hill. He saw Emmy in the passenger seat but her head was bowed. Cathal didn't look exactly full of the joys of spring, either. With white-hot panic boiling in his head, he opened up the throttle, bareheaded, his crash helmet still hanging on the fence. He didn't know how to get out of there fast enough.

17

DEAN WASN'T USED TO FEELING FRIGHTENED, HAVING DEVELOPED A high alarm threshold when he'd cut half his finger off with a Stanley knife at the age of eight and taken himself and the piece of digit to the hospital on the bus. His mother had been "missing" at the time, and when she went "missing" he and his brother used to fend for themselves until they ran out of food, then they'd go and get her from the pub. She always bought them double chips on the way back.

Life had continually thrown stuff at him, so he had grown up believing he could catch most things. But looking at Mog's blotchy face and wide, scared eyes, seeing the wet, slightly bloody sheets he had just taken off the bed, watching the way her back arched and her belly moved, he had an uncontainable fear that he was about to drop the one ball that really mattered.

He sat on a rickety painted stool next to the sofa on which Mog was immobilized and tried to keep his cool.

"Let me just take the motorbike up to the village and phone for an ambulance, yeah? I'll go like fuck. I'll be back before you even miss me."

He pulled the edge of his beard as he spoke. The skin was already red raw underneath.

"No," Mog begged. "I don't want you to leave me. I don't want to be on my own. Please don't go."

He held her left hand in both of his and squeezed. "You'll be all right. We're gonna 'ave a baby, be a little family, yeah?"

Mog's attempt at a smile failed. "It's happening again," she whimpered, lifting her bottom off the cushions and pulling his hand underneath the small of her back. "Can you push it there? Harder than that."

He put his rough splintered hand where she told him, and tried to take the strain. He knew that what she needed was force against force, but he was nervous of making it worse and he couldn't bring himself to press as hard as his instincts told him to. A strange moan kept coming out of her mouth but he could tell she didn't know she'd made a noise. Her taut, swollen torso shifted under her thin white shirt.

"I think these are just the early ones," she tried to say bravely when the contraction subsided. "I think they're going to get a lot worse than this."

He wiped her face with the flannel she boiled with the dishcloth and the tea towel every day. Her light hair was curling and damp round the edges of her face and she looked different, like a kid in bed with a temperature. They didn't have a watch or a clock so he was counting one Mississippi, two Mississippi, three Mississippi under his breath.

"I'll put some music on," he said. "What d'you feel like listening to?"

Mog shook her head and lay back on the pillow. Dean stood, pleased to have an excuse to look away. His legs were shaking and his hands fumbled through the wicker basket of tapes. He slotted a battered cassette the midwife had given them into their precious machine.

"When did we last charge the battery?" he asked, in a desperate attempt to hang on to normality, but she was too far gone for distraction. Her eyes were fixed on a distant internal horizon that he would never be able to reach, no matter how hard he tried.

Ambient ululations—whale noises or womb beats or something—filled the space, making the atmosphere even more surreal. He badly wanted a spliff.

As the plaintive baying on the tape began to compete with Mog's increasingly uninhibited wailing, the noise of a car engine broke through and Dean lost his last reserve of calm. He lurched from his stool, leaped across the floor, through the door and down the steps in one seamless stagger.

"Don't go," Mog shouted. "Please stay, Dean. Please!"

"I'm not going anywhere. There's a car out there. I'll be back in a minute."

Dean waved at Jonathan who felt a physical jolt at the promotion from stranger to friend. He had the Bedford Twin Steer aluminum sump pump in the back of his car between the fishing nets and the beach buckets, but he had a feeling that was no longer why he was here. For once, he had managed to be in the right place at the right time.

"Mog's having the baby," Dean screamed across the car park. "She's having the baby."

Jonathan turned to the four children in the car—his three and Scott—and spoke calmly. "Okay, looks like you may be rock-pooling on your own, kids."

"Why? Who's that man?"

"That's Dean."

"He looks mental," Scott said.

"I think he's trying to tell me his girlfriend is having their baby."

"Uuugh," Jay said.

"Gross," said Scott.

"So she won't be able to show us the sandhoppers?" Asha asked.

Jonathan didn't answer. He was too busy making sure he didn't run over Dean, who had his hand on the driver's door before the car had stopped moving. He saw his terrified face and remembered that alarm, that incapability to believe that anything good could possibly come out of such pain, that complete male helplessness, that awful creeping knowledge that you had led someone you loved to this place and now you had to leave her there.

He could have told Dean to dump it all there and then, because the place Mog was in would soon turn out to be so maternally absorbing, that she wouldn't necessarily notice if he was there or not. But Dean wouldn't have listened.

"Thank fuck you're here, mate," he blubbered. "I don't know what to do. We didn't have time to get into the village for the bus, or anything. It just started happening and she couldn't walk. I don't know what to do, man, I don't know what to fuckin' do."

"Well, the first thing you've got to do is calm down," Jonathan said in the measured voice he had heard Sita use with Jay lately. He hadn't noticed Dean's swearing, and if the children had they weren't showing it. With his dreadlocks pulled back off his face into a ponytail, Dean looked like a baby himself.

"Okay? Calm down," Jonathan repeated, getting out of the car. "Have you called an ambulance?"

"Haven't got a phone. She didn't want me to leave her. I thought I was going to have to . . ."

"Dad?" said Jay, who had got out of the car after him.

Jonathan put his hand on Dean's shaking shoulder. He felt paternal, a hundred years old. "Come on, it's going to be fine. Mog is going to need you to be strong."

"I can't, I can't, I can't. She was all right when we got up, and then . . ."

"We'll call an ambulance."

"She's not going to die, is she?"

"No, she's not." said Jonathan. "She really is not. Don't worry, I know what it's like. I've been through it three times myself. It's okay. It's nature's way. But it's bloody terrifying to watch, I'll give you that."

"Can you come and see her?"

"I will. I'll just deal with this lot. This is Jay."

"Hi," said Jay.

"Sorry, mate," said Dean, nodding at him in apology.

"Get your nets," Jay mouthed through the window to Scott. "Dad, what do you want me to do with Lila?"

"Leave her in the car until she wakes up. Keep checking her, will you? And don't wander off too far. And keep an eye on Asha. And don't go into the sea."

"Dad, I'm thirteen, not three," Jay said, looking at Dean for approval but Dean was heading back into the bus.

"Yes, I know. I'm sorry. But Scott——"

"Scott is fine."

"Good. Keep it that way. No showing off."

"Come on, you two. Leave Dad to deal with this."

Scott legged it out of the car and onto the beach as fast as he could, making sure he got as far away as he could from any possible blood or tears. He'd seen enough of those at home.

"Jonathan?" Dean shouted, reappearing. "She's just had two in the space of a minute."

"Two what?" asked Asha.

"Go with the boys," Jonathan said. "Be a good girl."

The inside of the bus looked different from the other day, smaller and scruffier. The sofa along the window was now a bed. Mog was lying on it, propped up with pillows, her legs open. When she saw Jonathan, she pulled a red Indian throw over herself.

"Hello," she said weakly. She sounded muffled, as if her body was conserving its strength.

"Hi, Mog. Don't worry."

She nodded and Jonathan saw a surge of energy ripple across her stomach.

"Here's another one," she said, bracing herself with a rush of panic. Her whine was barely audible at first and then, from her guts, it became an uninhibited groan. Oh shit, Jonathan thought, watching her bear down.

"Are you pushing?" he asked, failing to hide the alarm in his voice.

"Why? Is that bad?" Dean said.

"Do you feel like you need to push?" Jonathan repeated. He tried for eye contact.

"I think so," Mog sobbed. "I don't know. I don't know what to do. It hurts, it hurts."

Something bigger than him snatched at his insides. He scrabbled in the back of his mind for some forgotten piece of knowledge. First stage, transition, second stage. She was well into the second stage. Sita's labors had been long and slow but Mog had dived straight in at the deep end.

"You'll be okay. I'm just going to call an ambulance," he said quietly, hoping to God there would be a signal on his phone.

"No!" Mog shouted. "No, I don't want to go to hospital. No!"

Jonathan sat on the stool and took her clammy hand. Dean had taken up a new position by the door. He looked ready to run at any time.

"I don't think you've got time to get to hospital even if you wanted to, but listen, we can do this between us, if we all take things calmly, okay? Here's what we're going to do. Dean, you're going to hold Mog's hand and help her to take some long, deep breaths. Try not to push at the moment. Resist the urge if you can by doing lots of little quick puffs. I'm going to phone for an ambulance for back-up and then I'm going to call my wife and she's going to talk us through this, okay?"

He thought of the hushed calm of the delivery suites at the Portland Hospital in London where all three of his children had been born. Then he looked at Mog on the tangled heap of blankets on the sofa from the tip. Some of Dean's fear crept into his own thoughts.

"I'll be back in a minute."

In the car, a round, healthy Lila was sound asleep in her chair, her chin almost on her knees. Was her perilous journey into the world really only six months ago? His fingers trembled over the buttons on his mobile as he called for the ambulance. A pristine map in the driver door pocket told him the beach's proper name and even the grid reference for it. It was his old self's finest moment.

Then he pressed the speed dial button for Sita.

She answered immediately. "Jonathan? What's wrong?" She was on the attack again.

"The children are fine. I'm at the beach and Mog from the bus is in the second stage."

"The beach?"

"What should I do?"

"Mog from the bus? What are you talking about?" Her voice was sharp, impatient. "Where's Lila?"

"She's asleep, right next to me, in her car seat."

"Who's Mog?"

"The pregnant girl from the bus on the beach. I think she's about to have the baby. Like, imminently."

"No, I'm not with you. Start again. Which beach? What bus?"

"I haven't got time to explain fully, but I met some travelers at the beach. I thought I told you."

"Jonathan, we haven't been talking, remember?"

"I know. I'm sorry."

There was a silence while she assimilated the last two words. "So am I."

"Can you help me?" he said.

"Why?" Her tone was a little softer.

He told her everything again, more slowly and in order. It didn't make much sense but she understood one thing: he really did need her.

"I can't do this without you," he said.

"I'm right here."

"Thank God."

"First things first. Have you called an ambulance?"

"Yes."

"Fantastic, good, well done."

"But I don't think it's going to get here in time."

"Hang on."

He heard his wife speak into her desk intercom to the receptionist. Her measured efficiency made him feel a whole universe better.

"I'm back. I've stopped all calls. We'll do this together, okay? You tell me what's happening and I'll tell you what to do about it."

"Yes." His voice was tight.

"Jonathan, are you all right?"

"Yes. Are you?"

"Yes. Listen, I'm going to give you instructions, okay?"

"Yes. Yes, that's what I want."

"You won't mind me bossing you about? Giving you orders?"

"No."

"Sure?"

"Yes."

"Well, the first thing to do is to get something, a blanket or a towel or something, to keep the baby warm when it arrives. We don't want to waste precious time looking for something once the baby's out. That's really important."

Jonathan heard the word "we" and started to accept again that there might actually be a baby and not a tragedy at the end of all this.

"Okay, I'm going back into the bus," he said. "If I lose the signal, I'll phone you back. Or you could try me."

"Yes, don't worry."

"Dean," he said, leaping back into the bus, "I've got my wife on the phone. She's a doctor, and she's done this loads of times before from both ends. It's water off a duck's back for her. I'm going to take instruction from her and pass it on to you, yes? Okay, Mog? My wife is called Sita, she's right here, and she's really good at this kind of thing. We'll be fine now."

Dean nodded.

"She says we must find something to keep your baby warm. A towel, or a soft blanket or something."

"I'll talk to you about water off a duck's back later," Sita told him when he came back on the phone. "How far on do you think she is? Can you see the baby's head?"

"Not from where I'm standing."

It was her turn to think of the Portland. Jonathan had kept a safe distance from the sharp end of his children's births. He wasn't going to enjoy this. "You are going to have to look, Jon."

She heard him take a deep breath.

"Mog, do you mind if I just take a look to see if the baby's head is visible? Is that okay? Imagine I'm a midwife."

"Well done," said Sita. "Stay calm, help her to take long breaths. What can you see?"

Jonathan put his hand gently on Mog's left knee and parted it a little, but as he bent down to check the phone fell from under his chin.

"Dean, if I give you instructions, do you feel able to carry them out? I can't talk to Sita and do this at the same time." It was more appropriate anyway, for Dean to be close to Mog in that way.

Dean shook his head. He was holding Mog's hand and wiping her forehead with the wet flannel. Drips ran down her face and she pushed him away.

"I . . . I . . . no, I . . . I don't think . . ." he said. He looked green.

"Don't make him, darling," Sita said when Jon picked up the phone again. "You'll probably be more useful. Keep putting the handset down. I can hear you."

"Okay, Dean, it's okay, you just hang on to Mog. Sita, I'm putting the phone down on the sofa."

Sita heard the soft calm of his voice. "There it is. Hey, wow, I can see the baby. I can see dark hair."

Mog and Dean squeezed hands.

"Yes," he said, back on the phone. "I can see it."

"She's really close, then. You arrived just in time. Right, just let her push the baby out at her own rate now. The next contraction, she'll want to push, so let her."

Mog was already having one.

"Little pushes, Jon, if she can—try and get her to control them. Gentle pushes if she can."

"Okay, Mog, with me, little breaths like this."

Sita heard her husband doing what they had done together with each of theirs. She quickly brushed away a couple of tears.

The contraction ended. Mog was whining intermittently. She could feel her energy leaving her. "It hurts, it hurts, it hurts."

"I bet it does."

"Tell her she's doing well, to think how well she's doing. Come on, encourage her."

"Good girl, Mog. Nature does this all the time. You're doing really well. Be brave—you'll soon have a baby. Come on."

Another contraction came.

"And again?" Jonathan asked his wife.

"What can you see?"

"The head still."

"Keep her going."

"Go with it," Jonathan told Mog. "Go on, push. I can see the crown. Maybe even the forehead."

"That's it," Sita said down the phone, hearing Mog's familiar noise. "Good girl. Push as hard as you can."

"Push," urged Jonathan. "As hard as you can."

With one heave, the baby's head found its way out into the world, face down. It wasn't just blue, it was a deep shade of navy. Jonathan's heart banged against his chest.

"There, the head is out. Good girl," he said, already imagining the worst. He thought his own heart had stopped for a minute. "Sita? Remember Jay?"

She heard the sheer panic.

"Is it blue? Feel around the neck for the cord, feel for the softness of the cord. It's probably still pulsating. You'll be able to put your fingers under it if it's there. Can you do that?" She knew it was the equivalent of him asking her to jump out of an airplane.

"No," he said.

"Yes you can, you can. Imagine it is me. Imagine it is Lila in there. Please, quick Jon."

Jonathan put his fingers gently round the squashed wet little head of Mog's baby. "Yes. I can feel it." It was warm and throbbing and very very soft.

"Loop it over the baby's head. Hold the baby gently, don't pull it. See if you can gently loop it over."

He put his fingers under the cord and eased it out. For a moment, it felt as if it was too short, or stuck, but the blueness of the face, the thought of Sita and Lila, made him try again. It came in a trice, a quick slip.

"It's there," he told Sita.

"Good. Now watch this little miracle. The head should turn to the left or the right so it can get its shoulders out. You can ease them out if you want. Don't worry if it's still blue."

Sure enough, the tiny throttled head shifted.

"Yes," he spluttered down the phone. "Yes!"

"Oh, Jon, well done! Bloody good for you! Well done!"

Jonathan put his hands back round the baby's neck, and with a slither and a gush of fluid he delivered the baby up onto Mog's stomach.

"There's Mummy," he said, "Look, it's Mummy. That's it. Towel, Dean, quick."

The new father laid a light-brown towel and a knitted patchwork blanket over his silent child. Mog tucked it in and laid her hands on the small still body as she said, "Hello, hello, hello," over and over again, stroking the baby's rumpled, choked face.

"He's a little boy," Dean wept. "A little boy, are you? Hey?"

"I can't hear anything," Sita said quietly. "Jon, is the baby breathing?"

"I can't tell."

"Are the waters clear? Tell me if you can see any meconium—dark fluid." On the other end, she let the tears roll. The sensation of salt water on her cheeks was almost alien, it had been so long.

"I can't."

"Wrap the baby, darling, and keep it warm. Dry it as quickly as you can."

"It's wrapped."

"No!" Sita heard Dean shout as if he had come out of a coma. "Why is he blue?"

Everyone felt the same surge of alarm.

"Rub the baby gently with another towel, little circular movements to get its circulation going," Sita shouted. "Wipe round his mouth and nose, get the mucus out of the way if you can."

"Yes."

"Jonathan? I'm waiting to hear a cry. I really need to hear a cry." Even her voice was strained to the limit now.

"So do I. Shall I smack him?"

Everything was very, very quiet.

And then it happened: a little mew, followed by a slightly louder one which turned into a soft bawl.

"There it is! That's it!" She could tell Jonathan was crying too now. Suddenly, all talk merged.

"You did it."

"It was you."

"He's beautiful. Look at him, look at him."

"I love you."

"I'm so proud of you."

"I'm sorry. I'd forgotten how."

"So had I."

"Look at us."

Jonathan held the phone to his cheek as closely as Mog held her cheek to her little boy.

"Thank you, sweetheart," he whispered. "Thank you."

"You complete hero," Sita told him. "Well done, Jon, well done."

"Sita, can you come? I want you here."

"Do you?"

"Yes."

"Then I'm on my way."

And as Jonathan looked at Mog and Dean and their baby son, the blue of the fresh newborn face slowly and certainly turned to pink.

"Thank you," he said, into the phone, walking away for his own private moment. "I don't know what I would have done without you."

"You'd have coped."

"No, I wouldn't."

"Yes, you would."

"But thank God for you."

"And you."

"Yes."

"Just remember that," she said. "I'll see you in a minute. Put the kettle on."

"I will. I love you, Sita."

"And I love you too, Jon. I really do."

IN THE GARDEN, MAYA WAS WAITING FOR AN "I'M ME" MOMENT TO arrive. She hadn't had one for a while, not since Mum had started locking herself in her sewing room. She was really looking forward to one—that funny, slightly spooky feeling that she was the one and only, that confirmation that she knew exactly who she was. They never came when you summoned them, though.

"Whatever she's supposedly making in that bloody room, it'd better be good," Niall had said sarcastically at supper last night, when Emmy's chair remained empty yet again. "It isn't anything," Maya had told him in secret later. "I know what Mum's like. She won't let me in to have a look. If she had done something, she'd show me. I bet it's just a load of half-started stuff like it usually is. I bet she's not working at all. Can't you smell the smoke?"

Now that Maya knew eggshell days were a continuing theme, she had decided she could more or less ignore them. She had even nearly been brave enough to go to the beach with the others without asking, in a defiant stand against her recent enforced grounding, but she'd lost her nerve at the last minute when she'd seen the red rims of Emmy's eyes. Better to make her own fun outside, within shouting distance but out of hissing range.

There were some things still to be thankful for. In London she would have been cooped up in the flat, forced to be in a bad mood too. She could remember all too clearly the way she used to feel before venturing into her mum's tiny bedroom once the tiny television in the tiny sitting room got a tiny bit boring, and asking her in a tiny voice when she was going to get up. It was about being a tiny bit frightened of getting shouted at, a tiny bit frightened of seeing her mum crying again, and a lot of being utterly bored with it all.

Now she could look on the bright side. At least she wasn't the only one who had to deal with them. At least she had Niall on tap whenever she wanted him. At least everything here was the opposite of tiny, even if it was the bad mood.

She ran between the massive granite gateposts that led to the main road, and hopped back over the low brick wall. As she landed, she felt the boggy marsh mud seep into the gap between her ankle and her trainer. The noise it made when she pulled her foot out was lovely, but she was too concerned about the hacksaw and the pruning shears in her pocket to do it again. She patted the side of her coat. The tools she needed to cut a big enough gap in the bushes to get the yellow dinghy through were safe inside, ready for work.

She and Jay had discovered the dinghy in the store, folded up behind the tractor. At first they'd ignored it, stepping on it, thinking it was an old coat or something, but then she'd noticed the rope and the oar-locks.

Jay had only started to help once she'd shouted, "Boat," so really it was more hers than his. If she'd shouted, "Old coat," he wouldn't have bothered.

Never mind, she thought philosophically, you live and learn. When you find something you would prefer to keep all to yourself, you keep your mouth shut. He had found the foot pump, though, and he'd made his calves ache by inflating it so quickly, so she'd promised she wouldn't take it on the water without him. But he'd have to hurry up. If he wasn't back by the time she'd finished cutting back the bamboo, she'd told him, she would carry on without him.

EMMY SAT AT HER SEWING MACHINE, HER BOTTOM ACHING FROM THE hours and hours she had sat in the same position. The chair was hard and the wooden base pressed into her increasingly fleshless buttocks. She wouldn't be surprised if she had a bruise, or the equivalent of a bed-sore, if she could find the time to look.

Her foot pressed determinedly down on the pedal, her hands

splayed on the meter of red satin as it trundled through the machine. On the floor were piles of fur, net and canvas. On the shelves were bags of zips, velcro, buttons.

She seamed, she zig-zagged, she reversed stitch. She smoked, stood up, walked around, had a think, then she sat back down again and set the stitch selector from smocking to stretch.

She was working like a woman possessed, because she *was* a woman possessed. She was pushing herself beyond her limits for the second time in her life, whipped on not by her own body but by the demons in her mind. She had to exorcise them. She *would* exorcise them. She *would* rise out of these ashes. She had to.

She made blind hems, fancy hems and buttonholes. She smoked some more, carefully, out of the window, away from the fabric. Then she cut out appliqués, ignoring the sore pads on her fingers from all the scissor use, tacked in zips and attached velcro. When she made even the slightest error, she unpicked and repositioned. This had to be good. This had to be her best. She urged herself on. Come on Emmy. Push yourself. Believe in yourself. Show everyone you can do it. Get a life.

As she sewed, and pinned and tucked, she dreamed up things to say to Cathal, words to comfort Niall, examples to set Maya. When she thought she could do no more, she stretched her limbs, oiled the machine, replaced the needle, adjusted the bobbin. I will show them, she thought. I'll bloody show them. What she didn't realize was that she was already way into the second stage of showing herself.

THERE WAS A LOT OF WEED ON THE SURFACE OF THE POND WHICH MAYA decided to use to her advantage. If it was anchored by the green sludge, the dinghy was less likely to drift off before she was ready for it. She freed her trainers from the mud, took up the broom handle and pushed it as far as she could into the squishy ground. Then, using it as a stabilizer, she put one foot and then the other into the boat. It wobbled a little and Jay's pumping efforts began to look less impressive.

The front section could do with more air but she decided that the water was collecting in the bottom because she had climbed in too clumsily, and she was pleased with herself for bringing a beach bucket to bail it out.

She pulled the broom handle out and balanced herself with it. As soon as she found a little confidence in the floating properties of her vessel, she took her coat off and sat on it. The water permeated both the coat and her jeans, immediately soaking her bottom, not that she cared. Then she poked her stick into the bank to launch herself off, looking around for the oar she had brought from the store, a squat plastic paddle. She needed it to clear a path through the tangled weed, but it wasn't in the boat. Then she remembered. She had left it on the road, on the other side of the wall by the posts. Damn. Anyway, it was too late. She was away from the bank.

The boat could barely fight its way through the vegetation without help and she started to use the bucket. The water wasn't as cold as she'd thought it would be, but it was smelly, reminding her of rotten eggs or school cabbage.

If she could get to the other side of the pond without falling in, she would claim it as a success. She'd have to pick some of the yellow rhododendrons as proof, though, otherwise Jay would never believe her.

CATHAL HAD HIS PROOF BUT IT HAD GOT HIM NOWHERE, AND THERE was nothing left to do. He was giving in and leaving. As the wheels of his car crunched their way reluctantly down the drive, he wished he had at least been able to say good-bye to Maya properly.

He hadn't slept for more than three hours at a time for the entire duration of his stay, which felt a lot longer than a mere five nights. He could see the last few grains of sand in the egg timer of opportunity dropping through the glass. He had tried everything he could to encourage Emmy to see it from his point of view, but she couldn't. He had even tried to persuade himself to bulldoze through regardless, to tell Maya and Niall himself, to push on with disclosure, to deal with the fallout single-handedly. But he just couldn't do that, either. The only fatherly thing he could possibly do was to leave, and so restore the mother to the child. Everything else would have to wait.

A dull envy lingered in him as he pulled himself away. Apart from Emmy, everyone at Bodinnick had made him feel welcome. He wished he could have responded more enthusiastically, been freer with his usually easy sense of fun and his gratitude, behaved less like a guest and more like just another member of the household. But he had been permanently wary of his responsibilities, straitjacketed by a fear that Emmy would turn it against him. He had never reacted to warmth quite so gingerly.

He felt completely empty and barely knew which way to turn as he approached the gateposts, but as he did he caught flashes of an orange and purple hat through the bamboo, and a glimmer of hope reappeared. Maya? He'd thought she was at the beach with the others.

His mind had played enough tricks on him lately for him not to trust it, so he stopped the car and kept watch. The orange and purple hat flashed past again, and this time he could make out a slight body beneath it, sitting in an inflated craft. He could tell, even with all the bamboo in the way, that the boat was gliding quite proficiently.

From the car window, he saw the gap that had been cut in the hedge. The pruning shears and the hacksaw were on the ground and two huge gunnera leaves lay on the drive.

His car inched on over the stalks, his mind less committed to leaving now, past the huge Cedar of Lebanon, past the line of granite mushrooms, through the granite posts he'd probably never be invited through again. He pushed himself on. Then he saw the discarded oar.

That was it. The olive branch. The excuse. The prop that would allow him to say good-bye. He pulled his car to one side of the faded tarmac apron in front of the low wall and got out. Just a good-bye, until they could say a proper hello. With the oar in his hand, he had an excuse. A shout from the bank would suffice.

On the other side, the edge of the pond was only just discernible from the mossy bank. He walked along the narrow, marshy edge, following her footprints, occasionally accidentally turning his foot over and staggering into the water. When he reached the gap she had cut in the gunnera, he saw drag marks of what must be the bottom of the boat. He also saw the sharp stone sticking up like a shark's fin in the middle of them, and the possibility that she might have ripped the rubber planted itself in his mind.

Everything he could see was green. The edges of the pond were green, the hedges around it were green, the weed on the pond was green. He couldn't see any orange and purple flashes anywhere. He scanned the scene for color. Then, with a stab of alarm, he saw the yellow dinghy, floating on its own in the middle of the pond.

EMMY, STOPPING FOR A GLASS OF water, HEARD THE SHOUT AND WONdered idly what it was that Niall wanted Maya so urgently for. She thought he had gone cross country for an Aga part to see if he could get the cooker going again. A cold Aga was a strange and dead beast, she thought, touching it with her bare hand, which still throbbed from the vibration of the sewing machine.

She was in the kitchen, enjoying a freedom she hadn't tasted since Cathal's arrival. Ever since she had seen his good-bye note and checked that his car had gone, she had been wandering freely from room to room, taking stock of what had been going on in her enforced absence, enjoying the knowledge that she couldn't turn a corner or open a door and walk into him anymore.

Being downstairs again after so long in her garret reminded her of times in her childhood, before her mother had died, when she was allowed to get up after a day or two of illness. The house always looked tidier than she remembered it, more ghostly, like a stage set. Everyday things seemed unfamiliar. Smells seemed strange. There was the remainder of an apple crumble in the fridge that she hadn't seen either baked or eaten, there was mail on the side she hadn't sifted through, there was half a bottle of wine left by the Aga that she hadn't opened. It always struck her as otherworldly that normal life could go on without her.

"*Maya?*" she heard again.

This time, she turned off the tap and tried to work out what it was about Niall's voice that wasn't right. There was a politeness or a caution in it that wasn't usually present.

"*Maya!*"

The moment she realized what it was, she ran from the house in her socks, screaming the same name, only louder.

CATHAL WAS DOWN TO HIS BOXER SHORTS, T-SHIRT AND BARE FEET before he knew it. The coldness of the water didn't register as he waded in up to his knees, not even feeling the slimy clay and sharp grit between his toes. He yelped when the water hit his balls, but forced his cumbersome body to surge through the weeds, clawing back the green fronds, trying not to let them tie him down.

"*Maya! Maya!*"

He was breathless but his roar, which came from the pit of his stomach, could be heard at the farm. Not so far away, Mog was making a similar noise and Mrs. Partridge would later claim she'd heard that one, too.

The surface of the weed was broken around the boat, which bobbed knowingly up and down. Emmy's high-pitch scream reached his ears above the splashing:

"Where is she?"

He was working too hard against the vegetation to reply.

"Cathal! What's happening? Where's Maya? Is she all right?"

Emmy started to run round the pond's edge. It felt as if she had been scalped. Cathal was panicking—she could tell by the way his head swiveled, searching. Then she noticed his clothes heaped on the side. She had to reassess. He hadn't gone out in the boat with her. Perhaps he was rescuing her. Perhaps his presence was a godsend.

"Maya!" she shouted. "Maya, Cathal's coming. Hang on, Maya. Cathal's coming."

She ran, watching the surface of the pond, waiting for something to break. Cathal had reached the boat. He pulled the side down to check that the child wasn't lying still, for a joke, out of view. Maya's orange and purple hat was floating on the bottom, with her coat and four inches of water.

"No, no, no, *no!*" he heard himself cry. "Can she swim?" he shouted. His voice was breaking.

"Yes, she's a really good swimmer. What's happened? Get her for me, please get her!"

Emmy carried on running and he carried on swimming, moving toward each other. Cathal felt the far side of the pond scrape against his torso, and he hauled himself up, blue with cold. When he stood up, Emmy was right there. Weed hung from his hair and his wrists, and he was shivering with fear. The dread in their eyes was the same shade.

"Where is she?" Emmy sobbed. "Where is she? What happened?"

"We'll find her. Don't worry."

He pulled her to him, his hair dripping onto her, and put a tentative bare arm around her. She let him.

"It's going to be all right. She's okay, I know she is. It's just me. I panicked."

"*Maya?*" she shouted as loud as she could. "This is my fault," she said. "My selfishness. My—"

"No, stop that. It's going to be okay."

They started to run round the edge together, looking obsessively at the surface of the water, watching for something they hardly dared imagine.

"Maya?"

Cathal's feet were being cut to ribbons. Emmy's head was shrinking.

"I'm sorry, Cathal. I'm sorry I've been so, so, unable to cope."

"It's okay. Maya?"

The rhododendrons behind them rustled.

"Yes?" said Maya, coming out of the woods. She was clothed but shivering and she had a bunch of yellow rhododendrons in her hand.

Emmy fell on her. Cathal kept his hand on Maya's back, desperate to have equal contact. He let out short bursts of relieved laughter, the remnants of a panic so intense he had thought his world might end. Emmy was repeating her daughter's name over and over again.

"Have you been in as well?" Maya asked Cathal through chattering teeth. "The weed makes it really hard, doesn't it? I did a surface dive."

"Did you?" he tried to say. "Good girl." He spat a mouthful of saliva and pond water into his hand.

"You look like a weird fish," she told him as Emmy ripped off her fleece and put it round her daughter's shoulders. "A creature from the blue lagoon."

Cathal tried to suck in his cheeks. He looked like an old man with no teeth.

"Oh," Maya said, suddenly seeing him with entirely new eyes. "Look, Mum. I can't do that, either."

NIALL SAW THE THREE OF THEM FROM ACROSS THE POND. HE STOOD there, his feet on his brother's clothes, rooted to the spot. Then Cathal saw Niall. Emmy saw Cathal see Niall. Maya saw them all see each other. The earth stopped spinning on its axis for a moment.

"Look at these," Maya said, thrusting the yellow flowers under Cathal's nose. "This is proof, this is."

"I'll see them later," he said, looking toward his brother. "Go inside now with your mum and get warm. I've got to talk to Niall about something."

Maya waved across the pond at Niall.

Cathal looked at Emmy. His eyes searched hers. He was still shivering, still in his boxers, weed still hanging from him.

"Is that okay with you?"

"Yes," Emmy nodded, picking a string of blanket weed from his arm and preparing to usher Maya back to the house. "That's okay with me."

18

"WHY ARE YOU TAKING SO MUCH STUFF WITH YOU IF YOU'RE COMING back?" Maya persevered accusingly. She was leaning against Niall's bedroom door frame, noting every item he put into the three open cases on his bed. Books and music. An ashtray. A halogen desk light. He had already unplugged his computer in the library.

"To make room for Mog and Dean and baby Nathan."

"*Baby Nathan?*" she repeated. Niall was not himself. She looked at him as if to say, Do you think I'm stupid?

"They take up ten times more space than an adult, you know," he said.

"No, they don't."

"Go and take a look in Jonathan and Sita's room if you don't believe me. You can't move in there for nappies and powder, and vests and—"

"That's just them," she interrupted impatiently. "You know what they're like. They all have their own shampoos. And toothpaste. Asha's even got a different toothpaste from Jay."

"Whereas you clean your teeth with a stick and some salt."

"Yeah, and I wash my hair with my own spit."

Niall remembered the times he had taken her out with nothing more than a spare nappy and a packet of baby wipes in his coat pocket. She ate anything, slept anywhere, still did. Just thinking about her made the hole inside him even bigger.

"And my, how it shines."

Maya frowned at him. He could see that now was not an optimum time for joking, but he was doing his best to sound normal, to hide the fact that his heart had been wrenched from its casing and was hanging out on wires, like the light switch on the stairs the electrician was working on.

Twice, Emmy had tried to touch him, to see if she could ground him somehow, but twice she had got a shock. The first time was hardly surprising. It had been too soon after the whole ghastly showdown for there to be a safe connection. He had walked back into the house from the pond like a zombie, and she had leaped out at him from the shadows of the hall, mortified at her own behavior, desperate to talk, pleading with him to trust her, to speak to her. But he hadn't been able even to look at her. His worlds had collided, and the wreckage was still burning.

Niall couldn't shake off the memory of the way his brother's naked body had juddered in time with his voice.

"You need to know something," Cathal had stammered, dripping onto his clothes.

"I do, don't I? What's going on?"

"Nothing. It's not . . ."

"You and Emmy? I don't have a problem . . ."

"Not now, not for years. Just once."

"Once?" Niall had begun to laugh. "Jaysus, ye bastard, I thought you were going to tell me—"

"No, wait. Once, once is all it takes."

"You want to tell me you're in love with her?"

"No, I'm trying to tell you, I'm trying to tell you Emmy got pregnant."

"I know that."

"Not that time, another."

"What other time? How long ago?"

"Well, you know how long."

"W'd ye feck off?" Niall had laughed hopefully, but then he suddenly knew he had to accept it. "No. Not Maya." It wasn't even a question.

"I'm sorry. I would have told you years ago, except I didn't know. It's just come to a head in the last few weeks and . . ."

But coherent thought had stopped there for both of them.

"You must go," Niall had told him. "You must go. Just go. You can't be here. We can't do this. Go on. Go."

Cathal had put his dry clothes back on over his wet body and driven away, sodden and still trembling, because that was the only thing he could do to make it better.

It had been no easier to help Niall after Cathal had left. "I don't want you near me," he kept saying to Emmy, as if she was about to rip off her face mask and reveal an alien. "You feel like a stranger. Leave me alone. Don't touch me."

"I'm sorry," she kept saying. She wasn't crying, so he knew she meant it.

Maya hadn't become a stranger, though. She was still his girl, his lovely girl, and she wasn't prepared to take his exit lying down.

"Mog and Dean have got their own home. It's parked outside the door. Or haven't you noticed?" she persisted, coming in at last and sitting on the bed.

"But it's a bus, Maya. A knackered old bus. And this is a bedroom, in a house, with running water and electricity."

"The bus has got those things."

"Come on, stop being difficult."

"I don't want them here. I want them to go."

"How? Their bus has broken down. It was towed here, remember? Or are you going to push it for them?"

I would if it meant you would stay, she wanted to tell him.

"Well, how long are they staying, exactly?" What she meant was, How long will you be gone?

"They're going as soon as it's fixed."

"Can't *you* sleep in the bus till then? Stay. Please?"

The understanding was only just out of her mind's reach. Her mum seemed less stressed and yet Niall was leaving Bodinnick, Mog and Dean were taking his place and their baby both did and didn't have something to do with it. But to make sense of it, Maya needed the missing links, the other babies, the aborted baby, the baby she used to be. Only Emmy and Niall had those. Only they really knew the nature of the thin-skinned beast that stalked the house. Everyone else was left guessing at its curious footprints and unfamiliar cry.

"Well, I would, if this other problem hadn't come up."

"What other problem? Grown-ups are always saying they have to go because of something 'coming up.' I think it's just an excuse they use when they don't want to stay somewhere. They should be more truthful." She stared at him unforgivingly.

Niall didn't know how to answer. There was no point in fobbing her off, but he could hardly tell her the truth. I am going because I feel betrayed, because your mother has deceived me and my brother has defrauded me and I don't know who anyone is anymore.

He picked up a silver photo frame, a black and white picture he'd taken of her when she was two. All you could see was a chubby cheek, a strand of hair and one runny nostril.

"You're not taking that as well, are you? If you take that, I'll know you're not coming back," she said. She felt like crying. When she'd heard about his row with Kat and that Kat had gone back to London in a huff, she'd thought, Yippee, that's what we want. It hadn't occurred to her for a second that he might follow her.

"I was just looking at it," he said, changing his mind and putting it back on the tall chest of drawers.

"Are you going to live with Kat?"

"No."

"I mean, stay with Kat?"

"No, I'm not going to live with her or stay with her, not least because I wouldn't be welcome. You were right. Kat and I have split up. I'll be at my old flat."

"What about Chris? You said he could have it for at least three months, and it's only been two so far."

"I'll stay in the spare room."

"Stay in the spare room here."

"I can't, my darling."

"Why not?"

"I just can't."

His hand faltered over his Roberts Radio with the duck-egg-blue leather finish Kat had given him for his birthday. It had cost her a hundred ridiculous quid. "Do you want this in your room?"

"It's okay, thanks. Leave it here for the baby."

"Good idea. It's the right color, anyway."

He carried on packing and she carried on watching him.

Eventually, she spoke. "Niall?"

"Maya."

"Can I ask you something?"

"You can always ask me anything," he told her, feeling a shit for knowing he wouldn't always answer her honestly.

"If they wanted to name the baby after Jonathan, don't you think they should have called him Jo instead?"

Shit, he thought, winded by how much he loved her. I think I can live without Cathal and Emmy and Kat, but how the *hell* am I going to live without her?

DOWNSTAIRS, EMMY HELD NATHAN AGAINST HER SHOULDER AND walked rhythmically round and round the kitchen. She was singing a song, making it up as she went along, about sleeping and hope and riding life's storms. In a literary sense, it was rubbish.

But Nathan's birth had come to them all like a very small drop of extra-virgin oil on deeply troubled water, and that made no sense, either. The arrival of a new baby should wreak havoc in an already turbulent house, but somehow it had simplified it. He cried when he was hungry, and he slept when he was tired. He was showing them the secret of truly simple living. Perhaps Toby had sent him. Perhaps Toby had sent them all here, to burst her bubble, to set her free.

Emmy's bubble had finally burst, at the pond side. It had been such a precarious one, way too big for its own health, and it had wobbled and shaken and come so perilously close to so many sharp edges so often before that she'd always known it was going to burst one day. And now that it had, she felt released. As if it had been her prison rather than her sanctuary.

She had been bad. Worse than useless. Her breakdown—because that's what it felt like—had stretched the elasticity of friendship to the limit. It hadn't snapped it, but that was no thanks to her. That was down to Sita and Jonathan, Niall and Maya. It wouldn't happen again. She would make it her life's work not to let it.

Her free hand picked up one of the half-full packets of cigarettes that she had scattered around the house and her foot pressed the pedal on the trash can. As she threw it in, she took a lungful of the new air blowing through the kitchen and it tasted of reconciliation and acceptance. She could actually taste the calm after the storm.

Cathal's exit had been terrible, but at least it had brought a form of closure with it. The last she had seen of him was when she had picked the blanket weed off his arm, but that simple gesture and his simple question—"Is that okay with you?"—were a resolution of sorts, a good enough beginning and a fair enough end. She knew he had given control back to her. On her phone was one text message she had yet to delete which just said, THANK YOU.

Niall's departure was going to be even worse but, in the wake of everything that had already passed, it was nothing she couldn't cope with. They would sort it, somehow, sometime. It was a new experience to feel wrung out but not devastated. Eleven years of keeping a secret had come to an end, and she felt overwhelming relief peeping through the sadness.

It was good, too, being left with the baby. She felt endorsed by being considered suitable, by being viewed as the hands of experience, by enjoying the bestowal of someone's confidence.

Mog had wanted to wake Nathan and take him with her to go and get some cloth nappies and a feeding bra, but the only baby seat was in Sita's car and Sita was at work. Besides, it had been raining.

"He'll stay asleep till you get back," Emmy had promised. "He's just had a bucketful of milk. You'll be with him again in twenty minutes. It won't matter, I promise."

She'd made Nathan's tiny paw wave at Mog through the window as Jonathan's car pulled off. Don't worry, she'd mouthed.

Six days old. Warm and soft. Breathing and helpless. His own complete little independent soul. When she'd held Maya like this, she'd felt almost swamped by responsibility. She used to believe that every ounce of Maya's happiness, her character, her safety, her success, all of it depended on her own maternal strength. She used to think that Maya would become whatever she, Emmy, made her. It was a belief that both terrified and empowered her, but now, holding Nathan, she could see that she had been wrong. Maya was herself, the sum of nobody's parts. In the long run, it wouldn't matter too much who her parents had or hadn't been.

"As long as you all find a loving connection," she said to the white hump breathing into her neck, thinking it felt as if most of the last ten years had happened in the last ten days. Thank God that the choices she had made for Maya seemed to have had such little overall effect. There was no consistency, and yet Maya was entirely constant.

But it wasn't Maya who needed help, it was Niall. She kept seeing his ashen face, his body pole-axed in the hall. He had been motionless, as if someone had filled his boots with concrete, trapped him in a force field that she couldn't penetrate, one that he couldn't escape from, either.

The baby lurched in sleep, his tiny hands flying open, as if to catch a passing branch as he fell.

"Ch, ch, ch, ch," Emmy whispered but his eyes were already closed again.

Here was Nathan, dragged into the big wide world by naïveté and carelessness, already managing to be himself. His own sweet, pink-faced postnatal mother was somewhere else, letting out the invisible umbilical cord to an unimaginable length, painfully aware that every minute that passed was another minute away from her baby. But Nathan slept and dribbled against the ribbed cotton of an unfamiliar sweater, oblivious. The dark shriveled stump of his cord would soon fall off and reveal a perfect knot. He fed himself now.

"No one owns you, do they?" Emmy said to the crown of dark hair. "You own yourself." Her palm practically covered the baby's back, and she kept it firmly against the white ribbon-edged fleece of his tiny jacket, pressing him to her.

From behind, Niall could only see a rumpled forehead and two confused eyes peeping above the parapet of Emmy's shoulder. She had lost weight. Her checked drawstring trousers fell over her bottom more loosely than they had two months ago. Her hair was longer, tied in a simple ponytail. From the back, she looked twenty-one again.

He'd thought he was ready to leave, but seeing her like that, imagining she was holding their long-gone baby, he realized he wasn't. He realized he probably never would be. But he also knew he had no choice.

Supposing their own little fusion had made it farther than an embryo after all, supposing it hadn't been pulled away from its life-support system, picked like a flower still in bud, and chucked on the ground to die. Supposing they had got it right as Mog and Dean had, allowed it to stay in place, attached to the placenta, feeding and sucking and growing all its bits in the right places until it was ready to come out. And supposing it had come out in its own time, when it was ready, and no one in a green coat and a mask had dragged it out with sterile implements, or left it in a steel tray to wither and cease. What then?

He wanted to believe that the little ghost that floated somewhere at the back of their lives was not after all a ghost, but a human child that had once worn nappies and screamed and kept them both awake at night and was now a teenager, stropping around, putting its big feet all over the furniture, nicking beers from the fridge.

He also wanted to believe that Maya wasn't the product of a lazy shag between his ex-girlfriend and his greedy brother, that she was his, that she had been planned and wanted and conceived in excitement and anticipation and lust and love while their three-year-old, the little knitted slug that he had just seen in flashback on his mother's shoulder, slept in his cot.

Niall wondered if he was going stark raving mad.

"Hi," Emmy said softly. She'd sensed him behind her a while ago.

He raised his eyebrows in reply. His teeth were clenched behind his tight lips. He wanted to hold her, just once more, to feel a newborn baby between them.

"I'm on my way," he said.

"I wish you wouldn't go." She started to move toward him and felt a shot of pain as he backed off.

"I have to."

"Why don't you stay for Mog and Dean's send-off? They'll be gone soon. They really want you to."

"I can't."

"Please?"

He was silent.

"We should talk about it," Emmy said. "It could be a beginning."

"It's an end, Emmy."

Her hand left Nathan's sleep-suited feet and reached for his arm. He could smell the baby on it.

"Please don't say that."

"I will. I'm not going to say what I think you want to hear anymore. It's not good for anyone."

"I'm sorry."

"Will you say good-bye to Maya for me? I can't."

"I know you can't. Niall, listen to me."

"No, I can't listen to anyone."

And he walked back out again, placing one foot in front of the other, forcing himself not to look back but in no state to see very far ahead, either.

Jay found Maya crying in her bedroom.

"Sorry," he said.

"It's okay."

"I didn't know you were crying."

"Well, you do now."

"Do you want to talk about it?"

"No."

He had picked up a few useful hints about female behavior lately, so he stood there for a while, deliberating whether or not to admit something. Eventually, he found the courage. "I cried last night, too."

"Did you?" Maya was a little bit interested. Jay usually pretended he had something in his eye.

"Yeah."

"Why?"

"Because I don't want to go back to London."

"Who says we're going back to London?" Maya sniffed.

"What else do you think we're going to do if the house is sold?" It was the first time he'd said it out loud, and it made him feel even angrier than when he said it to himself.

Maya shrugged. She didn't care where they lived, as long as it was with Niall.

"We will, you know."

Maya still didn't talk.

"So I was thinking it might be time for some 'direct action,'" Jay said cautiously. He needed her with him on this.

She wiped her face, leaving dirty streaks across her freckled cheeks. "What's that?"

"It's when you take matters into your own hands."

"Oh."

"Do you want to tell me what you're crying about?"

She thought about it. Six weeks ago she wouldn't have told him, but then six weeks ago he wouldn't have asked. "I don't want Niall to go," she said.

"Well, the bad news is, he's already gone."

Her blotchy face crumpled again and he went to sit next to her, uninvited, on her purple appliqué quilt with the big pink stars.

"But he's coming back." Jay didn't believe it himself.

"Why did he go, then?" she snapped, as if it was Jay's fault.

"He had his reasons," he said darkly.

Actually he had no idea, nor did he understand why his parents had started to behave like themselves again, or why Emmy was up and about, leaving her sewing room, being normal. Or why there were travelers in a bus outside. Nothing that any of the adults had done ever since they got here made sense. Just as things were settling down, just as summer was really here, they were selling out. Most people came to Cornwall for the summer, not left.

"Do you want to go back to London?" he asked Maya.

She shrugged.

"Do you want to stay here, then?"

She shrugged again.

"Okay, do you want to be here more than you want to be in London?"

"Maybe." She didn't want to tell him that she wanted to be wherever Emmy and Niall were most likely to make friends again.

"Look, the grown-ups are crap. They don't really know what they're doing." Jay spoke in a conspiratorial whisper. He picked at a sticker she had put on her white wooden bedhead. "They should listen to us for a change, let us make some decisions."

"Oh, like they'd let us."

"Well, I think we should at least try. I've got no intention of going back, not after all this. We can't go back to our old houses. Other people live in them now."

"We can go back after three months, stupid. And another few weeks isn't going to kill anyone."

Jay ignored her. "Do you want to know a secret?"

"Yeah."

"Well, I heard them say they were definitely going to have another house meeting after supper, once we're in bed. I think it's the big one. We've got to try and listen. Once we know what the plan is, we'll have our own house meeting. We'll beat them at their own game. Come with me. Don't you dare say anything about this, right?"

The spy hole he'd found was perfect. It was down a medieval stone staircase which led from a closed door on the landing down to the kitchen. It was never used, because the door leading from the kitchen was permanently locked, besides being blocked by an oak church pew in front of it, and the key had been lost years ago. Anyway, in the winter, it would have been too cold to leave the doors open, either at the top or the bottom, because the staircase was a funnel for the wind. It was also a funnel for sound.

The back rest of the pew in the kitchen was a little lower than the keyhole, and the gap between the door and the wooden frame was just wide enough for you to press your ear against it and hear what people were saying. The most useful thing was that the pew ran along one side of the table, and Sita usually sat at the door end.

"If we're lucky, we should be able to get every word," Jay said.

"Not if the music is on."

"Nick the machine, then. Say you can't get to sleep without a tape."

"No," Maya said. "You say that. You're the one with sleeping difficulties."

He couldn't dispute it. "Anyway, the way Mum and Dad were talking, it's not going to be a music sort of evening," he told her grimly.

NIALL'S SWOLLEN FACE LOOKED AS IF HE HAD BEEN IN A FIGHT, BUT HE didn't care. He wanted to prolong the agony of his departure with one last pint in the Cott. He was still in that force field, not knowing how to break out, unable to remove himself from the place where he so wanted to be.

He knew he needed to leave Cornwall, but for the moment he couldn't. Beer usually helped, and he thought he had timed his drink carefully to avoid the regulars. Not carefully enough, though. As he walked out the back door from the public bar and up the slope that led to the car park, he bumped into Roy Mundy.

"Hello, boy. Why have you got a motorbike in the back of your van? I don't miss a trick, I don't."

"Yes, you've told me that before," Niall said joylessly.

"Well, I'm old. I repeat myself."

"I've got to go back to London. I've had to hire the van just to take my stuff back."

"Coming down again, are you?"

"No. It didn't work out."

"You've only just bleddy arrived. You can't tell me it's all over already."

"Yep." Niall kicked a few stones around to give him a reason for looking at the ground.

"You all right, boy?"

"I'll live."

"That's a shame." Roy tried a chuckle, but it got no response. "We'll miss you."

"Yeah. The others aren't leaving, though. They'll still be needing you."

"I wasn't thinking about work, boy. I was thinking about my lunchtime pint."

"You've got Jim. You'll be all right."

Roy thought he'd have one last crack. "Women troubles, is it?"

"You got it."

"That's all right, then. You'll be back," Roy said cheerfully. "I'll put a drink in d'rectly."

"I appreciate it," Niall said. "Cheers, Roy. Say good-bye to Jim for me."

"See you, boy." He limped into the pub, his hand up. "Go careful, mind."

The fat old plumber with the dodgy shoes and long line in acrylic school jumpers shouldn't have said that. It meant that Niall missed the opportunity to say good-bye to Jim Best in person, because when the electrician pulled in for his lunchtime pint Niall was too busy dealing with something in his eye to be able to look up and acknowledge him.

―――――

DARKNESS FELL.

"It's a lot of money," Jonathan said.

"A million pounds," Asha whispered too loudly outside the door behind the pew.

"I've told you," Jay whispered back crossly. "You're only allowed here if you keep quiet."

Maya watched her mother twist a curl of burgundy foil from the neck of the wine bottle round and round her index finger. Her nails were bitten to the quick.

"You might be better off with it in your bank account," Jonathan said.

"Money aside, I feel I ought to say sorry to you two properly," Emmy said. "I know I've made a complete mess of it."

"We've all done that," said Sita.

Maya looked at Jay. He grimaced and put his finger to his lips. Things were not looking good. He was right. This meeting did sound like the big one.

"So," asked Jonathan, "do we use Niall's departure as an incentive to regroup, or do we all pack up now and go with him?"

Maya's heart leaped. Jay's sank.

"We can't go anywhere until Bodinnick is sold," Sita said firmly.

"Why not?" Emmy said.

"Money?" said Sita.

"We can live without savings," said Jonathan.

"But we can't make a clean break if—"

"Don't. You know I can't do it without you," Emmy said feebly. "It's not just your money. I don't want to be here on my own."

"It's not only about you needing us, Em. We need you too."

"Why?"

"Well, for a start, we can't afford to buy Bodinnick off you."

"Have it."

"Don't be silly."

On the stairs, Jay put his head in his hands.

Emmy pulled the coil foil off her finger and stretched it. "You could always stay here and I could go back," she said. "Now that they're happy at school and everything."

Behind the door, Jay crossed his fingers.

"How?"

"You can live here as long as you want, for free. I mean it."

"No, we can't."

"Yes, you can. What's stopping you?"

"It's not right. That wasn't the vision."

"Well, visions change."

The children held their breath.

The adults shifted in their chairs. There was silence.

"Anyone want a beer?" Jonathan said.

"Bloody good idea," Emmy said. "God, I can't bear this." She got up from the table and wandered off, out of earshot.

"Damn," Jay shouted when all three parents had gone. "Why do they *never* stick at anything?"

AN HOUR AND A HALF LATER, MAYA SAT DOWN ON THE STONE STAIRS again, grateful for her slipper socks. It was funny to think they had all learned to deal with the little things like getting cold feet at night just when it looked as if they'd have to leave. Well, not funny, stupid.

She peeped through the gap. Her mum and Sita were back at the table, sitting opposite each other. They were talking in low voices, but she couldn't see or hear Jonathan. The wine bottle was empty and another one was next to it. Her mum was smoking, and Maya couldn't be sure but it looked as if Sita had a cigarette too. They looked like they had looked at the very beginning, when they'd first come here, before the eggshell days, before Sita started work, when Niall was here. More together again.

She wondered if she ought to go and wake Jay, but he was fast asleep in bed, having talked himself into a coma about Plan A and Plan B, real estate agents and sit-down protests.

She had drifted off next to Asha for a while but something had kept her from real sleep. She had intended to go straight back to her own room and fall asleep under her own duvet but the lure of the spyhole was too strong and she had crept down to find out if she could hear anymore.

The first question she heard almost made her laugh out loud. It sounded like the kind of thing she heard in the playground.

"Who do you think Niall hates most?" Sita was asking. Out of who? thought Maya. It might be the man who first invented Irish theme pubs. He was always going on about them. He'd once said he'd like to bomb them all.

"Both of us," Emmy said. Both of who? Sita and her mum? They were talking rubbish. Niall didn't hate anyone, apart from the pub man. Oh, and the Corrs.

"He won't feel like that for long."

"I don't know. It was so terrible, seeing him when he came back in. I've never seen anyone look like that, you know, as if his whole world had just completely collapsed."

"I have," Sita said. "I've seen you."

"I know. I'm sorry."

"I was seriously worried, you know."

Maya didn't understand. She was getting pins and needles and she shifted her position as carefully as she could. It took her a while to catch the words again after that.

Sita was talking. ". . . didn't occur to me that it was something to do with Cathal. I thought you were having trouble dealing with Niall and Kat. I can't believe you held it together as well as you did then, I really can't."

Maya saw her mother spray a mouthful of wine over the table as she laughed, but it wasn't the sort of laugh that other people joined in.

"C'mon."

"Have you told Maya?"

Maya jumped a little at her name and pressed her ear more tightly to the gap.

"No."

"Are you going to?"

"I don't know. My instincts tell me to trust the situation to work itself out."

"What if she asks?"

"I don't think she will."

"Cathal will stick with that, will he?"

Cathal? thought Maya, feeling the cold through her socks all of a sudden. What's he got to do with it?

"I've got to trust him, too. We both know it's got to be right. And what's he going to do? He's her father, for God's sake. He's going to want to get it right, isn't he?"

Father? Maya thought. Father? What father? Whose father? Then she remembered Cathal's fish face and how it had made him look like an old man.

Suddenly, she didn't want to hear anymore. She picked herself up and got herself back to her room as fast as she could, terrified that someone might catch her.

Her head spun for the briefest of moments. Cathal was her father. Was he? Was he really? Was that the question everyone was waiting to hear her ask? Was it? Well, it could wait. She didn't want to know. She was too tired. She was too disappointed. She wanted Niall. She wanted things to be like they were.

As she got into bed and turned to switch off the bedside light, she noticed Niall's black-and-white picture of her in its silver frame next to her bed. It had been put there to make her think he was coming back, but she knew now it was a good-bye present.

No. He wasn't allowed to say good-bye. If he wasn't going to come back on his own, she would go and get him. And if he had gone because of something to do with the question she was supposed to be asking, even if that question had something to do with Cathal, he could stop behaving like Emmy and grow up, as she had had to do, years ago.

SLEEPING IN THE BACK OF A TRANSIT VAN NEXT TO A MOTORBIKE IN AN unknown rest area because you were too pissed to drive was not very grown up at all, but Niall didn't feel like being mature. He had already made the most adult decision of his life by leaving Bodinnick. He wasn't ready to move on just yet.

The fat old plumber with the dodgy shoes felt like his only friend tonight, although what Roy would make of him chain-smoking, drinking Special Brew and listening to Elvis Costello in a van at midnight, Niall wasn't sure. But then he wasn't at all sure himself.

19

MAYA DIDN'T EAT MUCH BREAKFAST.

"I'm saving myself for Mog and Dean's send-off," she said, but the truth was she had no appetite. Her tummy was empty. It was making weird growling noises. But she couldn't think of one single thing she wanted to put inside it. Not even the smell of pasties in the Aga worked.

It was useful having everyone so preoccupied with Mog and Dean's departure. It meant she could do her own thing, which was turning out to be a strange, restless wandering through the house, going from room to room without purpose, unless it was to see if things looked different, now that she knew. They didn't. They looked exactly the same.

The sewing room door had been so firmly shut for so long that when Maya noticed that it was slightly open, she couldn't help herself. She kicked it open a little more, in anger. She was sick of secrecy. Her mum always used to say, "No secrets, eh?" and Maya had always truly believed that with all her heart. Now, of course, she knew differently. When grown-ups said they didn't want there to be any secrets, what they meant was they didn't want *you* to have any secrets from *them*. The other way round was fine. Apparently.

Her father wasn't a purple furry monster with three heads and eyes on stalks after all. He was Cathal, an ordinary man with a beer gut. Spot the anticlimax. She kicked the door again.

She felt as if she had lost something, but she was too young to realize that what she thought she had lost had never existed. Finding her dad had been a distant dream, and in it he had been whatever she wanted him to be. Now, though, he had to be Cathal. She couldn't pretend differently. It wasn't bad, exactly, it just wasn't the ending she would have written. If she had to have an O'Connor, she wanted Niall, but she had lost the choice, or, rather, her mum had taken it away from her.

If Emmy hadn't told Sita, Maya wouldn't have overheard, and then she wouldn't know—and if she didn't know, she could still dream. Her mum was a big mouth.

Perhaps her entire life was one great big cloak-and-dagger operation, perhaps there were all sorts of things Emmy pretended were one thing, but were in fact another. Perhaps she hadn't been sewing in her sewing room at all. Perhaps she had just been sitting in there, staring at the walls and smoking and talking to herself so she wouldn't have to talk to anyone else. Like Cathal, for example. At least some things made sense now.

Maya was frightened that nothing was what it seemed anymore. When she thought about it too hard, she felt seasick, as though the floor was rolling under her feet. She stood for a while outside the room, trying to pluck up the courage to go in. Now was as good a time as any to put Emmy to the test.

It was very dark in there. The curtain across the long narrow window was drawn and the light was off.

She thought about what she would say if she was caught, but realized she didn't care. She put one foot inside the door, and then the other, then slipped through the gap and shut it quickly behind her. In the shadows, she could see vague outlines of things hanging from the shelves, and she began to feel scared of what she might find. She remembered the look on her mother's face every time she had answered one of her knocks. Wild, tired, as if she had a ghost in there with her or something.

In a flash of uncharacteristic fear, Maya flicked the old light switch and the room burst into life.

"Uh!"

What she saw reminded her of when the old TV in the music room went wrong, got stuck on black and white and you had to bang it on the top to bring the color back. Bang! Pop! Color! It made her draw breath, and a little of what she had lost wafted back into her soul. In her excitement, she clamped her hand over her mouth to stop herself shouting.

"Mummy!" she whispered.

On hangers, suspended from the back of the door, from the edges of shelves, from the curtain rail and over the back of the chair, were costumes from every story she had ever been told.

There were petal skirts with layers of rainbow-colored floaty fabric, bright ribbon halos, miniature bridal gowns with lace-trimmed veils and rosebud bouquets, frothy pink net tutus and shimmering shifts with pearly drops and gauzy sleeves. There was a red satin cape with a black forked tail, a hood with matching horns, majestic ermine-trimmed cloaks and crowns, bejeweled headdresses, velvety hats, wicked-witch wands, and a purple wrap covered in moons and stars. A pair of angel wings flapped very gently in the breeze coming through the window.

She felt as if she had walked into a fairy's workshop in an enchanted kingdom. She thought of the Elves and the Shoemaker, and, funnily enough, she thought of Rumpelstiltskin too. Had some witchcraft gone on in here? Was this her mother's hand? It was unbelievable, fantastic, and utterly, totally mesmerizing. More than that, it was enough to make her forget everything she had held against Emmy since the night before. It was almost enough to make her believe that anything was still possible.

She stood rooted to the spot for a minute, and then she began to smile. The smile turned into a bigger one, and that in turn became a laugh. She sifted through the piles of discarded ribbons and rubbed her face in the fur on the table. She pulled at a length of silver chiffon that was poking from a heap of metallic remnants on the shelf and it went on and on and on and on, like a scarf from a magician's hat. When she finally found its end, she waved it above her head, making circles, and then, her arm aching, dropped it on the floor with the other piles and went to the window.

Hanging from the rail was a deep purple satin cloak, in the most beautiful color she had ever seen, covered with stars and edged with twisted gold braid. She felt it between her finger and thumb, and turned it to see its soot-black lining, scattered with moons. A piece of paper pinned to it in Emmy's handwriting simply said, *Magic*. You'd better believe it, she thought.

"WE JUST WANT TO SHOW YOU HOW THANKFUL WE ARE, BEFORE WE go," Mog said shyly, climbing the bus steps. She was still walking a little gingerly, the stitches so carefully administered by the community midwife occasionally reminding her of what her body had gone through.

She was nervous in her role as hostess. She and Dean had thrown parties before, but they had been scruffy affairs, with cans and cigarettes and loud music. This was a whole new world.

Dean had been into town on the blat to buy pasties which they had warmed in Bodinnick's kitchen, and saffron cake which Mog had spread out on a makeshift table covered with a Cornish flag and resting on trestles over the sofa where Nathan had been born. A big pottery jug on the side was full of cider, and there were small boxes of orange juice for the children. Balloons hung from the metal trim and a pickle jar of cow parsley and cranesbill geraniums sat on the side.

Mog didn't know how to do what she so badly wanted to. She wanted there to be some formality, for there to be one moment when they all recognized what they were there for. Nathan had changed everything, transported her from a world of drink and blats without petrol to a world where people said thank you to each other and put flowers in jars and planned ahead.

When Emmy hugged her, Mog felt a forgotten warmth dance right through her. This was how life was. Not like the coldness she had felt at boarding school, or the distance she had suffered at home, nor the self-conscious hardness of the travelers at the camp. For a split second, she thought of her mother, a woman who didn't do hugs or parties. But this time, there was no stab of pain. She realized now that things like that weren't genetic. You could learn them.

Dean winked at her, and she blushed, pouring the cider as Jonathan proposed the toast.

"To simple living," he said. And they all stood there with their mugs and their pasties, wondering if, at last, there might be the slightest chance of them all getting the hang of it. But Niall was missing, so it wasn't quite the hit it could have been.

IN THE SEWING ROOM, MAYA AND ASHA WRIGGLED OUT OF THEIR SNEAK-ers and jeans and dirty T-shirts, half terrified of discovery, half desper-ate to reveal. They stood giggling in their pants for a while, holding themselves as if they needed the loo. Lila was on the floor in the heap of ribbons, waving a wand and shrieking.

"You want to be a fairy, do you? A great big fat fairy?" Asha asked, pulling down Lila's elasticated floral trousers and squeezing her out of her green cotton top.

Maya found a small, soft, lined pink petal skirt with a stretchy bodice. "Do you think this will fit?"

It was for a two-year-old and the volume of shiny flimsy net turned the baby into an instant puff ball.

"Candy floss!"

"Mmm, let me eat you!"

They attached the fairy wings to the back of the dress, put a hairband on Lila's dark crown of silky hair and laughed. Lila laughed back. When people laughed, she laughed, and when people screamed, she screamed. Simple.

Maya went over to the purple velvet cape at the window and felt it again. "Do you think I should wear this?"

"Yeah. You could cast a spell over us, turn us all into frogs."

But Maya knew which spell she would use if she could. She took down the cloak and the long, pointed hat with the silver moons. Then she found a silver stick with an explosion of stars sprouting from its end.

"You *shall* go to the ball," she giggled as she tapped Asha's head.

Asha picked a fairytale princess, a reversible shimmery skirt, a spangly blue top, a sumptuous cape with a huge ribbon bow and a cone hat with a trailing chiffon scarf.

"Lady Asha awaits," she said.

"Pop! You're a frog."

They tiptoed along the landing, dragging Lila between them. In Emmy's room, they found the long mirror where she had once stood in her boots and jacket for Niall, and they twirled and danced and laughed at their new selves.

Then Asha sprang round to face the wizard.

"Come on, let's go and show everyone how clever your mum is!"

————

DEAN WAS OUTSIDE, FIDDLING WITH THE BATTERIES FROM THE BELLY boxes. They lay, battered and scratched, on the gravel drive next to a multi-pack of Special Brew which Niall had bought them before he had left. "Wet the baby's head for me," he'd told them. Inside the bus was his other gift, a bottle of champagne which neither Mog nor Dean had any idea how or when to drink.

An empty can rolled away as Dean attached wires to the back of Toby's ancient guitar amplifier. The volume dial was right up, from the last time someone had played with it hundreds of years ago, and a squeal of feedback orbited the bus as he made the final connection.

"Shit!" he shouted, throwing his head back, his dreadlocks flying all ways.

For a minute, Emmy wondered if the bus was going to take off, then, when the ambient whale noises the midwife had given Mog screeched into the air, she thought that perhaps it already had. "Not this," Mog called from the door. "I don't want this."

With Nathan in a black cotton sling, she grabbed the basket of tapes from the shelf and ran outside. Sita and Emmy followed, and at that moment, the two girls spilt from the house, clutching their pasties, flapping their capes and their wings and their ravishing gowns. They came flying across the lawn, with Lila in the stroller, her fairy headdress flopping over her eyes and her petal skirt bouncing up and down on every rut.

"Oh!" Emmy screamed. "Oh, my God! You look fantastic!"

Everyone looked up and saw the same perfect picture of three little girls floating across the green grass, seemingly conjured straight from the pages of a storybook. No one could believe what they were seeing.

Emmy certainly couldn't. It was the only time she had seen her work in broad daylight.

"Where did you get those from?" Sita asked.

Emmy's skin reddened, and an alien feeling of self-respect came over her. She hopped from foot to foot, not knowing how to accept the shrieks of impressed congratulations and amazement that were falling upon her.

"The sewing room."

"Emmy made them."

"But they're amazing."

"There are hundreds. We could be anything. We could be devils, dragons, knights."

"Or monkeys, or angels, or mermaids."

"Emmy." Sita came over to her, her arms out wide. "They're fabulous, Emmy."

"Are they?"

The girls were dancing round them and Jay was shaking a can of Coke furiously in front of them. Then, performing a trick he had learned from Scott, he shoved a pin in the side and an arc of sugary brown fizz shot into the air and began to spray Dean, who ripped off his wet shirt and started to chase him across the lawn.

"Watch those oufits!" Sita shouted. "Get them out of them, Emmy."

"No," Emmy said. "They can have them. Models' prerogative."

Jonathan staggered down the steps, too, accepting a drink from his racing son on the way, yanking back the ring pull and licking the foam from his wrist. Then he kissed Emmy firmly on the lips.

"Dark horse."

To say they presented an unusual tableau to the po-faced occupants of a white Japanese jeep as it crunched its way up the drive would be an understatement.

Then, when it was way too late, they were on top of each other. James Culworthy-King in a tweed jacket with leather elbow patches and sand-colored corduroys was already standing by the door of his Mitsubishi, looking at the thirty-year-old bus and the puddle of dried oil on the gravel with an expression one up from disgust. He opened his mouth to speak, but nothing came out.

"Turn that racket down," Emmy shouted, the last one yet to realize. Her twisted cotton scarf was now tied in a bow on her head. Lila was on her hip, chocolate smeared all round her mouth, her fairy headband at a lopsided angle, her wings round her waist. "The babies are going nuts.

"Ah," she said, seeing him at last. "Hello."

"Miss Hart," Culworthy-King said curtly with a slight nod.

The couple in the back of his car were making no move to get out. The man, wearing a pink crewneck sweater with a blue-striped shirt collar poking neatly over the top, was shaking his head. His pinched-faced wife was looking away in disdain.

"Did you call?" Jonathan asked. "I thought we said by appointment only."

"You clearly didn't get my message," James Culworthy-King replied. He was much less ingratiating than he had been on the first visit.

"No, clearly, I didn't."

"Well, you wouldn't have heard it over the noise, anyway. May I ask, is this a permanent feature?" He signaled toward the bus as if it was emitting a foul smell.

"Oh," Mog started to say, but Emmy spoke over her: "Semi permanent."

"Meaning?"

"Meaning it will go when it goes."

"I see. Well, it doesn't matter now. Mr. and Mrs. de Souza have obviously changed their minds, which is a shame since they are cash buyers." His face was red with anger.

"I bet they are," said Emmy, looking at their perma-tan. "Would they like a drink? We've got cider or Stella."

"I think not. They have other properties to see. Perhaps you would like to give me a ring when this, er, addition, has been removed. I really don't see we can market it while it . . ."

"Don't you like it?" said Jay, walking up, flicking drips of Coke off his soaking sleeve and swinging an electric guitar. "It's our new conservatory."

"I'll call you," Jonathan said to the back of the tweed jacket, glaring at his son. "So sorry to have inconvenienced you."

As the gleaming white back of Culworthy-King's car with its pristine spare wheel cover advertising his own firm disappeared back down the drive, the children cheered.

"I'll give you conservatory," Sita said to her son.

"I'd rather have a wetsuit," he answered.

Asha circled Lila's fairy wand. Jay put two fingers up behind his hand. Emmy didn't dare look, but she thought she could feel Sita smiling a little next to her.

Maya slunk upstairs again to pack.

I'M A STOWAWAY, SHE THOUGHT AN HOUR LATER, AS SHE FELT THE BUS'S exhaust rumble into action beneath her. To celebrate, she allowed herself a wriggle under the covers of Mog and Dean's "pit."

Her loose hair was sticking to the edges of her face and she was re-inhaling her own warm breath. She badly wanted to do more than wriggle. She wanted to crawl right out, not only because she was hot but because the milky-sweet smell of the bedclothes mingled with the petrol fumes, making her feel a bit sick. Or was it the saffron cake mingling with pasties and orange juice in her tummy?

She took her mind off it by imagining what would happen when everyone at Bodinnick realized she had gone. She could hear the phone conversation in her head. *Niall, is she there yet? Yes, she's just arrived. I'm coming back with her. Okay, see you both soon.* She hugged herself. It was going to work out fine after all. Direct action, Jay called it.

As the Bedford Twin Steer poked its flat nose out between the granite posts and turned left, brushing the hedgerows of tight young cow parsley and new foxgloves, she felt the back end swing and knew they were on the open road.

Pulling off the Indian throw and blankets, she blinked in the half-light. Her heart was still thumping, but the rumble of locomotion had already found a confident rhythm and she allowed herself a peep out of the small section of back window that hadn't been boarded up.

"Bye, Mum," she whispered as the lane slipped by. "Love you."

And then after she'd blown a kiss, she smiled. She was really doing it. One minute, she had been an apparently innocent member of the farewell party, giving Mog the card she'd made and kissing Nathan, and the next, she was running the length of the bus, diving for cover under the blankets. She'd fully expected to be dragged back out again, but it hadn't happened. The bus had started moving instead. She was really doing it. She was going to get Niall.

She breathed out, glad to be able to release herself from the darkness. From the back pocket of her jeans, she took the sheet of paper on which she had written her itinerary. 1. Hide in bus. 2. Get train to London. 3. Get tube to Tower Bridge. 4. Walk to Niall's. 5. Come home.

In her purse in her silver and fluorescent green backpack was a wad of notes she had taken from her millennium time capsule that morning. Forty-five pounds. In the top pocket of her denim jacket was another seven, in coins. She had taken three from the dressing table in Emmy's room, along with the mobile phone, and she'd left the note in their place.

In neat red ballpoint, it said, *I have gone to get Niall. I won't be gone long. Don't worry. I'll phone you when I get there. Love you lots, from Maya.* She had bordered it with kisses and propped it against a stack of Nytol and Silk Cut, knowing they were no longer needed.

She sighed. She wondered how far Mog and Dean would get before they discovered her and which train station they would drop her off at. She plaited a long strand of hair either side of her face. She played a game with her fingers, jumping from mirror bead to mirror bead on the throw.

Then she dug around in her backpack to find an apple but came across a tube of foil-wrapped ladybirds which Cathal had brought her. She hadn't eaten any of them before because it seemed disloyal, enjoying his presents when Niall was so sad, but it was different now. Needs must. Anyway, she ought to keep her energy levels up.

As she unwrapped it, she thought about the letter she had written to Cathal in her head. She told him she knew he was her dad, and she was getting used to it but, if it was okay with him, she would come and see him when she was older. Or when Niall was older. Or Emmy. That was what she wanted really, to put it all on hold. But she knew that grown-ups didn't like ignoring things, or if they did they weren't very good at it. Spot-pickers, they were. Squeezers. Pokers and prodders. You'll make it worse, she felt like telling them. And they always did.

20

AT THE VERY MOMENT WHEN NIALL THOUGHT THINGS COULD SURELY get no worse, they did.

Having finally found a tiny reserve of motivation to get himself back to London, he was now in Devon, at a filling station just over the county border. With Cornwall behind him, he had half expected to start feeling better. Distance had the same sort of healing properties as time, which was why in the past he had been so good at running away. It had worked miracles after his father died, and in the desperate months after Emmy's abortion.

He knew how to cut ties or make clean breaks in a way Cathal didn't, or couldn't. This time, though, the tie seemed made of extra-stretch elastic. He could feel it pulling him, ready to ping him right back to square one the moment he stopped. Now that he was finally moving, he needed to keep on moving, which was why vehicle-hire companies were currently top of his hate list. They always gave you the keys with an empty tank, the bastards. His hair needed a wash and it was sticking to his unshaven face. His eyes, swollen from self-pity and drink, stung when he tried to read the rapid green movement of the numbers on the pump's digital display. His fingers hardly had the energy to press the trigger on the handle. He was so tired he could barely stand up. He put in a full tank of Premium Unleaded, not caring that the price was day-light robbery. And then, as he was screwing the petrol cap back on his hired transit van, he remembered with one of those vein-stripping real-izations that it was in fact a diesel engine.

"Jaysus, no!" he shouted, thumping his fist against the tinny roof.

Feeling himself cave in under his own stupidity and fatigue, he put his forehead against the rim of the open door and groaned. He didn't want to have to think about what to do next. He wanted to stay there until someone came and told him to move—or, better still, moved him themselves. He banged his head a couple of times and groaned again. The forecourt attendant looked at him through her safety glass with disdain.

Then, as he leaned inside to get his credit cards to pay through the nose for the tank full of fuel that would now screw the engine and ren-der it useless, the old Motorola phone that had been lying in its death throes on his passenger seat bleeped.

"What bloody now?" he sighed, fumbling with the buttons. There was one bar left on the battery. Message. Read Now? OK. The machine didn't do anything as useful as display caller identity, of course.

"AM COMING ON MY OWN TO LONDON TO GET U. DON'T TELL MUM. TRAIN GETS IN AT 6. C U AT YR FLAT. LUV MAYA. XXXXXXX."

"No, I'm not there," he shouted in the emptiness of the van. "You stupid girl, I'm not there."

The car behind him sounded its horn and he stuck his head out to scowl. When he stuck it back in, the phone screen had gone blank. He switched it on again, swearing heavily, and it made the feeblest of noises before shutting down a second time. The battery had used the last drop of its power on getting Maya's message through to him, and he knew exactly where he had last seen his recharger: it was on the Welsh dresser at Bodinnick. Of course it bloody was.

The van wouldn't move, not even off the forecourt, so after paying up, he pushed it single-handedly over to the air and water and went to find a telephone.

"It's out of order," the girl in the red polo shirt unpacking crisps told him after five minutes of watching him try.

"Can I borrow yours, then? This is urgent."

"What number do you want?" she sighed.

Which was when he realized he didn't know. He had no idea which phone Maya had used but in any case all the numbers he needed were in the address book in his mobile, which was flat. Of course it bloody was. Bodinnick, he thought, call Bodinnick, tell Emmy. But as he pressed the numbers, he remembered with a piercing ache behind his eyes that Maya had asked him not to. She had given him her trust. "Don't tell Mum," she'd said. So he couldn't. He didn't have enough of her trust at the moment to fritter it away.

Back at the van, not caring that he was both behaving and looking like a madman, he pulled out his bike and started searching in the boxes and cases for his helmet. But he couldn't find it, could he? And nor would he. It was still on a fence post in the rest area at Boxtree. Well, of course it bloody was.

Under normal circumstances, he would have given up. He would have decided to write the day off and start again tomorrow. He would have gone and had a pint somewhere to think about it. But the thought of Maya setting off to get him and arriving at an empty flat didn't make him feel normal or thirsty or resigned at all, so he walked out onto the road, stuck out his thumb and looked so desperate for help that the next truck that passed actually stopped and gave him a lift to the nearest station.

AT BODINNICK, EMMY WAS TRYING NOT TO LET HER NEW SENSE OF achievement be smothered by her old creeping sense of failure. The house felt almost tragically empty. No Kat, no Cathal, no Mog or Dean or Nathan, no Niall, and now she couldn't find Maya. The place was so quiet. No newborn squeals, no music from Niall's room, no children fighting.

"Is anyone inside?" she shouted, her voice echoing around the new kitchen. Slate absorbed nothing. Perhaps that was why Toby chose the lino in the first place, to stop himself feeling so alone. Perhaps if she ended up living here on her own, she would start laying the lino back. There was usually a reason behind a reason behind a reason, she knew that now.

"Maya?"

She wasn't downstairs, but then nor should she be on a day like this.

Emmy found herself walking to the pond, a bubble of panic rising just slightly inside her, but this time the boat was on its side by the bull-rushes where Maya had left it and the surface of the water was perfectly still, like glass. Cathal's footprints were visible in the dark, damp earth and she put her own foot in one, just for the hell of it. She looked at the brown expanse, noticed a few new waterlilies and could hardly believe that the unraveling of her secret was only a week ago.

It was too beautiful to go inside, so she walked over to the chapel, across the daisies and the buttercups and the clover, noting that the track Jonathan had worn was disappearing again. She opened the door and heard it scrape the floor one more time. It smelled fresh and happy in there, as if it was relieved to be left to its own devices again, now that it was in better shape.

On the way back, she looked in the rhododendron bushes, behind the crumbling brick walls, in the farmer's empty barn and up the track, in all the dens and concealed corners where she knew her daughter had been spending too much time hiding lately.

In the top field, next to the bonfire remains, she saw Sita and Jonathan with their children, flying a kite, and she wandered over.

"Have you seen Maya?"

"I thought she was with you."

As she went back in through the front door, she looked at the patch of oil on the gravel drive and smiled to think of Culworthy-King's apoplectic face. She wouldn't have sold Bodinnick to people like the ones in his car, anyway. They looked the sort who might favor carriage lamps, or even put up a real conservatory.

"Maya?" she called half-heartedly up the stairs. "Maya?"

At least the emptiness wasn't inside her anymore. The overwhelming relief at Cathal's retreat had killed that, like the lancing of some ghastly boil.

We must be bloody mad not to make a go of this, she thought, admiring her newly exposed hall floor for the umpteenth time. From the table where the phone she had once been so frightened of ringing now sat silently, she picked up the glossy property particulars. Jay had defaced them already, crossing out words like "elegant" and "well-presented" and putting ones like "drafty" and "damp" in their place. Even without his added noughts, the price was ridiculous. Not half as ridiculous as we'll all feel back in London, she thought.

"Maya?" she called again as she walked up the stairs. "Where are you?"

She walked past Niall's space, and thought she could smell the faintest whiff of Camel cigarette smoke. I'll go and throw out that packet of Silk Cut on my dressing table, she decided. Then I'll suggest a barbecue on the beach and we'll go and have a look at some surfboards. It was a good plan. It could have been perfect. But thirty seconds after that, she found Maya's note.

"HAS NIALL CALLED YOU AT ALL?" CATHAL ASKED HIS MOTHER OVER THE phone from Bristol.

"No, why? Should he have?"

"No, I just wondered."

"Wondered what?"

"Oh, just wondered."

"I may be old, Cathal," she said, "but I'm not stupid yet. Best you tell me."

"Are you sure you want to hear it?"

"If I don't hear it, I'll imagine it."

So she heard it, from start to finish.

"Who are you concerned for? Your brother or your daughter?" his mother asked without admonishment.

"My brother," he mumbled, knowing it was the answer she wanted to hear.

"Then get on with it. Find him and put it right."

"How?"

"You'll find a way. Start with London. Make him talk to you. Tell him I say he has to."

"Should I not leave him to calm down for a while?"

"No," Mary O'Connor said emphatically. "You don't let the sun go down on this one, Cathal. Remember what I said. The thing is, we all think we have the time."

THE MOMENT OF DISCOVERY CAME JUST AS MAYA WAS PUTTING THE LAST chocolate in her mouth, but she was nearer London than she had hoped, so it didn't matter that she lost it somewhere in the bedclothes.

"Maya! God, don't do that to me."

Mog was standing in the doorway to the pit with Nathan attached to her left breast, his head covered by her stripy long-sleeved T-shirt. She had negotiated the walk down the length of the bus well, only having knocked her baby-free side once on the kitchen partition.

"Sorry."

"Did you fall asleep?"

"No. I tried but it was too hot." Maya was beaming, pleased to have someone to talk to after so long, but Mog looked worried, embarrassed, a bit disconcerted.

"Didn't you feel us moving? We've been traveling for hours."

"Yes, but . . ."

"Don't worry, don't worry, it's okay. We can easily turn round. We're not in a hurry."

"No." Maya climbed out, steadying herself against the wooden doorframe as the bus turned a corner. "You don't understand. I meant to come with you. I'm a stowaway."

"You are?" Mog didn't know how to tell her she couldn't be. She didn't want to be rude, not after all the help Maya's family had offered.

"Only as far as a train station. I'm going to London."

"You are?"

"If that's not too much trouble."

"Does Emmy know?" Mog asked, but she knew damn well Emmy did not.

"Not exactly," Maya said cautiously.

"So you've run away?"

"Not exactly."

Mog looked at her out of the corner of one eye. She saw a glimpse of herself in the child, a lack of fear and a self-taught independence. As she opened one of the two cartons of value orange juice left over from the send-off and poured juice into a chipped mug, she asked, "And what else is 'not exactly'?"

CATHAL WAS SO USED TO SEEING TEN-YEAR-OLD GIRLS IN THE STREET and imagining that they were Maya that when the ten-year-old girl in Niall's street really was Maya, he barely reacted.

He was sitting in his car, which was parked illegally on double yellows outside his brother's former council flat near Tower Bridge, wondering how much longer he should wait before he gave it up as a bad job.

He didn't immediately recognize Maya's orange and purple hat, the one he had last seen lying in a puddle in the bottom of a yellow dinghy, but why should he? He had been placing her in Cornwall, in the garden, on her bike. In fact, it wasn't until he watched her press the intercom and put her mouth close to it that he came to.

"Hiya, Maya," he said, out of breath. He'd made the same joke a few times in Cornwall. That they might be friends was about the best he could hope for.

She looked at him blankly at first. The tube from Waterloo had been busier than she remembered and the smell and noise were horrible. She could feel the fumes going up her nose and staying there. Everyone looked different. They all had gray or spotty skin and no one looked at you. She'd been beginning to wonder if she had shrunk in Cornwall, because London hadn't been this big when she lived here. And she'd begun to feel even smaller when Niall hadn't answered her ring.

"Cathal!" she said, dropping her bag at her feet.

There was no triangular formation this time, just a nice simple straight line.

"Are you all right, darling?" The parental concern was out before he could stop it.

"Fine, thanks." Well, she was now.

"What are you doing here?" Did she know?

"I've come to get Niall."

"So have I."

"Is he expecting you?"

"No. Is he expecting you?"

"I don't know. I sent him a message but he hasn't replied."

"Bit of a last-minute thing, was it?"

"Bit."

"You've come to get him? Where are you taking him?" He put his finger on the intercom too.

"Back to Cornwall."

"You came here on your own?" The penny was beginning to drop.

"Yes."

"Good journey?"

"Fine, thanks." She jiggled around, holding her legs together. "I wish he'd hurry up and answer. I'm bursting to go to the loo."

Cathal looked around. "Why don't we go over the road and get a pizza? You could go in there, and we can see from the window if he turns up."

"I'm not hungry. I've been eating those chocolate ladybirds you gave me all day."

"You kept them a long time."

"I know. I kept them for emergencies."

"And this is an emergency, is it?"

"You tell me," she said. She sounded so *old*.

"I think it probably is," he said truthfully.

They started to walk, but Cathal suddenly realized they had to do something else first. He had just seen it all from another point of view.

"Let's just tell your mum you're here, that you bumped into me, yeah? I've got my phone in the car. It's all charged up. It won't take a minute."

"I've spoken to her already."

"When?"

"On the train. She called me. I've got her phone."

"She ought to know you're here, with me."

"No, I don't think so," Maya said, shaking her head.

"I think we should."

"It'll just make her worry more. She'll think we arranged it."

"Well, we'll just have to tell her we didn't, won't we? We can't all carry on like this. It's mad."

"I know."

"She needs to know you're safe. I need her to know you're safe."

"Can we do it from the restaurant? Otherwise I'm going to pee all over the pavement."

———

EMMY ASKED THE GUARD WHY THE TRAIN WAS GOING SO SLOWLY.
"Track repairs," he said, not lifting his eyes from punching her
ticket.

"What, still?"

"It's not my fault. You want a safe network, don't you?"

She of all people did. She remembered a long-ago nightmare, of
Jonathan shouting, "Carriage C, Carriage C," and of her and Maya dying
in the wreckage to the sound of mobile phones and being matched in the
emergency morgue by their identical crooked little fingers. She thought
of the question they all used to ask themselves: If this was our time,
would we have died happy?

"Yes, I do," she told the guard. "Tell the driver to go as slow as he
needs."

"That's very kind of you," he replied sarcastically. "I'm sure he'll
appreciate your permission."

Emmy wished she had thought of changing from the clothes she
had worn for Mog and Dean's send-off, a ridiculously upbeat mix of a
tight green silk camisole top, a pink ruffle-neck jersey cardigan, and
cut-off jeans she had trimmed with a length of silver-beaded fringe. It
had been a conscious display of effort, wanting to show everyone that
she was making tracks to get back on course, ready to make the most of
what they had left. But now she felt ludicrous. She fiddled with her
cardigan, trying to pull it surreptitiously across to cover her breasts. She
put her ticket back in her sheepskin backpack and had the last slug of
Rescue Remedy. Maya's note was in there, too.

She tried to stop imagining walking the streets of London with a photograph of Maya in her hand, accosting tramps and policemen to ask if
they had seen her, to stop seeing her daughter's face on the front page of
the *Evening Standard* and on the television news. It was willful self-torture,
not least because she already knew Maya was safe. God bless mobiles!

Maya had been absolutely in control. "I'm on a train," she'd said. "I know how to get to Niall's, and I'll phone you when I get there." Which should be about now. According to Mog, her daughter could only be about two hours ahead.

Poor Mog had been so apologetic when she'd phoned Bodinnick. "I'm sorry. She wouldn't let me call until she was on the train."

"At least you've kept your promise to her. That's more than most of us have done. Did she say anything about why she's gone?" Emmy asked.

"Well, just that she wanted Niall."

"That's all?"

"I got the impression that was enough." She left out the rest. It was too complicated to simplify, and anyway Mog thought she owed it to Emmy to let her hear it firsthand.

The train chugged out of the tunnel and meandered along the Devon coast. Emmy had no choice. She would just have to put her faith in a ten-year-old. She looked at Sita's mobile. Any minute now it might leap into life and tell her all was well. As soon as it did that, it wouldn't matter how slowly the bloody train went. In the meantime, she just had to trust Maya to get it right. It wasn't as if she was Asha. She had negotiated the tube on her own to Niall's a few times before. She had defiance, she had money, she had her own two feet. But still Emmy imagined the tramps. Lesser fates never occurred to her.

She sat back, rested her head against the window, and looked out at the orange cliffs and the fishing boats on the murky green sea, wishing she had the peace of mind to enjoy them.

"DO YOU LIKE OLIVES?" MAYA ASKED CATHAL.

Neither of them had looked across the road for ages. They had forgotten why they were there. It was nothing to do with eating pizza or needing the loo or seeking sanctuary from the rain. It was as if whatever they had been waiting for had arrived, even though they had only just got hold of the menu.

"I love them. Do you?"

"Yes, but only the black ones."

"Oh, the green ones are horrible."

"Yuck! Do you like pepperoni?"

"Love it."

"And me. What about anchovies?"

"No. Vile things. You might as well lick the bottom of a boat."

Maya laughed. "Pineapple?"

"Like it cold, can't stand it hot."

"Snap." She turned over for puddings. "What would you choose out of apple pie or chocolate fudge cake?"

"Chocolate fudge cake," he said, crossing his fingers.

"Me too. Pecan pie or crème caramel?"

"Pecan pie."

"No," she said. "You're wrong. You wouldn't. You'd choose crème caramel."

"Oh, sorry, can you repeat the question?"

"Pecan pie or crème caramel?"

"That'd be crème caramel, definitely." He knew what she was doing.

"Right, what is your favorite color?" she asked.

He looked at her carefully. "Orange or purple," he hedged.

"You're only allowed one."

He drew in a breath. "It's a difficult one."

She took off her denim jacket and showed him her purple hooded top with the silver star.

"Purple, then."

"Is the right answer."

He looked at his watch. "Do you want to order?"

"Have we got time?"

"Read your mum's text again. What time's she getting in?"

"Paddington at 8:25. Is that long enough?"

No, Cathal wanted to say. It's not long enough at all. But it's a start.

"That's long enough for the pepperoni, the black olives, the choco-late fudge cake *and* the crème caramel if you want."

NIALL WAS SURPRISED TO SEE WRECKERS ALE FOR SALE AT THE STATION buffet. He had no real thirst for Roy Mundy's favorite tipple and just one warm can cost him more than an entire lunchtime round at the Cott but he slugged it back anyway as he wandered restlessly up and down the platform. He didn't particularly want to smoke, either, but he did that, too.

He knew he looked terrible—he had slept in his clothes last night, although sleep was a loose term for the twitching of his semiconscious body on the floor of the van—so he tried to keep his gaze away from people. When he had had enough of wandering, he found a space away from the benches and the waiting rooms and the information boards, put his hands in his pockets and stood. The only place to look was the floor.

When the train eventually trundled in, forty minutes late, he hung back. It came to a wheezy stop, not that he could see much of it through the ungracious scrabble of travelers fighting to get on and off. He stayed where he was, making no attempt to move forward, still staring at the dirty concrete platform. People tutted him, barged him, and thought rude things about him as they piled on, but he was oblivious. He didn't give a damn whether he was an obstacle or not.

When he looked up, he realized he was hallucinating. The woman sitting in the window seat that had come to rest at precisely the point on the platform where he had chosen to stand looked just like Emmy. She had pink sleeves round denim knees and her feet were on the uphol-stery. Her hair was hanging in a glossy curtain and she was dreaming about something.

Niall wanted to touch her, to feel a warm hand or a soft cheek or a curve through the cloth of her jeans, and because he was so tired and thought it wasn't really happening anyway, he tried. He reached out and put his hand against the cold window. Slowly, amazingly, another hand on the other side came up to join it. A hand with a hair tie around the wrist, hidden in a collection of silver bangles. A hand with a crooked little finger.

The explosive collision of their mutual recognition catapulted them both into action. He ran toward the door, which had already been shut by the guard in preparation for pulling out, and she scrambled in panic out of her seat, over her bag and into the fray. He yanked the metal handle, jumped on, and by the time he had slammed it behind him, there she was. Emmy.

"Are you okay?" she asked. His hair was sticking up in clumps for want of a good wash, but his brand of personal hygiene, or the lack of it, was again immediately familiar. It might even have been love at second sight.

"I will be," he said.

And they returned to her carriage and sat in silence with their eyes closed and their hands tightly in each other's, wondering what it was about trains and which single thing it was that had conspired to save them.

AT BODINNICK, SITA LAY ON THE LAWN, ENJOYING THE FEELING OF THE sun-warmed blanket beneath her and the burble of family life around her.

She watched the house martins dipping and diving in the brilliant blue sky, catching their food midair. Their fledgings were learning to fly, taking tentative excursions from their mud homes in the eaves, returning often, presumably to rest. Soon the colony would leave, without fuss.

That was the way to do it, she thought, thinking of the human chaos of the last few weeks. Will we still be here to miss you? she wondered.

In the distance, at the pond's edge, a group of mallards walked in file—a drake with its unmistakable green head and white neck ring, followed by his two adoring ducks. Their nests in the bamboo and reeds had been under constant attack from foxes and badgers. Asha had cried over the smashed eggs and sticky feathers, and yet still the ducks walked, heads up, expecting.

"It's nature," she'd told her daughter. "It's what happens."

She watched her own young, letting the soothing sound of their bike wheels on the gravel drive wash over her, not unlike waves over pebbles. From another corner of the garden, she could hear the sound of Jonathan hammering, mending a garden bench.

In the cushions next to her, Lila's chubby little hand reached out and picked up a toy cup, her fat wrist rotating in the air. Simple pleasures, Sita thought. Simple lives. Kind of.

The phone rang inside the house.

"Can you get that, darling?" she shouted to Jay. "You're faster than I am."

"I will," Asha cried. "I will."

Sita pulled herself up and started to walk inside after them, expecting it to be Emmy.

"It's James Culworthy-King," Jay said on the steps, trying not to feel as if he had just drunk a pint of lead. "He's got someone else interested. He wants to know when the bus is going."

The sound of hammering stopped. Lila dropped her cup.

Jonathan walked over to his family and the four of them stood by the oil patch, in the space where the wheels had once been.

"Well," he said quietly, "what do you think we should tell him?"

Sita, Jay and Asha looked at him hopefully.

"Go on. I'm listening."

"I think we should tell him it's still here," Jay said.

"And another one has come, too," Asha suggested.

"A peace convoy," Sita said. "To celebrate the summer solstice."

They trooped into the house together, and when they came back out a minute later they looked at the blanket on the lawn and saw that Lila was sitting up, straight-backed, perfectly balanced, without cushions, all on her own.

Discarded by
Westfield Washington
Public Library

FIC
Gregson, Rebecca
Eggshell Days

ED

DEMCO